What the critics are saying...

&

Sarael's Reading

"I've been watching Jory Strong since her debut and each time she writes another story I'm captivated by the characters and the plot. Her heroes are sexy and all male while her heroines can hold their own and usually take down the hero." ~ *Romance Reviews Today*

"Ms. Strong took a familiar vampire premise – breathing life and vitality into it. Ms. Strong demonstrates through her writing how a good paranormal tale should flow and grab the reader's full attention. The dialogues and thought sequences blend into perfect harmony. Ms. Strong is an author readers definitely need to keep a close eye on because her erotic voice is fierce!" ~ *Love Romances*!

"This story is sexually intense and downright carnal. With *Sarael's Reading*, Ms Strong has written an intense, erotic and enthralling book." ~ *JoyfullyReviewed*

"Vampire stories have been around forever and there are only so many ways you can make them unique. Ms. Strong has done that. Her characters were well-written ·and the plot suspenseful enough to keep you on the edge of your seat and yet not too distracting from the underlying romance between Sarael and Matteo. With her own take on beauty taming the beast, she has begun an amazing series." ~ *Fallen Angel Reviews*

Kiziah's Reading

"I have loved Ms. Strong's work for some time now and, in my opinion, this book is one of her best yet. She does a fabulous job of showing the conflict between societal attitudes and the needs and desires of the three main characters. Anyone who enjoys stories of threesome and same sex relationships containing paranormal elements should run, not walk, to purchase this marvelous book."~ *Coffee Time Romance*

"Once again, Jory Strong delivers an entertaining tale. I enjoy Ms Strong's books because they are character driven and this one is no exception...Magic, vampires, and love...*KIZIAH'S READING* has it all."~ *Romance Junkies*

"Wow, what a story! Highly erotic and difficult to put down...This book was impressive, I can't say enough about this awesome story! It truly deserves its 5 heart rating, and I can't wait for the next one in the series."~ *The Romance Studio*

Dakotah's Reading

"Jory Strong once again moves me with her latest release, DAKOTAH'S READING. Filled with emotion, torrid sex, danger, and fascinating characters, this book is a must read for all you paranormal romance fans."~ *Romance Reviews Today*

"With *Dakotah's Reading*, once again Jory Strong has written a perfectly wonderful novel that kept me spellbound from beginning to end. *Dakotah's Reading* is erotic, fast moving, and just delightful. When I read the last word, I was so satisfied." ~ *JoyfullyReviewed*

"Love scenes are wonderfully passionate and full of sensuality. Jory Strong is a talented author who creates tales of paranormal excitement that are sure to be remembered."~ *Romance Junkies*

Jory Strong
Carnival Tarot

ELLORA'S CAVE
ROMANTICA PUBLISHING

An Ellora's Cave Romantica Publication

www.ellorascave.com

Carnival Tarot

ISBN 1419955691
ALL RIGHTS RESERVED.
Sarael's Reading Copyright © 2005 Jory Strong
Kiziah's Reading Copyright © 2006 Jory Strong
Dakotah's Reading Copyright © 2006 Jory Strong
Edited by Sue-Ellen Gower.
Cover art by Willo

Trade paperback Publication September 2006

Excerpt from *Skye's Trail* Copyright © Jory Strong, 2005

Warning:

The following material contains graphic sexual content meant for mature readers. This story has been rated E–rotic by a minimum of three independent reviewers.

Ellora's Cave Publishing offers three levels of Romantica™ reading entertainment: S (S-ensuous), E (E-rotic), and X (X-treme).

S-ensuous love scenes are explicit and leave nothing to the imagination.

E-rotic love scenes are explicit, leave nothing to the imagination, and are high in volume per the overall word count. In addition, some E-rated titles might contain fantasy material that some readers find objectionable, such as bondage, submission, same sex encounters, forced seductions, and so forth. E-rated titles are the most graphic titles we carry; it is common, for instance, for an author to use words such as "fucking", "cock", "pussy", and such within their work of literature.

X-treme titles differ from E-rated titles only in plot premise and storyline execution. Unlike E-rated titles, stories designated with the letter X tend to contain controversial subject matter not for the faint of heart.

Contents

Also by Jory Strong

ဢ

Crime Tells 1: Lyric's Cop
Crime Tells 2: Cady's Cowboy
Crime Tells 3: Calista's Men
Ellora's Cavemen: Drams of the Oasis I
Fallon Mates 1: Binding Krista
Fallon Mates 2: Zeraac's Miracle
Fallon Mates 3: Roping Savannah
Supernatural Bonds 1: Trace's Psychic
Supernatural Bonds 2: Storm's Faeries
The Angelini 1: Skye's Trail
The Angelini 2: Syndelle's Possession

About the Author

ဢ

Jory has been writing since childhood and has never outgrown being a daydreamer. When she's not hunched over her computer, lost in the muse and conjuring up new heroes and heroines, she can usually be found reading, riding her horses, or hiking with her dogs.

Jory welcomes comments from readers. You can find her website and email address on her author bio page at www.ellorascave.com.

SARAEL'S READING

&

Dedication

୬

My thanks to Lisa Marie Rice — Ellora's Cave author of one of my personal favorites, Midnight Man — for looking over the Italian and offering some suggestions.

Trademarks Acknowledgement

୬

The author acknowledges the trademarked status and trademark owners of the following wordmarks mentioned in this work of fiction:

Denny's: DFO, Inc.

Chapter One

The tarot cards lay on black satin cloth. Three of them, lined up in a row.

The past. The present. The future.

Their backs glowed in lighting designed to produce just such an effect—one meant to awe the townies who ventured into the small carnival tent, most often on a whim, but sometimes because they truly believed.

Sarael Castillo fidgeted in her seat, wishing she could escape a reading that was unasked for, but presented all the same.

Helki sat across the table, her ancient, wrinkled face free of expression though her eyes were filled with too much knowledge. "You do not wish to see them?" the old woman asked, her voice holding a mild rebuke. A challenge. Something more.

Sarael ducked her head, shivering despite the jacket she wore. Did she want to see the cards?

A tendril of fear snaked through her. For days she'd felt as though a dark storm was gathering and would soon overtake her. Its arrival signaling the end of all that was familiar to her. And yet outwardly, there was no evidence that such a thing was true.

"I'll see them," she said, bracing herself as the cards were turned.

The Hanged Man.

The Tower.

The Moon.

Sarael looked at the cards, interpreting them for herself, but remaining silent, allowing Helki to have her say. "You have lived among us, adapting to a way of life you weren't meant for, held in limbo by choices that weren't your own—and yet the time wasn't wasted. You've learned much—more than you give yourself credit for. But now it is time to separate. To move away from what you know."

The elderly fortune-teller reached over and took Sarael's hand, turning the palm upward before removing the leather band from around Sarael's wrist, exposing the strange tattoo.

Helki tapped it. "Soon you will be joined with the one you were meant to be with, living in his world with him."

And Sarael believed, hearing prophesy in Helki's voice where often there was carnival showmanship and street cunning, the ability to read a person's expression and take an educated guess based on hard lessons and a lifetime of observation.

* * * * *

Matteo Cabrelli lounged in the back of the sleek black limousine, sipping from his wineglass, the dark red contents pungent with a strong mix of herbs. He'd grown used to the taste over the years, though it still remained foul, disgusting. But the penalty for not drinking it would be death—his.

Even with the herbs, it was often hard to control *La Brama*, The Hunger, the desire to drain everything from those he preyed on, to take their life essence along with each swallow of blood. But to yield to *La Brama* meant death at the hands of his own kind for a change, rather than by their enemies—the secret society of "Believers" who sought to destroy any being who could take the form of a human but was more than mortal.

From the very beginning there had been those who were aware of the existence of his kind, peasants and royalty and men of religion alike who feared and hated what they couldn't understand, what they saw as a threat, who wanted to destroy anything not human. The hysteria becoming so great that at one time they drove stakes into the hearts of their own dead or burned their bodies, thinking to keep them from rising as vampires. The hatred and fear passed on to their sons and daughters, to any who were willing to hunt and kill—the description of "human" narrowing as the years passed.

A grim smile played over Matteo's lips. Time had aided his kind. The great masses of humans no longer believed that there were creatures among them who could shift form, whose lives spanned centuries, and who fed on blood in order to survive. The masses no longer feared the dark, and many individuals embraced it, clamoring to clubs where they became easy prey — though they escaped with their lives. And still the Believers persisted. A society of intolerance, run by men who remained in the shadows, who fed on fear and lusted for power and riches.

Rage swirled through Matteo just thinking about those who hunted the Vampire, the anger forcing him to take another long sip from his wineglass. He had no time to worry about them now. No time to let hatred of them divert his attention from what was most important.

"Almost there, *Don* Cabrelli," the driver's voice intoned and Matteo's body tightened with anticipation. With need.

Almost there. Years and millions of dollars later, it appeared that the one who'd been created specifically for him had finally been found. A woman now. His to claim. To master. To feed from. To mate.

Sarael. He tasted the name. Let it coat his tongue. Its promise sweet where the herbs were bitter. Soon he'd be free of his daily ritual of herbs mixed in wine. Once he'd joined with her, there would be no chance of *La Brama* controlling him. Sarael's blood would sate him, her body would succor him, her life would give deeper meaning to his own.

Instead of centuries of meaningless conquest and feeding, of lone pursuits, he'd have a companion at his side, a woman who was his in every way. A woman who would give him sons over the centuries. Not many at any one time, his race was not a prolific one, but there would be children. A legacy. Something beyond himself.

Matteo's cock pulsed in anticipation. He would know immediately if Sarael was his. In truth, he had little doubt that she was. He'd needed to take his shaft in hand and find relief as soon as he saw the photographs forwarded to him by the American, Cable Luske, one of the *padrall* — the humans who had served Matteo's kind in one way or another since the very beginning, each generation passing the duty to the following one.

Sarael was the image of her grandmother — Angelique's mother. Small and feminine. Her features delicate, fey-like. Her eyes dark pools Matteo knew he would lose himself in. Her hair, thick and black, long enough to drape and rub against his body.

She was the one. He knew it. The picture only whetted his appetite. The leather band around her wrist was just another indication that his search would soon be over. His blood would confirm it when they finally arrived at the carnival and he saw her for the first time.

Sarael.

Soon she would be his bride. His *kadine*. The one who would satisfy all of his needs.

* * * * *

Sarael sat on the bed in the small trailer, twisting the leather wristband around and around, her thoughts an endless loop. She looked up only when her friend and trailer mate, Dakotah, plopped down at the end of the bed in a cloud of luxurious brown hair.

"They only give one possibility," Dakotah said, her eyes focusing on the three cards — not from Helki's deck, but from one of the many in their trailer.

"I can feel the truth in them," Sarael said, her stomach tense, her skin tight against her body, as though it was already too late to change the prediction.

Dakotah reached over, flipping the cards so they lay facedown. "You can change that truth."

Sarael rose from the bed and walked over to the screened door, seeing a sight she'd seen all her life. Though the faces and the locations changed, the essence of the carnival remained the same.

The trailer she and Dakotah shared was nestled among others just like it, cheap boxes of metal pulled by battered trucks and hidden by the tractor trailers that were used to move the rides and booths from city to city. "This is all I've ever known. I've never left the carnival. I've never stayed behind when it moved on."

And the carnival always kept moving. No place more than a week.

It suited most of the carnies. A lot of them were running—from the past, from themselves, from demons only they saw.

Sarael's mother had been running from something when she'd arrived with a toddler in her arms and found a home with the carnival. She'd run again a few years later, leaving her daughter behind.

But the carnies took care of their own. The old fortune-teller Helki had made room in her small trailer for Sarael. Never speaking of Sarael's mother or of the past. Never speaking of a future beyond the next town.

It was the only way of life Sarael knew. And yet, it no longer felt as though it belonged to her. The Tower burning, struck by lightning and crashing down around her, leaving her no options. Forcing her into a world that was frightening, unfamiliar, its rules and rhythms foreign.

Dakotah rolled off the bed, joining Sarael at the door. "Would it make you feel better if I told you that you haven't missed much? That for people like us, this might be as good as it gets. As safe as it gets."

"Do you really believe that?"

"I know it."

Nausea roiled in the pit of Sarael's stomach as old memories fought to surface. Of a small child who knew better than to wander from the carnival. A child bound and gagged and thrust into the trunk of a car by a man with a cute brown puppy. A child rescued by luck and not design when the man ran a red light. She pushed the memories down.

The Hanged Man rose in their place. All the years moving from town to town, the route identical some seasons, varying slightly in others. The faces of the townies blending and merging, changing over the years, appearing and disappearing, their stories tiny strands in the fabric of Sarael's life as she watched them, as she caught traces of their conversation, pieces of their happiness and sadness, their triumphs and tragedies—while safely removed from all of it and yet not untouched by it. "I'm a chicken," she whispered.

Dakotah snorted. "Hardly." She reached over and grabbed a jacket from a hook next to the door, hesitating for a second before saying, "You're one of the bravest people I know. You keep caring about others, even when you know they won't stick around."

Something in Dakotah's voice alerted Sarael. "You're leaving?"

"Not tonight, but soon."

Sarael nodded, saying nothing. An unwritten rule, a code among those who traveled with the carnival. Not to probe into another's secrets.

Dakotah put her jacket on. "I envy you."

A startled laugh escaped from Sarael. "Me?" She found it hard to believe. From the time Dakotah had joined the carnival, Sarael had wished she was as strong, as boldly confident as her friend.

"Yeah. You. You don't even realize how free you are, Sarael. How free you've always been." Dakotah opened the screened door. "I'm spelling whoever's on the Ferris wheel. You want to work there or are you going back to Helki's?"

"I'll work with you," Sarael said, glancing momentarily at the cards lying facedown on her bed before stepping out of the trailer.

Within a few steps they were back among the crowds. Surrounded by the sounds of the carnival. The music of the carousel with its colorful metal horses, the men and women calling out, trying to entice customers to their various games, the thumping and clanging as objects were knocked over or struck, the popping of balloons, the excited squeals of winners along with the crash of bumper car against bumper car.

The night air was a mix of popcorn and hot dogs, cotton candy and autumn leaves. Its breeze a whispered hint of the impending winter.

Families wandered, kids sticky from begged treats, some still high on sugar, others tired and whiny, up well past their bedtimes. Couples moved along with their arms around each other, the men and boys often stopping to throw softballs or basketballs or rings, trying to impress their wives or girlfriends by winning a stuffed animal.

Sarael and Dakotah took their places at the Ferris wheel, the routine so often done that only a few words needed to be spoken before those who'd been running the ride moved away.

Despite the lateness of the hour, there was a long line of people waiting to get on the wheel, teenage kids anxious to make out as they traveled around and around, up and down, more interested in each other than the sights from above the ground. Sarael and Dakotah shared a glance, both of them glad for the chill in the air. In the summer when clothing was skimpy, it was harder to operate the ride—the passengers often getting lost in their own world and forgetting how much of a show they were providing to those below them on the ground.

With easy precision, Sarael and Dakotah shepherded riders on and off, the time passing quickly, though as it did, Sarael grew more anxious, more unsettled. As though the gathering storm had finally arrived, stopping just short of touching her.

She looked around, noticing the local boys, the townies traveling in small packs. Most harmless, but some predatory— believing somehow that carnies were less, were fair game, the men for fighting, the women for easy sex.

A pack of three, each wearing a letterman jacket, had taken an interest in Sarael. Returning to the area again and again and positioning themselves so she could see them, could hear their comments about her body. She was at least five years older than they were, though she was small, delicate. Perhaps they thought she was still in high school so they stood a chance with her. More likely they didn't care.

But they weren't the source of her uneasiness. Not that she'd be careless and let them catch her alone. Small-town police departments weren't quick to apply a charge of rape when the boys were local—always from "good" families—and the girl was a carnie. She'd be careful. Very, very careful.

Her mother had always watched the carnival visitors around her as though she expected something dangerous to present itself. Or at least that's what her mother was like in the few memories Sarael had of the woman who'd given birth to her. Almost from the first, her mother had left her in the hands of the other carnies to raise. Creating a separation, a distance between the two of them that was rarely breached.

Sarael glanced at the leather wristband covering her tattoo. It was the one act of parenting her mother took seriously. Sometimes driving the point home with physical punishment. The sharp slaps and her mother's face etched deeply into Sarael's mind, along with her insistence that Sarael must always keep the tattoo covered. Though there was never an explanation for it. And her mother had no such marking on either of her wrists—that much Helki had been willing to tell Sarael.

Sighing, Sarael pushed thoughts of her mother—no doubt brought on by the tarot reading—away, and collected more tickets for the Ferris wheel, knowing by the feel and weight of those in her hand when she'd collected enough to fill the seats. She shook her head as a boy in line tried to hand her two, saying, "Next ride."

He took it with good grace, turning back to his girlfriend, the two of them talking quietly, staring into each other's eyes, the sight of it making Sarael fill with a loneliness she usually managed to keep at bay. She'd never been casual with her affections—not when it came to physical intimacy. Though she'd been tempted—more than once—to take a townie back to the trailer she and Dakotah now shared. But she couldn't bring herself to do it. To seek an empty comfort that would only leave her feeling lonelier when she moved to the next town.

"You're quieter than usual," Dakotah said after she'd set the Ferris wheel in motion, both of them keeping an eye on the riders.

Sarael shoved her hands in her back pockets, the move pushing her chest outward and gaining her a round of whistles from the boys who'd been watching her all night.

Dakotah snickered. "As if you'd waste yourself on them." She reached over and wrapped her hand around Sarael's arm, squeezing it. A gesture that always humbled Sarael. She was one of the few people Dakotah either touched or allowed a touch from. "Still thinking about the reading?"

Sarael shrugged. "Maybe. I just feel...different tonight. Hyperaware."

"Oh." Dakotah grinned. "Get laid then." Her head tilted in the direction of the three townies. "But not by one of them. Ask Cable or Fane back to the trailer."

"No thanks," Sarael said, meaning it, the images of the men who'd recently started hanging around the carnival flashing through her mind—their presence unexplained and yet seemingly accepted by the carnival's owner. The few times she'd seen them, she'd felt as though they somehow knew her, as though she should know them. And yet they kept their distance, not doing anything suspicious. Only speaking to her on one or two occasions.

Sarael frowned, wondering suddenly if they were the source of her nervousness and foreboding. But just as quickly as the question arose, she knew that they weren't.

She shivered, glancing up, looking beyond the crowds and lights and into the darkness that existed beyond the asphalt and dirt lot at the edge of the small town where the carnival had been set up. Into the nightscape dominated by The Moon.

* * * * *

Matteo watched from the shadows. His fury challenging the potency of the herbs he'd ingested earlier. He wanted to rip the three human boys apart for daring to stare at Sarael. For daring to comment on her breasts, her body. For even thinking of her in a carnal manner. She was his. As he'd known she would be. His blood roared with the knowledge, urging him to claim what belonged to him.

Perhaps he'd erred in not having Sarael brought to him. But he'd feared what the sight of another man touching her, what the scent of another man on her—even a padrall or a servant ordered to retrieve her—would do to him.

Matteo stirred. Angry. Impatient. Restless to end his torment. To get her back to the place he would use until he could return to Italy with her.

He was anxious to begin. To fuck her. To exchange blood with her three times. To make her first his bride and then his kadine.

His cock jerked in anticipation. His fangs itched to elongate. His mind reached to hers. Sensing her awareness of his presence—though she had no way of knowing he was the reason for her unsettled emotions.

When the time was right he would call her, compel her to come to him in the darkness. His blood already flowed through her veins. Given to her at birth by the padrall order charged with the duty of seeing to the creation of future kadines. His blood had been mixed into the ink used to create the tattoo on her wrist during the confirmation ceremony, marking her for him to claim in adulthood.

He rubbed his chest. Touching the matching tattoo over his own heart. Cursing Angelique for taking Sarael and running. The renewed rage thoughts of Angelique brought doing nothing to calm him.

Her family had long served his kind, gaining honor, prestige and great fortune by producing those who would bear future kadines and occasionally become kadines themselves. There were no females born to his race. But his ancestors had found a way to avoid extinction by adapting human women, by sharing blood with them so that their cells altered, forming a bridge between two species and creating a vessel that would accept their seed and produce a child who would ultimately be fully vampire.

In medieval times the process had fed the rumors of the undead, women with fangs who preyed on their neighbors and family members. Crazed beings without a conscience. Creatures who needed to be destroyed.

But that was no longer the case. Had not been in centuries, save for the few humans whose conversion had driven them insane, and for the most part those had been women without knowledge of the vampire world, women chosen as kadines by vampires who feared *La Brama* would claim them before they could arrange for a mate to be created for them by the padralls.

Renewed anger rushed through Matteo. It was never very far from the surface where Sarael's mother was concerned. He had cared little about Angelique's future and what she wished to do with it. But she should never have taken his chosen with her. She should have left Sarael behind so that she could be raised in such a way as to understand her duties to the one who would claim her as a bride.

Matteo's cock pulsed again, his body tightening. Hundreds of hearts beat near him, unaware of the predator in their midst, and yet for once *La Brama* didn't whisper through his veins, didn't call for him to feast and satisfy it.

Voices swirled all around him, and yet the only conversation of interest to Matteo was the unspoken one between Sarael and him. It pleased him that she sensed his presence. And with a thought he tested his strength against hers, sending a silent command that she push her hair away from her face and neck so he could see her more clearly. She hesitated, her hand lifting partway, her eyes moving again to the shadows where he stood, before she turned, her hand dropping to her side, denying his command.

Matteo straightened, surprised by her resistance but not worried. For a long moment he contemplated whether or not to reissue the command, to strengthen it. To insist that she obey him. Then decided to let it go.

In the end she would obey him in all things. But this was not the time to begin her training. He was not worried about capturing her. About finally taking possession of her. Even if she didn't come to his call later, as he anticipated, it would be a small matter to retrieve her. Despite the humans' myths, he could easily enter her trailer — with or without permission.

Sarael's words reached him despite the distance. "What are you doing after we close down?" she asked her companion.

"Some of us are going to the beach. We're going to build a campfire. Want to come?"

No! This time Matteo sent a sharp command. Already he had spent longer on this task than he'd intended to — his delay not fully explainable, even to himself.

No! The intensity of the thought jarred Sarael, making her heart jump. Making her mind spin with confusion and uneasiness. "No," she answered, thinking she was too jumpy, too nervous to be good company.

Dakotah shrugged. "Think about it. There's time to change your mind." She smiled slightly. "Fane and Cable might be there."

The words sent a rush of fear through Sarael. A sense of menace. She shook her head, moving into position so she could open the safety bars on the buckets and help the riders off the wheel as Dakotah controlled the ride.

They worked in silence after that, in perfect sync until there was no line of townies, until the carnival darkened booth by booth, ride by ride.

"Sure you don't want to go?" Dakotah asked after they'd turned in their receipts and gone back to the trailer.

"No. Not tonight."

"See you later then."

Sarael sat down on her bed and flipped the tarot cards over. Shivering as she saw them again.

The Hanged Man.

The Tower.

The Moon.

She traced a finger along the edges. Staring at them intently. Helki's prophesy ringing in her ears.

You have lived among us, adapting to a way of life you weren't meant for, held in limbo by choices that weren't your own—and yet the time wasn't wasted. You've learned much—more than you give yourself credit for. But now it is time to separate. To move away from what you know. Soon you will be joined with the one you were meant to be with, living in his world with him.

The Moon. Even now she could feel it calling her. Urging her to leave her familiar surroundings and the safety of the trailer.

Around her voices sounded—laughter, argument, passion— muffled only by thin metal and small distances.

Car doors slammed. Engines started. All of them helping Sarael to fight the need whispering through her mind, her body. The compulsion to return to the darkness of the carnival.

She fought it for as long as she could. But as the night grew quieter, as the carnies around her settled, with only muted conversation and television sets giving testament to their presence, the compulsion grew stronger until Sarael could no longer resist the call.

Chapter Two

Sarael stopped in front of the small, closed concession stand where hotdogs and hot pretzels with mustard were sold. The air around the stand was heavy with the smell of grease. Several yards away, the chrome on the bumper cars gleamed, quiet in the night, though in Sarael's mind, she could easily hear the shouts and laughter as they were slammed into each other.

Come.

She shivered. The need to keep moving making her heart pound in her chest.

The tattoo underneath her leather wristband felt inflamed. She twisted the band around and around. Using the movement as a distraction until the next undeniable impulse came.

Fear tried to swamp Sarael, but it was tempered by the same deeply held knowledge that had recognized the truth of what the tarot cards said. The accuracy of Helki's prediction. *It is time to separate. To move away from what you know.*

Sarael took a deep breath and tried to see into the darkness that swallowed everything up beyond the exit.

Come.

Stronger this time. Sending tendrils of sensation through her belly, her breasts.

She took a few more steps before grabbing the metal fencing used to form chutes for the crowds to line up in. The exit just on the other side of the carousel.

Her delay nearly cost Matteo his control. He was no closer to Sarael than he had been earlier, and yet now there was no one else around. No one to prevent him from closing the distance between them, from striding over and taking her in his arms, stilling any protest she might make by sealing her lips with his. Thwarting any attempt at escape with a show of strength.

His nostrils flared as a breeze brought her scent to him. His heart sped up, matching the rapid dance of hers. Two sides of a single coin. Prey and predator.

The urge to close the distance, to rush in, was nearly impossible to resist. His gums ached where sharp fangs fought to descend. His cock leaked, unwilling to accept the restraint he forced on the rest of his body.

Come. The command lashed out and she jerked in reaction to it. The deep night, the absence of others around them, making it easier to press his will on her. He'd held back earlier, but now he intended to begin as he meant to continue. To eliminate any resistance. Any thought to escape.

She had not been raised properly, trained, prepared. So now she must suffer the consequences of her mother's choice to run. Rather than moving easily and willingly — happily — into the life of a kadine, she would enter abruptly, her fate suddenly in a stranger's hands. One who would expect obedience. One who intended to own her, body and soul. And yet one who offered everything she could ever desire in return.

Frustration, impatience, made him command her again, this time with a hint of menace. The night was leaking away more rapidly than he wanted. They should be in the limo even now.

Sarael caught a glimpse of the man standing past the carnival entrance, his aura dark, his sudden burst of anger making it easier for her to fight the need to go to him. The way it struck at her reminding her of the slaps her mother had delivered more than once, the blows given over the then-hated wristband. The words that came with it as sharp as the sting from her mother's hand. *If you're found, your life won't be your own.*

An ominous warning left with nothing to put it into context, with no understanding of what it meant. Until now.

The Moon. On Helki's deck it rose, framed by ancient pillars. Both full and crescent. Beautiful. Alluring. Shining over a land of magic where souls could be trapped — or freed.

Soon you will be joined with the one you were meant to be with, living in his world with him.

A small sound escaped, a whimper, and Sarael tightened her grip on the metal railing, refusing to take another step despite the way her body fought to do so.

Come to me. Softer this time, though no less insistent as the man detached himself from the darkness, moving into the moonlight with flowing grace.

Sarael's heart sped up, her stomach fluttered at the sight of his handsome features.

"Come to me, Sarael," he said, his voice like pure honey, swirling around her, sweet and thick, trapping her so that in the end she stood in front of him, her breathing fast, her body slick with sweat, her face upturned, her thoughts in chaos.

He reached out, taking her hand and holding it against his heart while the other cupped her cheek, his thumb brushing over her lips. "I am Matteo Cabrelli."

She shivered, fighting to hold a part of herself separate as he forced her to meet his gaze. Their eyes locking, causing heat to move through her so that her body felt as though it wanted to meld, to blend, to become entwined with his. So that her nipples beaded, her vulva grew swollen, making her acutely aware of the place between her legs.

For long moments they stared into each other's eyes and her thoughts were scattered, lost. But finally she pushed a word through lips that were wet, parted, as though waiting for a kiss instead of an explanation.

"How?" she whispered.

"Because you are mine, *carissima*. From the moment of your conception you were destined for me." He brushed his thumb across her mouth again. "Over time you will understand, but now we must leave."

"No." It was barely more than a puff of air as she tried to step back. But his hold was too tight and her own body too uncooperative.

He leaned down and some instinct warned her against jerking away. Her breath caught in her throat but she was frozen in place, a whimper escaping when his mouth touched her neck, a gentle kiss followed by the feel of his tongue, then his teeth, lightly gripping her skin as the hand which had been cupping her cheek moved to stroke along her spine before pulling her against his body.

Instantly she was lost under wave after wave of sensation. Swimming through thick, unfamiliar desire. Barely able to think or breathe. To protest when he swung her into his arms and began walking.

Matteo cursed himself even as he stretched her out on the limo seat and forced his mouth away from her neck, her throbbing pulse leading him into a temptation he didn't dare yield to. And yet it was too late to keep from sampling what was his.

He'd thought to overwhelm her senses so that he could get her to the car, but once he'd touched her... Lust raced through him, a flame burning him with the need to claim her. He covered her lips with his, spearing his tongue into her mouth, dominating hers, thrusting in and out, a warning of what was to come. An imitation of what his cock would soon do as he mated with her.

She moved restlessly underneath him, her hands going to his sides, his hips. He pressed more of his weight down on her, reveling in the way her body was soft under his, already so submissive.

He lifted his lips from hers, meeting her eyes in the dim interior light of the car, reading them. They were dazed, feverish—leaving him dissatisfied and angry with himself. He'd moved too fast with her. Swamping her senses and enthralling her, treating her as though she was a female to be used without thought or conscience—not as his future kadine should be treated.

Matteo levered off Sarael, moving to the end of the seat and creating a distance between them. If she'd been raised properly then she would already possess enough of his blood that this wouldn't have happened. They would already know each other, be comfortable in each other's presence so that the first joining would be a much anticipated event. A mutual seduction entered into by both parties instead of a taking, an enthrallment better suited to dealing with prey.

There *would* be times between them when it became a taking, a commanding, an assertion of dominance—done both in play and with serious intent. But later. When Sarael was his kadine. Not now, when they were new to each other.

A low growl rumbled in Matteo's chest. Anger and frustration moving with it. What male wanted to wonder if his bride desired him only because she was drugged from a heady dose of the pheromones used to attract humans?

Sarael made herself sit up as the scorching heat and wild lust slowly faded. Her gaze found Matteo, wandering over him now that there was enough light for her to see him more clearly.

Her heart jumped in response, her eyes widening as she took in his dark, compelling beauty. The straight nose and masculine lips.

Cabrelli. Italian.

She was still wet, swollen, achy, but she forced herself to think. To question. "How can you…" She stopped, color rushing to her cheeks. "Make me do things?"

His nostrils flared and his eyes narrowed, as though she'd hit a sore spot. She tensed, bracing herself, remembering his response when she'd denied him what he wanted. But rather than swamp her with passion as he had before, his eyes became hooded, his voice carrying an edge. "Did Angelique prepare you at all?"

Sarael's eyebrows drew together in confusion. "Angelique?"

He bared his teeth. "Your mother."

She jerked, licking her lips but stilling when his gaze moved to her mouth and he leaned forward. "Angie. She went by the name of Angie," Sarael whispered, trying not to move, trying not to do anything to set him off, to make him pounce.

Fear moved through her, not the terror of someone who thought they were facing death, but the primitive response that came from being helpless, stripped of any control, any choice. He'd already proven that he could overwhelm her senses, could command her body at will so that it blocked out rational thought and left her at his mercy.

Matteo's jaw tightened. He closed the distance between them, his hand once again cupping her cheek, his thumb rubbing Sarael's bottom lip and making her breath catch in her throat. "What did she tell you?" Gentler this time, as though he was trying to rein in his emotions, to check his behavior.

Sarael hesitated, afraid that if she told him the truth, that she didn't know anything, then she would remain ignorant. He tilted her face, brushing his mouth against hers, giving her a small sucking kiss that encouraged her to trust him. That sent pulses of heat through her nipples and filled her belly with warmth but didn't leave her senseless. "Nothing," she whispered, feeling strangely compelled to add, "she left when I was small."

Rage whipped across his face and through his body, charging into her and making her try to ease away from him. He didn't let her escape.

Matteo gathered her into his arms and sat back, positioning her on his lap. "Take off the wristband."

She complied, not protesting when he took the leather strap and tossed it to the floor before taking her wrist and bringing it to his mouth, touching his lips to the place where her skin had been tattooed.

"You were created for me. You were born to be my other half," he said, punctuating each sentence with a kiss to her wrist. "You would know all of this if Angelique hadn't run and taken you with her. But it is too late to change the past. What matters now is the future." His eyes probed hers and Sarael tensed, a cold chill moving down her spine with the thought that he was trying to read her mind.

"Why did she run?" she asked, wanting to distract him but also wanting the answer.

Matteo's eyes narrowed and she felt the anger rise in him. "A man, perhaps. Who knows?" He stroked Sarael's cheek. "It's a good thing for her that I found you first, *carissima*, and have no need to keep searching for her." His voice was soft, but full of deadly menace and she couldn't suppress a shiver, her mother's words haunting her. *If you're found, your life won't be your own.*

He used his free hand to unbutton his shirt, parting it in order to expose the mark over his heart. Sarael couldn't resist touching the matching tattoo, tracing it with her fingers. She knew immediately that she'd made a mistake when his breathing changed and the waves of lust she'd experienced earlier began to swamp her.

This time Matteo fought the desire. Refusing to give in to the temptation to tumble her along the length of the seat once again and cover her body with his. Instead he concentrated on Angelique — his anger serving as a buffer, though he was no less aware of Sarael's fingers on his chest, her buttocks pressed against his erection.

"You are mine," he said, kissing her wrist again, tempting himself by tracing her claiming mark with his tongue.

Sarael shivered, unable to stop herself from leaning over and pressing a kiss to the mark on his chest, from imitating his action. From repeating it when he jerked under the lashes of her tongue.

But before she could do it a third time, he speared his fingers through her hair, forcing her away from his flesh, angling her so that his mouth could cover hers in a searing, punishing kiss. She yielded immediately, going soft and pliant. The shared tattoo somehow validating the rightness of being with him so that she enjoyed the heat and hunger that moved through her this time, instead of being overwhelmed by it.

She touched her tongue to his, swallowing his moan and whimpering when his hold on her tightened, when his tongue became even more aggressive, his body tense against hers. Sarael knew she should be frightened of him — terrified even — and yet her body recognized him even if she didn't, and her mind craved the answers he could provide.

This time Matteo felt only satisfaction when he raised his face from Sarael's and met her gaze, he saw only desire and a wealth of questions in her eyes instead of enthrallment. He kissed her again, a soothing, gentle kiss full of promise as the limo turned down the driveway leading to the house that would serve as their home until she was his kadine.

The car stopped and he adjusted his hold so he could easily slide from the limo with her in his arms, his servant and driver hurrying to get the front door of the house opened. He paused, a small smile on his face as he said, "After you attend to the matter we spoke of earlier, Pietro, you are free to entertain yourself. I will summon you when I next need you."

"Very good," Pietro said, a hint of a smile in his voice, though his ancient features didn't reveal any emotion.

Matteo navigated the darkness of the house, not bothering to turn on lights that weren't needed as he easily climbed the stairs to the second floor. Only when he got Sarael to his bedroom did he stop, taking the time to lock the door and then with a thought, start a fire roaring in the fireplace, his lips quirking upward at the irony of possessing such a talent. Fire was one of the few sure ways to kill his kind.

Sarael startled in his arms, her attention jerking to the fireplace. He'd planned to mate with her on the bed, but the warmth of the fire and its soothing effect made him change his mind and move toward it.

The room had been prepared for the claiming of a bride and so the area in front of the hearth was piled with plush, soft rugs. He lowered Sarael to them, immediately joining her, positioning himself on his side, his gaze capturing hers, his leg thrown over hers, preventing her from escaping him, his hand pinning her wrists above her head.

Desire such as he'd never known coursed through him, making his cock pulse in time to his own rapid heartbeat, making him clench his buttocks against the need to take himself in hand and release lest he move too quickly and take her as though she was nothing to him.

He had long ago tired of the endless string of women whose blood, even taken with sex, only sated him temporarily, who weren't even a fleeting thought once he'd risen from wherever he'd fucked them. He'd dreamed of this moment even before *La Smania*—the restless hunger and thirst for a mate—overtook him at the point when he became reproductively mature. He'd dreamed of this moment well before *La Brama* had grown to the level where he required the herbs to contain it.

A soul-deep need that entailed more than sex and blood rushed through him as he looked at Sarael. In her he could have everything he desired. That was the nature of one's kadine. But first he needed to make her his bride.

Sarael could feel the lust pouring off Matteo. It invaded her body, making her restless, achy with the need to touch and be touched. She tried to fight it, to push it aside long enough to question him, but when he leaned down, she could only meet his lips, opening her mouth willingly and welcoming his tongue against her own, a small cry of protest escaping when he ended the kiss, a whimper following when his lips moved to her throat, tormenting her with small, sucking bites.

She was shaking, covered with a fine sheen of sweat when he lifted his head moments later, his gaze going to hers, searching for something, the satisfaction on his face indicating he'd found it. "You're beautiful, Sarael," he whispered, "more so than I'd dared to hope for." His hand skimmed down the middle of her chest, settling on her quivering abdomen, his touch making her womb flutter and her legs part slightly. He gave her a kiss, a reward for her response and she touched her tongue to his in a silent request for more.

Matteo's cock pulsed, coating its head with a fresh wash of arousal. Every cell in his body argued that he had centuries to seduce and train her. That he should strip her and find his own satisfaction now.

He resisted. Forcing himself instead to slowly unbutton her shirt, parting it as his hand moved back toward the throbbing pulse in her throat.

"Beautiful," he said again after he'd unfastened the front clasp of her bra and peeled it back, exposing breasts capped with dark brown nipples. He leaned in, unable to resist the lure of them, relishing her cries of pleasure as he suckled, the pounding beat of her heart so close to his mouth that he ached to sink his fangs into her, to draw blood so he could truly feast at her breast.

Sarael writhed underneath him, still pinned down, unable to do anything but accept the pleasure he was giving her. A pleasure that was filling her up, making her feel as though she would burst. "Please," she whimpered, wanting so many things at once that she couldn't focus on any one of them.

Matteo stilled, his head lifting, his dark, dark eyes capturing hers, scaring her and thrilling her at the same time. "Please what?" he asked, his own features taut, strained.

"Let my hands go. Let me touch you."

He shifted, settling more of his weight on her, letting her feel the size of his erection through the layers of their clothing. "That would be very dangerous. You're not ready to take all of me yet."

She shivered, realizing now why she'd never let a man into her body before, why every time she'd gotten close, she'd become frightened...something warning that the consequences of yielding her virginity would become a horrible weight on her conscience in the future.

Looking up into Matteo's eyes, she knew he was the reason she had remained a virgin. Whatever it was that bound her to him, that allowed him to summon her, whatever it was, it had kept her from allowing another man to possess her. Subtly warning her that he would kill any man who knew her in such an intimate way.

Matteo used his free hand to finish unbuttoning his shirt, pushing it out of the way as he lowered his mouth to hers, allowing for the first contact of her breasts against his chest as he lay over her, imprinting more of his scent on her.

It had been a mistake to place her on the floor in front of the fire. He should have taken her to the bed, where he could tether her wrists and ankles when it became necessary. He wasn't sure he could remain in control if she touched him now, if she scratched at his back or wrapped her legs around him.

He craved her. Needed her. Wanted nothing more than to rip their clothing away and force himself into her tight sheath as his fangs pierced her skin and her blood flowed into him.

Instead he used his tongue, thrusting and twining, exploring her mouth as he swallowed her sweet cries and fed on her submission, on the way her body writhed underneath his, pleading with him to claim it, and her, for all time.

Sensation after sensation rippled through Sarael, beginning at the point where Matteo's hands held her wrists down, moving to where his lips and tongue touched hers, then downward, through her breasts, her abdomen, her cunt, even down to her toes. She moved restlessly against him, grinding against his erection until all of his weight was on her, holding her to the ground, pinning her so that she could barely move.

She was wet, painfully swollen. But a thrill of feminine pride whipped through her at the tightness of his body, at how he strained to keep from pumping into her, his breathing fast, his chest slick against hers, his mouth and tongue so dominant that she knew whatever power he held over her, she held some in her own right, to be able to make him desire her so.

With a groan, Matteo rolled off her, going to his knees, his hand gripping his cock through his trousers in order to keep from spewing his seed like an untried boy. He let her sit, but when she leaned toward him, reaching out to touch him, he halted her with a sharp command, reinforcing it with the strength of his will so that for an instant her hand hovered in midair between them before dropping to her lap, her face showing her confusion, her need to understand how he could command her in such a way.

"Take off your clothes," he ordered, chasing the question he didn't want to answer off her tongue, but at a cost. His cock pulsed, a hard warning as more arousal escaped through the slit in its head, his balls were tight against his body, already aching, burning with the need for release.

She obeyed. Easily shedding the shirt and bra, the shoes, socks and jeans. But then she stopped, remaining in a pair of black panties. The color hiding their wetness though the sight of her glistening inner thighs and the scent of her arousal were enough to force Matteo to move in, to once again put her on her back, this time with her wrists held at her sides as he knelt between her legs, mesmerized by the sight of her panties, by the smell of her.

He leaned down, pressing his face against the wet strip of cloth, breathing her in. He knew he should punish her for not obeying him completely, should use it as an excuse to move her to the bed and tie her there, but he was lost in her, enthralled. He turned his head, kissing her inner thigh, sucking, lapping at her escaped juices.

Growling a warning for her not to touch him, he freed her wrists long enough to dispose of the scrap of fabric between her legs. For long moments he stared, entranced by the sight of her swollen flesh, her clit, and then he was on her. Once again pinning her wrists in place as he devoured her. Exploring her slit with his tongue, fucking her with it, reveling in the way she thrust against his mouth, in the way she whimpered and pleaded for him not to stop, grinding herself against him and coming repeatedly, sobbing his name each time she did so.

She was shaking, shivering, completely submissive when he could finally drag his mouth away from her opening and move to her clit. And at the first touch of his lips there, she bolted into a sitting position, freeing her hands in a sudden spike of energy and spearing them into Matteo's hair, her breath coming in pants as she curled around him, gripping him, sometimes holding him in place, sometimes trying to pull him away as he alternated between sucking her swollen knob and twirling his tongue over and around it until finally she came again, uncurling and lying on her back, her legs spread, her body completely his.

He used his tongue to clean the evidence of her passion, to mark her with his scent, to further imprint himself on her. His fangs elongating as he licked over the artery in her inner thigh. She jerked when their sharp points grazed her, nicking the skin so that a drop of blood escaped. It was too much.

He struck, her scream too late as her hot blood poured into his mouth, her struggles — a confusing mix of terror and ecstasy — only adding to his lust so that he drank and drank and drank, gorging himself on her until her heart stuttered in warning that if he continued, he would kill her.

She was weak and soft, too drained to be afraid any longer by the sight of his fangs, by the knowledge of what he was when he settled his body on hers and pressed his cock to the entrance of her virgin channel, swallowing her small cry of pain as his penis became the first and only one that she would ever know. "Open wider for me," he said, cursing himself for his lack of control, cursing Sarael's mother for taking her away so that she hadn't been prepared properly.

But it was too late to stop the first claiming, the first exchange of blood. Matteo pressed his lips to Sarael's, growling when she tried to turn away at the metallic taste of blood that still lingered there, his hands going to her hair and holding her in place as he thrust his tongue aggressively into her mouth, building the passion again, pressing his cock into her an inch at a time, satisfaction rushing over him when her body responded, arching, inviting him deeper.

By the time he was fully seated, she was whimpering again, clawing at his back, his buttocks, shattering the rest of his control so that he pounded in and out of her, his reality centered on the need to feel his bride's sheath fisting around his cock, to fill her with his seed and give her his blood.

Fierce desire clouded Sarael's mind, taking the edge off the knowledge that he wasn't human — that he was a creature straight out of a horror film. A vampire.

There was no fighting him. No fighting herself. At least not now. Not with his cock inside her, not with her body wrapped around his, welcoming Matteo as though it had been created for him.

She arched into him, her nails digging into his flesh as orgasm slammed into her. As she felt his body go tight in the instant before wave after wave of his seed splashed into her womb.

Sated beyond all imagining she went lax, her eyes drifting shut, her thoughts scattered, unable to take form until he pressed her mouth to his wrist and his hot blood scorched her lips. She fought then, but she was no match for his superior strength as he forced her to take what he offered, to drink and drink and drink until it became a fine wine she couldn't do without. And only then did his touch change, his hand stroking her throat, along her spine, his voice praising her for each swallow, his words following her into the darkness of sleep. "Drink, Sarael. Tonight you are my bride. But soon you will be my kadine."

Chapter Three

Sarael jerked awake, her first thoughts following along their usual track. She needed to get up and get ready for work. Now that it was fall and school was in session for the townies, every weekend day counted, and Saturdays were the biggest draw. She'd promised to…

Her second thoughts cut off the first as she struggled to sit up, only to find herself held down by a heavy male body. Matteo. In a heartbeat the night came crashing back, making her struggle against his strength. But she was no match for him, and she stilled completely when his husky voice warned, "I will tether you to the bed if you continue to fight, Sarael."

She lay immobile, save for the rapid rise and fall of her chest, the thundering of her heart. He shifted to his side, his hand going to her breast, his thumb stroking over her nipple before he leaned down and took it in his mouth, suckling, the gentle pull of his mouth calming her so that she welcomed his touch, opening her legs for him when his hand glided over her abdomen and cupped her mound, his fingers sliding into a suddenly wet slit, fucking in and out until she was whimpering, coming at his command.

"Sleep," he said afterward, pulling her into his arms so that her mouth was positioned over the tattoo on his chest.

For a moment she remained trapped in a haze of sexual satisfaction, her mind and body content to obey him. She traced the tattoo with her tongue and he grunted, giving her a small slap on her buttock. "Enough, *carissima*, you'll wear me out before the night arrives if you tempt me into taking you now."

"How can you be awake?" she asked, her body telling her it was well past dawn.

He chuckled. "Over time we have come to call ourselves by the same name humans use for us, but human beliefs about vampires are incomplete at best, ludicrous at worst. If you open the curtains

36

and bathe me in sunlight you won't see me burst into flames — not as you might imagine. Nor will I turn into a corpse. I am not an undead human returned to feed on the living."

"What are you then?"

He sighed, the sound of a man who wanted nothing more than to sleep. "The one who claims you, Sarael. We are mated, joined for all time now."

She jerked in reaction, knowing by the strange heat burning through her veins and the complete certainty in his voice that it was true. She fought off her fear, suppressed the desire to protest. To engage in a battle that would lead her nowhere.

"You took my blood. You forced me to take yours." Her mind recoiled as she spoke the words even though her cunt pulsed with the feel of his erection pressing hot against her belly.

"Was it so bad, *carissima*?" he asked, stroking her hair and holding her tightly. Rolling now, his thighs forcing hers apart as his penis found its way home, forging deep inside her and making her whimper. "Did you hate it so much?" he whispered, shifting, urging her legs to bend so he could hook his elbows underneath her knees, changing the angle, turning her sheath into a vise around his cock.

Matteo clenched his jaw against the extreme pleasure, knowing it was a mistake to fuck her, knowing it would weaken him so that *Il Sonno* — The Sleep — would take him more deeply than he could afford to allow, so that should sunlight strike him, his cells would break down almost immediately, forcing him to shift to his second form — the form all vampires could assume, a survival mechanism that came with *La Metamorfosi*, when children born to pureblood vampires and their kadines shed the restrictions that came with their once fully human mothers.

Until *La Metamorfosi*, children slept during the sunlight hours, locked in bodies that were still part human, guarded by their mothers and the padralls who served the family. It was the only time during a vampire's life when he could be killed as easily as a human could be. But a measure of maturity was necessary in order to pull scattered cells together once the change had occurred. Preparation was required, knowledge, so that fear and confusion didn't give way to panic. The first change of form was painful, terrifying, exhilarating, empowering.

And now the future held sons for Matteo. As well as a kadine.

He looked down into Sarael's face and felt his heart swell. The need to claim her poured into him, but it was too soon to give her more of his blood. It was too soon to take more of hers. He had already taken too much during the first exchange, and yet he craved it—not with the mindless urgency of *La Brama*, but with the intensity of a male for his kadine.

Matteo took her body instead. His breath coming in pants as he forced himself in and out of a channel made small and exquisitely tight. His heart soaring at how she responded to him. With whimpers and tears and pleas for release. Accepting his right to her. His right to command her—to control even her pleasure.

He held off as long as he could, resisting until her inner muscles rippled and spasmed against his cock, drenching him with arousal and milking him of his seed, the hot rush of it through his penis making him weak and dizzy so that he collapsed against her, once again trapping her body under his.

For long moments Sarael lay in a fog of pleasure, sated, content. But slowly it faded, burned away by the strange heat moving through her veins. By the certainty that it was his blood, changing her, turning her into what he was—a vampire.

Her heartbeat spiked, racing, and she felt him tense. More questions pressed in on her, demanding answers, and yet she hesitated to ask them for fear he'd grow suspicious and worry she might escape—as her mother had.

Sarael shivered, fearing his reaction and yet determined to gain as much knowledge as she could. "Can you go out in the sunshine?"

"If I must, *carissima*, but I would not choose this form were I to do so." His eyes opened, locking to hers. And once again she had the sensation that he was pressing against some barrier keeping her mind shielded from his.

She wanted to ask what form he would take. But her survival instincts warned against further conversation so Sarael closed her eyes, forcing herself to relax, to snuggle against him as though she accepted her fate. She didn't doubt he'd do as he threatened and tie her to the bed. And if he did then she stood no chance of escaping.

Emotion rioted within her. The Moon against The Sun. Both of them trying to pull her into their realm and hold her there.

I can feel the truth of them, she'd said to Dakotah, the tarot cards laid out in front of her on the bed. *You can change that truth*, Dakotah claimed.

But could she?

Her mother had.

For the first time Sarael felt something other than pain over being abandoned. Had her mother left her with the carnival in the hopes she'd be safe there? In the hopes this day would never arrive for Sarael? A day when her body would betray her, leaving her defenseless against Matteo—even though he was a stranger, a man who would strip away the freedom she had taken for granted and turn her into... She shivered, not wanting to think about becoming a creature of nightmares. A creature whose world was governed by The Moon.

Three blood exchanges. Was it myth or reality?

She tried to imagine herself feeding and found it horrifying—until she became aware of Matteo's heartbeat, of the steady rhythm of his pulse only inches away from her mouth. Heat curled in her womb and her clit responded, stiffening, throbbing in time to the beats of his heart, stabbing against his body and making him chuckle.

"Sleep, Sarael, I will give you all that you desire when the moon rises again."

Contentment moved through Matteo, satisfaction. In his mind he kissed his way down her body, lingering to explore, to taste, to savor the sounds of her pleading, the feel of her hands in his hair as he slowly approached the small engorged knob indicating her arousal.

He could spend days with his face pressed between her legs. Kissing her. Licking her. Thrusting his tongue into her woman's opening. Sucking on her swollen cunt lips and straining clit.

Reveling in her.

Claiming her.

Heart and soul and cock swelling with the sounds of her pleasure.

His penis stirred, but he was too lethargic to act on his fantasy. Instead he had to content himself with the feel of her clit stabbing into him as he struggled against the heavy sleep of his kind.

He was mature enough that he wasn't completely helpless during the daylight hours, almost comatose as the very young were, but his ability to move around was limited, especially now, after mating with her during the morning hours. If she tried to hurt him, he could subdue her, but if she managed to get out of the house, he wouldn't be able to hunt her until dusk.

He'd already expended too much of his energy. And there were limits. A price that had to be paid for taking a human shape but maintaining the longevity as well as some of the abilities that had been the birthright of his alien ancestors.

Matteo shifted, placing more of her underneath him. She protested and his first thought was to restrain her even further, but then he felt the heat of her cheeks against his chest as she muttered, "I need to get up for a minute." A small shove of her hand punctuating the desire.

Matteo let her escape, watching through slitted eyes as she surveyed the room, quickly locating the bathroom. "Leave the door open," he said, prepared to enforce the command, but glad when she ducked her head and escaped into the bathroom without making it necessary.

When she returned, she joined him without urging, going willingly into his arms, making him smile against her hair, his heart filling with anticipation of what was to come. The second exchange of blood. With it his control over her would tighten, she would crave his blood desperately then. And with the third exchange, she would need it to survive.

His cock urged him to bury it inside her as they slept, his thoughts returning to the night, to the rush unlike any he'd ever experienced as he filled himself with her blood, reliving again the intensely erotic moments when she fed from him. It was all he'd ever thought it would be and so much more.

Sarael fell asleep despite her intentions not to, but as she eased out from underneath Matteo later in the day, she realized that she'd needed the sleep, just as desperately as she now needed to eat.

She was ravenous. Starving. The sensation almost painful it was so intense. She could smell the fruit left in a bowl on the dresser, could see it clearly even though the room was almost completely dark, the fire in the fireplace a dull red glow keeping the room warmed but providing very little light.

Her senses had always been sharper than those around her, but they'd never been this finely honed. She shivered, realizing that her blood still burned as it made its way through her body. She touched her tongue to her teeth, relieved to find them the same as they'd always been.

Her mind tried to shy away from thinking about the blood he'd forced her to take—but she couldn't ignore what had happened. It should have made her gag and vomit, instead his blood had slid down her throat so easily, filling her until she was willingly taking what he offered.

She needed to escape before it was too late. Before it happened again. And again. But even as she thought it, her body urged her to return to Matteo's arms. To find sanctuary there.

It was enough to scare Sarael, to call forth a primal instinct for self-preservation. She moved to the dresser, gorging herself on the fruit, the need to sleep pressing down on her as soon as she was full.

Then it was an effort to gather her clothes and slip into the bathroom so she could dress without fear of waking him. Her body continuing its demand that she return to Matteo and curl up next to him, allowing the heavy lethargy to overwhelm her. She fought the compulsion and dressed before looking out the partially open window, her pulse accelerating when she saw the drop to the ground. The only hope of escape from the bathroom was the tree that stood next to the house, rich with autumn leaves, its branches thick and sturdy—but a leap of faith away.

Could she do it if there was no other way to escape? Could she jump? Fear clogged her throat. And if she missed?

She remembered Matteo pausing at the bedroom door and locking it. But she hadn't been paying attention, didn't know whether he was locking them in, or others out.

It would be foolish to risk injury climbing out the bathroom window if she could escape through the bedroom door. Her hands went to the window. But it would be equally foolish to leave the bathroom without preparing for escape.

Whatever she was going to do, however she was going to leave, she needed to do it quickly. He was stirring, waking. Even without being in the same room with him, she knew it was happening.

Sarael forced the window all the way open, cringing when it screeched. A streak of ice shooting down her spine with his sharp command. *Come to me, Sarael. Now!*

There was no choice but to go out through the window. But she was unable even to lift her leg over the sill. He issued the command to come again, his will pelting her, beating away what little control she had over her own body, just as he'd been able to do at the carnival. The demonstration of his power over her more terrifying to her in that moment than his taking of her blood.

She fought his command with each step, her heartbeat a roar in her ears, but soon she was back in the bedroom. She'd expected to find him standing, ready to pounce. But he was sitting in front of the fireplace and she realized that he wasn't unaffected by the sunlight. That despite being awake, the lethargy which pressed down on her was probably only a fraction of what he was experiencing. But he was still powerful, his control of her body greater than her own.

"Get on the bed, Sarael." It was a hissed command full of menace. And in the dark room, his eyes glittered, reflecting the red of dying embers and giving him an alien appearance which only served to heighten her fear and desire to escape.

The sight of what waited for her on the bed—the restraints, one for each wrist and ankle—had her clutching at the drapes and trying to keep from obeying, just as she'd clutched at the metal railing near the carousel the previous night.

Now! It was a sharp command as he started to rise.

She jerked the drapes open without conscious thought. The fear of being tied, locked in darkness, helpless as she'd been once before as a child, the fierce primal desire to survive as fully human guiding her actions and flooding the room with sunlight.

Matteo recoiled, his face filled with anger and denial, his fangs exposed and glistening an instant before his image wavered, dissolved, turning into a mist that rushed toward her with enough force to press her against the window as though her body could block the sunlight streaming into the room. But then even the mist dissipated, though the air remained heavy with his presence, his menace, his silent promise that she would not escape him for long.

Sarael moved to the bedroom door, only to find the deadbolt locked and the key missing. She searched his clothing and then the room, tension building with each moment she remained in his house. Until finally she was once again in the bathroom, only this time she was crouched on the windowsill, steeling herself to jump, imagining herself grabbing the thick branch with her hands and swinging her leg over it.

For a moment she hesitated. Waves of lethargy striking her now that the sun was kissing her skin directly with its rays. And yet each passing urge to curl up and sleep seemed less intense than the last, until finally the desire became manageable.

Sarael looked at the ground far beneath her once more, but it didn't shake her resolve to escape. Too much was at stake. Her freedom. Something she'd always taken for granted. Her life. There would be no path back to The Sun if he succeeded in trapping her forever in the world of The Moon.

She took a deep breath and leaped, the movement smooth, her hands grabbing the branch, a sudden breeze gusting underneath her so that it became effortless to swing her lower body into position and secure herself by wrapping her legs around the limb.

She felt Matteo's angry presence as she descended, her pulse spiking with the realization that he could just as easily have sent her crashing to the ground when another sudden gust of air pressed her to the tree, keeping her from falling as she slid down a trunk whose lower branches and been removed in order to prevent someone gaining access to the upper floor by climbing.

A new fear filled Sarael when she reached the ground. She couldn't outrun the wind. She couldn't outrun the sun. Eventually the day would end and darkness would descend. And it would all be for nothing. Wherever she was, he would materialize to reclaim her.

And yet as soon as she thought it, she felt his presence fading away, then guessed the reason for it. The limo sat in the driveway, reminding her that the driver was also Matteo's servant.

Matteo would not let her run—even if the freedom was only an illusion—he would not let her escape if he could keep her locked in his house. She bolted then, pounding down the driveway and along the deserted road, heart thundering at the sight of miles and miles of beach to her left, at the thick, tangled woods to her right, giving the area a feel of isolation—as though finding someone who could help her would entail a miracle.

Chapter Four

Rage roared through Matteo's body, keeping *Il Sonno* at bay despite his slipping back into the house and returning to human form in one of the darkened rooms. He'd hated to leave Sarael, but the risk of her moving through the day, of possibly escaping him while he was nothing more than scattered particles had been too great.

His secondary form was geared toward survival, not the control of wayward brides. It made him very nearly impossible to kill. It allowed him to sneak up on enemies and prey alike if needed. He could become a small gust of air, the equivalent of a lunge. He could use his second form and his abilities with fire against his enemies, he could travel, but only at the speed he could do so as a human—unless the natural elements aided him, blending him into wind or breeze.

Some of his kind were blessed with an additional form, becoming a bird or animal that could move about in the daylight hours, but he could not. And even if he could, he could not command Sarael in such a form. Nor could he send Pietro chasing after her.

Renewed anger made him hiss in frustration. He'd been foolish. Overconfident. Drunk on her blood and sex.

He should have tethered her to the bed as he intended. Should not have forgotten even for a moment that the stain of her mother's choices now marked Sarael.

It would not happen again.

He focused inward, on the link that had first formed during the confirmation ceremony when the tattoos were drawn, a link that had strengthened with the first true exchange of blood done when he claimed Sarael as his bride. It was not yet strong enough to command her over larger distances, or to know her thoughts, but it still provided a way for him to make his will known. *Return to the house, Sarael. Now!*

Sarael stumbled as Matteo's voice whipped through her mind, followed by the sound of a car approaching. It would be the limo. She knew it with a certainty that had her scrambling into the woods and taking shelter behind a cluster of trees.

Within seconds the long, dark car came into view. Creeping slowly in her direction. Pietro scanning both sides of the road. Passing the spot where she hid.

She leaned against the tree in relief and tried to think. Almost instantly, Matteo's voice was there, insistent, ordering her to return. The command so strong that her heart raced and her breath came in shallow pants in reaction to it.

Sarael knew she needed to put distance between them. That the first step she took back to Matteo would mean the loss of her freedom. There would be no escaping him again.

The limo returned, gliding to a stop close to where Sarael has hiding. She was nearly paralyzed by fear when Pietro emerged from the car. What if Matteo could somehow take command of the elderly man's body? What if he could find and capture her using Pietro's form? But then the old man spoke, saying, "Come with me. *Don* Cabrelli will go easier on you if you come back to the house without trouble. Come. I'll fix you something hot to eat and find you some clean clothing. Come with me, please."

Sarael's eyes darted from the man to where the driver's door stood open, the engine running. If she could just beat him back to the car... But what if she couldn't?

The knife she carried was a heavy weight in her pocket. She knew how to use it. Along the way, the men and women passing through the carnival had taught her to defend herself. There was always the danger of being raped, of being fair game when you were a carnie. She knew that only too well.

What if she couldn't beat Pietro to the car? Could she attack an elderly man? Even for her freedom?

Pietro started to turn just as she spied a rock on the ground. With nothing to lose she picked it up and tossed it, sailing it away from her, its descent through the tangled woods diverting the elderly man, making him think she might be coming to his call. He moved further away from the car and she bolted, reaching it and thrusting it into drive even before she had the door closed.

As the miles passed, she calmed, her mind clearing of both Matteo's compulsion for her to return and the thundering roar of her own heart. She followed the ocean until she reached a small town. Different than the one where the carnival was camped. But it didn't matter. She knew she couldn't return to her own trailer.

Sarael parked the limo, placing the keys underneath the seat before getting out, locking the door and closing it afterward. The limo was too conspicuous. Too easily spotted, and though she hadn't seen evidence of great wealth, she assumed Matteo possessed it. He would send others besides his elderly servant to find her. Just as he must have had others searching for Angelique since the moment she first disappeared.

Sarael moved away from the abandoned car, putting as much distance between her and it as she could. When she could go no further, she found a payphone and called Dakotah.

"What's going on?" Dakotah asked, the sound of the carousel in the background.

"I need a favor."

"Name it."

"Can you bring me some of my things?"

Silence met the question, sending fear rippling through Sarael.

"You don't have them," Dakotah said, the tone of her voice, her statement warning Sarael that her things were gone.

She closed her eyes. Hearing Matteo's words from the previous night. *After you attend to the matter we spoke of earlier, Pietro, you are free to entertain yourself.* "Someone came and got them? An elderly man?"

"Yeah. I said no at first, but Helki appeared and insisted that it was all right. What's going on, Sarael? Cable and Fane are asking around about you. There are two other guys with them, also trying to find out if anyone's seen you."

Sarael's stomach tightened with familiar uneasiness at the mention of Cable and Fane. Matteo must have sent them to watch her before he arrived. They'd been harbingers of the storm she sensed coming, though their presence alone wasn't enough of a warning to make her run. "Who are the other two?"

"One of them is named Domino. The other's Italian."

Sarael's grip tightened on the phone. "Matteo?"

"No." There was a pause and Sarael could picture Dakotah digging in her pocket. "Alessandro Digate. He slipped me a card after the other three had walked away. He said he was a friend of Angelique's—like that's supposed to mean something."

Sarael closed her eyes, unsure whether or not she should involve Dakotah. They were best friends, or as close to being best friends as whatever Dakotah was running from would allow her to be.

That's the way it had been with all of the carnies who'd passed through Sarael's life as she was growing up. The things they were escaping brought them together, but beyond a certain closeness their secrets still kept them apart.

And now Sarael desperately needed help. She had some money in her pocket. Enough to get by for a couple of days. But not here. Not in this town. Not with the limo abandoned here.

"I need a ride. To anywhere. Just away from here." She paused for a heartbeat. "No questions asked."

"You got it."

And within the hour, Sarael was in strange city, with more money in her pocket than she'd had before, watching as the truck which had pulled the small trailer that had been her home since she was sixteen drove away.

Call me if you need more, Dakotah had said, pressing the money into her hand before hugging Sarael. Both of them teary-eyed.

Be careful, Sarael whispered. *I'm sorry for involving you. Please be careful. He'll be looking for me.*

I'll be okay. Call me if you need help.

But Sarael knew she wouldn't, couldn't. She shivered, remembering Matteo's earlier words. The deadly menace in his voice when he'd said that it was a good thing he'd found her before finding her mother. In her heart she didn't think he'd hurt Dakotah.

But she didn't doubt that he would seek Dakotah out—using his vampiric powers to wrest information from her.

Sarael's stomach knotted with worry, with guilt, with regret for involving someone else, but the only way she could get rid of it would be to return to the carnival and let herself be taken again. Pulled into the world of The Moon. A place of fantasy and nightmare. Illusion and alternate reality. A place from which she would never escape again. He would never allow it. He had made no pretense of hiding his intentions, his belief that she belonged to him. He could already compel her, command her—at least when they were near each other, and she knew his control over her would grow stronger each time she was forced to take his blood. She guessed he would soon be able to touch her thoughts, leaving her with no secrets. No freedom, either physically or mentally.

Tears sparkled at the tips of Sarael's eyelashes, left over from watching Dakotah drive away. Not just the loss of a friend, or the loss of what few possessions Sarael valued, but the loss of a way of life. The Tower in ruins around her.

She couldn't go back.

She couldn't stay where she was.

She needed to keep moving.

Alone now. Without a destination.

Running, as so many of those who found their way to the carnival were doing. But she ran without the chance of a sanctuary.

Matteo would never stop looking for her.

Fear rushed through Sarael, threatening to overwhelm her. To leave her paralyzed like a wild creature caught in headlights. It was the first time in her life she'd been completely on her own. And night was coming. The darkness descending earlier each day.

She forced herself to enter the restaurant where Dakotah had left her, to take a seat and order a meal. The sight of it when it arrived stirring her hunger, though the tightness of her stomach made each bite a challenge—even as each bite that stayed down was a victory—a reaffirmation that she was human and not vampire.

Sarael kept her head lowered and tried not to draw attention to herself as she ate. Even though the restaurant was empty save for several waitresses, she knew Matteo would come here looking for her, asking about her. Her hand went repeatedly to her front pocket, to the wad of money there. She knew she needed to move on, to leave this city. But the only way to do so without leaving a clear trail would be to ask a complete stranger for a ride.

She shuddered at the thought. At the danger inherent in getting into a car with someone she didn't know. Couldn't trust. Bile rising in her throat, churning in her stomach as memories from the past pushed in, of a friendly stranger with a cute brown puppy and an old black car.

Terror gripped her for a minute. Past horror colliding with a present one, each trying to control her movements, her decisions. But her options were limited.

Buses were out, even if she could find one. He would check there quickly and be able to intercept her—in person or with the aid of Cable and Fane, or the others. The same was true of a taxi. She might gain a head start, but it would cost her more than she could afford, and he would quickly find out where she'd been taken.

Sarael shivered, finishing the last of her meal and pushing the plate aside. Lingering in the safety of bright lights and people for precious minutes before paying her bill and slipping from the restaurant. Fear of leaving a trail kept her from asking for directions, so she wandered until she learned which road would lead her to the highway, her heightened senses making her jump each time a car approached, each time she heard footsteps or voices. The cold, sea-wet air clung to her face and hair, chilling her, making her hunker deeper into her jacket.

She was miles away from the restaurant, crossing at the edge of a nearly vacant parking lot when a car pulled in front of her, the door opening so quickly that she jerked, prepared to run, half expecting to see Matteo emerge. Instead a stranger wearing a predatory smile slid from the driver's side, their eyes meeting momentarily.

"Hold up, baby," he said. "I haven't seen you around here before."

Fear rippled through Sarael and she altered her course, traveling sideways so she could keep him in sight. He laughed, a sound that reinforced her fear, and she closed her hand over the knife in her jacket pocket, praying she could do what needed to be done if he assaulted her.

"Hold up," he said again, following her, gaining on her. "Come on, baby, don't be like this. I'm not going to hurt you. I just want us to have some fun together."

She started sprinting then, rushing in the direction of the few cars in the parking lot. He easily matched her speed, passing her, toying with her, getting in front of her and jogging backward, his smile all fun and games, amusement at her expense.

Sarael wheeled away from him, hope spiking when he stumbled — then receding just as quickly when he recovered before she could dodge him. Once again cutting her off before she could get to the cars parked in the lot and put something between the two of them.

"Come on, baby, this is getting old."

She pushed herself, despite the fire in her lungs and the ache in her side, aiming for the road now even as she heard him gaining on her again. The sound of an approaching car spurred her on, the sight of it slowing, stopping, nearly brought tears to her eyes.

When the driver emerged, her pursuer's footsteps faltered, altered, headed away from her. Sarael kept going.

"You okay?" the driver asked when she got to him, out of breath, her heart thundering in her ears.

Sarael's eyes met his. "Thanks for stopping."

"Fight with your boyfriend?" The man seemed reluctant to takes his eyes off her, but finally his gaze shifted. "Looks like he's decided to wait for you. Need a ride somewhere?"

Sarael looked at the car in front of her, shiny and silver, then took in the man, his suit only slightly wrinkled, his expression concerned, the graying at his temples making him look distinguished, trustworthy. She'd intended to hitch a ride to the next city and yet anxiety moved through her, trepidation at the thought of getting in a car, even with this man. But when she glanced over her shoulder, she saw that he wasn't lying. Her pursuer was casually leaning against his own car, confident, his arms folded as though they were lovers involved in a quarrel.

She looked around. Seeing the impossibility of trying to escape by foot and knowing she couldn't involve the police. "If you don't mind, I'd like a ride," Sarael said, forcing the words out. Her hand tightening on the knife in her jacket pocket.

"Hop in, it's unlocked."

She walked around the car, very nearly changing her mind when she felt his gaze travel over her body, but forced herself to open the door, the scent of leather making her think of Matteo's limo. Adding strength and courage to her resolve.

"I'm Ross," the man said, offering a hand.

"I'm Sar…ah. Sarah." She took his hand, their eyes meeting again, the look in his slightly disquieting. She broke the contact, pulling her hand away, glancing out the window to where the other man now waited in the driver's seat of his own car. "Where are you heading?" she asked, trying to remember the names of nearby cities—places the carnival had passed each year, but never stopped at.

The engine started with a deceptive purr and he shifted the car into drive. "Thomasville, but I'm not in any hurry."

Chapter Five

Sarael shivered despite the warmth in the car. Fear trickled in with each passing minute as the smell of Ross' arousal slowly filled the enclosed space.

Only the sight of the car in the rearview mirror kept her from telling him to pull over and let her out. She was beginning to think that the presence of her first purser behind them was the only thing keeping her safe now.

To her right was endless ocean. To her left, stretches of woods separating houses which were closed up against the darkness and fall chill.

"Doesn't look like he's going to give up," Ross said, his hand leaving the steering wheel and sliding across the seat toward her leg.

Sarael's thumb rubbed over the release on the knife in her pocket as she crowded against the passenger door, legs pressed tightly together, tensing when he put his hand on her knee, patting it at first as though offering comfort, but then leaving his hand there, making her stomach roil.

She took her hand out of her pocket and pushed his hand off her leg. "I don't like to be touched," she said, the words stark, ugly, a truth that hadn't existed for Sarael before. But she couldn't tolerate the feel of his hand, even through clothing. Her body wanted only Matteo's touch.

The car slowed. "Is that what you were fighting with your boyfriend about? Because you teased him, then wouldn't put out? Just like you're doing to me?" Ross asked.

He lifted his arm and Sarael flinched, wondering if he was going to grab or strike her. Instead he turned the overhead light on, taking his eyes from the road long enough to meet her gaze and send a renewed shiver of fear through her.

Realization dawned, forming a cold ball in her stomach and creeping outward when she viewed the mindless lust in his eyes, the flickering glimpses of confusion as though the man deep within was trying to fight a hidden enemy. Her heart began racing, the blood pounding through her veins, a thundering taunt in her ears, a rush that she had no way to channel or control.

Reflexively she reached over and opened the electric window, the blast of cold air filling the car, chasing away the heat and unintentional pheromones, causing the man's eyes to clear. He shook his head, as though coming out of a daze, his cheeks growing red — either from embarrassment or cold.

A sign loomed in front of them. "Take that exit," Sarael said, trying to pitch her voice the same way Matteo had when he stopped her hand midway between them — a small thrill of victory rushing through her when Ross immediately put the turn signal on. But the victory was short-lived, the shock of the cold air wearing off by the time they got into town.

His hand was on his cock then. Massaging his erection through the elegant trousers of his suit. His breathing coming faster, lust filling the car again despite the fresh air, his agitation growing, his eyes flicking back and forth, searching for a place to pull over and fuck.

Resolve filled Sarael and she leaned forward as if she too was looking for a likely place to suggest they go, but instead her hand crept to the door handle, grasping it, preparing to escape as soon as the car slowed.

A small measure of relief filled her when the car that had been trailing them got caught behind a stoplight. Then opportunity presented itself when the light ahead of them turned yellow and the car before them stopped.

She leapt from the car and ran, glad this city seemed busier than the last one, with some of the shops still open and people sitting in warmed cafés and restaurants. She darted into the first place she could, careful to keep her head ducked, to avoid making eye contact as she raced through, guessing there would be a kitchen entrance and a way to escape.

There were startled exclamations behind her, but no sounds of pursuit. Still, she kept moving. Escaping into an alley, and then another, weaving around until she spotted a bus with a female driver and only a few passengers.

Sarael climbed on, scared but knowing she had to take the risk. "How much?" she mumbled, head down.

The driver told her, adding, "This one's going to Leesburg. Last bus of the day, hon. You sure it's the one you want?"

Sarael nodded slightly and paid the fare, taking a seat as far away from the other passengers as she could and huddling, concentrating inward, on The Hanged Man this time and not The Moon. Finding a strange peace in doing so, a centering. Her mind reconstructing the card representing her past detail by detail. So focused on it that the trip to Leesburg passed quickly and without incident.

The exercise left her more aware than she had been. As the image of the tarot card dissolved, she could feel the very moment her body began calling to those around her, as though they were prey she would one day feed on. And in an instant, the peace she'd found disappeared.

She wandered after that, avoiding people, avoiding eye contact, desperately seeking a safe place. Wanting nothing more than four walls and a door she could lock. A place she could hide. Stopping only when she found a cheap hotel with a woman manning the desk.

* * * * *

Once again Matteo stood in the shadows of the carnival, watching, waiting. Only instead of Sarael, it was her friend — Dakotah — who shivered, aware on some level that she was being hunted.

Fane and Cable had questioned her early in the day, after Sarael had escaped with the limousine and Matteo had been forced to ask for assistance. When they'd spoken to Dakotah, she'd denied knowing where Sarael was. But later she'd been seen in the town where the limousine was abandoned, driving away with a woman who matched Sarael's description.

A growl rumbled in Matteo's chest. A sound of frustrated anger. It was a good thing this woman was Sarael's friend.

He was more dangerous now than he'd ever been. Despite forcing himself to swallow twice the amount of herbs than he usually required, *La Brama* roared through him, trying to overwhelm him.

The claiming of a kadine wasn't without risk and penalty. Something was gained and lost with each blood exchange.

He'd gorged himself on Sarael and now Matteo needed her blood far more than she needed his. His chest was tight, his body burning as every cell demanded he drink from her. He was parched and only she could truly quench his thirst.

If he yielded to *La Brama* now, if his fangs slid into a human, he would take everything, leaving a husk behind, drained of all life. And he would crave more. Taking the same again and again. Not ceasing until he'd once again pressed his mouth to Sarael and drunk from her.

It was a good thing Sarael cared for Dakotah. That alone might make the difference between life and death for her friend. He would not let anyone or anything stand in the way of reclaiming his bride, but he would prefer to go to Sarael with a clear conscience.

As he'd done so many times in the past, Matteo cursed Angelique for taking Sarael away from those who would have prepared her to come to his side. To find happiness there without suffering first.

Long ago his kind had come to the conclusion it was better to raise future kadines than to find them among the human population. To convert humans as adults was too arduous, too painful for all involved, and too many of them were lost in the process—dying, sometimes by their own hand, or going insane.

Though Sarael wasn't raised as she should have been, she had been created for him, his blood given to her at birth and during the confirmation ceremony verifying that she was indeed the female who would grow up to be his other half. She would never find true happiness anywhere but at his side. And he had little doubt that she *would* be happy. It could be no other way. With the third exchange of blood, they would be one. Her happiness would be his. Her misery his as well. Just as his needs and desires would become hers. There was almost no separation between a male and his kadine.

If Angelique had run before giving birth, before the confirmation ceremony, then he… Matteo shrugged the thoughts away. None of it mattered. Sarael was his. His claim was irrevocable. No other would do for him now that he'd tasted her blood and felt the welcoming heat of her sheath around his cock.

He shifted, restless, impatient. His thoughts going back to his earlier visit with Cable, the American padrall who had originally contacted him regarding Sarael's discovery.

Anger burned like a nest of hot coals in Matteo's gut. His pride still stung at having to admit that his bride had run from him, managing to escape when *he* should have made it impossible for her to do so.

It galled him that Alessandro Digate had been present to hear the admission, would no doubt enjoy carrying it back to Italy and the padrall order there — the same order which had been responsible for Sarael's conception and confirmation. "Perhaps you can now see how it was that the mother got away from us," Alessandro had said, as though Matteo needed a reminder of Angelique's escape and the suffering it had caused — not just for him but for her family and the padrall order which had been responsible for her.

Matteo hissed. He didn't blame the order for sending someone to serve as a witness to Sarael's status as his kadine, for wanting their failure to finally be a thing which could be left in the past. But he didn't like Alessandro and never had. Despite the great wealth Alessandro's family had gained by serving Matteo's race over the centuries, there had been times when Matteo thought he detected a hint of greed in Alessandro, a hunger for greater status and power.

Irritation moved through Matteo at wasting his thoughts on the other man. Of letting Alessandro's barb slide under his skin.

Sarael would be found and the remaining exchanges of blood would be made. She would be his kadine.

Matteo shifted, his senses suddenly alert, not for prey, but for another predator. His gaze quickly finding the source. Domino.

Obsidian eyes gleamed as the other man glided over to stand next to Matteo. "I'm surprised you haven't pounced." His smile widened as he shifted his focus to Dakotah. "So the friend helped your bride slip further away from you after all."

"Word travels fast."

"I encountered Fane and Cable earlier."

"Why are you here, Domino?"

"Hunting." Domino lifted his lips slightly, showing a hint of fang. "Like the good soldier that I am."

Just as long ago his kind had come to the conclusion it was better to raise future kadines than to find them among the human population, they had also decided it was better to create a soldier class, a line of men with the strengths of a vampire and yet who could move about in the sun. The humans once called them dhampirs, mistakenly thinking that they were vampire slayers.

But in truth, dhampirs could sate *La Brama* by feeding on the enemies they hunted, could even drain them of all life without sanction, but they could not survive without periodically drinking the blood of a vampire, most often feeding from the one who commanded them, overseeing their activities—at least until *La Trasformazione* occurred. Once that happened then dhampirs became fully vampire and reproductively mature, the children born to them becoming the next generation in a long line of soldiers.

"Our enemies are here?" Matteo asked, feeling a rush of fear unlike any he'd ever experienced—not for himself, but for Sarael. If she fell into the hands of those who called themselves the Believers...

"Yes, they're here," Domino said.

"How many of them?"

"One less than there were, but he was inconsequential, an idiot full of babble and rhetoric. And blood—at least for a short while." Domino shrugged. "I haven't been impressed by those I've encountered so far. They've been deviants who enjoy inflicting pain on others, hiding their sickness behind a cause they don't seem to fully believe in. Their lack of intelligence can only be an indication of how low our enemies have had to go in order to fill their ranks. Perhaps the time will come when they no longer exist at all."

"They are here for Sarael?" Matteo asked, anger and frustration joining the fear swirling violently inside him. He'd been careful to mask his arrival in the United States. Leaving behind those who usually accompanied him and bringing only Pietro. His ultimate destination — the carnival — known only by Cable, who had already asked the dhampir, Fane, to join him in ensuring Sarael's safety until Matteo arrived and could determine whether or not she was in fact Angelique's missing daughter.

"I don't know whether they are here for your bride or not. Fane said this place draws others who might interest the Believers. And tonight was the first time I stumbled on one of our enemy here — at the carnival. For the last months I've been watching a man called Byrd in the hopes he would lead me to those in greater positions of power. He came to a nearby town several days ago and others have since followed him." A smile slashed across Domino's face. "If your bride continues to elude you and you need to sate The Hunger, feel free to join Fane and me later for a hunt — I know where at least two of our enemies can be found with the approach of dawn. And their answers might be of interest to you."

"Sarael will not elude me for long," Matteo growled, irritation rippling over him at the amusement in Domino's obsidian eyes. "But I will consider your offer. If our enemies came for Sarael, then someone betrayed me."

"Then let us hope the presence of the Believers is just coincidence." Domino's focus shifted to where two men, hardly more than boys, had joined Dakotah, taking over the operation of the ride. His eyes narrowed as something one of them said made her laugh, the sound of it reaching the shadows where he and Matteo stood. "I'll grant that your missing bride is beautiful, but nothing is yet set in stone. Have you considered that perhaps she's more trouble than she's worth? I don't see it — giving up the freedom to sample a variety of different pleasures, all for the blood and cunt of a single female."

Matteo laughed, a genuine sound of amusement. "When *La Trasformazione* occurs you will see things differently and you will curse yourself for not going to the padrall earlier and arranging for a kadine of your own."

"So I have been told," Domino said, his eyes following Dakotah as she walked away, heading toward the back area of the carnival where the travel trailers were parked out of view from the crowds. "I will leave you to your hunting, and see you later perhaps."

Matteo nodded and moved away, following Dakotah. When she stopped suddenly and whirled around he had to admire both her intelligence and her courage.

"I don't know where she is. But I'm sure she'll find you if she wants anything to do with you," Dakotah said, somehow guessing who he was and what he wanted from her.

Matteo moved in closer, releasing the pheromones that fogged a human's mind, making them malleable and open to suggestion. "She left so quickly this morning that I'm not sure she can find the way home," he said, his voice like honey, a trap for the unwary.

Dakotah blinked, taking a step back from him, awareness battling the confusion and piquing his curiosity. She was not like other humans. If he weren't so intent on locating and reclaiming Sarael, if he weren't already sexually bonded to his bride, he would have enjoyed luring the female in front of him to a dark place and learning her secrets. "Where did you take Sarael?" he asked, moving in again, taking Dakotah's arm as he focused on her, trapping her with his eyes as wave after wave of pheromones struck her.

She fought and might have succeeded in freeing herself from one who hadn't reached reproductive maturity as Matteo had. But she was no match for him. "Where did you take Sarael?" he repeated when he knew she was helpless against him.

Dakotah shook her head, still fighting on some level, but the words tumbled out of her mouth regardless. "To Chesterfield."

"Where did you leave her?"

"Downtown."

He gave her a small shake, frustrated that she retained enough will to make him drag what he wanted to know out of her one question at a time. "Where did you leave her downtown?"

"At a restaurant."

"What was the name of it?"

"It was a Denny's."

"Do you remember a street name?"

Her eyebrows drew together. "No."

"What was around it?"

"Gas stations. Some hotels."

"Did you see where Sarael went?"

"Just inside. She said she was hungry. She didn't want me to know where she was going afterward."

Matteo released Dakotah but took her arm again when she swayed. "I'll help you back to your trailer," he said and her heart rate spiked, pulsing through her arm and into his hand like a lightning bolt, inadvertently stirring the bloodlust.

Fear could be a powerful aphrodisiac to one of his kind and he was not immune. His fangs elongated and for a long moment he hovered on the brink, the herbs and thoughts of Sarael only barely holding him in check and keeping him from doing something he would live to regret.

"I will follow you to ensure you are safe, as Sarael would want me to do. But I will not enter the trailer," he said, infusing his voice with calm, forcing his own body to echo the emotion as he released her arm.

Dakotah gave a small nod and turned, leading him to the trailer that she'd once shared with Sarael. Not lingering at the doorway when she got there, but hurrying inside and closing the door behind her. A small click telling him she'd also locked it.

For a minute Matteo hesitated, not quite ready to surround himself with people, to tempt himself with the steady, luring beat of their hearts. His gums were tingling from where he'd forced his fangs to retract. He closed his eyes and immediately the image of Sarael appeared — as he'd seen her last. Stretched out underneath him, sated and well-loved — seemingly content.

A hiss escaped with the last thought. Feelings of rage and betrayal rushed in. Matteo opened his eyes, fighting the need to strike out. To savage. Fighting the temptation that whispered through his veins, *La Brama*'s siren call offering him a chance to escape—at least for a little while—from the knowledge that his bride had chosen to run from him.

With a second hiss, he whirled, skirting the trailers housing those who traveled with the carnival, intent on returning to the limo. On taking up the search for Sarael once again.

She would not escape him. Not this time. Not ever.

He had erred in trusting her. Had misread the extent of Angelique's influence on her daughter—thinking the mother's absence meant Sarael was untainted. That she would accept her fate where Angelique hadn't.

He had learned otherwise.

Now he would teach Sarael that there were limits to his tolerance. Consequences for defying him.

If she feared him at first, then so be it. He would take her fear over her absence.

She'd been created for him. She belonged to him. In the end she would come to care for him just as deeply as he cared for her. It was her fate. One he wouldn't let her escape or deny.

* * * * *

Sarael dreamed of blood. At first it was a gentle call, drawing her to Matteo. Warming her as she took what he offered.

It was a sweet seduction urging her to take more and more until she was greedy for the taste, insatiable in her need for it.

And then there were thousands of hearts beating, luring her from Matteo's arms. Turning those around her into prey.

And they came to her, crowding in on her. Offering blood and sex. Their eyes glazed with lust, their hands reaching for her, grabbing at her, until she was forced to drive them back with her knife, slashing them until blood coated everything in sight.

* * * * *

Matteo prowled the bedroom. Ignoring the command to sleep that was being issued by the sun. Fighting against the lethargy.

Anger and fear warred inside him, frustration very nearly ruled. He hated relying on others to hunt for Sarael during the day, but there was no choice.

As Matteo paced, his mind ranged back to the Believers who'd provided some information — enough to make him fear for Sarael — and yet not enough to determine whether she was their true target.

"I heard two of them talking, we're here for a woman," the weaker-minded of the two Believers had said, falling easily under first Matteo's and then Domino's spell.

"What woman?" Matteo asked,

"I don't know. They haven't told us yet."

"Who are *they*?" Matteo asked.

"Chuck and Byrd, and the guy Chuck talks to on the phone. He's the one calling the shots."

Domino took over the questioning. "What are your orders?"

"To watch for vampires." The Believer clutched at the elaborate crucifix that hung around his neck. Its tip pointed and sharpened. A weapon neither Domino nor Matteo had seen the need to take away from him.

A grin spread across the Believer's face. "Byrd said at least one of them will probably show up, maybe more. And when they do, party time! If we have the girl by then, we're going to have a fuck-fest along with a nice little vampire barbeque."

Matteo's rage peaked with the image of Sarael being raped and he reacted, ripping the crucifix from the Believer's hand and shoving it into the other man's heart with so much force that he'd driven him backward and up, the sharp tip of the crucifix burying deep into the wall behind him so that when Matteo released his grip, the corpse hung, suspended, the Believer's feet dangling above the floor, rivulets of red trailing down the white wall.

"A waste of blood, a waste of life force, and a mess to clean up," Domino said. "But I agree, he told as much as he knew."

They'd turned their attention to the remaining Believer then, a hard-eyed zealot with a swirling red and black crucifix tattooed on his neck, his hands bound behind his back with his own necklace — a necklace made to double as a garrote, while the cross hanging from it would serve as a knife. "Do you care to add anything to what your friend said?" Fane asked, his voice silky, deadly, no less menacing for its softness.

The Believer spat at Fane. Hate burning in his eyes, a wet spot on the front of his pants where he'd orgasmed when Fane fed from him after subduing him.

Fane easily avoided the wad of saliva, shooting a look at Matteo. "There are times when the thought of reaching The Transformation is a welcome one." His smile widened, his fangs clearly visible. "But then moments like this occur and I am glad I can yield to The Hunger, and the rules that govern full vampires don't apply to me."

Fane grabbed the Believer, easily controlling the other man's body as he sank his fangs into the beefy, tattoo-covered neck again. Drinking, feasting, the man's cock hardening and erupting as he came repeatedly.

La Brama roared through Matteo at the sight of Fane feeding, taunting him, teasing him, urging him to sink his teeth into the Believer also, to experience the unparalleled high of taking everything—a primitive urge left from the days when his ancestors were trying to adapt to the hostile world they found themselves on—when they were experimenting, speeding the evolutionary process by taking the form of their prey, moving into its still warm body after they'd drained it of blood and left it an empty shell.

"Enough," Matteo growled, stepping forward, ready to rip Fane away from his victim if necessary. Despite his own killing of the first Believer, he would ensure that they'd gained every bit of information they could from this man before he was destroyed.

Fane lifted his head, his eyes momentarily feral, but then he resumed his questioning. "Let's start over again, tell us why you came here."

The man sagged in his chair. "Chuck called me. He said there was going to be some good hunting. The real thing, not the pathetic drugged-out assholes we've been practicing on."

"Practicing? Tell me about that." A sly smile formed on Fane's face. "Tell me about the pathetic drugged-out assholes. Tell me what you do when you practice."

The front of the man's pants tented in reaction to the question. He licked his lips. "We look for worthless scum no one will miss. And when we find them, we follow them, waiting for a chance to surprise them. Most of the time we take turns, seeing how fast we can strike with the knife. But other times we practice on our own."

Domino leaned in so that his face was only inches from the Believer's. "Those are the times you like best, aren't they? When you get to rape them before you actually kill them."

More ejaculate stained the front of the man's pants. "Yes."

Domino laughed softly. "How many Believers are here?"

"Chuck and Byrd and a couple of others. But more are coming. At least four more."

"And the woman you're here for?" Matteo pressed, feeling Fane and Domino's impatience to be done with this Believer and hunting the others.

"We're not even supposed to know about that. Chuck and Byrd haven't said anything."

Matteo returned home shortly thereafter, his worry for Sarael growing as the day grew brighter. His need for her building. His determination to recapture her unwavering. Two more exchanges and she would be his. Then he would take her to Italy. Away from the danger the Believers currently posed. Disposing of them was a matter for Fane and Domino, for the dhampirs, the soldiers of their race. His duties were encompassed by Sarael.

Chapter Six

Sarael eluded him for three days. But on the third night, he found her.

Satisfaction moved through Matteo, anticipation, as he stopped in front of her door, sensing her presence behind it. Sensing her awareness of him. Her fear.

He let the moments pass, let the fear build in her — retribution for what she'd put him through. A warning for the future.

She was weakened now, her will not nearly as strong. He knew he could command that she open the door, but he preferred to enter the room himself. Gaining the key from the clerk had been a simple matter — the ease of it only increasing his anger.

Sarael shivered, knowing the moment he was standing in front of the hotel door, dark and menacing, his arrival signaling the end of her freedom, and yet she very nearly cried in relief at his presence.

She'd been utterly alone, out in a world she'd never experienced before. One that had been made so much more dangerous by Matteo's blood.

Rather than getting weaker, its influence had grown stronger, making it difficult for her to leave the hotel room without being accosted by men. Most of them more frightening than any of those who came to the carnival looking for easy prey. More frightening than the face that used to haunt her dreams nightly as a small child, causing her to wake in a panic, tangled in sheets that reminded her of being tied and helpless.

She was afraid to go to sleep for fear the seedy hotel manager would sell access to her room and turn the other way as she was raped. And each time she did yield to exhaustion, she was haunted by dreams.

Blood dreams at first, then sexual ones. So intense that she'd wake abruptly and find herself feverish, needy. Her body coated with sweat, her hands between her legs or on her breasts.

She'd masturbated, trying to keep the memory of Matteo's touch from her mind as she'd plunged her fingers in and out of her slit, striking at her clit repeatedly, tweaking and tugging at her nipples. But the only way she'd found any relief was to let thoughts of him fill her, to relive those moments when his body had been on hers, his cock sheathed in her channel. It had barely been enough. And now he had found her.

Despite knowing he was there, she startled when the key slid into the lock, and remained motionless, watching — fascinated horror mingled with weary relief — as the knob slowly turned and the door swung open.

Matteo moved into the room and closed the door behind him. The fear that she was like her mother — and the anger that had accompanied it — had grown with each hour she'd eluded him. But his heart lurched at the sight of her, at the fatigue and vulnerability he saw in her face, at the way her body hunched in defeat and defenselessness as she sat on the bed, her knees drawn to her chest, her arms wrapped around her legs.

He'd thought to punish her, perhaps to tether her to his bedpost and use the flogger on her back and buttocks as a way of preventing further disobedience. But something inside him gave at the sight of her.

Matteo moved to the bed, sitting next to her and pulling her onto his lap, his heart and body leaping with pleasure and emotion when she didn't resist, but curled into him, her arms going around his neck, her face pressing against his skin.

He tightened his grip on her, breathing deeply and enjoying the feel of her soft hair against his cheek. "You shouldn't have run from me, Sarael."

She looked up, meeting his gaze, her own haunted. "I had to try," she whispered, licking her lips and sending a jolt of hot flame through his cock.

His hand came up, cupping her face, his thumb stroking over her cheek as he measured her words, hearing *her* truth in them.

Accepting it, but giving her his truth in return. "Never again, Sarael."

She gave a slight nod of her head and he leaned down, touching his lips to hers, the kiss one of forgiveness, of greeting, of reassurance, of understanding and promise. A slow exploration as tongues tentatively touched and welcomed each other, sliding and twining as the raw, unsettling, often violent emotions of the previous days slid away under growing desire.

With a groan Matteo stretched out on the bed, covering her body with his as he deepened the kiss. His tongue more aggressive now, his body tense with the need to reclaim Sarael.

She whimpered, holding him to her, her body restless under his, her legs going around his waist, her pelvis tilting and rubbing against him, her arms remaining around his neck. "Not here, Sarael," he said when he lifted his head in order to breathe. "Not here." And yet he couldn't stop himself from pushing her shirt up, from covering her nipple with his mouth and suckling, tempting his own control when his fang drew blood.

Sarael arched into him, knowing the instant when Matteo began drinking from her. Fierce need burned through her veins and arteries as her cunt wept, soaking her panties and pulsing in time to the strong, sucking pulls on her nipple.

She writhed underneath him, wanting to get closer, wanting to feel his skin against hers, wanting relief from the days of endless need and loneliness and fear. "Please," she begged, her hands going to his back, pulling his shirt up.

He jerked away at the first touch of her hands on his flesh, going to his knees and pinning her wrists to the bed as though she'd burned him. He was breathing in fast, shallow pants, his erection a hard line at the front of his trousers. "I won't take you here," he growled, more to himself than her. "I won't take you here."

For long moments he remained above her, his eyes dark and full of lust, boring into hers. Alien. And some of Sarael's fear returned. Her heart began thundering, the sound of it tightening his face and making him hiss, exposing fangs that only added to the roar of blood in her ears.

Her fear combined with the scent of her arousal was a heady combination. Striking the most primitive chords of his being. The part that was purely predator. Ancient. A throwback from when his ancestors had crashed on this planet and savagely fought for survival.

He would not mate with her in this cheap hotel room, he would not exchange blood with her here, but he would not leave without reclaiming a portion of her. Without proving his ownership of her.

"Grab the bedspread," he ordered, not releasing her wrists until she'd obeyed, and only then did his hands move to the front of her jeans, making short work of opening them and wrenching them down to her ankles along with her panties. When she let go of the bedspread he repeated his earlier command, this time enforcing it with his will so that the only movement available to her was the clenching and unclenching of her fingers on the coarse fabric of the bed covering.

Matteo pushed her knees apart, inhaling sharply at the sight of her wet folds, her cunt lips swollen, glistening, an open invitation for his tongue, his fingers, his cock.

He slid his hands along her inner thighs, her wild pulse and subtle shivering vibrating against his palms, her arousal coating them. He stopped when he reached her pussy, doing nothing but breathing in the scent of her and memorizing how delicate and feminine she looked framed between his hands as he held her open for his view.

He wanted to bury his face between her legs. Wanted to spear his tongue into her channel, to swirl it around her erect clit. For long moments he wavered, remembering what it had felt like to do the things he was imagining, telling himself that as long as his hands remained on her inner thighs, covering the places where he could easily feed, then he could resist. But as he watched her lower lips swell further, growing darker as they grew more flushed, and saw arousal seeping from her opening, he knew he couldn't risk even the first taste of her.

"Touch yourself," he growled, determined to prove to them both that he was in control. That she belonged completely to him.

Matteo's harsh command sent more blood rushing to Sarael's clit and labia. Fire streaked through her nipples, her pussy, and she pressed against his palms in an instinctual effort to close her legs.

"Touch yourself, Sarael. Pleasure yourself while I watch."

Her hands were shaking when she released the bedspread, tentative as they joined his between her legs. She coated her fingers with her own juices, sliding them back and forth over the mouth of her pussy without penetrating it, then moved to her clit, the fingers of one hand on either side of it as the tips of the other caressed along the underside and over the exposed head. A whimper escaped and her body jerked, her buttocks clenching as heated need shot up her spine.

Sarael's gaze flew to his face and her breath caught in her throat at the intensity of his expression. The mask of lust on his face. She started to pull her hand away, to beg for his mouth, his touch, but his hiss and his silent command stopped her, his will forcing her hand back down to her erect clit.

She closed her eyes then, giving herself over to his desire to see her masturbate, touching herself as she'd done for the last three days, only this time his presence gave her the relief she hadn't found before, so that her climax left her sated, content, sleepy.

With a curse Matteo stood, pulling her jeans and panties into place before lifting her in his arms and carrying her from the seedy hotel room. Pietro there to open the limousine door and take them home.

Sarael rested her head against Matteo's neck as he carried her into the house, her stomach rumbling at the smell of freshly baked bread. "You're hungry," he said.

She nodded, whispering, "It was hard to get food. Everywhere I went the men—" She broke off at the sound of his hiss.

He halted. "Did any touch you?"

She flinched at the menace in his voice. At the promise to kill she heard there.

"I wasn't raped." But more than once she'd come close. Her first blood dreams a prophecy of what was to come. The use of her knife the only reason she'd escaped.

He guided her face away from his neck, forced her gaze to meet his. "Any touch by another man is offensive to me, Sarael."

She wanted to avoid talking about the men who'd scared her with their unwanted attention. She didn't want their deaths on her conscience though some of them deserved to die. "Can I get something to eat now?" she asked, her stomach rumbling again.

Matteo's nostrils flared and she could see the struggle taking place on his face, the desire to pursue his questions versus the need to take care of her. Without looking away from her he said, "Prepare a tray of food and bring it to the bedroom, Pietro."

"Right away, *Don* Cabrelli," the elderly man said, closing the front door and scurrying off.

"We can eat in the kitchen," Sarael said, not sure she was ready to return to the bedroom now that the initial rush of emotion she'd felt when he entered the hotel room had calmed.

He ignored the comment, easily carrying her to the very room she'd escaped from. A spike of fear rushed in as she wondered if he planned to punish her. Instead he set her on the counter before moving to the old-fashioned tub, its clawed feet making Sarael look at Matteo's hands and wonder if that part of the vampire myth was true or false—if his nails could grow into deadly talons.

He turned the water on and returned to where she was sitting, his hands first stripping her of her jacket, and then going to the front of her shirt, unbuttoning it and slipping it from her body. Her bra followed, her shoes and socks next. The door to the bedroom opened and she jerked, covering her breasts with her crossed arms. Matteo turned his head slightly. "Leave it on the hearth, Pietro."

"Very good. Do you require anything else?"

"Privacy."

Sarael could have sworn she heard the elderly man chuckle before he answered, "I'll wait for your summons then."

The bedroom door closed and Matteo finished stripping her, then braided her hair, coiling it and securing it so that it wouldn't get wet, before he tested the temperature of the water and settled her in the tub.

When he lathered his hands with soap and began smoothing them over her neck and shoulders, her back, she had to look away, overwhelmed by a confusing mix of emotion. Even when she was a child, no one, not her mother nor Helki, had ever bathed her. Cleanliness was always a task, a hasty wash in a tiny trailer shower stall, and not something to linger over like he was doing.

"I can do it," she said, a flicker of independence and self-preservation rising in the swirl of confusion, a twinge of alarm at how natural it seemed to allow him to care for her in such an intimate manner.

He gave a small, husky laugh. "You can do it, *carissima*, but it is my right and privilege to do it for you. You are mine, Sarael. Mine," he said, punctuating the claim by gliding a soapy hand over her abdomen and between her legs, then along her inner thighs. She closed her legs in reaction to his touch, but only succeeded in making it worse by trapping his hand where he could drive the lust higher. His fingers manipulated her clit, sending ice-hot streaks up her spine and to her nipples. She whimpered, her back arching in reaction and he lowered his head, latching onto her nipple, his fangs retracted so that he could clamp down on it with his teeth, the sharp pain of his bite making her cry out.

He continued to hold her areola prisoner as his fingers found her slit, pressing into her, filling her, his palm repeatedly rubbing over the smooth, tiny head of her clit as his fingers fucked in and out of her, making her jerk against him, each jerk sending a fresh, sharp burst of pain through her nipple until she was thrashing, the water in the tub churning violently. He drove her up with his hand and mouth, taking her to the edge of release and then stopping, doing it time and time again until she was sobbing, pleading with him, shivering despite the heat of the water.

Lust roared through Matteo, along with anger at his own lack of restraint. He'd planned to bathe her, to feed her, to talk to her, to help her understand the world she now found herself in, to prepare her for what was yet to come. He hadn't meant to torment them both until it took every ounce of control he possessed to keep from pulling her out of the tub and taking her on the bathroom floor.

Matteo forced his mouth away from her nipple, fighting to ignore the pounding of her heart, the rapid beat of her pulse as he kissed upward, covering her lips with his. She was everything he would ever want, everything he would ever need. She was his! His! Created for him. His to pleasure and to gain pleasure from. His to feed and to feed from.

He lifted his mouth, fierce emotion charging through him as he looked at her upturned face, her naked body. "Now, Sarael," he growled, thrusting his fingers into her, wanting to watch her release, wanting to capture the image of it in his mind.

Her eyes fluttered open, dark and sensual, a timeless lure that would forever ensnare him. "Now," he commanded again, needing her helpless, wanting her completely obedient.

She whimpered, arching, the hard, glistening tips of her breasts beckoning for him to suckle them as her body tightened, as her sheath clamped down on his fingers and her clit ground into his palm. Release moved through her, flushing across her face and breasts. Pleasure warred with embarrassment, yielding to unstoppable need, to his command, his desires.

"You please me," Matteo said, kissing her afterward, reveling in the softness of her lips, in the way they clung to his as though he had become her world. He wanted her desperately, his cock arguing that he should take her. But he was afraid that if he began fucking her, he wouldn't be able to stop himself from making the second exchange.

Once that had taken place, she would become even more needy, for both his blood and body, their coupling continuing until the dawn. He owed it to her to make sure she was fed and cared for first. It shamed him that he'd already made so many mistakes with her. Her escape was his fault. He should have taken more time to talk to her before making her his bride. He should have tethered her to the bed while he slept — as he'd intended to.

She was young. Human in her thoughts and upbringing. Unprepared and untrained, despite the explosive desire that raged between them.

A cold fear had settled in his gut with her admission to being hungry and the reason for it. In his fury to find her, he hadn't considered even once that the first exchange of blood might have begun the process of turning her into his kadine, that it might have altered her body in a way that would make it hard for her to gain food or shelter for fear of being raped. He'd failed to take into consideration the kinds of places she would go with limited funds or experience beyond carnival life.

He needed to do better by Sarael. And yet it seemed an almost impossible task when she overwhelmed all of his senses, making it difficult for him to keep his hands off her. It was worse now that they'd exchanged blood. He'd known it would be, that it was part of the sexual bonding between a male and his kadine. He cursed himself once again for allowing her to escape, for not considering how alluring she would be to others until she was completely claimed. Completely his.

With a groan, Matteo forced himself to pull away from her mouth and lift her from the tub, hastily drying her then tossing the towel aside before carrying her to the bedroom, his will once again starting a fire in the fireplace, though this time he promised himself he would not take her on the rugs in front of it.

He settled her in front of the fire, leaving her there long enough to retrieve a hairbrush before sitting down behind her. "Eat," he said, uncoiling her hair and then unbraiding it, using his fingers to comb through it.

Sarael ducked her head, heat flooding her body at the picture they made, her naked while he was fully clothed. Despite everything they'd already done, she couldn't keep a blush from rising in her cheeks. "Aren't you going to get undressed?" she asked, her voice sounding self-conscious even to her own ears.

Matteo leaned closer, pushing her hair out of the way so that he could kiss along her shoulder and neck, one hand on her side while the other went around to stroke her abdomen. "In a little while, *carissima*. My control is not all that I wish it to be. Right now I want you to eat. I want us to spend some time together before… Eat, Sarael."

She ate, starting with the strawberries, moving to the peaches, the grapes, and then the cheese and fresh bread, her eyelids drooping with pleasure as he brushed her hair in long, sweeping strokes. "What about you?" she asked, "Can you…eat any of this?"

Matteo laughed softly, stopping his brushing of her hair. "Yes. But it's like candy. A little bit goes a long way. Too much, and it doesn't agree with me." He leaned down, pressing a kiss to her shoulder, his voice husky when he asked, "Would you like to feed me, *carissima*?"

Sarael ducked her head for a moment, her emotions swirling out of control. He confused her, beguiled her, satisfied her and yet left her needy for his touch, his approval…his caring.

She picked up a grape, offering it to him, her body singing with desire when he took it from her, his tongue licking over the tips of her fingers, his mouth sucking on them lightly before releasing them.

Sarael offered him more grapes then several strawberries, her nipples becoming hard, anxious pebbles when he sucked the last of the juice from her fingers, then took her arm, holding it as his mouth lingered over the pulse at her wrist, over the tattoo there before moving upward until he was once again brushing kisses along her shoulder.

"I want to care for you, Sarael, to protect you. To see to all of your needs. To be all that you desire. Your world, just as you are mine. You were created for me. You were born to be my other half. My kadine."

"You've used that term before," Sarael whispered. "Kadine. What does it mean?"

Matteo lifted his head, the softness in his expression melting her heart. He brought her wrist to his lips, pressing his mouth to the tattoo again. "A kadine is…everything…to the male she belongs to. She is his reason for living, his anchor in a lifetime that spans centuries. She is the mother of his children, the bride of his heart and soul, the blood that flows through his veins."

Sarael licked her lips, afraid to ask, but knowing that she had to. "And does she have a choice? Do I have a choice?"

Matteo's nostrils flared and all softness left his face. "From the moment of your conception, you were destined for me. There is no other choice, for either of us."

His fingers threaded through her hair, holding her immobile as his mouth hovered above hers. "Do not think to escape me again.

Do not think to escape your fate. You belong to me. Today. Tomorrow. Forever."

He kissed her then, a dominant claiming. A fierce press of his will against hers. A devouring that left her shaking, shivering, hungry for him—her body accepting his words though her mind struggled to rebel against them, to hold on to a small measure of freedom.

They were both breathing hard when he finally lifted his mouth from hers, his dark eyes staring into hers, his face taut. "Eat, *carissima*," he commanded gruffly, once again picking up the hairbrush. "The night is before us and I would have you ready for it."

She ducked her head and resumed eating. Her mind racing, trying to make peace with her body. And yet there was no peace to be found, especially when she no longer reached for the food on the platter and he changed the pattern of his brushing, the strokes becoming shorter, harder, so the bristles lightly scratched her back, making her nipples harden and her vulva swell.

Sarael stirred, self-conscious as arousal began seeping from her slit, wetting the carpet where she was sitting. "Stay," Matteo murmured, his hand going to her hip, his nostrils flaring, his cock rock-hard, wanting to bathe in her juices as it tunneled in and out of her channel.

It was all he could do to keep from tumbling her onto her hands and knees so he could cover her body with his, mounting her as a stallion mounts his mare. But if he started, he wouldn't stop until his fangs had pierced her skin and her hot blood rushed into him.

He didn't dare let that happen. Not until she was on the bed, tethered for her own safety, held open and helpless for him, her very helplessness giving him the edge he needed in order to control himself, to keep from taking too much blood and killing her.

If she hadn't run...if she hadn't eluded him for three days...then her safety would be assured. But now he hungered for her far beyond anything he'd ever known. Far beyond what was usually involved in the making of a kadine.

He wanted to drain every drop of independence from her, wanted to possess her so thoroughly that only *his* blood flowed in her veins, only *his* breath filled her lungs. It was savage and primitive. Lethal.

Chapter Seven

The very depth of his need to claim her completely, the violence of his emotions, fed his fear for her safety even as the scent of her arousal left his body coated with sweat, the head of his penis wet.

His cock burned and ached, his balls were tight and hard, painful.

He needed relief. Deserved it.

Matteo's nostrils flared with the thought and he dropped the brush, his gaze traveling over her naked, delicate body, devouring the sight of her slender figure, pausing at the dark pouty nipples, then lowering to the black curls between her legs.

She was his bride, his future kadine, and he needed relief. Deserved it.

Without a word he stood and removed his clothing. Satisfaction roaring through him at the way her gaze roamed over his body, her face growing flushed, her tongue darting out to moisten her lips as she took in the sight of him.

"Get on your knees, Sarael," he said, lust stinging him like the lash of an erotic whip when he saw a shiver of feminine fear move through her.

He opened and closed his hands, fighting the need to bury his fingers in her hair and force her to obey. A groan escaping when she complied, her eyes a wicked combination of sultry innocence, gazing at him through long eyelashes as her mouth trembled, her lips parted, wet.

Desire raged through him, making his cock pulse so that the only thing he could think about was what it would feel like as she sucked him into the sweet heaven of her mouth. He didn't bother with a command, knowing it was already too late, that he didn't dare risk that she'd deny him.

With a hiss he gave in to his impulse, spearing his fingers through her hair and pulling her forward, closing the distance so her face was buried in his groin, her lips on his shaft. She made a whimper of protest, her hands settling on his hips and pushing, sending savage impulses coursing through him, but as quickly as the violent emotion surged into his consciousness, it receded when he realized she wasn't fighting him, but was trying to position herself so she could please him.

Matteo loosened his hold on her, jerking when one of her hands circled his shaft and the other cupped his balls, massaging them, exploring them, making fire race up his spine. "Sarael." It came out a plea, a husky word of praise, a cry as her lips settled on the tip of his penis, slowly enfolding it and welcoming the engorged head into the wet heat of her mouth. "Sarael."

It was unspeakable ecstasy, unbearable pleasure to watch as she sucked his cock in and out of her mouth, driving him higher and higher by never letting him go as deeply as he wanted, by lashing at the sensitive head with her tongue.

In the end he was panting, his buttocks clenched tightly together, his body drenched with sweat and trembling, curled over her so that her silky hair brushed across his abdomen and thighs, his control very nearly in shreds. "Enough, Sarael. Enough!" But she knew it for the lie it was and tormented him further before letting him surge deeper into her mouth as her fingers explored the sensitive skin behind his balls.

Matteo came, her name on his lips as his seed escaped in a lava-hot eruption that left him empty and full at the same time. Weak and incredibly strong. Happy as he'd never been before.

He let her ease back down on the rug then, his cock hardening as he looked at Sarael's swollen lips, at the dazed expression on her face, the glistening arousal coating her inner thighs. He very nearly commanded her to lie back, to spread her legs and let him give her the same relief as she'd just given him.

It was tempting. So very tempting.

A temptation he knew better than to give in to. The last time he buried his face in her cunt as they lay in front of the fire, it had been his undoing. Had led to him rushing with her. Exchanging blood before he'd prepared her properly.

He knelt in front of her and wrapped his hand around her neck, pulling her to him and groaning with pleasure at the feel of her skin against his, holding her for his kiss as her pulse beat wildly in his palm—confirming his earlier thoughts, that he didn't dare urge her to spread her legs so that he could run his tongue through her slit and lap at the juices glistening on her inner thighs. He couldn't be so close to where her blood roared beneath delicate skin. "Sarael, you tempt me beyond measure," he whispered against her lips then moved to her ear, sucking on the lobe, teasing the delicate shell with his tongue before exploring the sensitive opening. His own heart thundering in his chest at the way her body molded itself to his, soft and submissive. Her whimper a siren's call so that he couldn't hold back the words. "I want you, *carissima*, on the bed this time."

She laughed, a soft, pleasing sound that curled in his belly and stroked his cock. "We can get on the bed."

He smiled, charmed by her innocence despite himself. Warmed by the forgiveness inherent in her simple comment—by the knowledge she didn't hold the last time against him. Perhaps didn't realize just how close to killing her he'd gotten. "I don't want to lose control, Sarael. You must accept being tethered this time."

Fear rushed through Sarael, chasing away all traces of languidness. She jerked, intending to scramble away from him, but his arms were like steel bands. "No," she said, continuing to wriggle and struggle until she was panting, pinned underneath him on the rugs, his erection pressed against her belly.

"It's necessary," Matteo said, his own breathing short, his earlier amusement gone in a flash of lust. "If you'd been raised as you should have been raised then you would already understand and accept it. But I will tell you since you have been cheated of the knowledge." He lowered his face to within inches above hers. His eyes were dark, compelling, the years of anger over Angelique's abduction of Sarael flaring to the surface. "I am trying to give you pleasure, to make up for my earlier errors and allow you time to accept what I am and what you will be to me. I am trying to keep from scaring you further, from taking you too roughly despite the fact that all I want to do is climb on top of you and claim you as I sate myself with your blood then give you mine in return. You need to be bound."

"No."

Her denial inflamed him further, pushed away all of his earlier intentions to be gentle, to take his time with her. His thoughts and emotions were volatile, chaotic. Dangerous. Fueled by an instinct more compelling than even *La Brama*. A male's need to claim and possess his kadine.

Matteo rose, prepared to use his superior strength to carry her to the bed and tie her there, but then she rolled to her hands and knees, perhaps intending to try and escape, and in a heartbeat he was on her, pressing her upper body to the carpeting, his knees forcing her legs apart so that he could thrust his cock into her tight, slick channel. She stilled under him, going soft once again, and it appeased him, forced the anger back so the fierce need to dominate controlled him instead of rage.

"Do not fight me, *carissima*," he said, giving her more of his weight, testing himself by brushing a kiss along her spine. Groaning when she dropped her head submissively, exposing her neck.

Sarael whimpered, frightened that he could reduce her to such helplessness, and yet she craved him. Craved the feel of his body on hers, craved his kisses, his touch, his words. His cock. "Please, Matteo," she said, shifting, opening herself wider, inviting him to press deeper, wanting him to plunge in so deeply that he could touch her heart, so deeply that the hot spew of his seed would wash away her doubts and fears.

His cock throbbed at the sound of her whispered plea, his balls tightened and he answered her call. The need to dominate driving him, and yet her submissiveness had enabled him to find a measure of control so that he moved in and out of her gently at first, building her trust, only becoming rougher, more forceful when she began writhing underneath him, sobbing, her body pushing into his thrusts, her cries hungry, needy.

His hand went around to her clit so that the thrust of his cock pressed her engorged nub into his palm. "Now, Sarael," he said, and she obeyed, coming hard and fast, gripping his penis in violent spasms that jerked wave after wave of seed from his balls and through his shaft.

They collapsed together on the rug, still connected, his body curled around hers, his hand still between her legs, both of them shivering, shaking in reaction to the intensity of their climax. "You undo me," he whispered, momentarily sated despite the call of her blood, despite the knowledge that he couldn't give her any more time. That the next time he took her, he would take more than her body, he would take her blood and with it a portion of her life into his keeping.

Even thinking about it was enough to stir his cock, to make it grow thick and full inside her until she was moving restlessly against him, her hand moving down to cover his so she could grind her clit into his palm. "I need you again," she said, and he could hear what it cost her to admit it.

Matteo's lips pulled back, a fierce baring of teeth as he kept himself from pumping in and out of her again. Anticipation burning through him at what was to come.

With the second exchange of blood she would truly need him. As often as he could take her and in whatever way he was willing to do it.

He placed his mouth next to her ear. "I'll give you everything you desire," he said, moving his palm over her clit in circular motions, groaning when she squeezed her legs together and tightened her hold on his cock. "But you must trust me, *carissima*. You must allow me to tether your wrists and ankles to the bed." He pressed down hard on her erect knob, a quick grinding assault that had her crying out in reaction. Old memories tried to influence her answer, old fears tried to control her, but when he did it again, sending fiery sensation through her, she gave him the answer he wanted.

"Yes," Sarael said, her body screaming in protest when Matteo pulled his cock free—then urging her to fight when he quickly lifted her into his arms and carried her to the old-fashioned bed with its elaborate, columned bedposts.

She was panting, panicked when he settled her on the mattress. And for a moment she kept herself from reacting, but as soon as he reached toward the head of the bed, toward a restraint that was already in place, she began struggling, fighting to get away from him.

He was on her in an instant, his body a solid weight, his hands pinning her wrists to the mattress. "Stop!" This time he used compulsion on her, blocking her mind's panicked commands to her limbs so that they went quiet while her blood thundered in her ears and her heart beat so fast it threatened to cease completely.

Matteo hissed, his fangs descended, sharp and glistening, adding to her primal terror and yet she was helpless to move. She watched in horrified fascination as he slowly lowered his mouth. But instead of going to her neck, he stopped next to her ear. "Don't fight me, Sarael. I don't want to hurt you. This is a dangerous time for both of us, *carissima*. There are men who have killed their kadines accidentally. You will find pleasure. Beyond anything you have yet experienced." He rubbed his cheek against hers. "Let me keep you safe. Please. Let me do this, for both of us."

"All right." It was a puff of air. An act of faith.

"*Grazie, carissima*," he said, releasing her wrists and rising to his knees, his body straddling hers so that his heavy balls brushed against the soft skin of her stomach, his smooth, hot cock gliding over her nipple as he leaned forward and once again reached for one of the restraints.

Sarael couldn't prevent herself from tensing when he placed it on her wrist, from pulling back slightly, though he allowed her to control her own body rather than forcing her into helplessness with a command. When she succeeded in allowing him to put the second restraint on without fighting him, he leaned down and covered her lips with his, praising her with his kiss, with the stroke of his tongue against hers, the lack of fangs demonstrating the truth of his earlier words, that fighting him made it more dangerous for her.

He lifted his face and her heart very nearly melted at the wealth of emotion she saw there. "You are my world, *carissima*. My life." He kissed her again, this time as his hands trailed down her immobilized arms, his fingers tracing her collarbones before settling on nipples that were tight and hard. His mouth followed, taking a different route, lingering over the wild pulse in her throat before brushing soft, teasing kisses across her nipples.

She whimpered and arched upward, her legs parting further, ready to lift and encircle him. "No," he said, his hands leaving her breasts and settling on her thighs, pinning them to the bed.

His teeth pulled on her nipple, the tugs causing heat to spiral in her belly as she remembered what it had felt like in the hotel room when he'd suckled, taking some of her blood with each erotic pull. As quickly as she'd been afraid of what was to come, she was now aroused by it.

"Please, Matteo," she said, her voice husky, needy, her body restless, her cunt and clit swollen.

He released her nipple, leaving her only long enough to tether her ankles. She shivered, fear and arousal colliding.

"Easy, *carissima*," Matteo said, covering her body with his, giving her his weight, his warmth, his comfort.

Now that she was safely bound, the crushing worry and fear he'd harbored deep inside—that he'd accidentally kill her— dissolved, leaving him nearly overwhelmed by the sheer pleasure of feeling her against him, of knowing he was taking care of her, seeing to her needs as he prepared to bring her more fully into his world. She was his life. His dream.

He closed his eyes briefly, savoring her scent, her softness. His cock hard and ready, wet with their shared passion and renewed arousal. "Sarael," he whispered, looking into her eyes before lowering his face and touching his lips to hers.

She responded by opening her mouth for him, by rubbing her tongue against his. For long moments they kissed, an erotic dance that built the desire between them until they were both shivering, him with the need to penetrate, her with the need to be penetrated.

He'd bound her ankles with enough slack to enable her to bend her knees and widen the spread of her legs. With a whimper she did so, arching enough so that his penis slid inside her welcoming channel.

In an instant the nature of the kiss changed. In an instant the coupling became a claiming.

Lust roared through Matteo, intense and powerful, primal. For Sarael's body, for her blood. For her heart and soul.

He swallowed her cries as he pounded into her, violently taking her, his entire focus on possessing the woman beneath him.

And Sarael writhed in pleasure, offering herself to him, responding to him in the way he'd long fantasized that his kadine would do. The emotions storming through him fierce, all consuming—more demanding than even *La Brama*.

Only when the tight fist of her muscles clamped down on him mercilessly as she climaxed did he give in to the desire to bite her. She screamed when he struck, but this time it was in pleasure and not in terror. And this time, with her wrists and ankles bound, he didn't lose control, didn't take more than he should, despite the hot rush of ecstasy her blood produced as it poured into him, becoming a part of every one of his cells, of his entire being—even as stream after stream of semen jetted through his cock, the pulsing release nearly excruciating in its intensity.

Sarael was relaxed, sated, thoroughly content when Matteo's tongue washed over her neck before he lifted his head. "My turn?" she asked, frowning slightly at the slur in her voice.

He laughed, a husky sound that had her nipples tightening despite the pleasure he'd already given her. "Impatient to become my kadine, *carissima*?"

Sarael tried to work up some fear, but none came. It felt right to be with him. To follow him into the world of The Moon. "Will you untie me, now?"

Matteo hesitated for a moment then set her free, immediately covering her body with his. "The changes will be more pronounced this time," he said, threading the fingers of one hand through her hair.

Some of the lassitude left her with his words. "What do you mean?"

He brushed his lips over hers. "Your body is changing, *carissima*. Adapting. Becoming more compatible, more receptive to mine. Without these changes it wouldn't be possible for us to have children, it wouldn't be possible for you to live as long as I'll live."

A small measure of her earlier fear returned, causing her pulse to beat more rapidly in her throat. The flaring of Matteo's nostrils and the stiffening of his cock telling her how attuned he was to the rush of her blood. "You're turning me into a vampire." This time her heart jerked in her chest and he groaned in reaction, shoving his cock into her channel.

"Remain calm, Sarael, or I will need to tie you again," he said, strain on his face.

The warning itself caused her to tense. Made her fight to stay quiet underneath him, even as she repeated her comment. "You're turning me into a vampire."

"No, *carissima*, not the vampire you call me, but a kadine."

"What's the difference?"

"You will understand soon enough, Sarael. But if it will ease your mind, then I will tell you this. You will be able to move around in the daytime if you desire. You will be able to eat and drink as you always have, but in addition you will need my blood to survive."

His mouth went to her neck and she forced herself to go completely soft and submissive underneath him. He lingered, first running his tongue over the place he'd bitten, then sucking on it, making her whimper and arch into him, her nipples hard, aching points, her cunt clenching and unclenching on his penis.

He laughed, amusement mixed with sensual torment, then lifted his face from her neck, shifting so his eyes could gaze into hers. "You tempt me beyond all measure, Sarael." His lips brushed against hers. "Do you drink willingly, *carissima*?"

"Yes," she whispered, watching as he used his fangs to open a vein on his own wrist. The fingers threaded through her hair tightened, but she didn't fight him when he pressed his wrist to her mouth. Instead she closed her eyes, concentrating on the memory of how it had been the first time, how rapidly his blood had become a fine wine she greedily swallowed.

It was even more potent the second time, burning its way through her body and becoming the sole focus of her existence. She drank, timeless minutes lost in a vortex of dark pleasure while his hand stroked her cheek, her throat, and his words of love and praise washed over her.

She protested when he finally pulled his wrist from her mouth, whimpering and trying to follow his movement. "You'll have more tomorrow, Sarael," he said, closing the vein with the swipe of his tongue. "And after that, we can share this as often as you wish." He leaned in, kissing her.

Sarael's legs went around his waist, forcing his cock deeper. Her body was burning, restless, wanting his seed now as desperately as his blood.

Matteo grunted, feeling the need in her, already connected to her so that her emotions flowed into him, amplifying his own. He'd expected it, wanted it, and yet the reality was so much more intense, so much more consuming than he'd imagined.

His cock grew larger, fighting against the tight fist of her muscles, and she began moving, the slick, hot feel of her sending jolts of icy pleasure through his balls and up his spine. He tightened his arms around her, answering her call, fucking her, their bodies so tightly melded it was almost as though they were one. But within seconds, the sound of her heart, the rush of her blood, her own desire for him to pierce her skin and drink had Matteo fighting for control.

With a groan he rolled to his back, his hands going to her breasts, pushing so that she straddled him. It was sweet torture to have her above him, dark hair and dark eyes, breasts heavy with desire, their hard tips pressed against his palms. It was pure eroticism to look down and see the place where their bodies joined, to watch as she lifted away from him, rising high enough that his cock nearly escaped the wet heaven it had claimed as its own, before she sank down, taking him willingly into her body. Swallowing him in slippery folds and feminine mystery.

She rode him mercilessly. As mercilessly as he'd ridden her earlier. Lowering her head and capturing his lips only in the final seconds, when they both strained against each other, slick with sweat, striving to be what their commingled blood claimed they were — one body, one heart, one soul — two halves of a single whole. Bound together for all eternity.

Afterward, Sarael lay on top of Matteo, needing his closeness. Needing the feel of his skin against hers. Needing his reassurance.

His hands stroked over her back. Comforting at first, then arousing. So that she began moving restlessly against him, her body burning once again, the sound of his heartbeat a roar in her head.

With a whimper she nuzzled his chest, his neck, putting her teeth on him and only barely able to prevent herself from biting. Matteo's arm tightened on her while one hand moved to cup her cheek, to force her face away from his neck and position it above his.

"I need you again," she whispered, her lower body grinding against his, her sheath tightening on his still-embedded penis.

He was ready for her in an instant. His body perfectly attuned to hers, prepared to give her everything she wanted—except for his blood. He'd taken them both to the very limits with the earlier exchange.

His cock jerked with the thought of her teeth on his neck. One more exchange and the adaptation would be complete. Her body would be fully compatible with his, and he would know the unparalleled ecstasy of her bite, the sharp sting of pleasure as her fangs slid into him. She would be his kadine in fact, her life irrevocably tied to his.

With a groan he rolled, levering himself away from her long enough to slip his arms under her knees, bending and guiding them so that they were draped over his shoulders, the position making her so tight and small that his penis had to fight its way back into her. The position making it easier to replace the desire for blood with the lust to fuck, to dominate, to satisfy the hunger burning in both of them.

And yet it wasn't a hunger that would be satisfied until the sun rose. He took her repeatedly, needing to tie her to the bed again in order to prevent himself from giving in to the sheer temptation she presented, the second exchange of blood making her crave his body and his blood desperately, sexually bonding her to him—just as the first exchange had bound him to her.

With the bonding she would gain control over the pheromones that served not only to lure prey but were part of a vampire's defense mechanism. Humans would be drawn to her, but only when she beckoned and she would be able to ensnare them in her gaze, directing their thoughts rather than being the victim of their sexual obsession.

A growl sounded in Matteo's throat at the thought of the men who'd tried to rape her during the three days when she'd eluded him. Never again. Never again would she be vulnerable, unprotected.

He leaned down and pressed his mouth to hers, his tongue as aggressive as his cock, pressing in and out of her in a show of dominance. Driving her higher until she was writhing against him, pleading with her body, held at the pinnacle of release until he allowed them both to tumble over.

Afterward he carried her to the bathroom, once again putting her on the counter while he filled the large, old-fashioned tub with water. Only this time instead of placing her in it alone, he scooped her into his arms and got in himself, settling her so that she was stretched out along his body, her back to his front, both of them immersed in the welcoming water.

Chapter Eight

Sarael closed her eyes and relaxed against him, enjoying the rippling warmth of the water and the lazy caresses as he smoothed soapy hands over her abdomen and breasts. "I could get used to this," she murmured, glad the fierce need and fiery restlessness that had assaulted her body for most of the night had loosened its grip on her.

Matteo laughed softly, his palms circling, gliding over her nipples, then retreating, stroking her stomach and thighs before his arms settled around her and he rubbed his cheek against her hair. "I am glad, *carissima*. I have savored you in my dreams for more years than you've been alive. But the reality, Sarael... The reality is so much more than the fantasy. You are my heart, my soul, my world."

Sarael laced her fingers through his. "What happens next?"

"Tomorrow we will finish what we have begun. And the day after, we will return to Italy."

Sarael's heart rate spiked and his arms tightened on her in response. "Italy?"

He rubbed his cheek against her hair. "I wish to return home with you, Sarael, to take you somewhere I can ensure your safety. We can visit the United States in the future, after you know more of our ways, and at a time when I can arrange for your security."

A whisper a fear moved through Sarael at the idea of leaving all that was familiar to her, at the thought of being trapped in a foreign land. A place where she didn't know the language or the people. Until he'd come into her life, all she'd ever known was the carnival. Traveling from place to place in a long circular route repeated each year. The rhythm of each day like a constant, steady heartbeat. "I'd like to stay here for a while."

"That is not possible. As I have said, we can visit the United States in the future. But as soon as you have gone through the last changes and become my kadine, then we must return to *Palazzo dei Venti Oscuri*."

Sarael heard the steel in his voice and knew it was pointless to argue. She heard her mother's warning. *If you're found, your life won't be your own.*

Her gaze strayed to the window she'd escaped through last time—noticing there were now bars covering it. She had no intention of running again even though the whisper of fear had become a sharper, colder breeze. Is this what her future held? Her choices always dictated by him? Her life always following the course he directed? Her own wishes and desires unimportant? "That's what you call your home? Palazzo dei…"

"*Palazzo dei Venti Oscuri*. Palace of Dark Winds. Yes. I have other estates, but it is the one I most frequently occupy."

Sarael shivered despite the warmth of the water. The name of his home and the sight of the bars over the bathroom window giving rise to the notion that it would be an elegant prison.

Matteo could sense the ebb and flow of her emotions, could almost taste her fear. It struck at his core, leaving him both raw and reactive. With the third exchange of blood, he would share her thoughts, but until then, he could only guess at them, could only anticipate what she might do.

But she was mistaken if she thought he would drop his guard and allow her to escape again. Especially with enemies lurking in the area.

For an instant he considered telling her about the danger the Believers posed, but then thought better of it. It was a lesson for another day.

Pride moved through him, desire, at how she had handled the second exchange. He'd been right to take his time with her, to spend precious moments gentling her and talking to her rather than punishing her for running and eluding him.

Matteo hugged her to him then rose to his feet, setting her out of the tub and following, reaching for a towel as he had before and drying her off before wiping the water from his own body. "We need to seek our rest," he said, feeling the creeping lethargy that heralded the arrival of the sun.

When he moved to lift her into his arms and carry her to bed, she flushed, ducking her head and saying, "I need a few minutes before I come to bed."

He cupped her chin, forcing her gaze to meet his, knowing she had already seen the bars installed over the window, but unable to prevent himself from saying, "Do not think to try and escape again, *carissima*." He released his grip and moved from the room, stopping just outside the door, but allowing her to close it.

Sarael breathed a sigh of relief. Thankful he'd given her some privacy as she attended to her needs. Thankful he'd given her a few minutes alone so she could think about all that had happened since he found her in the hotel room.

She already felt bound to him. Connected in a way that made her feel whole. She already believed she belonged in his world. The world of The Moon.

And despite the uneasiness that filled her at the prospect of being taken to *Palazzo dei Venti Oscuri*, she wouldn't fight it. Wouldn't fight him. It was too late to do so.

Sarael rubbed her finger over the tattoo on her wrist. Perhaps it had been too late from the moment of her birth.

Out of habit she gathered the clothes that lay scattered on the bathroom floor where he'd thrown them earlier, her mind immediately going to the knife in her jacket pocket. Her thoughts returning to the three days when she'd had to fend for herself in a world made more dangerous by his blood.

She left the bathroom with the clothes in her arms, now strangely reluctant not to have the knife near her. Matteo frowned but didn't say anything and she dropped the clothing in a chair next to the bed before sliding onto the mattress and into his arms. Willing to spend the day held by him, willing to sleep while the sun reigned and finish what they'd begun when it set and the moon ruled.

Matteo rolled her onto her back and settled on top of her, and despite the lethargy that was slowly invading her body, Sarael spread her legs and tilted her hips, ready to welcome him into her body. He gave a husky laugh and thrust, his cock sliding in easily, his strokes slow and gentle.

"*Carissima*," he whispered, knowing it was madness to take her, knowing it was foolish to make the same mistake a second time, to expend the last of his energy, enabling sleep to take him so deeply that it would be a struggle to wake during the daylight hours. But the feel of her slick flesh was more than he could resist. The sounds of her pleasure and the softness of her body a call he couldn't fail to answer. And so he yielded to temptation. Slowly fucking in and out of her, drawing the pleasure out as the sun rose higher in the sky, each thrust a victory against a world he couldn't fully live in, each thrust a reaffirmation of what they were to each other.

Only when Sarael cried and convulsed with pleasure did he allow himself to come. *Il Sonno* threatening to submerge him completely as he filled her with his seed and collapsed on top of her. Dark waves of sleep washing over him.

It took every ounce of willpower he possessed to fight the call of *Il Sonno*, to keep from tumbling into oblivion. But Matteo forced himself to his knees, finding satisfaction in the way Sarael frowned and mumbled when his body left hers. But when he placed the restraint on her ankle, her contentment left her in a rush and she jerked into a sitting position, trying to escape the viselike grip he had on her.

"No!" It was a protest from her very soul, rippling across his and making it feel as though a hand was squeezing his heart. "No." There was panic in her voice, confusion, hurt.

"Yes, *carissima*," he said, the violent swirl of her emotions battering him. "I can't take the chance that you'll run again."

Her eyes widened and she stilled, meeting his gaze with a pleading one. "And if I promise not to try and escape?"

He shook his head, feeling her need for him to trust her. Wanting to give his trust to her, but the stakes were too high. The danger too great. His dream of a kadine too close to being realized.

He'd promised himself not to err as he'd done before. Already it took all his willpower to fight *Il Sonno*, the hours hunting Sarael followed by the hours of pleasuring her, of filling her with his seed, had taken their toll on him. He would not be able to awaken quickly enough to race her to the door should she decide to leave him.

A frown came and went on Matteo's face as he realized he had left the door unlocked so Pietro could deliver a tray of food for Sarael. A quick glance and he could see the key sticking from the deadbolt on the inside, a lock he'd had installed when he first arranged to bring Sarael to this house. A lock that should even now be engaged and the key hidden.

He cursed silently. His attention had been so consumed by Sarael that he hadn't once thought of seeing to the door. And now his failure provided reason enough to tether her.

"I must," he said, regret in his voice, but also resolve, his heart weeping when he saw tears form at the corners of Sarael's eyes.

"Please don't," she whispered. *Trust me. Show me that what I want is important to you.*

"Just one ankle, Sarael. And I will extend the length of the tie so it doesn't restrict your movement so very much."

"I don't want to be tied at all. I've already told you I won't try to escape."

He shook his head, wanting desperately to give in to her plea, the very intensity of his desire to yield to her tears making his resolve firm. A kadine both strengthened and weakened the man who claimed her. But in this, he couldn't afford to weaken. He couldn't afford to trust her. He couldn't be certain that the taint of her mother wasn't still present in Sarael. She thought to stay with him *now*, but what if she changed her mind during the daylight hours and decided to chase after a freedom not meant for her?

"No, Sarael. Do not ask for what I can't give." His grip tightened on her ankle, though she made no effort to try and jerk it away from him.

"If you do this, Matteo, then I *will* try and escape again," she said, her voice shaky and yet full of conviction as he opened a leather pouch tied to the bedpost and removed a tiny silver padlock.

"Then I will warn you that you are doomed to failure, Sarael. And if you try to run away, then I will punish you—whether you are successful in the attempt or not." He closed the padlock at the point where the restraints met at her ankle, misgiving moving through him as he did so. Second thoughts arising as he lay down beside her and pulled her resistance-filled body against his own. "Sleep now, *carissima*. No purpose is served by fighting. The night will come soon enough, and with it, the completion we both desire."

Sarael couldn't stop herself from drawing her knee upward until the tether was taut, preventing her from further movement. "Please don't do this," she said again, her heart aching — torn by a confusion of emotion. Needing him to trust her. She'd accepted so many things, given herself to him willingly time and time again, even allowed him to tie her when he'd said it was important for her own safety — but this was not for her safety, this was *not* necessary.

This was a betrayal of her trust. This was a confirmation that he would think nothing of keeping her a prisoner. That her needs and desires would always be less important than his own.

"Sleep, Sarael," he said, sending a shaft of pain through her heart with his refusal to free her ankle.

She turned her back to him and closed her mind to the feel of his warm skin against hers. It was pointless to struggle. His arms were like steel bands around her, holding her against him. But she knew from before that once sleep claimed him, his grip would loosen.

Sadness pooled in Sarael's heart. Maybe this was the way it would always be. Maybe he'd always hold her mother's "sins" against her. Maybe he'd always worry that she was like her mother.

She fought to remain awake, but eventually exhaustion and then sleep claimed her. But unlike Matteo, it didn't hold her so tightly in its grip.

It was late afternoon when she woke. Sarael knew it without a clock telling her. She knew it despite the darkness of the room and the heavy curtains blocking all sunlight.

She'd shifted position in her sleep and so her first impulse was to place her leg over Matteo's and see if she could coax his cock into filling her. Because despite the slow, deep breathing which indicated he was asleep, his penis was rigid against her belly — standing ready to serve her.

But as soon as she moved her leg and the leather securing her to the bedpost became taut, she was reminded of what had transpired before sleep took them both. *If you do this, Matteo, then I will try and escape again.* Her earlier words rushed in, filling her thoughts so that she was at war with herself.

Her body craved him. Her blood sang his name. Her heart and soul insisted they belonged together. And yet her mind argued that unless there was trust then nothing else mattered, that all they had between them was an illusion, the result of whatever had been done to her with the tattooing of her wrist when she was an infant unable to make a choice about her future.

Sarael eased away from Matteo, careful despite the obvious depth of his sleep. The tether prevented her from getting very far, but it was still long enough. With one hand gripping the columned post at the head of the bed, she reached for the pile of clothing she'd placed on the chair, her heart plummeting as she wondered if some part of her had known she'd need the knife and that's why she'd picked her clothes off the bathroom floor instead of just leaving them there.

It was a simple matter to cut the leather binding, though the band around her ankle remained tightly in place, locked there by the tiny silver padlock — symbolic of a bondage she knew she'd never truly escape.

Matteo would find her. In truth, she knew she wasn't really running from him, but was trying to make herself heard. Trying to get him to understand that she needed his trust, she needed to feel…free…even as he held her tight and drew her deeper into his world.

She'd promised she'd escape if he tethered her. And she would see it through, going as far as the carnival so that she could glimpse her old life again before he took her to Italy and *Palazzo dei Venti Oscuri.*

A shiver moved through her as she remembered *his* earlier words — *if you try to run away, then I will punish you — whether you are successful in the attempt or not* — and her hands shook slightly as she got dressed, but she didn't let the threat of punishment stop her. She was prepared to accept the consequences of her actions. She needed to do this, not just to demonstrate that she meant what she said, but to prove to herself that she was strong enough to be

Matteo's match. That who she was wouldn't disappear, crushed by his dominant nature and the power he held over her.

Sarael moved to the door, was surprised when she saw the key in the lock. She'd had some vague notion of either using the knife to force the door open or pulling the heavy curtains aside and seeing if she could escape through a bedroom window. She hadn't anticipated escape would be so easy. Her pulse spiked and raced, her hand stilling on the doorknob. Was he testing her?

Confusion reigned for long moments. Indecision.

Her body urged her to return to the bed. To let him wake to find her still there, no longer tethered, able to escape but choosing freely to stay.

A new fear swirled in her heart. What if this was a test and she left? What if by leaving it meant he would no longer want her? That *he* would leave in turn, returning to Italy and seeking another female to be his kadine.

She very nearly gave in. Her hand dropped from the doorknob and she turned, taking several steps toward the bed before her earlier thoughts crowded in, her earlier worries about losing her sense of self. Of disappearing so thoroughly in the world of The Moon that she didn't exist other than to please Matteo. To be what he wanted her to be.

She forced her gaze away from him, halting, taking in the room—a room kept in absolute darkness and yet she could see perfectly. Her hands clenched into fists at her sides, her determination and confidence returning. His blood had already changed her. He would come for her. He had said time and time again that she belonged to him.

This was no test—other than one she needed to administer to herself. A smile formed on her lips when she spotted a small notebook and pen on the dresser. Without giving herself time to second-guess or question, she hastily moved to the dresser and left him a message. *You are asking me for everything but I need something in return. I need to know that what I want is important to you. I need to know I'm not a prisoner. I need you to trust me when I tell you something. I promised I would leave if you tethered me. And I have. You will find me at the carnival.*

She left then, moving quietly through the house, her senses now so acute that she could hear Pietro prowling around in the kitchen. She could feel Matteo in the depths of her consciousness, fighting through waves of cloying sleep, trying to surface and prevent her from escaping.

Adrenaline surged through her, quickening her footsteps. She paused only momentarily in the foyer, finding car keys on the small table just inside the front door. She recognized them instantly, grimacing at the thought of driving the limousine again, but glad she wouldn't be forced to flag down a passing motorist.

Nervousness skittered along her spine as she left the house and claimed the car. Memories crowded in of the men who'd been drawn to her the last time she ran. Her sole focus became getting to Helki's small trailer.

Chapter Nine

"Sit," Helki said and Sarael did so, holding her hand up as though to ward off a reading when the old fortune-teller picked up a deck of tarot cards. Helki laughed, a dry sound of amusement. "You have already found your fate, child, you have no need of a reading from me." She pressed the deck into Sarael's hands. "The cards offer you a story if you have the courage to hear it."

A whisper of amusement moved through Sarael as she realized the old woman had always used this method for getting her to accept change and uncomfortable knowledge, feeding the challenge and information to her in the form of subtle dares. Sarael shuffled the cards, cutting them before handing them back to Helki.

Helki removed the top five cards, her eyes never leaving Sarael's as she set the first on the table. It was the Page of Cups.

"Once there was a young girl. She was born to a family that had gained its prestige by providing brides for men such as the one who has claimed you. It was considered a great honor to be selected and at first, this young girl was thrilled by the privileges and adulation she gained. She was spoiled shamelessly by her family, and envied by her peers. But as the time grew nearer, she began to think about what it would mean to grow large with child, a child she would help raise until others took over the task. What it would mean if she was chosen to bear another child, and then another until her own beauty and youth had been diminished—never being selected herself as a bride. Perhaps if she hadn't been so spoiled by her family, she would have been content. But she was beautiful, and young, and headstrong, accustomed to men falling at her feet. And so when no offer was made for her, despite her attempts to attract one of the powerful men who desired a life companion, and she found herself pregnant, she turned her charms on a man forbidden her, a man who showed no interest in her at first."

Helki paused and flipped a card, revealing the Seven of Cups. "Daydreams soon filled this young girl's mind, of this man forbidden to her carrying her away and introducing her to a world different than her own. But this man was no easy conquest and his refusal only made her more determined to have him."

A third card joined the first two. The Five of Swords. "In the end, she got what she had pursued so relentlessly. But it was a hollow victory, one born of selfishness and deceit. The man she'd pursued so relentlessly finally came to her, claiming to have fallen under her spell. He helped her escape, convincing her that she should take her infant daughter with her. Though later she suspected his love was a lie."

Helki reached over and took Sarael's wrist, her thumb stroking over the tattoo. "The girl in this story gave in to her lover's persuasive arguments, to her own unworthy feelings of jealousy toward the daughter who would have the life she herself had wanted. Deep inside she knew it was wrong to take a child whose path was written in ancient blood, a child her mind wouldn't allow her heart to love."

"She found herself in the United States. Alone. Dependent on this man who sent money but found excuse after excuse not to join her. She became suspicious of his motives. She became frightened of the consequences which would result from not only running, but from taking the child. She began to fear for her life, seeing enemies all around who might want her dead."

Helki released Sarael's wrist. The Six of Swords joined the others on the table. "She ran. This time unaided—with few resources other than her stubbornness and pride, her beauty—trying to escape not only those who might be pursuing her but also from herself. Winding up here, traveling from town to town, growing older, maturing in many ways, but not in others."

There was a wealth of sadness in Helki's voice, an acknowledgement of a truth both of them had long known but avoided speaking of. Sarael looked up from the cards, her heart aching, filling again with a small girl's desire to be loved by her mother, with the remembered pain of thinking the fault was hers, that somehow she was unlovable.

"None of it was your doing, child," Helki said, placing the last card on the table. The Eight of Cups. The card of saying goodbye, of moving on, of ending emotional ties. "She chose her own path and had to walk it. She cared enough to ensure you would be taken care of before she left."

Sarael traced the edges along the Eight of Cups. Looking at the lone figure it contained, a figure walking away toward rugged mountains. "And now?"

"You have already found your path."

Sarael nodded, accepting the truth of Helki's statement. "What about her? Do you know where she is?"

"Will you seek her if I say yes?"

Even knowing some of her mother's story, the pain of her rejection and abandonment would forever linger in Sarael's heart. "No. I'd just like to know what happened to her after she left."

Helki reached for the deck of remaining tarot cards, cutting them several times before picking a solitary card and placing it on the table. Judgment.

Sarael tensed at the sight of it, but Helki gave a slight shake of her head. "It is not what you fear. She has made peace with the past and found a measure of happiness."

"I'm glad," Sarael said, finding that she meant it. Wondering why Helki had chosen to share this information with her now.

"You never told me this story before," Sarael said, picking up the cards and returning them to the deck.

"You didn't need to know it until today."

"Because of Matteo?"

Helki reached over and cupped Sarael's face, the tips of her fingers calloused from years of handling cards. She brushed them over Sarael's cheek in a rarely shown gesture of affection. "Child, why do you press me for reasons? I had a dream and just as it predicted, you arrived in time to hear the story the cards wanted you to know."

Sarael looked at the old woman who had shown her more caring than her own mother. It hadn't been a mother's love and yet it had soothed her, provided her with stability, a safe haven to grow up in. She felt her eyes grow wet with tears. "He's going to take me to his home in Italy."

"He'll bring you back here for a visit, child."

"You saw it?"

Helki chuckled. "I didn't need to. His nature is to dominate as well as to please you."

Heat moved through Sarael's face, a question as to whether Helki guessed at the exact nature in which Matteo *did* dominate and please. She looked away, letting the subject drop, slowly becoming aware of two men approaching the trailer. Their focus on her though they couldn't see her and she couldn't see them.

Sarael rose and moved to the window, understanding dawning when she saw Cable and Fane only a few steps away from the trailer. They'd made her nervous from the first moment she encountered them. But now she knew the reason for her uneasiness. Fane. He wasn't truly human.

She returned to the table, tears threatening as Helki stood, taking Sarael's hands in her ancient ones and giving them a gentle squeeze. "We will see each other again, child."

The metal door of the trailer rattled under a firm knock and Sarael clung to Helki's hands, holding on to the past for a moment more before letting go and moving to the door, opening it and stepping outside. Her heart both heavy and strangely light.

"Let's go," Fane said and Sarael turned her attention to the men who took up positions on either side of her but didn't touch her. Surprise rippled through her when she breathed in their mingled scent, realizing that both men carried the scent of the other on him, as though they'd been intimate with each other.

"You're taking me back to Matteo?"

Cable shook his head. "He'll come for you at dusk. Until then, you'll stay with us."

They got to the place she'd left the limo. It was gone. The key still in her pocket. A shiny red sports car parked where it had been.

Fane opened the door and folded the seat down, forcing her to climb into the tiny passenger compartment in the back. "It would be dangerous and foolish for you to run again," he growled, righting the seat and trapping her in. "Not only would you gain an even harsher punishment from Matteo but you risk falling into our enemies' hands."

"What enemies?"

The two men exchanged a glance, both of them scowling. "Matteo hasn't told you about the Believers?" Cable asked, starting the engine and shifting the car into drive.

"No. Who are they?"

"Humans who want to destroy anyone or anything with supernatural abilities," Cable said. "Particularly vampires. Or those associated with them."

Fane turned to look at her. His eyes angry and savage. "They're in the area searching for a woman. You maybe. And rape is on their agenda."

Sarael shivered, frightened by his expression and his words. "I didn't know."

Cable's eyes met hers in the rearview mirror. "And now you do. You were smart to leave a note telling Matteo where you'd gone. It'd be even smarter still if you don't force either one of us to touch you. It'll only make it worse if he smells our scent on you when he comes to reclaim you."

Sarael looked away, the mention of their scents making her aware of them again, of how obvious it was that the two men had been intimate, the hints of lust and satisfaction clinging to their skin despite the smell of soap and cleanliness.

"Where are you taking me?"

"To the place I'm renting." Fane's lips quirked upward in a slight smile. "For reasons known only to Matteo, he has decided that he prefers to have you guarded rather than returned and bound to his bed or locked in a secure room until nightfall."

Fane's answer caused Sarael's chest to flood with hope. Her leaving *had* made a difference.

She looked out the window, not surprised to find Fane's house was in a secluded area, completely surrounded by dark woods. Matteo would come for her soon, and when he did... Heat pooled in her belly and her breasts as a wave of anticipation and desire moved through her.

They escorted her inside where another man waited, excitement glittering in his eyes. She guessed he was the Italian who'd given his card to Dakotah. Alessandro, who claimed to be her mother's friend. "A call just came in," he said, directing his attention to Cable. "One of the waitresses in Chesterfield called the number you gave her. Four men sporting tattoos and the crucifix knives the Believers favor came into the restaurant. She said they walked across the street to the hotel there."

"Which restaurant?" Cable asked.

"Her shift is over now, but she said the room they went into was the last one to the right." Alessandro pulled a piece of paper out of his pocket and handed it to Fane.

Fane turned to Cable. "Sarael will be safe enough here with the two of you guarding her. I'll see if these are the men Domino and I learned of."

Cable's eyebrows drew together. "It feels wrong. It might be a trap."

"Let them try and spring it then."

"Call Domino…"

"He hunts elsewhere and you know it. I can't wait."

"I'll go with you then."

"Your duty is here, guarding Sarael until she's once again in Matteo's possession."

"I can stay with her," Alessandro said. "Despite her ability to escape from Matteo repeatedly, she won't get away from me."

"No," Fane said.

Cable looked at Sarael "She left a note telling Matteo where she could be found—and that was before she knew the danger the Believers posed. I don't think there is any danger of her running again. Is there?"

Sarael shook her head. "I'll stay here."

"It's settled then," Cable said. "There's no reason to think the Believers know about this house, and Matteo will be here soon."

Alessandro straightened. "If you will allow me to turn her over to Matteo, it would be a chance for my order to regain its lost honor over Angelique's escape."

Fane hissed, a frustrated sound. But Cable was already striding toward the sports car. And within seconds they were gone.

Wariness filled Sarael when Alessandro immediately closed the distance between them, taking her arm in his hand, a tight grip meant to restrain. "I've waited all my life for this opportunity. Come on, we need to hurry. Your mother is waiting. She's anxious to see you, to apologize, to explain why she had to leave you at the carnival long enough for Matteo to find you and make the first two exchanges with you." He laughed. "What a miracle that you managed to escape before the third one! We'd planned to try and rescue you, but we couldn't find out where Matteo had you hidden. He refused to tell any of us."

Sarael's pulse jumped. The story Helki told her with the tarot cards racing through her mind. The last one, the Judgment card, an indication that her mother had made peace with the past and found a measure of happiness. She knew he lied, that he wasn't taking her to Angelique.

"You helped my mother escape the first time. You convinced her to take me with her." Some of the smooth charm dropped from Alessandro's face, and Sarael raced to gain some answers, forcing her voice to sound small and frightened. "Please, tell me why she wanted Matteo to find me, why I had to endure what he did to me."

Alessandro's face became sympathetic. "We're both sorry for your suffering, Sarael. But it was the only way. For years the vampires have used humans. Generation after generation of us has been born into their service. Gaining wealth, but not what they have! Centuries of life." His hand tightened on her arm. "But your blood will change that, Sarael. As long as Matteo lives, you live. And through your blood... Come on, we need to leave. Your mother is beside herself waiting for this reunion." He took a step toward the door and she went with him without resistance, knowing that at some point he'd have to let go of her arm.

The knife was in her jacket pocket. Close, and yet she knew there was no way she'd be able to get to it fast enough unless she could put some distance between them.

A black car waited in the driveway. "How far away is she?" Sarael asked, forcing excitement into her voice. Her question a false indication that she believed his story.

"Several hours. But by the time Matteo realizes you've been taken and Fane and Cable determine they're chasing a phantom enemy, it will be too late. We'll be long gone with no trail left for them to follow."

She tried to maintain the fiction that she believed him as she waited for the moment when he'd loosen his grip on her long enough for her to escape. But when they drew close to the passenger door and she saw the handcuffs in the seat, she couldn't stop herself from reacting. In a heartbeat she began struggling, her forehead connecting with his nose hard enough to loosen his grip on her so she could gain her freedom and run.

"Bitch!" he screamed, delayed for several precious seconds by pain and the blood gushing from his nose. But then he was chasing after her.

Chapter Ten

Sarael darted into the woods, using the gloom to her advantage. Matteo's blood allowing her to see perfectly, while the darkness slowed Alessandro down.

She ran until her sides ached. Hoping that he'd give up. But he didn't and so she altered her course, trying to circle back to the house, the car, where, if nothing else, she could get a door between them until Matteo arrived.

Alessandro caught her a few steps away from the front door, lunging and taking her to the ground, then rolled her over, straddling her and forcing the knife from her hand before tossing it a short distance away. "Bitch!" he said, striking her face in mad fury when she continued to fight him, blood streaming from her lips.

Sarael saw the instant his gaze latched onto her mouth, his attentions so riveted that she knew what she needed to do in order to ensure her survival. The feel of Alessandro's body touching hers made her stomach roil. But if she could just keep him occupied…

The time spent evading him in the woods had been enough. She could feel Matteo getting closer. Timing his arrival so he could reclaim her only seconds after the sun set.

She continued struggling, squirming, allowing the pheromones she'd gained with Matteo's blood to work to her advantage, to distract Alessandro. He struck her again. This time licking the blood from his hand. His dream of a life beyond what a human could have, flowing from her lips in scarlet temptation.

He was on her in a second, his body holding hers down, his mouth covering hers, so absorbed in what he was doing, in keeping her subdued that he was unaware of Matteo's arrival until he screamed in agony, his shirt bursting into flames, causing him to jerk away from her and meet death.

Sarael scrambled to her feet just as Matteo dropped Alessandro's lifeless body to the ground, the neck broken with a quick decisive snap. She didn't resist when he pulled her to him, licking over her bleeding lips, healing and cleaning them. "Where are Fane and Cable?"

"On their way to Chesterfield. He told them four Believers had been seen there. But it was just a lie to get them to leave."

Matteo set her aside. "Get in the car." His voice promised retribution despite the tender way he'd taken care of her injuries.

"I..."

"Do not add to your troubles by arguing with me, Sarael. Get in the car."

She retreated to the limousine, watching as he disappeared into the house with Alessandro's body. Emerging a few minutes later and stopping only long enough to pick up her knife and slip it into his pocket before joining her in the car.

They drove home in silence, despite the fact that Matteo held her on his lap, his arms unyielding around her waist, his erection pressed against her buttocks. Several times Sarael thought to speak about what had happened, but something in his manner stopped her.

Like a movie rewound so a scene could be repeated yet again, the limo glided to a halt and Pietro opened the door so Matteo could exit with Sarael in his arms, then hurried to the house, enabling Matteo to move inside and directly to the bedroom without pausing.

He took her to the bathroom, setting her on her feet and finally speaking. "Take a shower, Sarael, before the scent of another man on you drives me to do something I will regret."

Her hands went to her shirt, shaking at the hot, dangerous anger she saw in his face, shaking in delayed reaction to what had transpired at Fane's house. She didn't bother asking Matteo to leave. The harshness of his expression and his stance told her he had no intention of letting her out of his sight. Feminine fear moved through her, laced with anticipation. In his presence her body was already starting to burn, her blood was whispering through her veins, anxious to blend with his.

She stripped out of her clothing, her nipples tightening and her cunt lips swelling, tingling, so that she pressed her legs together as his gaze traveled over her naked body, his eyes going from dark polished stones to molten lava. "Get in the shower now." It was a growled command, a warning, and she obeyed. Stepping into the modern shower that was a short distance away from the old-fashioned tub. Knowing he watched through the clear glass as she pooled liquid soap into her palms and then ran her hands over her skin.

Giddy relief chased away her fear in the same way as the hot water cascaded over her flesh, carrying the soap away, leaving her feeling renewed, refreshed — reckless. His lust was a tangible thing, touching her despite the distance and glass that stood between them, and she reacted to it. Cupping her breasts, tweaking her nipples, then slowly smoothing a hand downward, stopping when it was wedged between her legs, her palm massaging a clit that was hard, erect, its hood already pulled back, her fingers slippery, not from soap alone but from arousal.

Fire roared through Matteo's cock and mind, burning away all other emotion except the primitive desire to fuck his bride as he fed from her, as he claimed her completely, opening a vein and experiencing the dark pleasure of her mouth pressed against his skin, his blood and will flowing into her as she drank of him.

He wrenched the shower door open and jerked her out, pausing only long enough to turn off the water before he hauled her against him and kissed her. A dominant claiming that had her whimpering and going soft in his arms, submissive, her body molding itself to his in an offering that took all he had to refuse.

With a hiss he forced his lips away from hers, tangling his fingers in her hair in order to control her, to keep her from nuzzling against him and diverting him from the course he was determined to take. He would fuck her. He would bite her and be bitten in return. He would know the ecstasy of claiming and taking the last step necessary to make her his kadine. But he would punish Sarael first for escaping to the carnival.

He grabbed a towel, pressing it into her hands and taking a step backward, his body still burning from where it had touched hers. He stripped as she dried off, taking her upper arm when they were both done and guiding her to the bedroom, halting at the foot of the bed where cuffs hung from the corner post.

She stiffened and tried to pull away at the sight of them but she was no match for his superior strength and he easily secured her wrists so that her arms were above her head, her movements limited. "I understand why you left, Sarael. And just as you kept your promise, I will keep mine."

He moved to the dresser and a bolt of shock ripped through her when he picked up a flogger before returning to where she was restrained. She pulled at her bindings, primal instinct demanding she try and avoid the stinging bite of leather whipping across her back and buttocks.

Matteo stilled her struggles, pressing his front to her back, his palm cupping her breast, stroking her abdomen before his fingers grasped the ends of the flogger straps, pulling them tight. "You must learn to obey me, Sarael. To accept the things I do in order to ensure your safety, to gain peace of mind for myself. I am almost impossible to destroy. But you, *carissima*, even with my blood racing through your veins, you are still vulnerable. The idea of you being killed, of you being taken by our enemies is intolerable." He glided the taut leather back and forth over her pebbled nipples, then downward, the cool feel of the material against her belly making her quiver. "I'm not sure what I would do if such a thing occurred, but I fear I might become the monster of your human stories. Tonight you will go through the final changes and become my kadine. Already it is too late to undo what we are to each other."

He dropped the flogger ends, forcing her legs open and reaching between them from behind, grasping the leather strips again and pulling them taut so they pressed against her swollen, slippery folds and engorged clit. "I have made mistakes with you," Matteo surprised her by admitting, his mouth brushing a kiss across her shoulder and up her neck, his hands sawing the strips of leather back and forth across her aroused flesh. "No doubt I will make other mistakes in the future, Sarael. But we have made a good start in showing that we both can keep our word." His fangs grazed her skin and she whimpered, arching her neck in offering.

"After your punishment," he said, and she shivered when he stepped away from her, the leather straps of the flogger trailing over her inner thigh as it retreated with him.

Anticipation moved through her, an addictive erotic fear she'd never experienced with any other man. She tensed, bracing herself for the first strike, but it didn't come immediately.

Instead he waited, letting her grow more anxious, more needy, more aroused, until her inner thighs glistened with moisture and her nipples were so hard that she leaned forward and rubbed them against the bedpost in an effort to find relief.

"No!" Matteo hissed, his command blending with the soft rustle of leather as the straps moved through the air, landing on her buttocks with a sting that was painful pleasure. A contradiction that had her hungry for more, willing to accept this form of discipline from him. "Your release will come from me, Sarael," he growled, the second strike coming more rapidly, once again lashing across her buttocks as did the following two, the next several moving higher, until the eighth one struck the flesh over her shoulder blades, the very tip of the leather curling around and stinging her nipple with its bite.

She was shaking then, shivering, her body painfully aroused, her senses so heightened that she cried out when his arms went around her, pulling her back against his front once again, one hand going between her legs, the other cupping her breast, his fingers ruthless on her clit and nipple until he gave her the relief he'd said would come only from him.

Satisfaction filled Matteo. Lust. Pleasure. Anticipation.

Sarael's body was soft and submissive in his arms. Humming with the aftermath of orgasm—and yet he knew that with only a few strokes of his hand, the touch of his lips or fangs to her skin, she would be ready again. Needy for all he had to offer.

His cock was rock-hard against her back, wet with his own arousal, pulsing in time to the rapid beat of both of their hearts. "Eight lashes, Sarael. That was your punishment for running. But what I have given you as a punishment can be given in reward as well."

She whimpered in response, rubbing against his erection and making his body sing with joy, not only at her acceptance of what he'd done to her and her desire for him to do it again, but at the trust she was showing him.

With a groan he forced his hands away from her breast and cunt long enough to free her wrists and lift her into his arms, carrying her the few steps necessary to place her on the bed. "You are my heart, my soul, my world, *carissima*," he said, covering her body with his, pushing into the wet heat of her when she immediately wrapped her legs around his waist.

"You're the same for me," she whispered, the first time she'd made such an admission. Their movements stilling, their gazes locking, emotion flowing back and forth between them.

Matteo lowered his head and captured her mouth, his kiss gentle, loving, an echo and reaffirmation of the words they'd both uttered. She wound her arms around his neck, offering him everything with the way her lips clung to his, the way her tongue yielded, her body open and receptive underneath his.

They remained unmoving except for the sensuous dance of tongue against tongue, the subtle press of skin to skin, two bodies trying to meld into one until the urge to mate, the call for blood became impossible to ignore.

Matteo began moving then, long, forceful thrusts meant to claim, to dominate, to pleasure, content to swallow Sarael's cries until she began writhing against him, the movement inflaming him, pushing him to the limits of his control, then toppling him over when his fangs elongated and her tongue slid across the sharp points, filling his mouth with the taste of her blood.

The heavy bed shook with the force of his thrusts, the room filled with the sound of flesh striking flesh, with whimpers and moans, pleading and guttural sounds of release.

He drank, filling himself with her, then offering her the same, letting her suck at his wrist until she was momentarily sated. *Do you feel the last of the changes beginning, carissima?* This time he spoke mind-to-mind, seeking the connection which had opened at her birth and been reinforced with the tattooing done during the confirmation ceremony, a connection widened and deepened with each sharing of blood until it was no longer a pathway for him to control her, but a part of their irrevocable bond with one another. *Do you feel the last of the changes beginning, carissima?* he repeated, lying heavily on her, her wrists now held to the bed, his body already aware of the changes taking place in hers, anticipating the moment when her fangs would emerge.

She startled underneath him, her heart racing, and he could feel her confusion, her surprise, the small layer of resistance before she accepted. *It burns. It's worse than the last time.*

It'll pass soon, carissima. Don't fight it. But he knew she wouldn't be able to prevent herself from doing just that as the heat built, as the last of her cells adapted and changed, becoming as alien as they were human. The perfect blending to allow for the creation and survival of their children. Children who would begin more human than vampire—so they could be cared for by their mother when they were young, but would be fully vampire when *La Metamorfosi* occurred.

It burns, Sarael said, arching, writhing against him, reacting to the searing heat coursing through her veins with an intensity that bordered on painful, just as the sting of the lashes she'd felt earlier had. Tears formed at the corners of her eyes and soon her body was slick with sweat, shaking, her gums tingling and the roar of blood drowning out the ability to think about anything other than the need to nuzzle against Matteo's chest or neck, to bite him so hard that she broke the skin.

Almost there, carissima. Open for me now, he said, not waiting for her to spread her legs, but forcing them apart with his own. Plowing into her just as her canine teeth elongated and she lunged for his neck. With a hiss he changed his grip, holding both of her wrists to the bed with one of his hands so that the other was free to tangle in her hair and restrict her movements.

She fought him like a wild thing, bucking and struggling, giving him the right to tame her, to use more of his strength against her, to subdue and control her until the maiden rush of *La Brama* passed and Sarael lay beneath him, panting, eyes and body hungry, and yet submissive, waiting for him to provide what she needed.

He dared to lean down then, to kiss her, to explore her smaller fangs with his tongue. To test her.

She held steady, her only movement the rapid rise and fall of her chest, the rubbing of her tongue against his in an effort to appease him, to apologize for lunging at his neck so savagely.

Now that the bond was forged, the connection between them completely open, Matteo couldn't resist the urge to touch her thoughts, to reassure himself that she was truly his, that she harbored no desire to escape from him.

He moved through her mind, anger flaring up at the images of Angelique striking Sarael, warning her that her life wouldn't be her own if she was found, the anger giving way to regret when he saw how his own actions, his own impatience and lack of control had caused his kadine to suffer needlessly, to be afraid when she didn't need to be. The regret yielding to a mix of softer, more tender emotions when he found what he was looking for. Her acceptance. Her willingness to belong to him. Her trust.

He had made mistakes with her. Painted her with her mother's sins. But he *would* do better in the future. He would ensure that she knew just how important she was to him. She was his heart, his soul, his world, everything he longed for.

Matteo lifted his head, touching her lips briefly. *I will give you what you need now, Sarael. I will always provide for you.* He shifted position, releasing her wrists so he could hold himself above her. *Feed now, carissima, feed while we make love.*

Sarael nuzzled his chest, making him groan as her tongue swirled and teased over his flesh. She was aware of every place where their skin touched, aware of his cock deeply embedded in her channel. His heat surrounded her. His body hovered over hers, dominant, protective. She belonged to him. Every cell sang the truth of it. And yet she could also feel his need to please her, his need to ensure her happiness in the world she was now a part of. A fantasyscape existing under The Moon.

She touched his thoughts and found his joy during the confirmation ceremony, his suffering when she'd been taken, his fear as he'd searched for Angelique. She found his regrets at having misjudged her, his anger at himself for not controlling his own needs, for not being able to bring her gently into his world. She saw his resolve to do better and was humbled by what her acceptance, her trust meant to him.

She licked over the tattooed mark on his chest and felt a burst of heat in the one on her wrist. *Sarael!* It was a command, a demand echoed by the sharp thrust of his cock.

Need rushed through her. The desire to be one with him. His strong heartbeat filled her with a sense of homecoming. She did as he commanded, nearly orgasming as her fangs slid into his chest, dark pleasure and ecstasy flowing into her along with his blood.

KIZIAH'S READING

ഇ

Dedication

ॐ

For Jennifer K – Head Cheerleader and Chief Nag.
May this story inspire you!

Trademarks Acknowledgement

ॐ

The author acknowledges the trademarked status and trademark owners of the following wordmarks mentioned in this work of fiction:

Suburban: General Motors Corporation

Airstream: Airstream, Inc.

Chapter One

The scene in front of Kiziah Stillwell was just like she'd experienced it in her dream. Cheap carnival rides under a star-speckled autumn sky. The air brisk, chilled, loaded with the smell of hot dogs and cotton candy, filled with tinny musical themes and the voices of carnies vying with one another, each trying to entice the men strolling with their wives and girlfriends to stop and try their luck, to part with their money and attempt to win a stuffed animal.

Kiziah stopped in front of the fortune-teller's tent. Madame Helki. She hadn't seen the name in her dream, but she'd seen the red hand painted on the canvas front, a spread of tarot cards above it.

"You've come for your reading?" a voice questioned from the darkened interior of the tent, startling Kiziah with the wording. Could the fortune-teller really know about the dream?

Kiziah touched her fingers to the base of her throat, gently outlining the small dreamcatcher she wore underneath her jacket and shirt. It was the only link she had to the nomadic silversmith who'd died before she was born, unaware even that he'd fathered a child.

Her father's people, the Chippewa, believed all dreams came from external sources and not from the subconscious of the one experiencing them. That's why they had originally fashioned the dreamcatchers, to trap the bad dreams but allow the good ones through.

Maybe the old woman had sent the dream. Kiziah's hand dropped from the necklace. Or maybe her mother's spirit had, knowing that today of all days, Kiziah would be thinking about the past, aching for the return of old times, for something of her mother.

Kiziah moved into the tent and took a seat, ignoring everything but the ancient fortune-teller in front of her and the deck of cards now in Madame Helki's hands. The cards were the only important *thing* in the tent, everything else was just a special effect put into place in order to create a setting, an atmosphere, a show for those who viewed the reading as entertainment—or needed to see something different than what they saw in their everyday environment in order to believe.

Kiziah knew better. She had a lifetime of memories proving it didn't matter. Readings done in restaurants, at playgrounds, while sitting in the backseat of her mother's car and leaning over the front so she could view the cards a traveling companion was interpreting as they drove to yet another psychic fair—their travel trailer, their home on wheels, being pulled behind them.

"You've come for your reading?" the ancient fortune-teller asked again, understanding in her voice, the merest hint of amusement in her eyes.

"Yes."

Madame Helki handed the cards to Kiziah, not asking for a specific question but waiting patiently. Kiziah shuffled them, opening herself up to the message she felt sure was out there for her. The reason for the dream and her presence in the garish tent, a metal creation covered with tarp to make it seem more than just a carnival amusement.

She stopped shuffling when it felt right to do so. Cutting the deck and restacking it before handing it back to the woman across from her. In quick succession three cards were placed on the table.

The past. The present. The future.

The High Priestess.

The Hermit.

The Wheel of Fortune.

Madame Helki leaned over the cards, nodding slightly. "Much of your life has been influenced by a woman. A woman who introduced you to the mysteries of a world that can't always be seen. But she is gone now except in dreamscapes where spirits can sometimes touch the lives of those who are important to them." Sympathy moved through the fortune-teller's face. "So now you maintain a distance from others, traveling alone, living a solitary life. Seeking. Trying to find meaning, a place for yourself. A belonging." Her fingers settled on the table, underlining the Wheel of Fortune. "Soon. Very soon, an opportunity will present itself. A destiny not planned for, even by those who will draw you into their world. But you are well suited for it. You need only to use the strength and courage you have gained and the wisdom bestowed on you by The High Priestess in order to grasp and hold what fate will soon offer you."

* * * * *

The warm water struck Cable Luske's body, chasing away the chill he'd gained during the boat ride out to sea in order to dispose of the body. Christ. He hadn't seen that one coming.

He would never have guessed that a fellow padrall—one whose family had served the vampire race for more generations than his own—would try and abduct a kadine, a vampire's mate. What insanity.

His own reputation would suffer for it. *If* Matteo Cabrelli chose to make an issue of Cable's failure to keep Sarael guarded until the very moment when Matteo came to reclaim her. But how was he to know there was an enemy in their midst?

Cable tried to work up some concern at the prospect of being lectured by the higher-ups in his order, by his father, of possibly being reduced to errand boy for a while, but couldn't. Not when the rest of his life was about to crash down around him. Not when he felt like things were coming to an end with Fane.

Sorrow moved through him. Pain. The fingers of future heartbreak reaching back and stroking him. Yeah, he'd get over it eventually. It was just getting *through* it that he had to manage first.

Fane was a dhampir. A soldier of the vampire race, a man born to protect his kind until The Transformation, when he became a full vampire. A reproductively mature male who would want a bride, a kadine, a woman who could give him the children who would become the next generation of soldiers.

Two years ago when the relationship had begun, the prospect of Fane's Transformation hadn't bothered Cable. Fane's parents had been alive, as had his brother.

But now they were gone. Killed by the Believers, the secret society whose original mission was to destroy any creature that could take on the form of man, but was more than mortal.

Vampires had been the primary target of the Believers. But over the centuries their description of "human" had narrowed, and those they'd chosen to hunt, kill and persecute had expanded to include witches, psychics and anyone with supernatural ability or talents.

During the last year Cable had managed to ignore thinking about the truth of his future with Fane, to avoid facing it or discussing it—even though he believed that in the end Fane would feel he owed it to his father's memory to not only avenge his death but to produce the next generation of dhampirs. Cable had helped Fane gather information, eventually finding a name to go with the bomb that had killed Fane's family. But now Cable knew he couldn't avoid the future any longer.

The Transformation was approaching. Cable had been around enough dhampirs to recognize it—even if he wanted to ignore it, wanted to pretend it wasn't so close.

But he could sense the restlessness in Fane. The Hunger. The Heat.

Cable's cock grew hard thinking about how aggressive Fane had become in bed. How insatiable. How dangerous.

There were times when he'd avoided being bitten only because Fane had been underneath him, tethered or with his face pressed against the mattress in order to maintain control. Cable closed his eyes, taking his shaft in hand. Pumping up and down. Christ, he was horny. He longed for the feel of fangs sliding through his skin, dreamed of the ecstasy of being taken while Fane fed, of taking Fane while the other man bit him.

It was madness. The consequences serious for a padrall who became obsessed with that particular high. Nothing was as addictive as a vampire's bite when the one being bitten was allowed to experience it without the fog of enthrallment.

There were places, brothels, where padralls who'd succumbed to the lure and the addiction were kept to service vampires and dhampirs who preferred their prey aware. The fallen padralls were little more than whores, never trusted again because of fears of what they might do if they found themselves repudiated or replaced. A large number of them died by their own hand once their looks had faded and they were no longer favored by the men who visited the brothels.

He'd avoided Fane's bite not just because of the possible consequences but because it would only make him desire Fane more desperately. Christ. He should have stuck to women, a pleasure Fane had only occasionally indulged in. Or blonds. He and Fane were alike in that regard, usually avoiding dark-haired partners.

Hell, maybe it said something about both of them that they could easily pass for distant cousins. Their bodies similar in build, their eyes so brown they appeared almost as black as their hair.

Cable closed his eyes and tilted his head back, wishing the hot water could pound the desire for Fane out of his head. He needed to put some distance between himself and Fane. To walk away from the relationship before Fane came to him and asked for him to arrange for the creation of a kadine—a mate.

Who else would Fane trust with such an important undertaking? And yet to undertake the task would be a living hell. One that could extend for decades—unless one of the women who were little more than breeders, their rights to their daughters nonexistent from the moment of conception—was selected.

Pain speared through Cable's chest. Fuck. Would Fane expect the two of them to stay lovers until Fane claimed his bride, until he sexually bonded with her as he turned her into his kadine? And then what? Stick around, helping them raise their children, aging quickly while they aged over centuries?

Christ! What a future that was. And Cable wanted no part of it. No part of any of it.

Long ago, the alien race from which the vampire had evolved had come to the conclusion it was better to raise future mates than to find them among the human population. To convert humans as adults was too arduous, too painful for all involved, and too many of them were lost in the process—dying or going insane. They'd found it easier to cultivate families who would offer their daughters for money and power.

In those early days, daughters were chattel, bought and sold, their fate of little concern in the human world. But as civilization changed and the padralls became wealthy, powerful families in their own right, their daughters became desirable wives to kings and lords and merchant princes, and they no longer wished to turn them over to the vampires they served. And so another source was cultivated, families who would gain riches from allowing their daughters to provide female children whose blood would be altered at birth and who would be taken away as soon as they were weaned, raised from infancy to take their place as vampire mates.

It was still possible to convert full humans, but it was a painful process. Only those who were born to be brides, who were given their future mate's blood at birth and at the confirmation ceremony were spared the excruciating agony that becoming biologically compatible, able to bear a vampire's children, entailed.

Cable grimaced, finding the system of creating brides distasteful, but he was in no position to change it. True, the padrall families had prospered and gained power with each generation, but their livelihood and survival was irrevocably tied to the vampire race. There was no escape. No breaking the bonds forged so long ago that there was no written record of it. Betrayal—on any level—was a death sentence.

The bathroom door opened and Cable knew without looking that Fane had entered the room and stood watching him through the glass shower stall as he slid his hand up and down his cock. He should turn his back, or better yet, get out of the room and out of the house completely.

But he didn't.

What he felt for Fane went beyond sheer lust, though there was plenty of that. It was love. A hopeless, destructive emotion when it was directed toward a dhampir, one who would soon change into a full vampire and need to breed, one who was consumed with revenge—against the Believers in general, and the bomber who'd killed his family in particular.

The shower door clicked open, allowing cool air and Fane's scent to swirl around Cable. He tried to ignore them both.

It was impossible.

A calloused hand stroked along his spine. Another covered his own where it was wrapped around his cock, pumping up and down for several strokes before leaving in order to cup Cable's balls and make him groan.

"Something's bothering you," Fane said, tightening his grip, knowing just how much pressure to exert, knowing just where and how to touch another man. Where and how to touch Cable.

"Yeah. What's new?" Cable turned his head away slightly, his eyes remaining closed as he tried to minimize the impact of Fane's presence, the desire to turn into him, to allow their bodies to touch, trapping their cocks against one another as their tongues met and dueled in a wet, heated kiss.

"Matteo won't make an issue of what happened with Sarael," Fane said, crowding closer, his water-slick penis hard against Cable's side, swamping him with a lust that had nothing to do with vampire pheromones. "By now he's no doubt made the third exchange of blood and she's already gone through the last changes. He'll be content to take her back to Italy and begin an investigation within the padrall order there."

"Great," Cable said, the tone of his voice conveying how little he cared. His continued failure to open his eyes and look at Fane a subtle challenge he knew wouldn't go unanswered. It was insane. Pushing Fane's buttons would only escalate the situation.

Cable groaned when Fane's arm went around his waist, his hand coming to rest on Cable's hand again, his thumb brushing over the tip of Cable's cock, making it pulse and leak, the fingers of the other hand tightening and releasing on Cable's balls before lightly exploring the place behind them. Cable clenched his jaw against the pleasure of Fane's touch and closeness. He told himself that he should push Fane away and get the hell out of there.

He opened his eyes instead and turned to Fane, angry at himself, angry at Fane. His emotion making the kiss they shared aggressive, a ruthless struggle for control instead of a lazy exploration of passion.

Within seconds Cable found himself pinned to the wall, Fane's cock hard against his own, rubbing, pressing, while their tongues dueled and their hands roamed, relentlessly finding each erogenous zone, a battle for dominance, a dance that in the beginning of their relationship had been safe. A contest fought for enjoyment, to heighten the pleasure between partners whose future blended easily. Who had found companionship and love when neither had been expecting it.

A tremor of fear mixed with longing shot through Cable when Fane's canine teeth elongated into fangs. One slip-up, one careless movement and his tongue would bleed.

Neither one of them was prepared to deal with the consequences if that happened.

Need roared through Fane. The press and slide of Cable's tongue against his, the nearness of it to his fangs a maddening temptation he couldn't endure.

With a deep hiss of frustration and anger, he ended the kiss and stepped back. His skin felt too tight for his body, his cock pulsed in angry demand, his gums ached. He wanted to fuck, hard and fast, without restraint. He wanted to do it as he gorged himself on Cable.

It was primitive instinct and violent emotion combined with The Hunger, The Heat. And the sound of Cable's rapid heartbeat, the hint of fear coupled with the knowledge that Cable was trying to pull away from him only drove the lust higher.

The Transformation was drawing near. Fane knew it. He cursed it as deeply as other dhampirs desired and welcomed it.

With the change came the need to drink a foul mix of herbs in order to control The Hunger. He would no longer be free to drain everything from those he hunted — from the Believers — to take their life essence along with each swallow of their blood. He'd be relieved of his duties as a soldier for the vampire race, expected instead to take a kadine, to mate with her so a new generation of dhampirs would be created.

Rage rushed through Fane. Hatred toward all Believers but especially toward the one who called himself The Apostle, the one who'd created the bomb that killed his parents and brother as they drove away from the theater, no doubt lost in a discussion of *The Phantom of the Opera*.

Until that had happened, Fane had thought to take Cable as his lifelong companion when the change occurred and he became fully vampire, to make the required exchanges, sharing blood three times so they would be sexually bonded, so Cable's life would be irrevocably tied to his. So Cable would need his blood to survive.

Such a thing was condemned by most of the padrall orders, a leftover tenet from the past when the earliest of them had altered the course of their own history by choosing to serve without benefit of extending their lifespan. Those early leaders fearing the loss of their souls with centuries of life.

Fane had not broached the subject with Cable, believing there was plenty of time. Not wanting a confrontation—or a rejection. Knowing that not only would Cable be condemned by his own order if he agreed to tie his life to Fane's, but some would revile him, seeing a male companion as weak and submissive. Though there was no truth in that characterization of their relationship, and among Fane's own kind there was no reduction in status for either a vampire or his male mate. With existence spanning centuries, it was foolish to choose unhappiness when selecting a companion. And while Fane had fucked women, he had never shared as much of himself with any other human as he had with Cable. Had never felt as deeply about one as he felt about Cable.

With an older brother to carry on the line, and parents who had only borne and raised the first generation of sons, and who would continue to raise more, two or three during each quarter of a century, there had been no pressure for Fane to reproduce. But all that had changed with their deaths. Now he would need to take a kadine. He owed it to his father and brother.

Anger howled in Fane, mixing with the lust as the scent of their combined arousal surrounded him, as his eyes met Cable's. He moved in again, pressing his body to Cable's, hissing when his penis rubbed against Cable's, when Cable's hand dropped, encircling both their cocks, pumping up and down so that exquisite heat shot up Fane's spine and made his balls pull tight against his body.

"Turn around," he ordered, feeling the wildness growing, the need to dominate. The very heat and hunger that drove a vampire to take a bride, a kadine.

"It's too dangerous," Cable said, his other hand lowering, grasping Fane's balls and pulling them against his own, fondling, squeezing, showing that he commanded Fane's body as thoroughly as Fane commanded his.

Fane closed his eyes. Gathering his resolve. He needed to fuck tonight, not get fucked. "Turn around," he repeated.

Cable soaked in the sight of Fane. The taut face, the tense, water-slick body. It had been days since Fane had taken the dominant position, controlling the pleasure. He leaned in, pressing his lips to Fane's, his tongue twining with Fane's before lightly tracing Fane's fangs — testing Fane's control and sending a pulse of desire through them both.

With a groan, Cable pulled back, freeing his hands and using one of them to reach for the lubricant they kept next to the shampoo, handing it to Fane. Fane's nostrils flared, his eyes darkened.

Cable turned around and braced his hands against the wall, spreading his legs, his balls hanging between them — a sight he knew would further inflame Fane. Just as it never failed to drive his own lust higher.

With a hiss, Fane moved in, reaching around and taking Cable's cock in his hand, sliding up and down so that Cable bucked, so that arousal leaked from the swollen head. The lubricant bottle dropping to the floor in the second before Fane's fingers circled the pucker of Cable's back entrance then slipped in and out, preparing him, both of them growing harder, hotter, more anxious to couple, to connect, to ignore the future in favor of the wild pleasure of the moment.

And then Fane was there, panting and groaning, working himself in as he continued to manipulate Cable's cock. It was heaven and hell. A dark ecstasy for both of them.

When he was fully seated, Fane pressed his chest to Cable's back, savoring the slick feel of flesh against flesh, his lips brushing across Cable's shoulder and neck. Every cell in his body screaming for him to strike, to pierce Cable with his fangs as thoroughly as he was piercing him with his cock.

"Christ," Cable panted, fucking his cock in and out through the tight grip of Fane's hand, pushing backward in the process and driving Fane's penis deeper, the movement scraping the pointed tips of Fane's canine teeth against Cable's neck and drawing blood.

It was too much. Temptation too long denied. Desire held in check when the heart wanted a consummation.

Fane couldn't resist. His fangs sank deeper, his mouth forming a seal against Cable's skin. He drank as he fucked. Feasted as he made love. Taking everything, body, soul, blood. Only lifting his head at the end, to shout in pleasure as he came, as Cable's body shuddered and jerked against his, as wave after wave of semen jetted through their cocks.

They sagged against the water-warm tiles of the stall, stood as the hot blast from the showerhead struck them, washing away the seed but not the memory of what had happened. They didn't speak as the barrier of the future rose between them.

Fane closed his eyes, knowing he should say he was sorry. But the words would be a lie. His cock pressed against Cable's buttocks, need and desire having already filled it again. Fantasy flooding his mind. He wanted to leave the shower, to take Cable on the bed, to let Cable take him, blood flowing between them. A sacred covenant bonding them together.

A hiss escaped when Cable tensed underneath him, the dominant urges of the vampire race swirling in Fane. He was so close to turning, so close to needing a companion in order to control The Hunger. To cope with the changes that would occur when he went through The Transformation, when he lost the ability to maintain a human form as he moved about in the daylight hours.

Cable stilled. Cursing himself. Cursing Fane.

He closed his eyes. Fighting off the pleasure that still lingered. Willing his cock to go limp. He was hard again, on the verge of selling his soul in order to experience the ecstasy of Fane's bite along with the forbidden pleasures he'd fantasized about.

It was insanity. A path to hell, paved by heartbreak and suffering. "Get off me," Cable said, the muscles of his arms bunching. His chest tightening.

Fane tried to step back, but The Heat and Hunger ruled. His body was screaming for him to strike again, to gorge himself on Cable's blood even if he had to pin Cable against the wall and swamp him with the pheromones used to lure and control prey. His cock was throbbing, aching, his heart was howling at the choices being forced on him.

"I'm almost out of control. I need a kadine." It came out harsh, guttural. Tortured. The words powerful enough to force some distance between their heated, water-slick bodies.

"Yeah. What's new?" Cable said, escaping from the shower and taking only enough time to dry off and dress before leaving the house and driving into the darkness. Putting physical distance between, wishing the night would allow him to hide from the heartache that had finally found him.

Chapter Two

Kiziah paused as she exited the fortune-teller's tent, a tingling along her spine forcing her attention away from Madame Helki's words. She rubbed her arms and concentrated on the source of her uneasiness, wishing she had more psychic ability, though she was glad she had enough to determine that the cause of her sudden wariness was human instead of supernatural.

She glanced around, focusing on the individuals rather than the broad landscape of the carnival. No one was looking at her and yet her gaze was drawn to a man throwing darts at a booth a short distance away.

He seemed oblivious to anything other than the dartboard, but something about him scared her. Something beyond the buzz cut or the ornate cross tattooed on his neck. She knew better than to go by external appearances. She'd grown up around men whose looks spanned the range from long-haired sixties hippy to tattooed biker-bad.

The man finished with his darts and turned slightly, his eyes meeting hers and she knew she'd been right in picking him out of the crowd. Something dark and twisted lived inside him. Something that enjoyed inflicting fear and pain.

She broke off the eye contact and moved away from Madame Helki's tent, shivering as she felt his gaze on her back. Her stomach knotting as she thought about where she'd left her car. The distance and the darkness adding to the sense of foreboding.

Cable's body responded to the sight of the blonde emerging from the fortune-teller's tent, his cock going rock hard so fast that it made him dizzy. Christ. Like he needed to add more insanity to his life. He was still reeling from what had happened with Fane. Still hurting from hearing Fane acknowledge the truth they both knew.

Knowing that they'd finally reached the break-point in their relationship.

He adjusted his jeans, trying to gain some relief from the press of them against his erection, disgusted with himself for coming to the carnival in the first place. What did he expect the fortune-teller and the cards to tell him that he didn't already know?

The blonde stilled, her body language causing Cable to step into the shadows and look around. Something was bothering her.

It took only an instant for Cable to spot the Believer. Fuck! His hand slipped into his jacket pocket for the cell phone. Where there was one Believer there might be two.

The blonde turned and began walking. The Believer pushed away from the booth where he'd been playing darts and followed her. Cable flicked open his phone but before he could touch the first button, an amused voice said, "I believe I can handle this without assistance."

Cable snapped the phone shut, irritation scraping over him and making him grit his teeth. "I'll leave you to it then," he said, walking away without looking at Domino Santori. The last thing he needed was to be in the presence of another dhampir tonight.

Cable paused at the entrance to Madame Helki's tent just long enough in ensure that she was alone. "Ah, I was expecting you," she said, and he closed his eyes briefly. Christ. Was this what a descent into madness felt like? Even *he* recognized that his emotions were all over the map tonight. But he took a seat across from the fortune-teller, his heart racing when he noticed the cards. Three of them, lined up in a row. The past. The present. The future. The High Priestess. The Hermit. The Wheel of Fortune.

He tensed. Despite the number of times he'd visited with her when he was guarding Sarael, she'd never giving him a reading.

The old fortune-teller laughed, an amused sound that reminded Cable of Domino. She leaned forward, turning the first two cards over and leaving the third exposed before picking up the deck of remaining cards and handing it to him. "Choose one."

Christ. He couldn't believe he was doing this. But he couldn't prevent himself from obeying her, shuffling the deck and cutting it until he felt compelled to stop and remove the card that had risen to the surface of the deck.

Madame Helki took it from him. Nodding to herself as she placed it across the Wheel of Fortune.

Everything inside Cable tightened at the sight of The Lovers. A man and a woman standing naked underneath a tree.

"You have reached a turning point, a place with many possible outcomes and a chance for great happiness," the fortune-teller said. "You must recognize and reconcile your own needs in order to fully embrace the opportunity that will soon present itself to you."

"A woman?" Cable managed, his voice very nearly a croak. He hadn't been intimate with one since meeting Fane, though his thoughts went immediately to the blonde who'd been in the tent before him. Were the three cards on the table hers? Were the two of them linked by the Wheel of Fortune?

Madame Helki's eyes crinkled with amusement as she gathered the cards and returned them to the deck. "I can't tell you anything more."

* * * * *

There was a moment of disorientation, an elongation of reality in the instant before Kiziah's surroundings snapped into focus. And then fear raced in.

She was walking in the direction of her car, crowded by darkness and surrounded by empty streets as heavy footsteps followed a short distance behind her. Their owner projecting a menace she recognized from outside of the fortune-teller's tent.

The man with the ornate cross tattooed on his neck.

Kiziah knew it with certainty even before she looked back and saw him. She opened her mouth to scream, but the sound was trapped in her throat, held there as though phantom fingers were preventing it from escaping.

True terror tried to push through the barrier but the only sound to escape was a small whimper.

Her heart raced, beating so fast that pain rippled through her chest.

She stumbled and very nearly fell, then regained her balance and began running.

The man raced after her and she could feel his anticipation, his enjoyment of her fear. His utter belief that he'd catch her before she could escape.

And then just as quickly as she'd first become aware of him, the sound of his footsteps ended and didn't resume. His menace replaced by that of a supernatural presence behind her.

She kept running, daring a glance backward and seeing nothing, but she didn't stop until she was locked in her car and driving away. Her body shaking in reaction. Her lungs burning.

God! What had just happened? Why had she left the carnival without an escort? She could have asked someone to walk with her or begged a ride from someone. Instead she couldn't remember leaving at all.

Miles from where she'd escaped the man pursuing her, she pulled over so she could gather herself, so she could force her thoughts back to the moment she'd stepped out of the fortune-teller's tent, to her first awareness of the man who'd been following her. She remembered deciding then and there that she wouldn't walk back to her car unless she was sure it was safe.

What had she done next?

Kiziah rubbed her eyes. The move triggering a memory, a sense of being in the presence of something supernatural, a touch on her shoulder so she'd turned, a glimpse of obsidian eyes, a desire to go to her car, followed by a haze of nothingness until reality returned.

Her heart jerked. Her mind sharpened with understanding.

She'd been hypnotized. Used for bait to draw her assailant into the darkness.

She shivered, the Wheel of Fortune rising, a specter in her mind, and with it, Madame Helki's words. *Very soon, an opportunity will present itself. A destiny not planned for, even by those who will draw you into their world.*

Kiziah had been aware of supernatural presences before, but she'd never had one touch her life so directly. Was this the beginning then? The point of divergence? The place where the influence of The Hermit yielded to that of the Wheel?

Unbidden, tears came to her eyes. The thought of The High Priestess putting them there. The card of the past. Of the mother who had also been her best friend, her confidant, her teacher.

Pain speared through Kiziah. A year ago on this very day a driver running a red light had collapsed her world. Crashed into it and created carnage. Leaving death and destruction behind as he'd walked away with only a few scratches, so drunk he was hardly aware of what he'd done.

Kiziah fought against the tears welling up. Braced herself to endure the tight fist of agony as her heart was squeezed mercilessly by the loss of her mother.

She took a deep breath, her earlier thoughts returning, lending her strength. Maybe her mother's spirit *had* sent the dream that guided her to Madame Helki's tent. Without the dream, she would have bypassed this town and the carnival altogether. She would have gone straight through to Ashburg, settling in at the campground where many of the men and women she'd grown up among were already camped, waiting to set up booths at the psychic fair.

She pulled the dreamcatcher necklace out from underneath her clothing. Whether or not her mother's spirit was behind the reading, or responsible for the presence of the supernatural being who'd both used her and saved her, Kiziah knew tonight wasn't a good night to be alone. She needed bright lights and people. A warm place to sit. Music to fill her mind and crowd her thoughts out.

She put the car into gear and drove into town. Relief pouring through her when she spotted a brightly lit coffee shop, the sign out front announcing that a local band was playing. She traveled another block then parked. Laughing at herself when she caught herself glancing back to check the travel trailer—the one currently at a nearby campground and not being pulled behind the car.

The Hermit. It was an honest representation of the last year. More than once she'd thought about how her life resembled a turtle's. Solitary. Moving from place to place, her home with her wherever she went. A place to retreat, to close the door behind her when she wanted to block out the world around her.

Not tonight though. She didn't want to climb into the Airstream and be alone in her shell.

The realization of how deeply her need for companionship was on this particular night made her heart ache, made her realize that the need was deep enough that despite what would come in the morning—the awkwardness, the hollowness, the loneliness—if she had a chance…

Yeah right. This was small town America and she was a stranger. The few times she'd given in to the need for physical intimacy had been when she was working a craft fair or a psychic fair, the men she sought comfort with also working the fairs or with someone she knew.

She entered the coffee shop, the artsy-crafty feel of it making her feel at home. There were empty chairs, but the tables were full with groups of people or couples laying claim to the area around them. A few of them glanced in her direction before refocusing on their companions. The warmth of the room, the mellow music, wrapping them in a cocoon of togetherness.

Kiziah leaned against the serving bar. The coffee mug hot against her palms doing its best to thaw the ice-cold spot at her center.

This isn't going to help. This was a mistake.

The music. The couples. The groups of friends. They only emphasized how alone she felt. A truck stop with rowdy, laughing men, twenty-five-cent table jukeboxes and whiny, fighting kids being attended by tired, irritable parents would be better. It was easier to lose herself in that kind of a crowd, to keep her thoughts at bay.

A silent laugh lightened her spirits, pulling the corners of her mouth into a tiny smile as the image of The Hermit formed in her mind again. She had to believe that something important was about to happen, that something in her life was about to change. Otherwise the dream sending her to the carnival was just a dream. The card reading just an entertainment. And the surreal events afterward unexplainable.

So rather than retreat she claimed a two-person table near the door when it became available and concentrated on the warmth of the coffee shop, the smells. Forced herself to sink into this place at this time, to avoid thoughts of the past or the future as the music flowed over and through her.

She wasn't aware of the time passing. Couldn't have said how much of it had gone by before the door behind her opened and closed, the cold fall air rushing over her along with a crisp masculine scent.

Kiziah looked up, immediately caught in dark chocolate eyes, her pulse jerking and racing when a smile formed on kissable lips, when the stranger cocked his head and asked, "Is this seat taken?"

"No."

His smile widened. A hand settled on the back of the chair. "Is it all right with you if I claim it?"

"Yes."

He laughed, a warm, husky sound. "Save it while I get a coffee?"

"Sure."

She grimaced. Her answers looping through her mind as he moved to the counter and ordered a drink. Great. He was going to think she was queen of the monosyllable.

Her heart lurched and her body tightened traitorously. If she'd dreamed up a man to spend the evening with, he would look like this one. Dark-haired. Dark-eyed. Totally masculine. And yet...his laugh, his eyes, he wasn't a man who was afraid to feel.

So what was he doing here? Alone?

Kiziah wrapped her hands around her empty coffee mug and forced her eyes away from the stranger. Maybe he was a traveler, just passing through town. A man who didn't want to spend the night holed up in some dismal hotel room.

The fact that he came here instead of a bar told her something about him. She shivered, aware of the moment he turned away from the counter and headed toward the table.

The loneliness and need for companionship that had driven Kiziah into the coffee shop returned, bringing a ripple of nervousness with it, an ache that settled in her belly. This was the part she wasn't very good at. The reason why her sexual encounters were few and far between.

She forced herself to take a deep breath. To concentrate on the here and now again. This was something. Better than what she'd had a few minutes ago. She'd get herself another mocha and enjoy the music. She'd sit back and soak in the cozy illusion of being here with a gorgeous man, one who would probably star in her fantasies when she returned to the camper, alone.

Desire moved through Cable, along with an unexpected tenderness as he focused on the blonde who'd agreed to share her table with him. Did she have any idea how vulnerable she looked? How desirable?

There was a sadness radiating off her. A loneliness that found an echoing chord inside of him.

Christ, he'd been thinking about the reading. About The Lovers. About her. And here she was. Here they were together.

Hell. Maybe this was exactly what he needed. A night in a beautiful woman's arms. A night with his cock pumping in and out of a woman's slick, welcoming channel.

He didn't even know her name yet, but he could already imagine himself stripping her out of her clothing, peeling each layer away in order to reveal a body made for pleasure. She was lithe, her breasts the perfect size, large enough to claim his attention, and yet… He gave a small laugh, knowing there were men who claimed breasts could never be too big. But he and Fane both favored— Cable's thoughts veered off, but returned to their original destination. Both he and Fane favored women who looked like this one. Blonde, dark-eyed, soft. Though they'd never shared a woman.

Hell, Fane probably couldn't even remember the last woman he'd been with. And it had been over two years since Cable had been with one.

He rubbed his chest, wishing he could ease the ache in his heart. He couldn't risk being alone with Fane again. Couldn't even be angry over what had happened in the shower. Fuck!

His cock responded to the word. To the images. To the lingering sensations coursing through him, starting at the point where Fane had bitten and streaking through his nipples, his sac, his penis.

Cable forced his attention back to the woman as he took his seat and they introduced themselves. Making small talk and listening to the mellow jazz for a while, becoming comfortable with each other, forming a barricade of warmth against the chill of the deepening night.

Kiziah tried a hundred different conversation starters in her mind but didn't utter a single one of them. Pathetic. She might as well have a capital "L" on her forehead when it came to men. Not that she couldn't talk to them, she could. She could talk their ears off when she was working and they stopped by her booth and expressed an interest in her dreamcatchers.

That's because you're in your comfort zone, Kiz. Maybe it would have been better if we'd stayed in one place, instead of traveling all the time. Then you would have had a normal childhood. I should have…

A lump formed in her throat as her mother's clear voice echoed in her thoughts. She could see her mother's features soften and grow sad. Could read the guilt there over the nomadic lifestyle—the traveling from psychic fair to psychic fair, to weekend festivals and craft shows.

No way, Mom. I love this!

Promise me that if you meet a man…

Kiziah looked down at the table. The sadness she'd been trying to escape when she sought refuge in the bright coffee shop suddenly catching up to her again. A year ago today she'd been "out on the town"—at her mother's urging. Trying to find something in common with the friends of a friend of a friend's client who had invited her to join them while they went from bar to bar looking for "Mr. Right" or at least for "Mr. Tonight". If she hadn't been with them…

Maybe she'd have been killed too when the drunk driver ignored the stoplight and plowed into her mother's car. Or maybe she would have been able to prevent it. Maybe since she would have been driving…

"Something wrong?"

Cable's voice pulled Kiziah out of her thoughts. She gave him an apologetic smile. "Sorry, I guess I'm not very good company tonight."

He gave a soft, husky laugh, surprising her by taking her left hand in his. "That makes two of us." He brushed his thumb over the backs of her fingers. "Let me guess. Boyfriend troubles. That's the only reason I can think of for someone as beautiful as you are coming here by herself. Or maybe you were supposed to meet him, and he didn't show?"

Heat moved through Kiziah's face, embarrassed pleasure. Did he really think she was beautiful? She avoided answering by turning the conversation back on him. "If neither one of us is good company tonight, what's your story? You're more tempting than dark chocolate. Girlfriend problems?"

Cable's smile was a irresistible mix of sad and wry. "Boyfriend problems. A breakup that's been inevitable for a year."

"Oh." *Yeah. It figures.* Kiziah suddenly felt deflated.

The fist that had been holding Cable's heart in a vise grip loosened. Christ, she was so soft, so vulnerable, so genuine. He wanted to wrap his arms around her and shelter her from loneliness and pain. He wanted to find refuge from the same emotions in the heaven of her body.

He squeezed her hand and met her gaze, steeling himself for her reaction. "I haven't been with a woman in over two years."

Kiziah's eyes widened slightly and Cable felt a laugh building. Just being with her lightened his spirits.

"Oh," she said. "Oh."

The laugh escaped. "Yeah—oh." He leaned over and looked into her empty coffee mug, making a show of inhaling. "Mocha? So you find chocolate hard to resist?"

She was finding *him* hard to resist. Something inside of her loosened, making room for a small flicker of courage to flare and take hold. Whatever happened between them, she was going to make the most of this night.

Chapter Three

Fane prowled through the darkened house. Every cell in his body screamed for blood while his cock raged for sex. He was more dangerous now than he'd been when he encountered Cable in the shower.

Anger howled through him. Frustration. Regret.

I need a kadine.

As soon as he'd uttered the words, he'd wanted to call them back. Wanted to retreat to the bedroom with Cable, to fuck until The Heat and Hunger faded and they could talk about the future.

Fane closed his eyes, covering his jeans-protected cock with his hand as his body shuddered in remembered pleasure. As he relived those moments in the shower when Cable's hot blood had rushed into him as they'd fucked.

Could he really give that up? Could he really give Cable up?

There were other dhampirs. Other families to produce the soldiers needed in order to keep their race safe. Children weren't required of him.

And yet... He owed it to his parents not to be all that was left of their union. Owed it to his father to produce sons. But even as he thought it, he could picture his mother's gentle smile. Her lips pressed against his forehead, her whispered words, *Be happy, Fane.*

How many times had she told him that? Even when he was a grown man?

Would he be happy if he gave up Cable?

Maybe there was a way to have both what he wanted and what he needed. In the long history of the vampire race, there had to have been men who enjoyed women as well as other men. Men who wouldn't choose one over the other when it came to taking a companion.

A trickle of fear slid into Fane's heart. A possibility that he rarely faced head-on. Even if he could claim a kadine as well as Cable, there was still no guarantee Cable would suffer the condemnation of the other padralls and agree to bind his life so completely to Fane's that Fane's death would trigger his own.

Fane's hand tightened on his cock. His blood roared through his veins as the primitive instincts of his ancestors flared to life. A dark ruthlessness that lurked in the deepest region of a vampire's soul. There was no law that said companions had to bind themselves willingly.

In the very beginning, none of the humans had been willing.

In the end. It didn't matter.

After the three exchanges of blood were made, a vampire and his chosen were almost one being.

Fane tried to force his mind away from such thoughts but a hint of them still lingered. Driving him to start pacing again. Prowling through the house like a caged predator.

Where had Cable gone?

To Domino Santori?

He doubted Cable would seek the company of another dhampir tonight. Especially one like Domino, whose sense of humor could be dark and biting. One who still believed he could avoid the hunger for a kadine in favor of fucking a variety of women.

Had Cable gone to the carnival, then?

It would be closed by now. But that wouldn't matter. They'd spent so much time there guarding Sarael that they easily fit in. And Cable had visited with the fortune-teller, Helki, more than Fane thought was wise. Would he seek a tarot reading in order to deal with what had happened in the shower? In order to deal with Fane's careless words regarding a kadine?

Fane's chest tightened, his heart aching as though a hand had reached in and wrapped it in a fist. His guts burned. He had no control over what the cards and the fortune-teller might say to Cable. He had no control over what Cable might do.

Without conscious thought, Fane moved to the door. He would go to the carnival in search of Cable. And if he didn't find him there, then he would seek out Domino and together they could hunt a viable prey. He was too close to turning now to risk hunting alone. If he found no one deserving of death, he wasn't sure he could stop from killing an innocent once the first hot splash of blood filled his mouth. Even for a dhampir, such a thing could warrant a death penalty.

* * * * *

Kiziah rubbed her palms against her jeans in an effort to both warm them and to still the slight trembling as she walked over to the travel trailer where Cable was already out of his car and waiting.

They'd been the last to leave the coffee shop, retreating to the nearly abandoned campground at the edge of town, the place Kiziah had unhitched and set up the Airstream before going to the carnival and then into town.

She rubbed her palms against her jeans again. Nervous. Not for her safety. There were a few campers scattered around the site and she trusted Cable. Otherwise she would never have led him back to her home on wheels.

She wanted this. She needed it. Even if it was only for one night. Only an illusion of real intimacy. She didn't want to be alone tonight. She wanted to be held, kissed, made love to. And she wanted to give comfort in return. Cable needed what she had to offer just as much as she needed what he had to offer.

Cable's heart melted when he saw the nervousness in Kiziah's face. He pulled her into his arms and pressed his mouth to hers in a coaxing first kiss.

Christ. It felt so good. So different than what he'd been used to for the last couple of years.

Tender. Welcoming. Two people who could please each other without first having to struggle to see who was going to be the dominant partner.

He traced the seam of her mouth with his tongue and she immediately opened for him, her body going soft against his. Her arms going around his neck as her tongue responded to his, letting him lead, letting him take charge of the kiss, the night.

He groaned, trapping her against the door of the trailer and deepening his assault on her mouth, twining his tongue with hers, his hands smoothing over her back and sides as his erection throbbed against her front.

They were both flushed, aroused when he lifted his mouth from hers. Cable wanted to get inside, to peel her clothing away and explore her body, to get lost in her wet heat, but he didn't want to let go of her long enough to do it.

He lowered his head and recaptured her lips, his hands tugging her shirt out of her jeans this time so that he could feel her smooth skin against his palms as they traveled up her sides, pushing underneath the camisole she wore, stroking her nipples with his thumbs so that she whimpered and he swallowed the sound, taking it deep inside himself, reveling in her need.

His cock pulsed and he ground his pelvis into her, covered her breasts with his hands so that her nipples stabbed his palms in silent demand. Christ, she was perfect.

He forced his mouth away from hers, trailing kisses along her cheek, her neck, fantasizing about what it would be like to feel her lips on his skin, to feel her teeth and know it was safe. "Let's go inside," he whispered when he reached her ear. But instead of releasing her, he explored the sensitive canal with his tongue until she was shivering against him, her hands trying to get underneath his jacket and shirt so she could touch him.

With a groan he stepped back, giving her room to unlock the Airstream and then following her inside. Taking a moment to notice that the travel trailer was warm and welcoming, done in blues and beiges. Soft and muted. Peaceful, with dreamcatchers hanging in front of the windows.

"This is nice," Cable said, pulling Kiziah into his arms again and nuzzling the side of her face. "But this is nicer."

Kiziah wrapped her arms around his waist, enjoying the hard strength, the heat. This time she succeeded in finding skin, her hands exploring the muscles of his back as he once again pressed his mouth to hers and coaxed her lips open so that his tongue could slide against hers, could move in and out, making her labia swell and ache, making her body feel restless and needy.

When the kiss ended he shrugged out of his jacket as her fingers made quick work of unbuttoning his shirt. "Definitely more tempting than dark chocolate," she said, pushing the material off his shoulders, her breath catching at the sheer beauty of him. He was the closest thing to a fantasy lover she would ever get.

Cable laughed, a husky sound that forced her eyes off his chest and abdomen and up to his face. "Fair is fair," he teased, getting rid of her jacket and the flannel shirt she was wearing, leaving the ultrafeminine camisole so that he could torment them both by teasing over the rigid points of her nipples, sucking and biting through the thin material before kissing along her shoulder and neck.

Her hands went to his sides, his hips, the front of his pants and he growled against her neck but didn't stop her when she unbuttoned the top button and then carefully lowered the zipper, heat rushing into her when his cock sprung free, brushing against her hand as though demanding attention.

She wrapped her fingers around his penis and it jerked in response, making him groan and lift his face. Cable's hand covered hers, tightening, pumping up and down, both of them watching as the head of his cock beaded and grew more flushed. "I won't last if we keep this up," he said, "and I want to. I want to take my time with you."

With a groan he pulled their hands away from his erection, this time finishing what he'd begun and stripping her out of her camisole before kneeling to remove the rest of her clothing.

Christ, she was exquisite. He hadn't been with a woman in so long, but even then, he couldn't remember a time when he felt this enthralled by one. Kiziah was flushed and wet between her legs, her cunt lips bare and her mound waxed except for a small strip of honey-dark curls. He leaned in and nuzzled her, licking along her slit and over her tiny, erect clit, consumed with the need to thoroughly explore her feminine flesh.

Kiziah jerked in reaction to his touch, hunching over and burying her fingers in his dark hair, not sure she'd be able to remain standing if he continued his assault. Her legs very nearly giving out when his tongue dipped into her channel, stroking in and out before he returned to her clit and began sucking.

Cable lifted his face and her stomach fluttered at the raw desire she saw there. Her heart swelled with a wild mix of emotion. No man had ever looked at her like that. No man had ever taken this kind of time with her before.

"Christ, you're beautiful," he said, sliding his hands down from her hips and using his thumbs to open her wider.

She shivered under his regard, her labia growing more swollen as arousal seeped from her opening, coating her lower lips as though trying to tempt him into a kiss.

Cable groaned, leaning forward once again, licking her, sucking her, claiming every inch of her cunt with his tongue as she clung to him, whimpering, panting, straining toward a release that came all too soon and yet not soon enough.

This time when he pulled away one of his hands dropped to his cock, encircling it, squeezing it as though he was on the verge of losing control. His face was taut, strained, flushed.

"Let's get on the bed," Kiziah whispered, trailing her fingers over his cheeks, his neck, his torso as he rose to his feet.

"Let's," Cable said, covering her mouth with his, kissing her, sharing the taste of her own arousal with her before stripping out of his remaining clothes and taking her hand, leading her to the large bed at one end of the travel trailer.

"We'll have to improvise later," Cable joked, dropping six brightly colored foil packages next to the pillow as he settled on top of Kiziah, kissing her before adding, "It's been a while since I needed them and that's all I could scrounge up in the car."

Kiziah laughed, twining her arms around his neck and rising up to press her lips to his. "You think we'll need more than six?"

"Oh yeah."

Cable closed his eyes and rested more of his weight on her, just savoring the feel of her underneath him as their tongues glided against each other, the softness, the curves, the smooth place between her thighs. A place nature had designed for a man's pleasure, a man's cock.

It felt so good. So right.

He'd forgotten—or maybe it had never been this way with a woman before. He didn't know which. He didn't want to think about it.

He just wanted to feel. To lose himself in her. To forget everything else and be in the moment. With her.

"I won't last long the first time," he warned. Opening his eyes and looking into Kiziah's, his heart expanding and beating wildly when her face warmed with color, when she said, "It's okay, you've already…it's already been good for me."

"It'll get even better," he said, nuzzling her nose with his, kissing her, building the passion again until she was whimpering, writhing, her hands destroying his control, her arousal-slick folds coating his penis until it was equally wet, engorged to the point of pain.

With a groan Cable levered himself away from her long enough to slip on a condom, shaking his head when she offered to do it for him. He was too far gone. Just the sight of her hands on his cock would be enough to cause him to erupt, spewing his seed on her mound, on her stomach.

Christ.

His cock jerked in warning at the images alone. Screamed in protest at the latex barrier. He wanted to feel her wet heat. To slam in and out of her without anything between masculine and feminine flesh. He wanted to know Kiziah as thoroughly and as intimately as a man could know a woman.

She welcomed him with open arms and legs when he settled over her again, wrapping them around his body while her own hand guided him to her entrance. He groaned as he slipped inside her, shook with the need to rut on her wildly. "Kizzy," he whispered and she bit him for using the nickname, unleashing a rush of hot emotion, of savage need—the bite a reminder of what had happened in the shower with Fane.

Cable couldn't fight the lust burning through him. Couldn't stop it from overwhelming his desire to go slow and savor every second.

He thrust in and out of Kiziah. Swallowing her cries even as his tongue mimicked what his cock was doing. Both of them straining, panting, pressing against each other as though they were trying to become one, the tight fist of her sheath around his cock as she climaxed triggering his own eruption, making Cable cry out as he came in a long, shuddering eruption of seed and pleasure.

* * * * *

"You're close to turning, my friend," Domino Santori said as Fane slid into the sleek black sports car and closed the passenger door behind him.

"Close, but not yet there."

"Close enough that I can feel The Heat radiating off your skin. Close enough that The Hunger rides you so fiercely that you smell of it—among other things. You're prepared? You've made arrangements for someone to guard you during The Transformation, to give you first blood so that you won't be forced to hunt immediately?" Domino cocked his head. "You've arranged for Cable to continue making himself scarce?"

Fane stiffened. "Don't worry about it."

"How can I not? If precautions aren't taken, I might be forced to hunt you." Obsidian eyes gleamed in the reflected light of the moon. "Even as a fully turned vampire, you would be no match for me. What fun would that be?"

Fane hissed, his eyes glowing red, his fangs flashing, but Domino only laughed and said, "It's a good thing you called me. I've already seen a brother through what you'll soon be facing. When the need arises, I'll stand with you." He laughed again. "Or on you, if that's what's required of me."

For a long moment Fane's body remained tense, anger pulsing through him along with the desire to attack, to savage—to gorge himself until only one heart remained beating in the confines of the small car.

The thought brought him up short. Sent a shiver of real fear down his spine.

Domino was a fellow dhampir. A man who had been friends with Fane's brother. Who had been like an older brother to Fane on more than one occasion.

"Have you learned anything more about the bomb-maker's whereabouts?" Fane asked, forcing his attention away from the rush of Domino's blood, channeling the primitive emotions that rode close to the surface as The Transformation drew near toward the Believer who'd murdered his family.

"Nothing is certain, but I think one of the others will soon lead us to The Apostle — or will be persuaded to tell us where he is."

"You think The Apostle is coming here?"

Domino shifted the car into reverse and shot down the long driveway. "I don't know. But perhaps we'll get lucky and find someone to ask tonight."

"What about the Believer you've been following for the last couple of months?"

"Byrd? He's still useful, at least for a few more days." Domino easily shifted gears, moving through the lower ones until they were racing along the deserted highway. "Don't worry, when the time is right, I'll gather everything he knows. In the meantime, I found another one of our enemies prowling around the carnival tonight, long after Sarael had been returned to Matteo. He knew next to nothing. He was like the others I've encountered so far. A deviant who enjoyed inflicting pain, hiding his sickness behind a cause he didn't fully believe in. Until tonight I thought the lack of intelligence and belief was an indication of how low our enemies have had to go in order to fill their ranks. But now I'm beginning to wonder if those we are finding and destroying are nothing more than cannon fodder. A distraction to keep us occupied or to gain information about how many of us are in the area and how effective we are."

"A trap?"

Domino shrugged. "Maybe. Maybe not."

"And the woman we thought they were hunting? Sarael?"

"The Believer I encountered knew nothing about her. His interest was in the fortune-teller, though the prospect of raping and killing her was not nearly as appealing to him as doing the same to a beautiful blonde who emerged from Helki's tent."

"You eliminated him?"

"Of course."

Fane shifted in his seat, thinking about what Domino said. It meshed with the vague feelings of uneasiness that occasionally fought their way to the surface of his consciousness.

He'd had little time to think about them until now. Even before Cable discovered the woman who was most likely Matteo Cabrelli's missing mate and they'd come to guard her until Matteo could arrive from Italy, Fane had been fighting the beginnings of The Transformation.

A chill moved through him at the possibility that an elaborate trap was being set by their enemies. Distraction could be deadly for a dhampir.

Unlike what he would soon become — fully vampire — he was still human enough to die if he became careless. True, he wouldn't be killed easily. He had strengths, powers that made him a difficult target, an affinity for knives that allowed him to use and control them with his mind alone — but he was still trapped in a human body. He was without the vampire's most effective self-defense mechanism, the ability to change into mist and dissipate into the air. Once The Transformation had taken place that would change and he would be very nearly impossible to kill. But the price he would have to pay in order to gain the unseen form of his alien heritage would be the loss of his ability to remain in the sun in a human shape.

It was a price he wanted to delay paying until the Believer who called himself The Apostle had been found. Until he had the satisfaction of draining the bomb-maker's life one swallow at a time, reducing him to an empty husk, a corpse to be eradicated in a great ball of fire, consumed by one of his own bombs.

It was Fane's obsession. The sweet thought of revenge the only thing he'd fantasized about in the last year — other than having Cable at his side during the centuries that lay ahead.

Cable. Fane's cock hardened thinking about him. Renewed frustration and worry moved through him. Domino had already said that he'd seen Cable for a brief moment at the carnival. But by the time Fane arrived, there was no trace of Cable and he wasn't answering his cell phone.

What if he'd fallen into the hands of their enemies? He was fully human. Easily killed. Fane growled. Perhaps he should abandon this hunt and look for Cable instead.

"Trouble in paradise?" Domino asked, his amusement like sandpaper over Fane's skin. The knowledge that Domino was aware of his arousal and could guess the direction of his thoughts grating on Fane's nerves.

"Don't concern yourself with my affairs."

"Affairs? That surprises me. You're so often in each others' company, cheating would seem impossible."

Fane ground his teeth together. "You know what I meant."

"You want me to 'not worry about it' just as I'm not to worry about how close you are to turning? I would hardly be honoring your brother's memory if I left you to make mistakes you'd live to regret. So I will give you this bit of advice. Don't be so quick to throw away your happiness. Find a woman you like." Obsidian eyes gleamed with amusement. "Or allow Cable to find one. Keep them both."

"After the first exchange of blood, after the first fuck, I'll be sexually bonded to my bride. You know that."

"So take her at the same time that Cable's cock is buried inside of her." Domino's laugh held a wealth of amusement. "Unless the thought of a cunt repulses Cable. Then again, if the tight fist of a woman's channel is not to his liking, perhaps he could close his eyes and thrust into her back entrance and pretend it's you."

A low growl sounded deep in Fane's chest. A warning that he'd only take so much of Domino's humor. "Cable has no problem with women. If anything he has more experience with them than I do."

"There you go then. Problem solved. You can have Cable as well as a kadine if you handle it correctly. I've been told that one of my early ancestors found a way to do it. Once you and Cable have reconciled, have him check the records that the padralls are so obsessed with keeping. It's possible that my ancestor shared the details of his mating with one inclined to preserve it for future reference."

Domino's teeth flashed white in the darkness. "And then all you'll need is a woman. Perhaps the fortune-teller can assist you in finding a third for your bed. Despite the difficulties Matteo experienced in claiming Sarael, Helki's reading did ease the way for Sarael. But if you insist on following tradition when it comes to a kadine, then choose among the women who provide the future brides rather than asking that one be created and raised specifically for you."

Fane shifted in his seat. The thought of going to the padralls and arranging for introductions, of "shopping" for a potential bride—of no doubt having to appear as though he and Cable were no longer together—settled heavily in his gut, chasing the blood from his cock and leaving it unenthused.

He closed his eyes and tried to remember the women he'd been with before Cable. Fleeting images came to mind. All of them blonde, all of them easy prey. Forgettable as soon as he'd pulled from their bodies.

Unlike Cable, who enjoyed women and men equally, Fane had more often been drawn to those of his own sex. Perhaps that was why he was finding it so hard to reconcile what he felt he owed to his father, the taking of a kadine and the birth of sons, with what his mother would say were she still alive. *Be happy, Fane.*

Be happy. Fane hit the redial button on his cell and his call once again went directly to Cable's voice mail. A small hiss escaped. A surge of anger moved through him. A trickle of fear following in its wake. *Where the fuck was Cable?*

Chapter Four

Kiziah smoothed her hand over Cable's chest, exploring his small hard nipples with the tips of her fingers as she rested on an elbow and looked down at his face. God, he was gorgeous. But even more importantly, he was nice. Funny. Ultramasculine and yet gentle at the same time. Sweet, though he would probably object if he heard her call him that.

She laughed softly, watching as his cock filled again as a result of her attention. He hadn't been joking, they just might have to improvise by morning. Half of his supply of condoms was already depleted and he didn't show any sign of slowing down.

Or hurrying.

It felt like they had forever.

Kiziah's heart lurched in her chest but she refused to think beyond the here and now, beyond enjoying and savoring this time with him. There was no point in setting herself up to feel let down when he left.

"My turn now," she murmured, changing position so that she was straddling him, teasing his mouth with kisses, sighing with pleasure as his hands immediately went to her breasts, cupping them, rubbing his thumbs over pouty nipples.

She closed her eyes, soaking in his touch, savoring the kiss. Memorizing them so that she could relive the pleasure over and over again in her fantasies.

If she could have conjured up a man, Cable would be him. He was a dream lover, and yet so much more. A man she could grow to love if she had a chance. A man she could easily envision at her side.

Kiziah forced the thoughts from her mind. Concentrating instead on the stroking and twining of her tongue against his. On the slow buildup of pleasure, the fullness as blood rushed to her labia, making it swell so that her cunt lips parted in preparation for his cock.

She wanted to give him the same pleasure he'd given her earlier and so she reluctantly left his lips, trailing down his neck, licking over his masculine flesh and thrilling at the way his body tightened and strained underneath her wet kisses and sucking bites.

"You're killing me, Zia," he groaned when she took his nipple between her teeth, arching so that his engorged penis rubbed against her slick folds. "You're killing me."

But she knew it was a small death he gladly sought. And she wanted nothing more than to give it to him.

She tightened her grip on his nipple and reveled in the way he cried out, spearing his fingers through her hair and holding her to his chest as his breath quickened and his cock leaked. When she bit down harder, he groaned, panting now, urging her to move lower, to taste more of his flesh, to take his straining penis into her mouth.

She allowed him to guide her. To hold his own cock as she took everything above his hand into her mouth. Tormenting him with her tongue, with the threat of her teeth, with short sucks, and the feel of her lips against his engorged head as she teased him, sliding up and down on him.

Cable was in heaven and hell. Ecstasy with the threat of torture hanging over him. Each time her lips settled on the tip of his penis he jerked for fear that she would lift her face and leave him.

"Zia," he groaned, unable to articulate more than a shortened version of her name as his buttocks clenched and his balls pulled tight. Aching. In desperate need. And then there was no room for any thought. For any words as her hand covered his, feminine strength added to masculine power, both of them holding his cock as she drove him to a release that had him bucking, grunting, shuddering.

* * * * *

Fane shifted position in the confines of Domino's sports car as they waited for the Believers they were hunting to emerge from the hotel room. He felt restless, irritable, as though his skin could no longer contain his body. "Why delay any longer? Let's take care of them now and be done with it."

"And risk having the police called? We can't be sure how many are in the room or how quickly they can be brought under our control."

Fane snorted, but before he could comment, the door they'd been watching opened and a Believer emerged, followed by two others. All of them dressed in black, their expressions serious, men embarking on a task.

"A little different than those we've been encountering," Domino commented.

"We can take them."

"Of course."

The men climbed into a dark sedan and drove away from the hotel with Domino following at a distance. They headed into a wealthy section of town where large homes built in an earlier century waited at the end of long, tree-lined driveways.

"Not their usual prey," Fane said, anticipation building. "Perhaps they're meeting someone."

Domino's teeth flashed in the dark interior of the car. "We can only hope."

The sedan continued to travel for several blocks before easing to a stop underneath a huge oak tree. Domino pulled the sports car over as well, its headlights off for most of the time they'd been following the Believers.

Fane looked around, trying to guess where their enemy was heading. Most of the houses were darkened, the occupants asleep, their cars tucked away in garages. But one house glowed with muted light, its driveway lined with cars.

"It might be wise to call some of the others," Fane said, referring to the dhampirs and vampires who'd come to the area to hunt the Believers.

"Perhaps," Domino said, but neither or them reached for their cell phones immediately. Instead they watched as the three men moved around and lifted the sedan's trunk, pulling out an assortment of guns. Domino laughed. "And perhaps not. It looks like our prey has gathered for a kill of their own. Do you have a preference?"

"If they make it as far as the house, I'll take the right side."

"Fair enough."

They slipped from the sports car, blending with the darkness, their eyesight well used to seeing in the dead of night. As they'd guessed, the Believers headed for the house whose occupants were entertaining guests, bypassing the front door in favor of trying to enter the residence where the trees and darkness could hide their activities.

The Hunger rose in Fane as he stalked his prey, a burning that had his stomach spasming and his fangs fully extended well before he'd gotten close enough to his victim to hear his heartbeat. Thoughts of blood filled Fane's mind, thoughts of sinking his fangs into human flesh and feeding as a life was ended. The intensity of his desire to kill, a need that had nothing to do with his prey being one of their enemies, sounded a warning in Fane's mind, but he didn't listen, didn't stop.

He drew close to the first Believer as he was crouched next to a window looking inside where the residents were gathered around a table, chanting ancient words that had the hair on Fane's neck rising in alarm. Witches. Warlocks. A coven gathered to summon power or information from the dead who lingered with unfinished business.

Fane had intended to take his enemy to the ground and feed, but the presence of the coven made him hesitate and draw a knife instead. The release of his enemy's life force might well impact whatever was going on inside the residence, but it couldn't be helped.

With a hiss Fane closed the distance, not bothering with the pheromones which could enthrall, determined instead to enjoy some measure of revenge for the death of his family, even if The Hunger wouldn't be sated.

In Fane's hand the knife parted skin and muscle as easily as if it was cutting butter left out on the dining room table. Blood gushed from the opened throat, slick and shiny in the moon's light, coating the black leather of the Believer's jacket as his heart emptied him of life with each panicked beat.

It was over too quickly as far as Fane was concerned. A waste of blood and a far gentler death than his enemy deserved.

Fane dropped the body to the ground, his nostrils flaring at the scent of so much blood, his body shuddering painfully, angrily as The Hunger snarled and raged, scraping his insides like a caged beast. He took a step forward and stumbled, The Hunger not yet ready to loosen its grip on him. To stop its knife-sharp rebuke, the rake of talons through his internal organs and across his skin. Fane hunched for long moments, willing the pain away, but if anything it grew more intense, nearly dropping him to his knees.

Domino emerged from the darkness at the end of the house. His expression mocking for one instant, but as soon as he saw Fane, his amusement disappeared. "The Transformation is upon you," he said, reaching Fane's side and taking his arm. "Those we saved tonight will have to clean up after us if I can't return in time to do it." Obsidian eyes gleamed as humor reappeared. "Can you walk or do you wish to live with the memory of being carried back to the car?"

Fane hissed, his fangs extended, a flash of threat as he forced himself to stand, though he didn't shake off Domino's hand on his arm. "You took care of the other two?"

"Yes, and even managed to extract information from the second before wondering if you'd encountered trouble or were just playing with your food."

"What did you learn?"

"I believe I have found the reason so many Believers are in the area. Several of the witches inside are just passing through, on their way to a psychic fair in another city. The men we disposed of followed them here and learned of tonight's activities, then received orders to kill them here."

Fane hissed. Anger and hatred leaving little room for an awareness of the pain spiraling through his body. "The Apostle. He'll strike at the psychic fair."

"Most likely."

They reached the car and Fane jerked to a stop, gasping and bending over, pain streaking across his abdomen, so intense he felt as though he was being disemboweled. It came in jagged strikes, each one expanding and lengthening to cover more area, working upward to concentrate on his heart and lungs, so that his body was coated with sweat by the time he could get into the passenger seat.

He'd known what to expect since childhood, but there was no way to prepare for The Transformation, for the intensity of the pain that screamed through him as his body altered—the alien cells multiplying rapidly, mimicking the information contained in the part of him that was human then savagely attacking and eradicating all traces of his humanness. The Hunger of a full-blood vampire would follow, a bloodlust that would make him extremely dangerous until he'd fed for the first time after The Transformation. And even afterward, he'd need the herbs to manage it until he took a mate—the exchange of blood coupled with sex triggering a survival mechanism that would temper his needs.

Fane was barely aware of the drive. Barely aware of the trip down to Domino's basement. But when Domino disappeared, only to return carrying silver bindings studded with bloodstone, every cell in Fane's body screamed for him to escape, to fight like a man possessed, to kill a fellow dhampir if that's what was necessary in order to avoid being bound.

He'd allowed Cable to tether him to the bed more often lately, but the soft strips of leather had been symbolic, a reminder to help Fane maintain control over The Heat that was a harbinger of The Transformation. To keep him from biting Cable and exchanging blood with him.

The bindings in Domino's hand were a true prison. They would paralyze Fane's limbs once they encircled his wrists and ankles. They'd make him completely helpless until the conversion was complete and he gained a second form.

Fane hissed, filled with a swirling wildness. The need for blood and freedom temporarily displacing the agony of his cells changing. Without thought he reached for his knives, anger joining the mix when he found that Domino had removed them.

For long moments they faced off. Domino blocking the only exit. Fane battling against the riot of ruthless, feral impulses that had served his ancient ancestors well in the primitive surroundings they'd found themselves in, but would create havoc in the modern world.

Bit by bit Fane gained control of himself, using remembered conversations with his father and brother to do so. He would not fail them by turning into a rogue, by forcing Domino to hunt him. "Do it," he growled, holding his arms out in front of him.

Domino glided over, silently clamping a band around one wrist and then the other before taking one of Fane's limp arms and guiding him to a pile of blankets on the floor. Their presence making Fane's eyes narrow with suspicion, making him glance around at the lack of windows, the door which sealed firmly, allowing no escape of air. A vampire needed only a small gap in order to enter and exit in their dissipative state. "You're about to change."

"I'm close. But not as close as you apparently." Domino placed the bands on Fane's ankles and helped him to lie down before settling a few feet away. "I'll stay with you until it's over and be here to give you first blood." A flicker of amusement followed the comment. "And to make sure you take your herbs like a good boy."

Fane's response was lost in a gasp as his body went rigid with agony, the pain once again making itself known.

* * * * *

Cable woke to light streaming through the dreamcatchers that hung in front of each window. His first thoughts were about the night, about the woman who lay snuggled against him, her back to his front, her buttocks pressed against a cock that was already standing at attention and ready to serve.

He smiled and rubbed his cheek against her hair, tightening his arms around her for an instant before relaxing his grip. It felt good to be with her. It felt right. Peaceful. Normal. As though none of the rest of his life existed, except in a nightmare. As though there were no vampires, no dhampirs, no padralls or kadines.

He closed his eyes and just savored the feel of her, soaked in her warmth, her softness, how good it felt to be wrapped around her. How good it felt to lie with a woman — with her.

He'd had girlfriends in the past. And he'd been faithful to them. But he wasn't going to lie to himself about his needs. He wasn't going to promise something he couldn't give—long-term monogamy—one man, one woman. He couldn't have promised a male lover either, though a different set of rules applied with Fane.

Cable rubbed his cheek against Kiziah's hair again. Christ, it hurt to think about Fane.

He didn't think he could make the arrangements for the creation of a kadine for Fane. He sure as hell couldn't take part in overseeing how she was raised, what she was taught, what her life experiences were so that her interests and personality would meld with her future mate's.

The thought of it sickened him on so many levels. Left him feeling heart-sore—though he knew Fane hurt too.

He should have fought the attraction early on. God knows, he'd been warned off Fane by most of the padralls in his order. He'd been sent on errands that would separate the two of them. He'd even been sent to the order's version of a chaplain-shrink, not just in the hopes of "curing" him of Fane but of "curing" him of men in general. The second a request by his father no doubt, who still had not reconciled himself to the truth that his youngest son was not solidly heterosexual.

Cable sighed. Maybe he should have tried harder to look beyond the pleasure of the present and concentrated instead on the pain of the future.

Yeah, so what was new about that thought?

The trouble was, until Fane's parents and brother had been killed, he hadn't seen a future that didn't include Fane. They were good together, they enjoyed each other's company. They balanced each other out. They were friends—and lovers. They had fun and yet despite the intensity of their physical attraction, it wasn't all about sex.

Maybe he would have eventually gotten the urge to be with a woman again, maybe Fane would have too, but dhampirs and vampires were free of human diseases, so there was no risk of getting a disease from or giving one to Fane.

Maybe they would have finally broached the subject neither one of them had dared think too deeply about. A centuries-long bond formed by three exchanges of blood. A bond that would alter the cells of his body so that he would gain fangs and need to feed, not on strangers, but on Fane.

The padralls had records that spanned centuries so Cable knew that taking a male companion instead of a kadine had been done many times before—though he'd been extremely careful not to let any of the others know what he was researching. If they suspected he might be willing to break a long-held taboo and bind his life so thoroughly to Fane's, he'd find himself permanently assigned to some task that allowed little contact with either dhampirs or vampires.

Kiziah sighed and shifted, turning in his arms and nuzzling his chest in her sleep. The smooth flesh of her cunt and the small strip of downy softness rubbing against his cock in the process, making it jerk against her.

His body tightened. A wave of heat moved from the place on his shoulder where Fane had bitten, surging along his spine and through his penis so that arousal leaked from the head and onto her abdomen. He gritted his teeth against the impulse to urge her legs apart and slip inside her. To feel her sheath clamp down on him, to feel the wet heat of her with nothing separating them.

He wanted to bury himself in her. To stay lodged inside her and forget everything else going on in his life. And yet it was so much more than pure escapism. Being with Kiziah felt as right as being with Fane.

The moments in Madame Helki's tent replayed themselves. The Wheel of Fortune crossed by The Lovers.

You have reached a turning point, a place with many possible outcomes and a chance for great happiness. You must recognize and reconcile your own needs in order to fully embrace the opportunity that will soon present itself to you.

Cable laughed despite the confusion of his emotions. Despite the conflicting desires. The painful hopelessness of one relationship and the unexpected, unlooked for possibility of another—because now that he'd been with Kiziah, he intended to stick around and spend more time with her.

Hell, when he called in to report after he visited Matteo Cabrelli and verified that Sarael had been fully claimed and made a kadine, all he would have to do is mention that he'd met a woman and his father would insist he take a vacation, all in the hopes that Cable would end up married with a pregnant bride. That's the way his father thought. Fuck, that's the way most of the padralls thought. They might be living in the twenty-first century, but their culture often seemed as though it had barely crawled out of the middle ages.

Cable smoothed his hand over Kiziah's buttocks, his awareness shifting to the feel of her breasts against his chest. His thoughts looping back to an earlier thread but weaving a different design.

Even for Fane, he didn't think he could give women up. And that was the catch. A vampire and his kadine—or male companion—were sexually bonded so that neither could willingly take another lover. It was a survival mechanism, not only for the individual but for the race.

There were no exceptions to the rule. At least none that Cable had been able to find. He grimaced—not that he'd had a chance to go through every ledger recording the history and lineage of every dhampir or vampire family in the order's possession, much less visit other orders and review their books. Nothing was computerized.

Kiziah mumbled in her sleep, draping her leg over Cable's and pressing closer, adjusting her position just enough so that her erect clit pressed against his shaft like a tiny penis and sent icy-hot pleasure jolting up his spine. This time when his cock pulsed, she whimpered and arousal seeped from her opening, wetting more of his penis than the moisture-beaded head.

He groaned, rolling them over so that his cock was trapped between them, ready to hump against her mound and belly if necessary.

Chapter Five

Kiziah woke with a smile and wound her arms around Cable's neck, making his heart dance just from looking at her. Christ, she was beautiful, inside and out, soft and gentle, a balm for a soul that felt as though it was being shredded.

"About time," he teased.

She laughed, rocking against his cock. "You've been *up* for awhile?"

"Oh yeah, a *long* time."

"Well, we're both awake now."

Cable leaned down and took her bottom lip between his teeth, giving it a gentle nip. "There's a problem."

"Let me guess. A *big* one."

"Huge actually. Enormous."

Kiziah snickered. "Yeah. I can tell."

He laughed despite the ache in his cock and balls. "Worse than you're imagining. We don't have any protection left."

Her eyes widened. "Oh."

Cable rubbed his nose against hers. "Yeah. Oh." He kissed her, a slow lingering touch of lips and tongue. When he lifted his mouth from hers, he said, "I'm clean, if you want to…"

"I'm not on the pill." Color flooded her face. "I don't do this very often. I mean, I don't… There haven't been many."

Tenderness filled Cable. Surprise. *Fuck.* What was wrong with the men she knew? How could they be around her and not get her into bed and into their lives and keep her there?

Cable pressed his mouth to hers again, savoring the softness of her body underneath his, the way she responded to him, letting him lead, trusting him, making him feel as though he was home. He trailed kisses over her cheek, then explored her ear, tormenting her, knowing how sensitive she was there, how much she liked it, her whimpers only inciting him to drive them both higher.

Kiziah writhed against him. Wrapped her legs around his waist and clung to him. She was almost sorry she'd told him she wasn't on the pill. Almost.

She ached. Not just with physical need. But with the need for intimacy. For closeness.

But she was the end result of a night of reckless passion—at least on her father's part—and she wouldn't do that to a child of hers. She wouldn't do that to Cable. She already knew he wasn't the type of man to walk away from responsibility.

Emotion filled her as he raised his head and she saw the tautness of his features, the desire. No man had ever responded to her like he did, had ever made her feel like he did.

Their eyes met and he moved his hips, sliding his cock against her clit, her belly, sending heated ecstasy straight to her breasts so that her nipples tightened into painful buds. He groaned, ducking his head, suckling, biting, laving the pebbled tips until Kiziah was straining against him, hot, desperate for more intimate contact than the rub of flesh against flesh.

When his mouth returned to hers, she closed her eyes for an instant, gathering her courage before whispering against his lips, "We could do it...you could go in the back way."

Cable's cock jerked against her abdomen. "Have you ever done it that way?" His body tensed with anticipation.

"No, but... You've been with...you've had..." Once again her cheeks heated. "I trust you to know what to do."

Christ, she undid him. Claimed parts of him that had been waiting just for her. There was no way he could refuse her offer. "It'll be easier with lubricant. I've got some in the car."

"There's some in the nightstand."

The blush deepened and Cable was completely lost in her. She was the perfect mix of innocence and knowledge. A woman who wasn't afraid to be passionate but who wasn't cynical and brazen like the women he and Fane usually encountered when they were out at clubs.

He levered himself off her and retrieved the lubricant, then settled next to her, kissing his way down her body, rebuilding the passion as his fingers prepared her, their bodies glistening with a sheen of sweat, both of them close to coming by the time his tongue and mouth found her straining clit. She arched upward with a cry as his sucks and licks drove her to orgasm, sending arousal washing over his fingers and providing even more lubrication for his entry.

In a heartbeat he rose above her, guiding the tip of his penis to her back entrance. His lips covering hers as he slowly worked himself into her virgin opening.

He wanted to shout from the overwhelming pleasure of it. He wanted to cry at the sheer intimacy of it. He wanted to plunge in and out wildly. And he wanted to stay completely still, savoring and memorizing every moment as her unused muscles fisted and unfisted on his cock, as her whimpers and shivers corralled his heart.

He began thrusting, shallow digs at first, his breathing hard from the effort to go slow. To control himself and give her time to adjust. But when she began moving against him, accepting his rhythm, arching into him, all he could think about was the extreme sensations rushing through his cock and up his spine. Christ. He couldn't hold back any longer.

Cable covered her mouth with his, twining his tongue with hers as his hand slid between their straining bodies, his fingers going to her clit, stroking over the naked head and underside until they both cried out, shuddering in release.

They lay together peacefully for a few minutes before taking showers and returning to bed, snuggling and dozing. Waking up in each other's arms. Cable's first thoughts about Kiziah. His second about Fane.

He couldn't move forward with his life, take time off to be with Kiziah until he talked to Fane. If he was honest with himself, he shouldn't have let things get this far with her. But he couldn't feel sorry for it. Fuck no. He couldn't feel sorry for it. If anything, he felt like it was inevitable. Destined.

His fingers explored her spine. He breathed her in. Soaked her in. Madame Helki's words returning in that moment. Flashing into his thoughts again along with the image of The Lovers.

You must recognize and reconcile your own needs in order to fully embrace the opportunity that will soon present itself to you.

This time a deeper understanding came with the words. A truth he couldn't ignore.

He wouldn't be truly happy if he had to give up women. Not just because of the sex, but because of the tenderness that came with the closeness.

Christ, Fane would go through his skin if he tried to cuddle him like this. Hell, *he'd* go through his skin if Fane tried to do it to him.

They had raunchy, rough sex as well as easy, I-love-you sex. They traded off who was the more dominant partner and they liked to be close to one another afterward, often ending up in a tangle of arms and legs when they woke up together, but they didn't do snuggling.

For an instant he imagined what it would be like to have Kiziah in bed with them. To share her with Fane, to experience this same closeness afterward. He and Fane cuddled against her. The three of them content, happy. Complete.

His heart squeezed painfully, filled with longing until he had to push the images aside. Fuck. He needed to finish things with Fane but he couldn't face doing it just yet.

Cable pressed a kiss to Kiziah's forehead just as his stomach gave a low rumble, a reminder that he couldn't live on sex alone. He chuckled. "How about we go out to dinner, my treat." He brushed his hand over her buttocks. "And then we can swing by the drugstore and wipe out their supply of condoms."

Kiziah smiled against his chest. "Maybe we should hit more than just one drug store."

He grinned, rolling to his back and pulling her on top of him. "You think I'm that good?"

"Definitely." She traced his eyebrows, his nose, his lips. Then trailed her fingers down his neck and across his chest, stopping at his nipple.

His cock jerked in reaction and he covered her hand with his. "Food first. Condoms second. Another errand third. Then we can come back and resume from this position."

"It's a deal," Kiziah said, making him groan as she slid off him and got to her feet.

"Christ, you're gorgeous, Kizzy," Cable said, sitting up and watching as she bent over and rifled through a dresser drawer.

She paused and looked back at him, eyes dancing though she sent him a frown. "Don't call me that. Kizzy morphs into Dizzy and when you're blonde…"

He laughed and stood, unable to stop himself from going over and taking her in his arms, pulling her back to his front, the sight of them in the mirror sending a rush of blood to his cock and making him groan as fantasies of bending her over and taking her as they watched in the mirror flooded his mind. He forced himself to let her go, to put on his jeans so he could retrieve fresh clothing from the car.

Kiziah dressed, fighting against the hope that was starting to form in her chest. She'd expected to wake up and say goodbye, not have him laugh and tease, invite her to dinner and imply they'd be spending another night together.

She'd planned to head to Ashburg today. She'd been looking forward to the psychic fair, to being among friends, people she'd known her entire life, people who'd known her mother. But now…

The Wheel of Fortune surfaced in her thoughts and with it the feeling that she was where she needed to be. She smiled slightly. Too bad the third card hadn't been The Lovers. Cable felt so right. She could easily imagine him traveling with her. She could easily imagine settling in one place with him.

The Airstream door opened and Cable came back inside to finish dressing. "Ready?"

"Ready."

They took his car, settling on a small, home-style restaurant and lingering over dinner. Joking, teasing, touching frequently as though needing the reassurance of the contact.

"You said you had a third stop to make," Kiziah prompted as they slipped from their booth and left the restaurant. Deciding to walk to a drugstore several blocks away rather than get back into the car.

"I need to visit someone before they leave for Italy. It'll only take a few minutes." Cable glanced at the sky and then at his watch. "But we'd better hustle."

They paused at a street corner and Kiziah's gaze landed on a newspaper rack, shock coursing through her when she saw the face staring back at her from the front page and read the caption. *Police Seeking Information.*

"Fuck!" Cable said, his hand going to his pocket to retrieve some change.

He shoved the change into the coin slot and opened the front of the rack in order to retrieve a newspaper, the display copy the only one remaining.

They both read the short article about the body of an escaped convict being discovered near the carnival, the article ending with a request by police that anyone who'd seen the man or knew anything about his activities to come forward with the information. Kiziah shivered, wondering what the police would think if she told them that he'd been following her—until something supernatural killed him.

She shivered again and Cable put his arm around her, pulling her against him. "You saw him last night, playing darts."

Kiziah jerked in reaction. Her eyes going to his. "How do you know that?"

"I saw you come out of Madame Helki's tent."

Confusion filled Kiziah. Uncertainty. He couldn't have followed her to the coffee shop. Could he? He wasn't the one who had hypnotized her and used her as bait, then saved her. Was he?

Cable stroked his thumb over the frown lines between her eyebrows, smoothing them out, his face taking on an uncertain expression.

"You saw me leave Madame Helki's tent..." she prompted.

"Yeah. And I went in afterward. For a reading." His embarrassed laugh sent a burst of warmth though Kiziah's heart. "There were three cards on the table when I walked in. The last one was the Wheel of Fortune." He hesitated for a second. "I thought maybe they were for me. But Helki took the Wheel and crossed it with a card she had me draw. The Lovers. I wondered... Then when I walked by the coffee shop and saw you in it..." He shrugged and looked away, vulnerable, confused, torn. "My life's a little insane right now."

Kiziah pressed a kiss to his cheek and then nibbled over to his mouth, swallowing his groan of pleasure and glorying in the way he held her tightly against him as their mouths fused together and the kiss deepened.

"I don't want to talk to the police about seeing him last night," she said when they parted in order to breathe. Wondering what Cable would think if she told him what had happened while he was in the fortune-teller's tent.

"I'm sure they've got plenty of people volunteering information." Cable pressed a quick kiss to her mouth. *What had Domino been thinking to leave the body where it could be found?* Christ. One dhampir in his life was enough to worry about. He couldn't worry about Domino too. Cable folded the paper, abandoning it on the drugstore counter after he and Kiziah had spent a few lighthearted minutes in the contraceptive aisle before purchasing condoms and leaving.

It was full dark when they got to Matteo Cabrelli's, though the moon shone down on the old house with a sinister cast. "You want to go in or wait in the car?" Cable asked.

"In."

He leaned over and gave her a kiss. "This'll just take a few minutes."

The front door opened before either of them could knock. "*Don* Cabrelli and his wife are in the drawing room," the elderly man who stood in front of them said, frowning when he saw Kiziah but stepping aside to let them pass.

Kiziah's breath caught in her throat as soon as she crossed the threshold. Her lungs seeming to fill with ice, freezing with instant fear as the aura of the supernatural washed over her. Its intensity stronger than anything she'd ever experienced. She let out a strangled gasp and stumbled, only to have Cable steady her, his expression concerned. "You okay?"

"Yeah," she panted, wondering if a ghost haunted the house. It was spooky enough on the outside to lend credence to the theory.

Slowly the weight and cold disappeared though the awareness of the supernatural remained, tempered by the realization that it lacked menace despite the lethal edge she could sense in its depths. "I'm okay," she said, touched by the concern still evident on Cable's face.

Cable squeezed her hand, cursing himself, realizing too late that given what she'd told him about her mother and her childhood, Kiziah might possess some measure of psychic ability, might be picking up on just how deadly Matteo was, even if she didn't believe in vampires.

They moved into the drawing room where he introduced her to Matteo and Sarael. Despite what Cable had been telling himself, it was a relief not to be on the receiving end of Matteo's hostility. If anything, the Italian vampire was at his most charming, though his possessive gaze repeatedly returned to Sarael, traveling over her body with so much heat that she blushed.

Kiziah's presence was a complication until Matteo drew her into a conversation about the dreamcatchers she made, his interest appearing genuine as he asked her to do some sketches, accompanying her to a desk against the wall and standing with her, their backs turned toward Sarael and Cable.

"It's done?" Cable whispered and Sarael nodded, parting her lips slightly so that he could see the fangs she'd gained after Matteo had exchanged blood with her for a third time. For an instant Cable felt relieved. The task he'd been given would be considered finished as soon as he contacted his father and told him that he'd confirmed Sarael's transformation from human to kadine.

But following the relief came a wash of guilt and sadness along with thoughts of Fane. He couldn't go back to the Airstream with Kiziah and fuck the night away like he'd intended to without seeing Fane first.

Last night it had seemed so right to be with Kiziah, so easy to put aside thoughts of vampires and dhampirs in favor of The Lovers. But coming here reminded him of the world he was a part of. Its restrictions. Its harsh realities. The painful knowledge that in the future Fane would also have a kadine.

They left a few minutes later. Spending most of the drive back to the campground in silence.

When they pulled up in front of the travel trailer Kiziah closed her eyes against the pain that had started to ripple through her heart. Against the laughing moments they'd spent earlier, as they'd joked about condoms in the drug store. She knew without being told that they wouldn't be making use of them tonight.

Forcing her eyes open, she reached over and took Cable's hand as he switched off the ignition, neither of them making a move to open their doors. "You're thinking about him," she said, pleased that her voice sounded so calm.

"About Fane. Yeah." He turned toward her. "I need to go back to the house. I need to settle things with him."

She squeezed his hand. "It might turn out better than you think."

Cable gave an unhappy laugh before leaning in and pressing his mouth to hers briefly. "It won't. I want to see you again, Zia. How much longer are you going to be camped here?"

For a split second she thought about saying she'd wait until she heard from him, but she didn't let those words escape. She'd never expected more than a night together. Though for a few hours, after he'd told her about his visit with Madame Helki, about her own Wheel of Fortune being covered by the card he'd drawn, The Lovers, she'd allowed herself to hope, to dream, to wonder…

But he was right. He needed to resolve whatever was going on with his boyfriend. And she already cared enough about Cable to hope that things worked out in a way that would make him happy.

Yeah, she'd probably cry all the way to Ashburg, but she didn't regret the time she'd spent with him.

She needed to leave. She needed to put the fantasy aside in favor of the reality of her life. "I should already be in Ashburg. I've got a campsite and a booth at the fair already reserved, but location is on a first come, first serve basis. By the time I get there I'll be relegated to the worst possible spots in both places."

Pain rushed through Cable at the thought of her leaving. He felt as though he was being torn in two. "How far is Ashburg from here?"

"A couple of hours."

"I'll meet up with you there. Tomorrow sometime. After I've seen Fane. Okay?"

She bit her lip, wishing he hadn't said that. His words were fuel for a hope she knew she couldn't afford. He was rebounding, and despite the fantasy night they'd had together, Cable still cared about his partner. There'd been a wealth of love and heartbreak in his voice just saying "Fane".

She squeezed his hand again and reached for the door handle, swallowing against the thickness in her throat and chest, knowing she was going to break down and start crying if they dragged goodbye out much longer. "Maybe you can still work it out with him, Cable. Don't give up. If I don't see you in Ashburg... You better get going. So should I."

He wouldn't let her escape so easily. His hand tightened on hers. "Where can I find you?"

Kiziah gave him the name of the campground. "You won't have trouble finding the psychic fair. That's where I'll be most of the time."

"Psychic fair?"

Kiziah stiffened at his tone. Her heart sinking when she risked a glance and saw the tight expression on his face. She'd told him a little bit about her childhood as they'd been snuggled next to each other in the darkness. And he'd been interested in knowing about the dreamcatchers she made. He'd even admitted to visiting Madame Helki and yet now he sounded upset about the fair in Ashburg. "Yes, a psychic fair."

"A big one?"

Kiziah's eyebrows drew together. "Pretty big. Why?"

Christ! What could he tell her? *You remember the guy who followed you last night and was found dead this morning? Well, he was part of a secret organization that kills vampires as well as any humans who might have supernatural ability.*

Yeah. Right. Kiziah would think he was a nut case.

A knot of fear and dread formed in Cable's gut. He needed to let Fane and Domino know. This had to be the reason so many Believers were streaming into the area.

His stomach roiled just thinking about the man who'd been waiting near Madame Helki's tent. If Domino hadn't been there... Shit! He'd just assumed the Believer saw Kiziah and went for her because she was beautiful. But what if he knew she was heading to the psychic fair? What if she'd been his intended target all along? What if the Believers were attacking and killing fair attendees far enough away so there wouldn't be an obvious link between targets?

"I want to go to the psychic fair with you," Cable blurted out. "Stay here for one more night. Please."

When she started to shake her head, he tightened his grip on her hand. Christ, he couldn't show up at the house with her and he didn't want her traveling alone, much less camping among people the Believers might have targeted. He could call and ask Domino to protect Kiziah while he dealt with Fane...if she'd agree to stay. "I'll be back as soon as I can, Kiziah. By morning, for sure. I promise. Give me until then."

She hesitated and he leaned forward, stroking her cheek before spearing his fingers through her hair and forcing her to turn and face him, his heart aching when he saw the conflict in her eyes. Hope pitted against the need to avoid getting hurt. The desire to be among friends rather than to wait alone in a nearly abandoned campground while events she had no control over unfolded elsewhere. "I'll be back. I swear it. Just give me tonight to sort things out with Fane."

Kiziah nodded slightly then wrote down a phone number and handed it to him. "If you work it out with him, just call me. Okay? It'd be too hard to say goodbye again."

Chapter Six

Cable barely got into the house before Fane was on him. Coming out of nowhere. Attacking. The two of them rolling around on the floor, crashing into furniture as clothing ripped and bodies writhed.

They'd fought before, wrestled for fun as a prelude to rough, sweaty sex. But Cable knew within seconds that this was different. A battle on more levels than just the physical.

"You've been with a woman," Fane said, anger roaring through him, mingling with The Hunger, The Heat, as he finally cleared the tangle of fallen furniture and pinned Cable underneath him, not bothering to limit himself to a human's strength as he usually did when they were playing. Wondering in that instant why he bothered to limit himself at all when it came to Cable.

Fuck! A woman. Her smell was all over Cable. Claiming him, taunting Fane with the knowledge that Cable had been with someone else. That he was going to lose Cable if he didn't act to keep him.

Fane struck. Driving his fangs into Cable's neck in a primitive instinct to take what he wanted. What his soul screamed he needed.

The hot rush of Cable's blood was a reward in itself. And he gorged. Taking so much that Cable's heart stuttered in warning before Fane stopped and ripped his own wrist, pressing the gushing vein to Cable's lips and forcing him to drink. Only the smallest part of Fane's sanity keeping him from fucking Cable, only the echo of Domino's words, *You can have Cable as well as a kadine if you handle it correctly*, keeping him from binding himself sexually to Cable.

"I could finish it now," Fane snarled, anger and hurt still churning inside of him. Joined by lust. He was rock hard. His erection pressed against Cable's. "One fuck is all it would take."

Cable jerked his mouth from Fane's wrist. "Christ! Get off me."

"How badly do you want her?"

"Get off me and I'll tell you!"

Cable closed his eyes against the lust that was swamping him, burning through his veins like lava as his heart thundered in his chest. If Fane didn't get off him they were going to start fucking like minks. And it wouldn't end there. Two more nights. Two more blood exchanges and his life would be tied completely to Fane's.

Yesterday he would have welcomed it. But today...

Maybe you can still work it out with him. If I don't see you in Ashburg...

The image of Kiziah's soulful eyes and gentle smile gave him the strength to push Fane away. To sit up and ensure there was some distance between them. Fuck! Fane was a full vampire now. He'd been around enough of them to recognize when a dhampir had gone through The Transformation.

Cable rubbed the place where Fane had bitten, groaned when pleasure radiated from it, shooting down his chest and making his cock pulse and leak. Making heat curl in his balls and around his shaft so that his hand dropped to cover his erection.

A hiss from Fane warned him that they weren't out of danger yet. Fuck. He could hardly believe they'd stopped at all.

"Who is she?" Fane asked, his eyes flashing with wild emotion and Cable heard the hurt underneath the anger in Fane's voice.

Guilt cooled some of Cable's desire. Misgiving. But Fane would recognize Kiziah's scent as soon as they got to the psychic fair. "Her name's Kiziah. You'll like her."

"I'd better." Fane moved in, nostrils flared, closing the distance between them. "If you want her, Cable, then I'll make her my kadine." His lips pressed against Cable's in a firm, hard kiss before he added, "And I'll convert you at the same time. I don't have the luxury of waiting and the padralls will never sanction what I want."

Cable's heart jerked in his chest. Disbelief and hope warred inside him. His cock surged, arousal leaking from its tip as his earlier fantasy of having Kiziah snuggled between Fane and him returned in a rush. "It's never been done."

"You're wrong. One of Domino's ancestors had both a kadine and a male companion."

"Domino knows how his ancestor managed it?"

"The records of the Santori are in the possession of your order. I can hold out long enough for you to check them." His eyes met Cable's. "I can give you that much time. But now that we've made the first exchange, the herbs won't curb the need for long."

For an endless moment Cable's conscience tried to impose itself on him. A kiss, a touch, a show of willingness and Fane wouldn't wait. All it would take was one fuck now that they'd exchanged blood and Fane would be sexually bonded to him. Kiziah would be safe then, but he'd lose her. And Fane would lose the chance to father children.

Fuck! It was madness to consider it. It was insanity to refuse.

Christ! It was the completeness he'd longed for as he lay in Kiziah's arms. The very scene he'd imagined, Fane in bed with them, the three of them together.

Madame Helki's words rang through Cable's mind. *You have reached a turning point, a place with many possible outcomes and a chance for great happiness.* Had she guessed? Had she really seen this possibility in the future? Or was he just using the reading as an excuse to suppress his conscience and make a grab at happiness?

"I'll leave tonight," Cable said, rising to his feet and offering a hand to pull Fane up. "But we need to talk first."

* * * * *

Kiziah hitched the trailer to the Suburban, trying not to see it as anything other than a necessary preparation. Whether Cable returned or called to say that he and Fane had worked things out, she needed to be on the road tomorrow.

She rubbed her hand over her heart, trying to smooth away some of the ache there. She didn't regret a single moment spent with Cable, but she knew it would be a long time before she invited another man back to the Airstream, or went home with one.

The truth was that she wasn't cut out for casual sex. She couldn't separate her body from her heart and mind. And the night with Cable had made her realize how empty her life was now that her mother was gone, how she'd just kept on doing what she'd always done — traveling across the country — without ever stopping to consider whether or not it was the lifestyle she wanted as opposed to the only one she knew.

She thought about the dream that had sent her to Madame Helki's tent. About the card of her present, The Hermit. And she knew with a certainty that she was ready for change.

Maybe not with Cable, though her chest grew tight at the prospect of not seeing him again. But she couldn't hope that he and Fane were separating permanently — not when it was obvious how deeply Cable cared about Fane.

She'd been a chicken not to ask questions. She wished now that she had, that she knew what the breakup was about.

What if it was over women? Maybe Cable needing both a boyfriend and a girlfriend while Fane didn't.

Kiziah's face flushed with heat. Her body reacted, her imagination filling with images of sharing Cable with another man, of watching the two men together.

She laughed, a small sound of amusement tinged with sadness. Maybe it was a good thing she hadn't asked Cable what Fane looked like. Maybe it was better if she didn't know anything more about the two of them.

The loneliness she'd been escaping last night was already back, the hollow place larger, expanded by hope and the time she'd spent with Cable. She lightly traced the dreamcatcher necklace, its shape reminding her of the card representing her future. The Wheel of Fortune. *Very soon, an opportunity will present itself. A destiny not planned for, even by those who will draw you into their world.*

Kiziah allowed herself to fantasize that *their world* meant Fane and Cable's world, that *The Lovers* Cable had drawn when he visited Madame Helki's tent, overlaid on the card of *her* future, was a symbolic link, a mystical connection with roots in the dream that had sent her to the carnival in the first place.

Only reluctantly did she push the fantasies and hopes aside and reach for her cell phone, suddenly longing for a familiar voice. Surprised pleasure filling her when she learned that Margo and

Walt, a witch and warlock she'd known all her life, were in town, delayed themselves because they'd been guests at an important coven meeting.

"Come and play cards with us," Margo said as soon as she learned where Kiziah was camped. "In fact, I insist! Walter is on his way to pick you up right now."

And Kiziah didn't protest. She gathered several dreamcatchers to give as gifts to the coven that was hosting her friends, then left the nearly abandoned campsite, glad the long hours until she heard from Cable would pass a little more quickly.

* * * * *

Fane paced the short length of the Airstream, emotion churning through him with each step. Cable's scent was everywhere. Mingling with Kiziah's. Overlaid with sex.

Even knowing what to expect, Fane had felt a surge of pain when he'd slipped into the trailer and was confronted by the lingering scent of passion, by the reality that Cable had truly been with someone else. In that instant he'd been tempted to leave, to prowl the campground for prey—The Hunger whispering in his ear that blood would soothe him, would fill the hollowed-out places in his soul.

He'd whirled and taken a step toward the door, his quick movement stirring the air in the small confines of the travel trailer and sending the dreamcatchers dancing in front of the windows. That's what had caught his attention at first, but then his gaze had lowered and he'd seen the photograph.

Now he was rock hard, unsure whether it was the lingering reminder of Cable's presence here or the prospect of claiming a bride that had his cock full, aching for release.

Kiziah. Cable hadn't lied when he'd said that she was beautiful. Honey-blonde hair and dark, dark eyes. A tempting blend of sensuousness and softness, gentleness.

Fane picked up the photograph and studied it again, seeing the details as clearly in the moonlit trailer as most would see during the daylight. She was standing arm-in-arm with another woman, her mother, both of them smiling into the camera, at peace in the moment, neither of them knowing what was to come.

He ached for her. For himself. Cable had told him that the previous night marked the one-year anniversary of her mother's death. How well Fane knew that pain. Not just for a mother. But a father. A brother. The latter two nearly impossible to kill—though Fane knew that even if they'd known in the instant before the car they were in became an inferno, even if they'd had that split second to become mist, particles in the air, neither his father nor his brother would have abandoned his mother.

The need for revenge burned in Fane's gut. The thought of his family's last seconds, the image of the three of them together, debating the merits of a theater production as they were prone to do after a show, seared his heart and mind and soul.

Anger flashed through Fane. What was Cable thinking to allow Kiziah to remain in the travel trailer where a simple bomb or a spray from an automatic weapon could kill her? So what if he had called Domino? Though Domino liked to think he was invincible, he was only one dhampir.

The memory of Domino's amusement when Fane arrived at the campground only to learn that Kiziah was missing still rankled. His obvious enjoyment of Fane's fury and possessiveness—over a woman—made Fane hope that he was around to witness Domino's Transformation. To watch as Domino succumbed to The Heat and took a mate.

And yet, despite Domino's often abrasive humor, Fane would step forward in a heartbeat should Domino need his help. Just as he knew Domino would do for him—their parting conversation adding to the debt Fane owed.

Once she arrives, I will continue to stand guard while the two of you become…better acquainted. But I trust you won't want to remain here for long.

I can't believe that Cable left her here to begin with!

He should have brought her home, like a stray kitten? You would have welcomed her with open arms and an open fly?

I will take her back to the house as soon as possible.

Call me and I will help you. I have touched her mind before and though she emerged from my compulsion earlier than I intended, I can aid you in getting her to your house without her awareness. It would be best to take her car and trailer as well, to leave nothing of her behind for the Believers to find.

Fane put the photograph down and moved away from it, calming himself. The past had to be set aside, at least for tonight. He needed to be in control when he met his future kadine. He wouldn't risk exchanging blood with her tonight, nor would he tempt himself by feeding on her. Not until Cable returned with the results of his research.

He would fuck her though. He would claim her body and he wouldn't wait for Cable's arrival to do so. He would set the ground rules of his relationship with Kiziah tonight, mounting her until she was completely submissive, until she acknowledged who was the master—though it was much more complex than that simple word implied. With the third exchange of blood the three of them would become almost one. Kiziah's happiness would become their happiness. Her misery would be theirs as well. There was almost no separation between a vampire and his kadine—and in Fane's case, there would be almost no separation between him and Cable either—though he had little worry about *that* relationship.

It was different with Cable. The primitive instincts of Fane's ancient, alien ancestors flared up but were easily overcome—recognizing that Cable was not a means to the future, a means to a new generation. Until the approach of The Transformation, it had been easy enough to alternate who was the dominant partner—and with a little effort, a trust built over the last two years, Fane thought he could return to the place where they had been before, to a relationship of equals.

Love moved through Fane at the sacrifices Cable was willing to make in order to be with him. At the depth of Cable's caring and commitment.

Cable's father and brothers might well shun him for his choices. And in binding his life to Fane's, Cable might well be giving up the possibility of siring children of his own, though perhaps the records of the Santori would say otherwise. Regardless, Kiziah's body would be altered by the blood exchanges, made as alien as it was human in order for Fane's seed to take root, for Fane's children to grow there.

Desire rushed into Fane's cock with the thought of those children. But just as quickly, the lust for sex turned into the lust for blood, his body tightening, preparing itself for attack as a car stopped in front of the trailer, its doors opening, two people exiting. A female who could only be Kiziah. A male who wasn't Cable.

Fangs emerged and primitive urges threatened to overwhelm Fane, to force him into acting without thought. Demanding that he destroy any competition, anything that might stand in the way of claiming a bride, a kadine, a mate.

Kiziah shivered as she neared the Airstream, her footsteps slowing, a sudden fear gripping her, the eerie presence of the supernatural making her reluctant to go inside her home.

"I don't like seeing you parked in a nearly empty campground like this," Walt said, his hand moving to rest on her shoulder. "The folks hosting Margo and me wouldn't mind one more rig in front of their house overnight. And if you come back, we could play another couple of rounds of cards."

Kiziah patted the hand. "I'll be fine, Walt. Honestly. You know Mom and I camped here plenty of times. And it's not completely deserted."

Walt's heavy eyebrows drew together as they halted in front of the door. "There's a presence here. Do you feel it, Kiz?"

She almost wished that Walt hadn't said anything, but she answered, "Yes."

"I've felt this one before," he surprised her by saying.

"Is that a good thing or a bad thing?"

He took a long time answering. "I'm not sure. It happened last night, while the coven was gathered in a circle. I felt this presence just before a rush of incredible magic and power. I've never experienced anything like it, even during ceremonies where a sacrifice was made."

"I'll be fine," she repeated, "and I'll see you and Margo in Ashburg tomorrow."

Walt pulled Kiziah against him in a fierce hug. She returned the hug then watched him get in his car before unlocking the door and moving inside the Airstream.

Fane didn't allow her time to panic. To scream or run. He swamped her with the pheromones of his kind, a potent mix that rendered humans dazed, helpless, easy prey.

"Come to me," he commanded, seeing why Cable had fallen so completely under her spell. She was exquisite, sleek lines and gentle curves, soft in all the places they were hard.

Kiziah moved to him, her scent reaching him first, swirling around him, mixed with Cable's and reminding him that she was not prey to be used and forgotten. Reminding him that Cable would care not just how Fane took her, but about her willingness to be taken.

It was a good thing for all of them that the man who'd brought her home was just a friend. Otherwise Fane wouldn't have found the strength to control the alien instincts roaring through him. Wouldn't have been able to find that small illusory piece of him that remained human after The Transformation, a conscience sparked by the love he held for his once-human mother and the knowledge she would not approve of him taking a woman against her will, forcing his attention on one who hadn't offered herself to him.

"I'm Fane," he said, reducing the pheromones and letting Kiziah slowly surface from the enthrallment that held her.

Kiziah blinked, trying hard to overcome the confusion and lust swamping her. Had she invited him in? She couldn't remember doing it, and yet here he was. She glanced toward the bed, almost expecting to see Cable lounging there. "Where's Cable?" she asked, her heart beginning to race.

"He'll join us when he can."

She shivered, not sure she wanted to be alone with Fane. Wondering why he was here at all. There was something about him that frightened her, stirring up a primal instinct to flee in the presence of a deadly predator.

Kiziah tried to take a step backward but didn't, the thought leaving almost as quickly as it had arrived. The fear receding, pushed deep inside until it was caged and ignored in favor of the lust washing over her. Images of Fane thrusting his cock into her filled her mind, heating her face and tightening her nipples, sending blood rushing to her clit and labia.

Some part of her knew that what she was feeling didn't completely originate within her, and yet she didn't resist the powerful sensations. She remained mesmerized, lost as Fane stroked her cheek. But when his hand moved lower, to cup her neck so that her pulse beat against his palm, the fear surged wildly inside of her, trying to break through its restraints, pushing her heartbeat up until it thundered in her ears — becoming both a siren's song and a curse to Fane.

Fane only barely suppressed a hiss as he struggled to keep his fangs from extending. Fear was a heady aphrodisiac to his kind. The lure of it, the ease in which it became an addiction in itself was part of the reason why laws were put in place forbidding full vampires from killing their prey by draining them of life, from feeding on both their blood and their fear. They couldn't afford for their existence to become widely known, especially now, in a world with advanced technology. Their kind did not reproduce so quickly that they could afford the loss of their women and children. They were not as indestructible as they were once.

He'd come here angry and hurt even though he knew his losing control in the shower, first biting Cable, then telling him that he needed a kadine had been the catalyst for Cable ending up in Kiziah's bed. A part of Fane had wanted to strike out at her because she'd claimed a piece of Cable for her own. But as he looked at her, as his cock urged him to hurry and take her, to know her in the same way Cable did, a sliver of guilt edged its way into his chest so that he found no satisfaction in her fear.

She had not asked to be pulled into his world. Had not been prepared for it.

Unlike his mother, who had been created for and raised to be his father's kadine, who had been given her future mate's blood at birth and during the confirmation ceremony so that when the time came, her body would burn with the change but accept it easily — Kiziah's own conversion would be nearly as painful as The Transformation had been for him. She *would* suffer, and he would witness it, helpless to do anything to spare her.

Be happy, Fane. His mother's gentle refrain eased some of the anger and hurt inside him.

Here was a chance to have both a kadine and Cable. Here was a chance at happiness.

She was beautiful and he trusted Cable's judgment when it came to women. And then there was the fact that his body responded to her. His cock had grown limp, unenthusiastic at the prospect of searching for a bride among the women who bear the kadines. But now it was hard and full, impatient for Fane's thoughts to catch up with his desires and accept what had been obvious to it from the moment Fane had stepped inside the travel trailer and inhaled her scent, seen the picture of her. She was his. His to fuck. His to breed. His to share with Cable.

Fane allowed the pheromones to swamp her once more, to force her fear back again so that her pulse was a smooth, steady beat against his palm. He pulled her body to his, burying his nose in her silky hair and breathing her in. "Don't be afraid," he found himself murmuring, allowing a moment of gentleness, offering reassurance. "You're safe from me." His lips suckled at her earlobe. His tongue traced the delicate shell of her ear. "Can you imagine us together?" he asked, letting her surface from the enthrallment though his voice was a dark seduction in and of itself. "You and me? Then with Cable joining us?"

"Yes," Kiziah whispered, trying to remember how she'd ended up in Fane's arms, her nipples tight and her cunt flushed, his erection pressed against her belly. She didn't even know him and yet she wanted him desperately. Couldn't imagine turning away from him.

A whimper escaped when he let her go, stepping back, the expression on his face so carnal that she shivered in response. Her own need so great that she didn't hesitate when he commanded her to strip.

Her clothes fell with a soft rustle of fabric. Her gaze never leaving his, though her heart began thundering in her chest once again when his expression grew more possessive, when something primitive, alien flickered in his eyes.

There was no escape for any of them.

The sight of Kiziah standing in front of him, naked, vulnerable, her body primed for his had stirred up The Heat beyond anything Fane had ever known. Beyond anything he would have guessed he could feel for a woman.

In a heartbeat he understood why it was so often necessary to restrain a female in the early stages of the claiming and making of a kadine. One wrong move, one hint that she thought to resist or flee, and he would become little more than a beast intent on subduing and taming his mate.

With Cable he could suppress the urge to dominate. Not with Kiziah. It was a shout in every cell. A deep-seated need. A programming that couldn't be ignored.

"Get on the bed," he growled, tensing, a part of him wanting her to disobey — the saner part, the part connecting him to Cable, praying that she would do as he'd ordered.

She hesitated and his cock pulsed with anticipation, beaded with arousal, a lubrication that would aid him if he was forced to pounce and mount her roughly.

Fire burned through his veins, an inferno that filled his chest and abdomen, growing more intense when her head ducked in submission before she moved to the bed and crawled onto it.

He didn't remember closing the distance between them or stripping out of his clothing. In an instant the sight of her on her hands and knees, her slick, pink vulva peeking from between her thighs became the center of his awareness. The center of his existence.

He pinned her down, his chest against her back, his breath coming in heavy pants, his hand pushing between her legs so that his palm cupped and rubbed her mound, glorying in the smooth curves and tiny clit, the bare skin and soft strip of pubic down.

It was easy to see now why Cable had become entranced with her, enthralled. She was exquisite. Intoxicating.

Fane's gums ached with the need to allow his fangs to descend, to pierce her neck so that he could take her blood at the same time his cock surged into her and bathed in her sex. He forced himself to deny the first need, but there was no denying the second.

With a groan, he covered her fully, using his thighs to widen hers. His mouth going to her neck and shoulders, kissing, nipping, sucking, building the need in both of them until she shifted the angle of her pelvis just enough so that his cock slid in.

At the feel of her clamping down on his penis, slick and hot, lust roared through Fane, a wild rush that left little room for thought. His lips pulled back in a snarl of ecstasy as he thrust in and out of her, using the weight of his body to hold her down, not because she needed to be restrained but because the alien stamp of his ancestors was imprinted so thoroughly that there was no denying it.

He soaked the fevered heat of her skin in through his, drank her cries of pleasure and drowned in the scent of her arousal, knowing as he did it that no other woman would ever satisfy him now.

Chapter Seven

Cable contemplated parking the sports car at the gate of his father's estate and walking in but then thought better of it. That'd be even more suspicious than arriving long after everyone should be in bed and going directly to the vaults.

If he got lucky he could be gone within an hour, without anyone knowing he'd been there. Shit. He was still reeling. Riding a roller coaster of hope and disbelief. Almost unable to accept the possibility that he could have what he wanted most. Fane and Kiziah.

He touched his neck. Pleasure still radiated from the spot on his neck where Fane had bitten, this time marking Cable by leaving a bruise along with the barest hint of twin puncture wounds. It'd taken forever for the hard-on he'd had to go away.

Cable parked, moving quietly from the car into the house, slipping downstairs and tapping in the first of a sequence of codes allowing him access to the parts of his father's estate reserved for padrall use. The areas no woman routinely stepped foot in—though in his mother's case, he suspected she knew much of what happened in the order without ever visiting the secured rooms.

Guilt attacked Cable. The same sickening crush he'd experienced off and on since his discussion with Fane. But just as he'd done in the car, he pushed it away.

Kiziah was the perfect choice for them. She already knew about Fane and despite the fact that she hadn't been raised to become a kadine, she'd grown up among psychics and those who dabbled in the supernatural. She would be able to handle the knowledge that vampires and dhampirs existed. And once they were bound together, changed by the exchanges of blood, there would be almost no barrier between the three of them. They'd know each other more deeply, more thoroughly than was possible for a human. They'd be able to touch each others' thoughts and emotions at will.

Warmth filled Cable, flooding in with the memory of Kiziah's soft eyes and gentle smile. She'd forgive them for pulling her into their world. And they'd spend a lifetime making sure she was glad they'd done it.

Cable stopped in front of the door to the vault, the library where the records maintained over centuries were kept, keying in the last set of codes and hearing the click indicating that the lock had disengaged, moving inside and going to the book which indexed where each volume of history resided. Within minutes he had several heavy tomes in front of him, all detailing the Santori history and lineage. If only Domino could have come up with an ancestor name, even a reference to a period of time…

Cable sighed and reached for a book. While he'd been driving, he'd had plenty of time to contemplate how he was going to approach the task. He started in the early years of Julius Caesar and moved forward, finding what he was looking for in the year Rome burned while under Nero's rule.

Domino's ancestor laid out what he'd done clearly, probably viewing the padrall who'd dutifully written down those since-translated words as little more than a scribe. Cable could barely contain his excitement as he read the account, so intent on what he was doing that he was unaware of his father's presence until a heavy sense of foreboding began to smother his exhilaration.

Fuck! He flinched when he saw his father in the doorway but tried to brazen it out, casually closing the book as he said, "You're up late."

"As are you. No one mentioned you'd come back. Is the matter with Matteo settled?"

"Yes. Sarael's completed the transformation to kadine. I verified it earlier in the evening. They're on their way back to Italy now."

"Good." His father moved to stand next to the desk, his glance taking in the tomes spread across the polished wood. "You're researching the Santori?"

Cable shrugged, worry tightening his stomach. There was no good reason for him to be here at this time of night. "Domino is on the scene. I thought I'd update the records, then became curious as to how close he was to the change and got sidetracked."

His father nodded, but something in his eyes only intensified the dread in Cable's gut. "And Fane? Has he been through The Transformation?"

Cable had no choice but to tell the truth. Fuck! Why hadn't he mentioned Kiziah as soon as he saw his father?

"Yes. I'll update the Mercier records as well since I'm here." He shifted in his seat, having to decide in a split second whether late was better than not at all. "I'd like to take some time off. I've met a woman. Someone I'm serious about." His father's eyebrows lifted in silent question and Cable continued, "Her name's Kiziah. I think you'll like her."

"I'm sure I will." His father moved to the door, pausing there. "When did Fane change?"

"Last night, when he was hunting with Domino."

"Domino gave him first blood?"

"Yes."

His father nodded once again. "I'll leave you to updating the records then."

Cable tried to feel relieved when his father left. Instead all he felt was a sense of impending doom. Fuck, he needed to get out of here, but now he had to delay long enough to write something in the records.

He rose and moved over to where the Mercier records were shelved. Going immediately to the volume chronicling Fane's history — or what was known of it. The ancient vampires had loved to provide information, seeing it as a testament to their importance, their invincibility. The more modern ones were wary, aware of how dangerous information could be in a time when cyberspace was open to anyone.

The door opened just as Cable placed the tome on the desk. This time there was no way to maintain the illusion that everything was okay.

His father entered, along with his three older brothers. Any one of them was large enough and strong enough to prevent Cable from leaving the room, the three of them together were a wrecking crew.

"We can do this the easy way or the hard way, son. Take off your shirt."

Christ! Cable shut his eyes briefly. There was no defending himself, no point in saying a word or trying to avoid his father's edict. They'd never hear a thing he said and even if he was foolish enough to resist, they'd tear his clothing and beat him to a pulp if necessary if they thought they were saving him from disgrace and a centuries' long mistake.

He took off the jacket and shirt, draping them over the back of the chair and standing straight as his father prowled around him while his brothers continued to block the door. "Just the one exchange?" his father asked, knowing that the presence of the marking signified that blood had been shared.

Cable ground his teeth together. They'd force him to strip completely if they thought he was lying. "Yes, just the one." And because he knew what was coming and that Kiziah might be his only chance for escape, he added, "Fane's not sexually bonded to me. He lost control when he found out I'd been with Kiziah, but he regained it before it went any further."

His father reached down and gathered Cable's shirt and jacket, retrieving Cable's cell phone and putting it in his own pocket before picking up the volume of Mercier history. "You've been saying for years that we should enter all the records into the computer. Maybe revisiting the past as you input the data will open your eyes to what vampires are really like. You'll remain down here until I determine that it's appropriate to allow you to leave the estate."

Cable had expected as much. He scooped up the Santori chronicles since he had no way of knowing how much of their history his father was aware of, and he had no intention of letting him stumble on the very information that had brought him to the estate. A small measure of relief settled in Cable's chest when he was allowed to keep the books, his brothers escorting him, blocking any chance of escape as his father led the way to a rarely used room that was, in truth, a holding cell.

"Sleep, son. We'll talk more in the morning," his father said before closing the door, the sound of a deadbolt being keyed into place filling the silence left behind him.

* * * * *

Kiziah woke with the same disorientation, the same elongation of reality that she'd experienced the previous night when she'd left the carnival without being aware that she'd done so. Only this time, instead of finding herself on the street, heading to her car, she found herself in a strange room, a strange bed, with a man she didn't remember meeting, though she knew who he was and what they'd done together in the Airstream.

"Where's Cable?" she asked, suddenly needing him to be with her, needing answers, needing…

Fane covered Kiziah's body with his own, swamping her with just enough pheromones to alleviate her anxiety and suppress her rising panic. "He'll be here soon," he said before pressing his lips to hers and demanding entry with his tongue.

He hated the necessity of enthralling her in order to control her fear, but there was no way he could allow her to escape or to remain in the travel trailer now that he'd started dreaming of the moment when she'd become his kadine. It still shocked him just how much he desired her. How his cock filled with blood and need just looking at her, how the scent of her, the softness of her skin and feminine curves were a potent lure.

The attraction would grow in intensity after the first blood exchange, after he and Cable had taken her at the same time, their cocks rubbing against each other in the depths of her body as they fucked. At the moment, the pheromones were reducing her fear and inhibitions, but Fane wanted to believe her responses weren't only the result of enthrallment. He wanted to believe that she found him as intoxicating as he found her.

"More," Kiziah whispered, embracing the dream-like fog that made it seem perfectly normal to be in bed with Fane. She'd fantasized about it, hadn't she? She'd wondered if the fortune-teller had seen a future that included both Fane and Cable.

She shifted restlessly underneath him. Wrapping her legs around his waist as she wound her arms around his neck and pulled his face down for a kiss, savoring the way he took control immediately, used his tongue to force her own into submission. Used the hardness and weight of his body to assert his dominance.

"I need more," she whispered when the kiss ended, tilting her pelvis in order to entice him to enter her again.

Fane shuddered as she drenched his cock with her arousal. The Heat raged through him, demanding that he give Kiziah what she was asking for—and then some. That he drive his fangs into her soft neck and feast on her as he fucked her.

With a groan he levered himself up so he straddled her, the rub of his cock and balls against her belly almost undoing him. Her whimpered protest making his penis jerk in protest.

He didn't trust himself to have his mouth anywhere near her, not if she was going to wrap him in her arms and legs, surround him with her scent and slick desire as she pleaded for more from him. He was too close to claiming her completely. One drop of blood and even his love for Cable wouldn't keep him from sexually bonding himself to Kiziah. The instincts of his alien ancestors, the drive to survive and procreate was too strong, too deeply programmed into Fane's cells.

He had to withstand the temptation she presented, at least until Cable returned. And then he would gorge himself on her. Would savor the incredible rush that came with an exchange of blood.

And yet he needed relief. His cock screamed to feel her wet heat.

"Please," she whispered, rising onto her elbows, and Fane's gaze focused on her mouth. On lips left swollen by his kisses.

He rose from the bed in a fluid motion, his hand going to his cock, his mind prepared to command her if necessary, but after a small whimpered protest at his leaving, she came to him on her own, came to him on hands and knees, the delicate line of her spine and the curve of her buttocks driving more blood to a cock that was already engorged to the point of pain, to balls that were already heavy and full.

"Yes!" he hissed, his fangs elongating at the first touch of her lips to his penis, his hands going to her head, his fingers spearing through her luxurious blonde hair, steadying her, holding her in position as one of her hands cupped his sac and the other encircled his shaft.

Her touch was different than Cable's, softer, gentler, and yet within seconds Fane knew that he'd forever crave the feel of her hands and mouth on his cock. She squeezed him, teased him, tormented him, refused to grant him the release he needed until he was draped over her, moaning in ecstasy, shivering under the lash of her tongue, crying out as she sucked him, as she manipulated his testicles and explored the sensitive skin behind them, the tip of her finger drawing close to his back entrance, making him crave Cable's presence, making him fantasize about having Cable penetrate him as Kiziah pleasured him.

With a groan Fane tightened his grip on her hair, tried to drive himself deeper into her throat, wanting her to swallow him, to take everything and still plead for more. And yet she resisted, warning him with the press of her teeth against his swollen cock that she wouldn't be rushed, her small defiance driving him higher, taking him dangerously close to the point where he would lose control.

She ignored his commands until he was panting, his buttocks clenched, his fists curling and uncurling in her hair, his body straining. Until he was a breath away from savagery, a shiver away from simply overwhelming her with his physical strength. And then she relented, letting him thrust against the back of her throat as she swallowed. Her capitulation a command instead of a surrender. But he couldn't stop his body from obeying her, couldn't stop his seed from burning through his cock in a lava-hot rush that left him dizzy, momentarily weak, sated. Hers in a way that he had never belonged to any woman.

He actually cried out when her mouth left him, his hips thrusting, his cock beginning to fill, wanting to enjoy the sweet torment of her mouth again. She laughed, a husky sound of female power that reawakened his primitive instincts and brought the urge to dominate crashing through him, a beast let out of its cage though it remained leashed.

Fane fell on her then. His mouth covering hers, his tongue thrusting aggressively against hers, his hands pinning hers to the mattress.

He knew he should lash her wrists and ankles to the bed as a safeguard against his own hunger, but he wanted Kiziah to accept being tied without the calming effects of the pheromones. He wanted Cable present to share those first moments of absolute trust when she allowed herself to be rendered completely helpless.

He rode the edge of control, drinking in her cries of pleasure as his body held hers to the bed. Her whimpers and pleas feeding the primitive parts of his soul.

She was soft and slick, utterly mesmerizing. His. And the desire to mark her became unbearable.

He left her mouth, reveling in the way she arched upward, offering him her breasts as he tormented himself by kissing her neck before moving lower, licking and biting, sucking on nipples that were much different than his own or Cable's. He'd thought to bury his face between her thighs, but as she writhed against him, her body an inferno of need, he gave in to her pleas, driving her to orgasm again and again with his mouth and teeth on her nipples, his cock a hard ridge against her tiny clit.

Only when she was limp underneath him did he cover her body completely, pressing his cock into wet heat and feminine mystery, his own breathing coming in fast pants as he tried to go slow, to savor the feel of her. But it took only a whimper, a single "Please, Fane," and he was helpless to do anything else but yield, to thrust hard and fast, his own release ripped from him when she came, arching into him, driving him deeper, the tight fist of her inner muscles squeezing him mercilessly until his sac was completely empty of seed. And even then, he didn't want to leave the heaven of her body.

He collapsed, shifting their position so that his penis remained embedded in Kiziah's channel as she snuggled against him, a small sigh escaping her as she fell into an exhausted sleep. The Heat was still present, urging him to claim her completely. The Hunger echoed the desire. But with her relaxed in sleep and his thoughts filling with worry about Cable, Fane was able to resist the dual call of his ancestors. To resist the urge to exchange blood.

It was nearing dawn. He could feel The Sleep closing in on him.

Cable should have called by now, even if only to say that he hadn't yet found the information he was looking for. Cable *would* have called to ensure that Kiziah was okay, safe, and to satisfy his curiosity about Fane's reaction to her.

Fane smoothed his hand up her spine before tangling his fingers in her silky hair. His worry deepening. It was all too easy to guess the reason for Cable's delay.

No doubt Cable's father had seen the bite mark and restricted Cable's movements in order to make it impossible for the second and third exchanges to take place. If Cable weren't a padrall, then one exchange alone would be enough for Fane to assert his claim. But the relationship between vampire and servant was complex, made more so by the wealth and power, the knowledge that the padralls had gained over the centuries. Fane doubted he would prevail in a challenge until after the third exchange had been made.

His stomach twisted with fury, despair, frustration. To be so close…

Kiziah made a distressed sound in her sleep, as if sensing the turmoil of his emotions, and Fane's heart experienced a jolt of warmth. He'd never thought there was much pleasure to be had with a woman, other than for a quick fuck, a release that didn't require an investment of time and emotion. But one night with her and he knew he would enjoy having a kadine, having *her* during the centuries that lay ahead, though it didn't lessen the desire for Cable.

Fane's hand slipped lower, smoothing up and down her spine, knowing that she was the key to Cable's freedom. And yet he couldn't compel her to act. He had only a vampire's ability to enthrall, to blur short-term memory in order to subdue prey and feed.

In frustration Fane concentrated on a black-handled knife lying on the dresser, using his mind to hurl it across the room and drive its sharp point into the wall. For once he wished he had Domino's ability to hypnotize and control instead of his own special affinity with knives.

Reluctantly he eased away from Kiziah, his cock protesting the loss of her warmth when he pulled it free. The familiar rage swamping him, at having gone through The Transformation before he was ready to give up the ability to move about during the day in a human form.

He removed the knife from the wall, dropping it on the dresser as he paced. Misgiving swamping him as a plan formed in his mind. Uncertainty making his chest tighten.

The Sleep was pressing down on him and he couldn't see any other option but to present Kiziah with the choice of helping Cable and hope that she cared enough to do it. If she chose to run, then he would contact Domino when night fell. But until then, she was the key to Cable's freedom.

Fane stopped next to the bed, unable to resist tracing his finger over her eyebrows, her nose, across her lips. She was truly exquisite. He had to trust Cable's judgment when it came to her. He had to believe Cable wouldn't have fallen so quickly for Kiziah if she wasn't the right woman for both of them.

A small laugh escaped. And perhaps he had to trust the tarot cards, though it still amused him that Cable had sought a reading from the carnival fortune-teller. Fane leaned down, compelled by a strange tenderness to brush his lips against Kiziah's before leaving the room in order to prepare his message for her.

Kiziah woke and for all of a second she thought the previous night with Fane had been an intensely erotic dream. But as soon she stretched and felt the sheet slide across nipples that were sore, she knew it hadn't been. And then when she opened her eyes and saw a bedroom instead of the interior of the Airstream, she accepted that all of it had happened—despite the dream-like quality of her time with him.

She slipped from the bed and moved to the window, opening the heavy drapes and flooding the room with sunlight. A smile escaped when she saw clothing scattered about and knew that this was the bedroom Cable and Fane shared.

A part of her still couldn't believe she was here, a part of her remained troubled that she couldn't remember being brought here. But none of her was sorry for what had happened.

Kiziah laughed, thinking about The Hermit. She'd decided she was ready for change, she'd fantasized that the tarot reading meant she would be with Cable and Fane, but she hadn't allowed herself to truly believe it would happen.

She showered, selecting one of their shirts from the closet until she could retrieve her own clothing from the travel trailer, then went in search of them. Her happiness fading, replaced by uneasiness when they couldn't be found. By a deep pool of worry when she saw the tarot cards on the kitchen counter.

The High Priestess, The Hermit, The Wheel of Fortune, and on top of the Wheel, The Lovers, held down by an ornate ring and resting on a folded piece of paper.

The note was written in bold strokes. *Cable has not called or returned from his parents' estate, which can only mean he isn't free to do so. The ring is a betrothal ring. It will gain you access to his family estate and hopefully to him. Today the choice is yours whether or not to help him. Fane.*

Chapter Eight

The estate was like something out of a fairy tale. Gleaming towers rising out of mist-enshrouded lands. Imposing and majestic. A place of wealth and privilege and quiet luxury.

Kiziah rubbed her left hand against her thigh, hyperaware of the ring Fane claimed would gain her access to the estate, to Cable. Looking at the scene in front of her, she could believe it was a place of secrets, a place where Cable's family held him prisoner.

Despite the subtle threat contained in Fane's note, it was the message in the tarot that made the decision to come here easy for Kiziah. The belief that her mother's spirit had sent the dream directing her to Madame Helki's tent, where their lives had first touched, their futures linked by the cards.

She rubbed her hand against her thigh again, ridding it of moisture as she gathered her courage, parking the car on the long circular driveway and walking to the front door. The loud sound of chimes announcing her presence as soon as she pressed the doorbell.

A butler answered. His black suit and haughty manner purposefully intimidating.

"I'm here to see Cable," she said, hating that her voice held a tremor of nervousness.

"Wait here," he said, leaving her standing in the foyer, a subtle rebuke for arriving unannounced.

Kiziah stayed put, not giving in to temptation and moving to take a closer look at the artwork on the walls, priceless pieces done by long-dead masters. She shoved her hands into her jacket pockets, huddled against the old wealth surrounding her until the sound of footsteps approaching made her heart leap and race.

Anticipation filled her, only to be smothered when an older man entered the foyer, followed by two others who had to be Cable's brothers. "You're here to see my son?"

"Yes." She wiped the nervousness from her hands before pulling them from her pockets, offering her right one to Cable's father though his eyes appeared riveted to the ring on her left hand. "I'm Kiziah Stillwell."

He took her hand, clasping it between his instead of shaking it. His gaze finally lifting from the ring to Kiziah's face. "Cable spoke of you."

A thrill of pleasure pierced her heart despite the aura of foreboding pressing down on her. "Can I see him?"

"Let's discuss it elsewhere."

He left her little choice other than to fight to reclaim her hand or to follow where he led. A third son joining the other two a minute later, making her feel more like a prisoner being escorted to the gallows than a guest visiting one of their family members.

They moved through art-rich hallways, passing through several doors that required a code to unlock, until finally entering a spacious den, a masculine haunt furnished in leather and wood.

Cable's father released her hand, pausing momentarily before saying, "I'm sorry that this is necessary, but you'll need to take off your clothing before you'll be allowed to see my son."

Heat poured into Kiziah's face. Shock and disbelief rushed through her mind. "Excuse me?"

He didn't flinch. "If you want to see Cable, then you must disrobe first."

She could see that he was serious. She could also see that it wasn't a lewd request.

One of Cable's brothers spoke. "Do you want me to bring Mom down? She could…"

"No." His father's tone was brusque. "I told you earlier, I don't want her to know Cable is here. Not yet. She worries enough, and she's soft, especially when it comes to him."

"I'm not carrying a weapon if that's what you're worried about," Kiziah said, surprised they couldn't hear her heart thundering in her chest. "If you want to pat me down instead of..."

Cable's father looked at his sons, then at Kiziah. This time he took her left hand in his, rubbing his thumb over the ring, but he didn't relent. "I'm sorry. This has to be done, with witnesses. If you want to do it in stages, that's fine. It can be done quickly, but it must be done."

She thought about the doors they'd passed through, each with a keypad, each requiring a code to unlock it. "I'm not carrying a listening device or anything else to spy on you."

Something flickered in his eyes. He smiled slightly. "If you'd prefer to leave, one of Cable's brothers will escort you out."

"Can you at least tell me why?"

His thumb grazed the betrothal ring again. "Once you're fully committed to Cable, he'll provide an explanation."

The answer was more ominous than the setting, sending a shiver along Kiziah's spine as she pulled her hand from Cable's father's hand.

She tried to close her mind, to concentrate on Cable as she removed her jacket. Her fingers were trembling so badly that it took several attempts to unbutton her blouse and shed it.

The four men moved closer, staring intently at bared flesh. Flooding her with discomfort.

"Now the bra." It was a gruff command and she obeyed, grateful that there was no passion, no undertones of arousal in the older man's voice.

Once again she felt their eyes on her body, looking for something, the father's clinical, almost embarrassed when he saw her love-bruised nipples, the brother's appreciative and yet not lustful as color flushed over her breasts and into her face, making her ask, "Can I put my clothes back on?"

"Yes."

She hurried to cover her upper body. Then without being told, she released the hooks on her long skirt and let it fall to the ground, widening her stance, praying that they wouldn't ask her to remove the barely-there panties that afforded her a small measure of modesty.

"Good," Cable's father said, the single word signaling she could gather her skirt and refasten it as he shifted his attention to his sons. "Bring Cable in."

They left without a word, the thought that it took three of them to ensure Cable's compliance filled Kiziah with anxiousness and foreboding, so that his arrival only a few moments later had her rushing into his arms, clinging to him.

He hugged her to him, his lips covering hers in a long sharing of breath and existence. A welcoming of two souls already connected, already finding a home in each other.

"It seems like we've been apart forever," Cable whispered when their mouths finally separated.

He wanted to ask her a hundred questions but couldn't. He wanted to get the hell off the estate but knew it wouldn't be as easy as Kiziah showing up—her presence the proof his father desperately wanted to believe, that Cable was returning to the heterosexual fold.

Anger moved through him. They would have made her strip before they brought him out. They would have made sure she hadn't been bitten, wasn't somehow in Fane's control. He tightened his grip on her, kissing her again, this time in apology for what she'd suffered on his behalf. What she was yet to suffer.

Part of him wanted to be noble. To tell her to leave. To spare her. She hadn't asked to be pulled into his world. Into Fane's. But now there was no escaping it. And so he once again promised himself that he would spend a lifetime ensuring her happiness.

"Christ, I missed you," he said, trailing his hand down her arm, pulling it from his waist so that he could make a show of kissing the ring on her finger, though he doubted Fane had discussed the full implications of wearing it. That once a woman entered their world, the only escape from it was death.

He kissed her again, his cock hard against her abdomen, his tongue more insistent this time, his hands moving over her body, touching her in ways he knew would arouse her. His own body becoming more feverish as hers softened and molded against his, as she followed his lead, whimpering in need, clinging to him, uncaring about their audience.

She jerked when his father's voice intruded, a gruff, "Escort them to the bedroom," and Cable let her take a step backward, grimacing when the other men in his family quickly checked to make sure the front of his trousers indicated that Kiziah had aroused him. He squeezed her hand in reassurance and continued to hold it as they moved back in the direction of the room serving as his prison.

Kiziah tensed when she saw the deadbolt on the door and noticed that there were no windows in the bedroom, but she allowed Cable to lead her inside. "It'll be okay," he said, hugging her as the door closed behind them, both of them listening for the sound of a lock being keyed into place and relaxing slightly when it didn't come. "It'll be okay," Cable repeated, smoothing over her hair, rubbing his cheek against hers.

"That's really your father? Those are really your brothers?"

Cable laughed, a sound that managed to contain a hint of amusement. "We've been having a little disagreement," he said, kissing her forehead before leading her to the bed and sitting, pulling her down next to him. "Believe it or not, most of the time we get along."

Their eyes met, she opened her mouth to ask if the disagreement centered on Fane. He gave a slight shake of his head and brushed his thumb across her mouth to keep her from speaking, then eased her onto her back, positioning himself along her side.

"You're okay?" he asked, leaning over her, his expression telling her he knew she'd been forced to strip. The tone of his voice telling her how guilty he felt.

"A little nervous," she whispered, the warmth in her face echoing the more important warmth in her heart. "It's better now."

"Zia, I'm sorry…"

This time Kiziah brushed her thumb across his mouth to silence him. "It's okay. As long as you tell me we're going to be able to leave — together."

Cable sighed, tracing her eyebrow, her nose, smoothing over her cheek with his knuckles before picking up her left hand and kissing the ring. The guilt resurfacing.

She was here, which meant Fane had sent her. She was in the room with him, which meant Fane hadn't bitten her. And yet he couldn't imagine Fane hadn't been with her, hadn't fucked her. Didn't want her as his kadine.

Christ! What insanity. She might be his only hope of escaping the compound, but at the same time he couldn't stomach the thought of trapping her — not if Fane had decided to let her go.

Cable released her hand, his fingers going to the front of her blouse, his gaze locked on hers as he slowly undid the buttons, fire surging into his cock when her eyes widened slightly with arousal, when she shivered in anticipation. Fuck! He wasn't sure *he* could let her go. She filled empty, needy places in his soul, places he hadn't even been aware of before she came along.

She whimpered when he pushed the fabric of the blouse aside and opened the front clasp of her bra, brushing the material away and exposing taut, well-loved nipples. His cock pulsed and leaked at the sight, satisfaction roared through him with the knowledge that Fane had been with her.

There was a flicker of guilt in her face, trepidation when he shifted his focus from her nipples and met her eyes. He leaned down and kissed her, his palm covering her breast, massaging the hardened, bruised tips. "Are you okay with this?" he asked, praying Fane's jealousy and hurt hadn't mixed with The Heat and Hunger in such a way that he'd taken her when she wasn't willing.

"Yes." It was a soft whisper but it sounded as loud as a shout in Cable's heart.

"I'm glad." He kissed her again, long and deep, languid, as though they had all the time in the world though he knew they didn't. He hadn't found the cameras or microphones, hadn't bothered looking, but he knew the room contained them. He knew his fathers and brothers were watching, listening, waiting to see if he'd fuck her, and after he did, they'd return with the padrall chaplain for a shotgun wedding — orchestrated by the groom's family instead of the bride's. They knew him too well, knew he'd never stray from Kiziah if he married her.

He had to hope she wouldn't balk, that the presence of the ring on her finger would prepare her to play it out so they'd be allowed to leave. He could only be grateful his fathers and brothers hadn't read the Santori histories or stumbled on the knowledge that a vampire could have both a kadine and a companion.

A chill moved through him. A doubt.

If they had, then this would serve their purpose just as easily. They could hold the two of them on the estate until Kiziah was pregnant with a son.

Even though he'd exchanged blood with Fane, the conversion process wouldn't begin without sex. He was still fully human, as was Kiziah, and there were rules even the vampires must abide by. Fane would be considered rogue—marked for extermination—if he converted Kiziah and a padrall fetus died as a result.

Fane would never risk it. *He'd* never risk it. None of them could afford to gamble with such high stakes. Their lives would be forfeit along with Fane's.

Christ! When had his life become such a mix of heaven and hell?

But there was no way to alter the course they were on. No other choice but to gamble a future that suddenly seemed perilous.

He kissed Kiziah again. Her gentleness and acceptance a balm for his soul. The twining of her tongue with his making him suddenly desperate to feel her wet sheath fisting around his cock, holding him inside her.

Cable shifted, trailing kisses down her neck, over the slopes of her breasts, then lower, licking and suckling the tender, bruised nipples, his ministrations making her arch into him as her fingers speared through his hair, holding him to her.

Sensation surged through Kiziah, a blend of pleasure and pain she was starting to crave. There was still a dream-like quality to the time she'd spent with Fane, but this was real, intense. She moved restlessly against Cable, wanting him to bury his face between her legs and give her clit the same attention he was giving her nipples.

She wanted him to slide his tongue in and out of her hungry channel, to devour her.

She cried out when he bit her nipple, her hands clenching and unclenching in his hair, a tortured "Please" jerked from her as she rubbed her clothing-covered mound against his erection.

Cable groaned and lifted his head from her breast, shifting just enough so that he could pull her skirt up and push her panties down, the wanton display making her blush even as her cunt lips flushed with pleasure and slickened with arousal.

"You're so beautiful," he murmured, gliding his fingers along her slit, coating the bare skin of her labia with her own juices.

"Please, Cable," she whispered and he laughed, a warm husky sound that was music to her heart, a stroke to her feminine pride.

"Please what?" he teased, unzipping his jeans, jerking when she immediately encircled his cock with her hand, groaning when her thumb rubbed the swollen, sensitive head, wetting his heated flesh with the arousal she found there.

This time it was Kiziah who laughed, rising up to press her mouth to his. "Please make love to me. I need you."

He didn't bother to remove any more of their clothing. Didn't bother with additional words other than a single command, a request she found it easy to grant. "Put me inside you," he whispered, and she guided him home, both of them shivering as his unprotected cock pushed into her for the first time, a throbbing hard presence in a hot, tight channel. A coming together as they were meant to be, with nothing separating them.

Cable sealed her mouth with his and began thrusting, the feel of her so exquisite that he knew it'd be over too soon. Christ, it was impossible to care about anything else when he was with her.

The narrow bed shook with the violence of their passion. The room filled with the sounds and smells of sex, ending in a crescendo of swallowed moans and whimpers as their tongues and mouths touched, fused together by shared need and desire.

They were still joined, struggling for breath, hugging each other in the aftermath of pleasure when the door opened and one of Cable's brothers stepped into the room.

"Go away, Levant," Cable said.

"Get cleaned up. Marshall is on his way here. Dad's explaining the situation to Mom."

Even though he'd expected it, Cable's gut still tightened. "Can we have a little privacy here?"

His brother hesitated, knowing Cable was referring to the hidden cameras and microphones and not his presence. His gaze flickered to Kiziah and then back to Cable. "Fair enough. You've only got a few minutes."

He ducked out of the room and Kiziah asked, "What's going on?" Fear moving in again, edging toward terror. There were so many undercurrents swirling around her. With Fane. With Cable's father and brothers. She shivered, picturing the lock on the opposite side of the door, a deadbolt meant to keep occupants in rather than out.

Once again Cable picked up her left hand, kissing the ring, knowing there was no way to break it to her gently. "Marshall's the chaplain who serves my family."

It took Kiziah a few seconds before she understood what he was really saying. Shock coursed through her. Uncertainty. Confusion. "They expect us to get married? Now?"

Cable squeezed her hand. "You can say no. You can say you planned on a long engagement. They'll let you leave. Maybe even let you come back. They'll watch you to see if you're pregnant or not. But you'll be safe."

"And you'll be here."

"Yeah. I'll be here."

"And if I go through with the ceremony?"

He hesitated, but in the end he had to be honest with her. To allow her a solitary chance to escape. "Even then, there aren't any guarantees they'll let us leave, Zia." He rubbed his thumb over her knuckles. "They may still keep me here, they may keep us both."

"Why?"

Cable shook his head slightly, not willing to risk mentioning Fane despite Levant's agreement to allow them privacy. His brother's intentions would yield quickly to their father's command.

"I can't tell you. Not now." He cupped her breast, playing with the nipple Fane had loved so thoroughly. "I know it happened fast, Zia, but I can't imagine not having you in my life." His gaze met hers. "*We* could be happy together. Happier than we'd be separately."

Kiziah's cunt clenched, the emphasis on *we* and the way he was toying with her nipple a confirmation that their relationship would include Fane. She shivered and he leaned over her, kissing her, a tender joining as his hand glided over her abdomen. "I can't tell you the things I think you should know before we get hauled out of here for my father's version of a shotgun wedding. But I can tell you that if you say yes, I'll spend the rest of my life trying to make you happy."

His words rang in her ears, joined by the fortune-teller's admonishment to grasp and hold what fate would offer her. The Wheel of Fortune had stopped spinning, revealing a path, presenting a choice, and she could say *no* but the opportunity might disappear completely.

The door opened again. This time a different brother entered the room. He shook his head and smiled slightly when he saw that they were still on the bed, their clothing still undone. "Time to go. Marshall's here." He folded his arms over his chest, his stance an indication that he intended to wait for them.

"Your choice," Cable said, brushing his lips against Kiziah's before shifting position and zipping his pants, then sitting, using his body to shield hers so she could reorganize her clothing before they both got off the bed.

They held hands as they moved through the estate, Cable's other two brothers joining them before they left the secured section of the house. Closing ranks as though they were afraid their prisoners were going to make a break for it when they stepped through the courtyard door and into the sunshine.

For a minute Cable was overwhelmed by emotion. Christ! A part of him had felt like a condemned prisoner, afraid there were going to be endless years of being trapped in the tiny room.

Kiziah squeezed his hand and he looked at her, his heart turning over when he saw the concern and understanding in her eyes. *You okay?* she mouthed and he stopped so suddenly that his brother crashed into him and cursed, even as Cable's mouth was covering Kiziah's, his tongue stroking against hers as he held her against him.

Shit! He was losing it. Unraveling when he needed to hold it together.

He knew his father and brothers acted out of love and he couldn't hate them for it. But he also knew they wouldn't relent, wouldn't let him out of the compound until they believed that he was unavailable to Fane, or Fane was unavailable to him.

He hadn't realized how deeply the loss of freedom had affected him until he stepped outside and breathed in the crisp smell of late fall, felt the warmth of the sun as it kissed him.

Christ, if Kiziah said no... He didn't think he could walk quietly back to his cell and calmly accept his fate.

Chapter Nine

Kiziah's eyes burned with unshed tears as she became aware of the tiny tremors going through Cable's body. His turmoil reached inside her, taking her heart in a painful grip and squeezing mercilessly. She tightened her arms around his waist, hugging him, trying to convey with the slide of her tongue against his that she wouldn't abandon him.

Only when their lungs began to burn from lack of oxygen did they separate, and even then, only enough to breathe. She rubbed her cheek against his, enjoying the rough feel of stubble. "They're waiting for us in the chapel. The sooner we get through the ceremony, the sooner we can leave and start our unplanned honeymoon."

Relief rushed through Cable. Joy. Blocking his throat for a minute so words were impossible. When he could speak again, he laughed, a rough, husky sound. "Oh yeah, I think I'm ready for a honeymoon." He kissed her, a quick press of his lips to hers, and they resumed walking, hand-in-hand, not stopping until they stood at the front of the chapel.

The ceremony was simple. The words standard — though the way the chaplain emphasized *until death do you part* unnerved Kiziah, making her grip Cable's hand tightly as undercurrents swirled around her, chilling her.

There was nothing romantic about what happened in the chapel, no smiling faces or congratulatory hugs, even Cable's mother seemed tense and unhappy, worried, her gaze flicking back and forth between Cable and Kiziah, her eyes telegraphing a message that she wished they could talk together, but her husband's constant presence and the hand he kept on her arm made it clear that such a thing was impossible. Kiziah's hand shook slightly as she signed her name underneath Cable's in an old leather-bound book recording their marriage. Her nerves stretched to the breaking point when she was led into a small office off the main chapel, photographed and fingerprinted as though she were being identified and incarcerated for life.

"Can we go now?" she asked when it was done, her voice strained.

Cable tensed, his gaze shifting from the chaplain to his father. "My *wife* has gone through enough for one day. I assume you've seen everything you need to see and you don't need to witness our wedding night. I'd prefer not to spend it here if it's all the same to you."

The chaplain was the one to answer, shooting Cable's father a look as he said, "Our marriage vows are sacred and permanent, our protection extending to those taken as wives. I see no reason why Cable and his bride can't embark on a honeymoon."

Cable's father nodded stiffly. His body posture revealing that he wasn't happy about granting them freedom. But Cable and Kiziah didn't hesitate to make their escape.

"What about your car?" Kiziah asked a few moments later, after they'd cleared the gates of the estate, Cable driving her Suburban, their hands clasped.

"It's safe where it is. And besides that, we'll need this one to move your travel trailer." He squeezed her hand. "You know it can't stay at the campground?"

Kiziah shivered, the events of the day finally catching up with her. Even now, in her own car, she felt nervous, paranoid, worried that something would go wrong and they'd end up back in the small room with the deadbolts on the outside of the door. "Is it safe to talk?" she asked, thinking of the obvious wealth of Cable's family, the hallways full of priceless artwork, the doors she'd seen, with their keypads and coded locks. It was easy to imagine listening devices in the car.

Cable laughed, but the sound held no humor. "Probably. But it would be smarter to save the serious discussion for later." He rubbed his thumb over her knuckles. "I'm sorry you had to meet my family this way. Believe it or not, they're not always so intense—well, not my brothers anyway."

"But your father is."

"Oh yeah." Cable sighed, a deep unhappy exhalation and Kiziah knew he was thinking about Fane. "I'm the youngest, so he blames himself for the way I turned out."

"The male lovers?"

"My father views sexuality as a choice and according to him there is only *one* correct choice. Heterosexuality." He risked a glance at Kiziah. "Does it bother you?"

"That you've been with men?" *That I'll see you and Fane together?*

"Among other things."

"No. I haven't had a conventional upbringing. Will it bother you to go to psychic fairs with me or to know that's where I am? Around people who dabble in the supernatural?"

Cable tensed. Christ! They were going to have a battle on their hands when she tried to do that. And he'd be in the middle, seeing her side as well as Fane's.

Fane would never allow her to be in a place were the Believers might target her or where she might be caught in the crossfire. And even if their enemy wasn't present, he'd still forbid her from being in a place where he couldn't guard her personally. Vampires and dhampirs might associate with individuals who possessed supernatural abilities, but they didn't willingly wade into a crowd of them and advertise their existence.

He forced the tension from his body and pulled her hand into his lap, rubbing the back of it against his shirt-covered abdomen. "I'm glad you had the upbringing you did," he said, evading her question about attending psychic fairs. "I'm glad you're open to the possibility that there are…" He foundered, wondering if he should ask her if she believed in vampires. Wondering how much of her time with Fane she remembered.

He almost asked. He was desperate to bring the conversation fully out into the open. To hear her say she was willing to share a bed with Fane and him.

Would it turn her on to see Fane fucking him? To see him fucking Fane? Would she like having both of their cocks in her, knowing they enjoyed the feel of each other as much as they enjoyed being held in her hot depths?

Cable shifted their hands so that hers was pressed against his jeans-covered erection instead of his belly. Christ! He wanted to pull over and find a hotel room — or better yet, just pull over and fuck in the back of the Suburban.

"Zia," he warned when her hand wriggled away from his and went to his zipper.

She laughed, a husky sound that had him leaking, panting, grabbing his cock when the zipper slid down and his penis sprung free. "Put both hands on the steering wheel," she ordered, shocking herself with her sudden intention. *What was it about Cable that made her want to do things she'd never even fantasized about doing?*

"Fuck!"

But he obeyed. His abdomen becoming taut, his breathing ragged as she leaned over and touched her lips to his shaft. Nibbling along its length as he clenched his buttocks and pressed against her mouth.

She wanted to see Cable and Fane together, she wanted to have them both at the same time. The night with Fane might have seemed more like a dream than a reality, but it had fueled her fantasies. It had fueled something else too, the need to hold her own, to explore her own feminine power. To take as well as to give. To claim as well as to be claimed.

The car jerked and swerved, coming to a stop at the side of the road as Kiziah swirled her tongue around the sensitive tip of his penis, grasping his shaft in her hand before slowly allowing the head of his cock to push through firmed lips and enter her mouth. He shuddered as she began sucking him, laving him with her tongue. And she reveled in the way he cried out, in the way he panted and writhed, his groans becoming whispered pleas, filling her with wonder and pride that she could reduce him to begging. That she could give him so much pleasure.

Fire roared through Cable's shaft, hotter even than the vampire blood Fane had forced him to ingest. He wanted to spear his fingers into her hair and fuck in and out of her mouth, but his hands remained locked on the steering wheel, the fear that she'd stop what she was doing keeping them there.

"Christ, Zia!" he said, his spine arching, his head thrown back as he tried to drive his cock through her fist and into her throat. He wanted her to swallow him whole, to take everything he had to offer.

She responded by sucking harder, more aggressively, her moans joining his as she loosened her grip on his shaft and took him deeper.

Cable lost all control then, couldn't think beyond the wet heat of her mouth, the absolute ecstasy of what she was doing to him, his climax coming in a rush that left him dizzy and weak, hunched over the steering wheel with his eyes shut, his fingers still locked into position on the gray vinyl.

"Give me a minute and I'll take care of you," he managed, already imagining himself thrusting his tongue into her slit and feasting on her clit as mercilessly as she'd just taken his cock.

Kiziah cuddled against his side and put her head on his shoulder, laughing softly when she realized the Suburban's engine was still running. She traced her fingers over his abdomen, his sweat-slick shirt clinging to his skin. "It's almost dark. Let's wait until we get back to the house."

The words penetrated the thunder of Cable's heartbeat and the fog of pleasure in his mind. "House?"

She smiled against his shoulder. "I was there this morning, when I woke up—alone—and you weren't back yet."

Cable closed his eyes. Fuck. He wished he knew whether or not his brothers had planted a listening device in her car. He wanted to be able to talk to her without worrying about whether or not they were listening. He should have guessed that Fane wouldn't leave her at the campground—especially in a trailer that could be blown up or attacked.

"Is the Airstream parked at the house?"

"Yes."

He grimaced at the puzzlement he heard in her voice. Guessing that she didn't remember moving it.

She rubbed her cheek against his shoulder and sighed. "I need to get to Ashburg. My friends are probably starting to worry and my booth should already be set up. The psychic fair has started."

"I've got money to support us," he said, wanting to head off the confrontation he knew was coming.

She moved away so she could see his face, circling back to the very thing he wanted to avoid. Repeating her earlier question. "Will it bother you to go to psychic fairs with me?"

Cable zipped his pants, his cock protesting the confinement, willing to fill once again and offer Kiziah a different type of pleasure. He shifted the car into drive and pulled back onto the road, then reached for her hand. "We need to talk about that."

Now that they were married in the eyes of his order, he could share information with her without the risk of being sanctioned. Without worrying that it would put her in danger.

The vampires were merciless when it came to betrayal. The padralls were every bit as merciless when it came to maintaining secrecy. *Until death do us part* wasn't a figure of speech but a literal interpretation of the vows that bound the wives who hadn't been born into their world to their husbands. Women didn't leave and take their padrall sons with them. Widows didn't stay widows for long unless they were elderly, their trustworthiness proven over the course of long marriages.

Cable rubbed her hand against his leg, the nervous gesture making him grimace. "I don't know how we're going to work the psychic fair thing out," he admitted. "Do you remember the guy at the carnival?"

"The one the police found dead?"

"Yeah. He followed you after you left Madame Helki's tent. But you were never at risk."

She stiffened but didn't pull her hand from his, hesitated before asking, "Do you believe that supernatural...things can exist?"

A startled laugh escaped before Cable could suppress it. She tried to pull her hand away. He tightened his grip. "Sorry, you surprised me. I was going to ask you the same thing." He risked a glance at her, cringing inwardly when he saw her disbelieving expression. "I mean it. Now tell me why you asked."

When she didn't answer he contemplated pulling to the side of the road and seducing her back into the easy companionship they'd been enjoying. Instead he pressed the back of her hand to his mouth, nibbling on it. "Please, Zia."

"You'll laugh again."

"No I won't. Promise." He squeezed her hand.

She sighed and admitted, "I don't remember leaving the carnival. I still don't remember it. There's just an impression of obsidian eyes. Then I was on a dark street and the man with the tattoo on his neck was following me. I started running. I felt...a presence...then it was gone and he was gone."

Cable rubbed the back of her hand against his cheek. "He was part of a secret society that kills people who aren't 'human' enough to suit them. They call themselves True Believers. Most of the American members seem to favor the crucifix tattoo on their neck." He risked another glance, saw Kiziah's wariness and added, "That's why I was going to ask you if you believed supernatural things could exist."

Her eyebrows drew together. "You said I was never at risk. You knew about the presence?"

"His name is Domino Santori. For better or worse, you'll probably end up meeting him."

The fortune-teller's reading came instantly to mind. And Kiziah could see now that it held so many different meanings. Not just accepting Fane and Cable as lovers, or dealing with the strange swirling undercurrents of Cable's family, but embracing the supernatural in a way that was more personal than anything she'd known.

Despite a childhood spent among psychics and witches, charlatans and true believers, she didn't consider herself blessed with any true power or ability. Even the awareness of the supernatural she possessed, she attributed to having grown up accepting it rather than denying and blocking it.

But almost from the first moment her life had intersected Cable's, the instant she'd emerged from Madame Helki's tent as he was contemplating entering it, she'd come into contact with one supernatural force after another. The presence on the darkened street, Domino, what she'd felt when they visited Matteo and Sarael, and then last night—with Fane.

"Are you a warlock?" she asked and Cable choked back a startled laugh.

"No."

"What about…" She stopped before she said Fane. "What are you then?"

"Just a man, Zia. Your husband." He squeezed her hand. "I can't tell you anything more right now. But I meant what I said before they dragged us to the chapel. I'll spend the rest of my life trying to make you happy."

"I believe you," Kiziah said, snuggling against his side, pressing a kiss to his cheek.

They drove in silence after that, both of them aware of the rapidly darkening sky, but for different reasons.

Kiziah's thoughts were on the psychic fair, on the dreamcatchers she'd spent long hours creating in order to have them ready for this particular event, the friends she'd looked forward to seeing, on Margo and Walt who were expecting her and would start to worry if she didn't call them soon and tell them she was okay.

Cable's thoughts were on Fane. On what would happen when they got to the house.

His cock was hard and his conscience was in overdrive. He could rationalize not talking about Fane, not warning Kiziah. He could tell himself that he didn't dare say anything for fear that his brothers were following them, listening in to the conversation, prepared to swoop in. But it didn't ease the ache in his heart. The worry that she'd feel betrayed. That she'd be terrified in the moment when she realized what Fane was.

With the third exchange of blood the three of them would be able to touch each others' thoughts and memories, to communicate without words, to feel each others' emotions. She'd know the agony he'd experienced at each point where his decision brought her a step further into his world.

He wanted to believe she'd forgive him. He thought she would. But he found the prospect of her fear and pain intolerable.

"Do you believe in vampires?" he asked, the words tumbling out, pushed by conscience as the last turn before Fane's driveway came into sight.

Kiziah jerked in reaction. Her eyes meeting his in the mirror, and Cable eased the car to the side of the road so he could turn and face her. Knowing in that instant that this had to be her choice too.

"Is that what Domino is?" she asked, the steadiness of her voice giving him hope.

"Almost."

She frowned but let it pass. "Matteo and Sarael?"

"Matteo. Sarael's still partly human. She'll always be partly human." He leaned forward and rubbed his cheek against hers, a small measure of relief filling him at the unexpected opportunity to provide her with information. "Sarael can go out in the sunlight, she eats like she always has, but she needs Matteo's blood to survive. Just his. She's got a foot in both worlds. It's the only way vampires can reproduce. They're not humans who have died and risen from the grave, they're a different species altogether."

Kiziah closed her eyes and Cable grimaced. Christ. Hearing himself say it out loud made *him* sound crazy.

For a moment, a bubble of hysteria formed in Kiziah's chest. For a split second she wondered if she'd somehow stumbled down the rabbit hole into an alternate reality—or worse, that she'd reached such a desperate state of loneliness that she was willing to believe anything in order to share her life with a man.

But just as quickly as those thoughts rose, memories of the dream which had sent her to Madame Helki's tent in the first place pushed them away. Whether it was fate or her mother's hand, something had set her on this course and she *was* well suited for it— if she had the courage to continue.

Cable had stopped here to give her a choice. Just as he'd done on the way to the chapel. He hadn't intended for her to be pulled into his world. She was sure of that. She was equally sure that he was trying to do the right thing, his honor and integrity shining through.

She made an intuitive leap then, her heart racing as she replayed what he'd just said. *Sarael's still partly human… It's the only way vampires can reproduce.*

If she hadn't been with Fane already, she might have been angry, offended. Terrified at what lay ahead.

She took a deep breath, the movement making her aware of her love-bruised nipples and causing heat to curl in Kiziah's belly at the reminder of how thoroughly Fane had dominated her the previous night, how possessive his expression had been while he was doing it. He might have agreed to include her because he wanted children, but last night hadn't been about reproduction.

And yet she wanted to know she wasn't something to be used and then disposed of. "If Sarael has to have Matteo's blood in order to live, what happens if he grows tired of her?"

Cable's laugh held honest amusement, though the look in his eyes told Kiziah he understood what she was really asking. "A vampire and his kadine…his wife…are sexually bonded to one another. They're almost one person."

He hesitated and Kiziah thought he was going to say more. When he didn't she reached over and unbuttoned the first few buttons on Cable's shirt, opening it to expose the love bite on Cable's neck. Now that she was studying it closely, she could see the faint hint of fang marks.

Color rushed to her face along with the memory of being required to strip in front of Cable's father and brothers. Realization dawned. They were making sure she hadn't been bitten by Fane as well. Perhaps wondering if she'd been sent to try and "break Cable out of prison".

Kiziah had to smile at the thought, though she shivered just thinking about the small room with the deadbolt lock on the outside. Her fingers went to the bite mark and Cable jerked, his body going tense, his breathing changing with a sharp inhalation that had Kiziah looking down at his lap.

A fierce rush of desire swamped her when she saw his hand gripping his jeans-covered erection. Blood pooled in her labia and she knew the time for questions was nearly over. She wanted him.

She wanted Fane. She could guess what was going to happen when they got to the house, but she wanted to hear it confirmed.

"You said Sarael's still partly human. Does that mean she used to be completely human? Did it take three exchanges of blood to do it?" she asked, pinching the love bite between her fingers and growing hotter when she saw how it affected Cable. How his face went taut and his eyes closed, his tiny male nipples tightening into hard points as his hand squeezed his cock.

"Yes, and yes," he answered, nearly panting. His arousal fueling her own so that she leaned in and pressed her lips to his, the kiss becoming so carnal that within seconds her shirt and bra were open and his hand was on her breast, mercilessly driving her higher with his assault on her nipple.

When their mouths parted, it was Kiziah who whispered, "Let's get to the house so we can start our honeymoon."

Chapter Ten

Fane sensed that Cable was near and settled on the couch to wait, his cock protesting the position, but he was tired of prowling and stalking around the house. It did nothing to relieve the tension. In fact, it only seemed to escalate it, leaving him feeling like a caged beast.

He needed to fuck. He needed to feed.

And his body didn't particularly care which order he did it, though his mind knew it mattered. He had to maintain control, to wait long enough to find out what Cable had learned from the Santori histories.

And if Cable was alone? If Kiziah wasn't with him?

Fane hissed, erupting from the chair and going to the front door, only barely able to stop himself from flinging it open and waiting outside. Irritation moved through him. He didn't trust Cable's family. They might well have surveillance equipment in place, knowing that if such equipment was discovered they could claim it was done for Cable and Fane's protection. He couldn't risk advertising his presence, not tonight.

They'd be gone from this place tomorrow. Safely housed in a secluded rental near Ashburg.

Fane's cock pulsed in warning and he gripped it through his jeans. Wishing he knew how far away Cable was and whether Kiziah was with him. He wasn't surprised there'd been no call. He hadn't expected Cable to risk one, especially if it had been difficult escaping his father's estate. Still, Fane's resolve not to go outside, not to rush, was tested when he heard the sound of the Suburban's engine and guessed they were together.

It seemed to take forever for them to park and get out of the car, each moment of their delay increasing the hunger in Fane, the need. The anticipation of what was to come.

The smell of sex assaulted him as soon as Cable and Kiziah came into the house. The scent of it triggering primitive impulses which were impossible for Fane to control. He crowded them, his attention split for an instant between the two of them before he pressed Cable against the back of the door and fused their mouths together in a kiss that was part relief and part carnal intent.

It turned Kiziah on to witness it. It shocked her just how much she liked watching their hands roam and seeing how they ate hungrily at each other's mouths.

She was primed for this. Primed for them. Wet. Swollen. Achy from pleasuring Cable in the car but insisting they wait until they were back at the house before doing more.

With a groan Fane released Cable and turned, reaching for Kiziah and wrenching open her shirt and bra before pulling her against him, pausing long enough to allow Cable to move in behind her and gather her hair to the side, exposing her smooth neck. Fane captured her lips, one of his hands going to Cable's side while the other covered her breast.

White-hot need poured into Kiziah, sliding along her tongue and down her throat, blossoming from her nipples and streaking to her swollen cunt and engorged clit. Fane's kiss alone was enough to make her whimper, but the feel of Cable's mouth on her neck was sweet torture.

She shivered in anticipation when Cable released the catches on her skirt and it dropped to her ankles in a pool of color. Her breath caught in her throat when his hands moved around, forcing their way between Fane and her in order to unzip Fane's jeans. All three of them moaning when Fane's cock sprung free to be captured by one of Cable's hands while Cable's other slid into Kiziah's panties, his fingers brushing over her clit on their way to her opening.

Christ! It was hard for Cable to think about anything beyond somehow getting their clothes off and his cock inside of Kiziah while Fane did the same. He was about to come just from grinding against her buttocks, from pumping his hand up and down Fane's shaft while his fingers fucked in and out of Kiziah.

He lifted his mouth from her neck just as Fane's lips left hers, their eyes meeting, Fane's full of the same wildness Cable had seen on the night Fane forced him into the first exchange of blood. "Do it," Cable said. "It has to be done before we can go any further. Just don't come."

Fane's nostrils flared in reaction to the words. Savage victory filling his eyes. "It was in the histories?"

"Yeah."

Fane needed no further urging. He leaned forward and pressed a kiss to Cable's lips before returning to Kiziah's, thrusting his tongue against hers, every cell in his body screaming for him to allow his fangs to descend.

This time when the kiss ended he went to her neck, tempting himself with the siren call of her blood, the pounding, erratic beat of her pulse against his lips. His fangs slid free, but he didn't give in to the urge to sink them into her delicate neck. Her nipples lured him and he lowered his mouth to them, the change in position forcing him to take his own cock in hand, but it increased his excitement to have Cable's hand move to her breast, to cup it as Fane laved and sucked a nipple that still bore the marks of his attention the night before.

Kiziah's moans and the scent of her arousal tested Fane's control. The knowledge that her reactions were freely given, a result of what they were doing to her and not enthrallment was a powerful aphrodisiac.

With a groan, Fane forced his mouth away from her nipple. His cock was engorged past anything he'd ever known. His balls full and aching. He tightened his grip on his penis and closed his eyes against the rush of need pulsing through his shaft.

A tremor of fear moved through him. *Don't come*, Cable had said.

Fane knew it would take every ounce of control he possessed in order to avoid spewing his seed—both in the instant he sank his fangs into Kiziah and in the instant when he pressed her mouth to his chest and their fate was sealed with the first swallow.

He delayed by removing her shoes and stockings, mesmerized by the sight of Cable's hand disappearing into the feminine scrap of black material, The Heat burning hotter with the sounds of her soft gasps as Cable's palm grazed her clit and his fingers slipped in and out of her slit.

One again Fane took his cock in hand, tightening his grip to the point of pain. A reminder. A warning. He couldn't come. "Slide them down," he growled, The Heat roaring through him when Cable complied, sending her shirt and bra as well as her panties to the floor so that she stood naked between them.

It was more than Fane could bear. He leaned in, his mouth going to her wet folds, his tongue fucking into her channel, tasting Cable as well as Kiziah.

His! The single word reverberating through every cell in his body, along every nerve ending. With every heartbeat. His! Both of them were his!

It was a primitive chant. A thunderous demand.

A compulsion more powerful than even the strongest vampire's. To take. To dominate. To possess.

Kiziah writhed between them, bombarded by sensation. Reduced to a sensual being whose only reality was the pleasure her lovers were giving her.

Her whimpers turned to cries and then to a litany of pleas. She begged for release and Fane gave it to her. His mouth going to her clit, sucking the small organ, torturing it with his tongue until she climaxed, flooding his senses with her orgasm.

Fane pulled her leg over his shoulder then, his nostrils flaring at the arousal coating her inner thigh, his heart beating in the same wild rhythm as hers. She jerked when his fangs slid through skin, but she didn't fight him, and soon she was burying her fingers in his hair, holding him to her as he took her life's blood.

Fane consumed her, devoured her, lost himself for long moments as The Heat and The Hunger merged, becoming one in a way that only occurred with a bride, a kadine, a lover who would be bound to a vampire for centuries. It was a dark ecstasy like no other, to take from a willing partner until their heart stuttered in warning, to know the pleasure he gave them was so great that they'd trade their lives for his bite.

He very nearly killed her. But the touch of Cable's hand on his face, Cable's urgent, "Christ, Fane, stop!" pulled him from the darkness of his own primitive nature.

Fane ran his tongue over the bite, sealing it, though satisfaction rippled through him with the knowledge that the mark would remain until the claiming was finished. He rose, his gaze taking in her closed eyes and pale features, her shallow breathing—Cable's angry, worried expression as he held Kiziah upright.

With a sharp mental command, Fane summoned a knife from a table in the living room, grasping it when it came to his command, using it to open a wound in his chest before pressing Kiziah's mouth to the opening. Both he and Cable coaxing her to drink with murmured words and soothing strokes, both of them filling with relief as she responded, taking from Fane as he'd taken from her.

When it was done, Cable swung Kiziah into his arms and carried her to the bedroom, gently placing her on the bed and coming down after her. "Okay?" he asked between kisses.

Kiziah laughed, joy filling her heart at the caring she saw on his face. "It wasn't horrifying at all."

"Good," Fane growled, dropping to her side, his expression fierce, though she saw a hint of worry in his eyes.

She smiled and brushed her fingertips across his lips. "How come I'm the only one naked?"

Something dark and feral moved through Fane's eyes and her body tightened in reaction, blood rushing to her labia, filling her cunt lips, making her restless to spread her legs. And as if scenting her renewed arousal, Fane's nostrils flared, his lips parted slightly, the hint of fangs causing her nipples to bead and her clit to stand erect, to throb against the rough texture of Cable's jeans.

She shivered when Fane's hand moved to Cable's back, tracing his spine and causing Cable to pump against her in reaction, to groan and say, "Christ, my cock is about to explode."

"Let's finish what we started then," Fane said, rolling from the bed and removing his clothing, his cock bobbing in greeting when Kiziah's gaze focused on it.

Kiziah sat up when Cable stood in order to strip, her hand going to Fane's cock, her thumb teasing over the flushed, full head as she drew him to her. He grabbed her wrist as though he was going to stop her then hissed as if the thought of losing her touch was more than he could stand.

Feminine satisfaction filled Kiziah and she leaned forward, intent on taking him into her mouth, but Cable stopped her, his laugh husky as he pulled her away, positioning her so that she was on top of him, his cock a hard, demanding presence against her mound. "He can't come until we're both inside you, Zia. That's why I was at my family's compound, to research how the three of us can be together."

Cable shifted, impaling her with a single thrust and making her cry out in pleasure. She shivered when his hands went to her buttocks, tensed when Fane positioned himself behind her. "Relax," Cable said, kissing her, luring her tongue into his mouth as Fane's hands went to her breasts, the two of them building the heat into an inferno of need so that Kiziah was once again writhing between them, pleading with her body for them to take her, to satisfy her, to claim her as theirs.

They commanded the pleasure and she went where they took her, loving the intimacy, the knowledge that they needed her just as much as she'd come to need them. She whimpered when Fane's penis slipped into her back entrance, cried when he was all the way in, the pain-pleasure of the dual penetration, the fullness, the feel of their cocks rubbing against each other while they fucked a dark enthrallment that she'd forever crave. The shared release a pinnacle beyond anything she'd ever dreamed was possible.

* * * * *

Kiziah woke between two warm male bodies and stretched, smiling when she realized that she wasn't sore even though she should have been. Oh yeah, she should have been. In the last couple of days she'd had more sex in more ways then she'd had over the rest of her life put together.

It was daytime. She knew it even though the windows were covered with heavy drapes.

Fane stirred and she turned on her side, running her hand over his chest, unconsciously looking for the place where he'd cut himself before pressing her lips to his skin. He stirred again and her gaze shifted lower, to his cock. Her hand followed and his eyes slitted open.

"You're awake," she said, sensing that she had the advantage for a change.

"The Sleep doesn't hold me completely yet." His face tightened as his cock pulsed against her fingers. "Straddle me, Kiziah."

She laughed. A husky sound of feminine power.

He hissed, flashing his fangs, but the sight of them only made her feel more reckless.

Kiziah slid her leg over him, pressed her mound against his erection and measured it with the rub of her clit along his engorged flesh. "I'm entitled to some answers. Can you go out in the sun?"

He jerked and hissed, but he answered her question. "Not in this form."

"What form then?"

"Mist. Particles in the air."

Lips brushed across Kiziah's shoulder. A hand reached around to cup her breast and tweak her nipple. Cable. "I'll answer your questions later, Zia. Hurry up and fuck him. I want my turn while The Sleep tames him."

The comment brought a dark look to Fane's face, a promise of retribution to his eyes that sent a gush of arousal from Kiziah's swollen pussy. She shifted, reaching down and guiding Fane's cock to her wet, ready entrance, teasing him until he surged upward and filled her completely, taking control, teaching her that *tame* wasn't a word she could apply to him.

He commanded her body and it obeyed him, he made her beg and she did it, but it was a sweet surrender that left her sated as she slipped to Fane's side, content to watch as Cable pinned Fane's wrists to the mattress before covering Fane's body with his own, the kiss they shared an aggressive duel, a struggle until a hidden accord was reached between the two of them and Fane spread his legs so that Cable's cock could lodge in his back entrance.

In a heartbeat, the need for release returned and Kiziah's hand went to her cunt, her fingers stroking her clit and plunging into her channel in time with Cable's thrusts. She whimpered as they moaned, her breath grew short, matching their pants, her body arching and straining for relief as their movements became violent. Until finally she cried out as they did, lost in a haze of satisfaction.

Kiziah closed her eyes and snuggled against Fane as Cable left the bed, and then against Cable when he returned from the bathroom, fresh from a shower and Fane rose, his movements echoing the lethargy Kiziah was starting to feel. The heavy need to sleep that was beginning to press down on her. Unnatural in its intensity.

She became aware of the burning in her veins and her heart rate jumped in response. A moment of alarm, a tremor of fear moved through her when it took every ounce of willpower she possessed to open her eyes and sit up.

As though sensing her distress, Cable rose and helped her to her feet, holding her against him. "It'll get easier, especially once you're out in the sun."

"This is The Sleep?"

"A diluted version of it."

A few minutes later, Fane stepped out of the bathroom, his skin still glistening, as though he'd only taken enough time to hastily dry himself. "We can't stay here," he said, his attention directed at Cable. "Domino's rented a place outside of Ashburg. I left the directions with the car keys. He's already there." Fane's lips quirked upward. "As is the carnival apparently."

"You'll sleep on the way there?" Cable asked. "We could tow the Airstream."

"Leave it. And check the car in case your family is monitoring your movements and conversations."

Cable grimaced and nodded. Kiziah started to say something about visiting her friends at the psychic fair but thought better of it when she remembered the conversation she'd had with Cable.

Though she'd only been with Fane and Cable a short time, of the two of them, she already knew Cable was the most reasonable, the one who was more likely to bend, to compromise. The one most likely to tell her what she needed to know in order to warn the people who were like family to her.

True, the people she'd grown up among were used to being careful, to dealing with those who didn't approve of their lifestyles and abilities. She'd never been to a psychic fair where hellfire-and-damnation protestors weren't gathered outside, chanting and carrying placards. But if the danger this time was greater, the threat of physical harm more real, then she would do what she could to protect her friends.

A shiver moved down her spine. A realization.

Was this why the dream of Madame Helki's tent had been sent to her? Why she'd been set on this path?

"Hey, you still awake?" Cable teased, gently shaking Kiziah and making her aware of how completely she'd been lost in her thoughts.

"Just thinking." She glanced at Fane and tensed when she saw his expression. His dark eyes were boring into her, so focused that she had the fleeting impression he was trying to read her mind. "I think I'll take a shower," she said.

Cable pressed a quick kiss to her shoulder. "I'll scrounge up something to eat. See you in the kitchen."

The mention of food had Kiziah's gaze flicking back to Fane's face. The dark intensity had been replaced by the gleam of anticipation. "It will be difficult, but I can last until tonight," he said, making her womb flutter and her nipples tighten with his slow perusal of her body.

She escaped to the bathroom, laughing at herself when moments later she started wishing that Fane or Cable, or both, had followed her into the shower. Sex under steamy hot water had always been a fantasy of hers. But given the dimensions of the stall in the travel trailer, she wouldn't have even considered trying it there.

As the water cascaded over her, she inventoried what she wanted to take from the Airstream. She assumed they'd come back and get it later, but she could see the wisdom of not taking it with them.

Even under the hot blast of the shower, she felt chilled just thinking about her trip to Cable's family estate. It wasn't difficult to imagine them putting devices in the cars and continuing to watch until they were sure Fane wasn't around — or until it was too late to do anything about the situation.

Kiziah closed her eyes. Once again seeing the anticipation glittering in Fane's eyes. Hearing his words as his gaze traveled over her body, settling for an instant on the bruised bite he'd left on her inner thigh.

She'd had no idea just how intensely erotic it would be, how the place where his fangs had pierced would become an erogenous zone. If she stood under the shower much longer, allowing the hot water to strike the mark, she'd end up masturbating until she came and even then it wouldn't be enough. She'd end up back in bed all day and then all night. They couldn't afford for that to happen. They needed to get to Ashburg.

Kiziah forced herself to leave the shower, to dry off and return to the bedroom. A smile formed when she saw that Cable had gone out to the travel trailer and brought in a selection of clothing for her to choose from. She went for comfort — jeans, a blue flannel shirt, tennis shoes — then located Cable assembling sandwiches at the kitchen counter.

"Thanks for getting my clothes," she said, slipping her arms around his waist and hugging her front to his back.

"It was a sacrifice. I'd rather keep you naked."

She laughed and rubbed her cheek against his back. "Where's Fane?"

Cable pressed the top piece of bread to the sandwich he was making and then turned in her arms, a small, worried frown on his face. "Can't you feel him?"

And she did. Not in a location that could be pinpointed, but more in a general sense, a possessive presence that hovered around them. "He's in his other form?"

"Yeah, he can remain awake that way. Otherwise he'd be crashed on the bed. Some of the really, really old vampires can fight The Sleep in their human form and move around inside a dark house during the daytime." Cable grinned. "But Fane's just a babe."

Kiziah snickered. "You're a babe too."

Cable nibbled on her bottom lip. "I'm crazy about you, Zia. You know that, right?"

"The feeling's mutual."

They ate and afterward Cable disappeared into the bedroom in order to pack clothing for himself and Fane. Kiziah took care of the few dishes they'd dirtied, then decided to get the Suburban packed with the clothes and dreamcatchers she wanted to take with her.

The first hint of trouble came when she stepped outside and the air around her began vibrating with menace. Her heart jerked, shooting adrenaline through her veins, and she actually turned to get back into the sanctuary of the house, but as she stepped through the doorway, she realized the source of her fear. Fane. Who apparently didn't want her to leave the house.

"I'm just going out to pack the car," she said, feeling self-conscious about talking to thin air.

The menace intensified as soon as she stepped back outside, an unseen presence that swirled angrily around her as she transferred everything she needed from the Airstream to the Suburban, coming across a package that had gotten relocated to the backseat when they abandoned Cable's car at his father's estate and drove away in hers. A package she'd promised to deliver to a shop in Waynesville when she passed through on the way to the psychic fair.

Kiziah looked up when Cable emerged from the house carrying a couple of suitcases, her heart spasming at the frown that immediately formed on his face when he saw her at the Suburban. "We're taking the sports car," he said, nodding to the much smaller black car—Fane's probably since they'd left Cable's behind.

"I don't want to be stranded, Cable. I'm sure there are going to be times when you need to be off doing errands." She wasn't about to bring up visiting the fair or the campground where many of her friends would be staying.

Cable grimaced and she imagined he was feeling the same lash of frustrated anger from Fane that she was. "I can understand that, Zia, but..."

She gave a slight shake of her head. Glad that if they were going to have a first fight, that it would be outside in the sunlight, where it would remain one-against-one instead of two-against-one.

She might be at a disadvantage, not understanding much about Fane and Cable's world, but she didn't intend to be made a prisoner of it. "We can stay within sight of each other. We can talk on the cell phones."

"Christ, Zia," he said and she could hear in his voice that he really did understand and that he wasn't going to try and force her into the sports car.

She left the protection of the heavy Suburban and went to him, putting her arms around his neck and pressing her lips to his. He dropped the suitcases and pulled her into a hug. "This is going to make things very intense later."

"I'll deal with later when it gets here."

"Easy for you say." His grip tightened momentarily. "It may get rough. Will you be able to handle that, Zia?"

She shivered, the images coming to her mind so erotic that her cunt and clit responded in a flash of heat and blood. "Will you?"

He laughed. Husky, masculine. "It's different for me."

"Then I'll deal with later when it gets here," she repeated before stepping away from him.

Chapter Eleven

They traveled to Waynesville without any sign of being followed, Kiziah and Cable talking on cell phones, laughing and teasing mostly, though Kiziah used some of the time to find out more about the world she was now a part of, about vampires and dhampirs, kadines and padralls—and especially about the Believers.

Her heart ached when Cable told her about the death of Fane's family. Her stomach tightened with fear for the safety of those attending the psychic fair and she almost suggested they forget about stopping to deliver the package, but she'd promised, and it would only take a few minutes to accomplish.

The small shop she needed to visit was in an old section of town, redone to attract tourists who came for the picturesque setting and the chance to marvel over the beauty of autumn. The street was lined with cars, though the sidewalks were empty save for a handful of elderly artists with their canvases lined up, each of them painting their interpretation of a fountain turned green with time.

A burst of warmth blossomed in Kiziah's chest when Cable got out of the sports car and immediately jogged the block that separated them, pulling her into a hug and kissing her, Fane's irritable presence hovering around them. "You need help carrying anything?" Cable asked.

"No, thanks. I can manage it." She glanced at the coffee shop down the street. "But I wouldn't mind having a mocha." She gave him a teasing smile. "And take *him* with you. Please! I thought I was going to suffocate in the car."

Cable's gaze traveled the length of the street as the air around them thickened with Fane's dislike of the idea of them separating. "Or we could deliver your package and then go for coffee together."

"That's fine too."

Cable grimaced. "I have this overpowering compulsion not to let you out of my sight. And it's not my own."

"I know, but I don't think we were followed."

"We weren't."

"Then why don't we do the most efficient thing. You get us some coffee and I'll run into the shop. Whoever gets done first can meet the other one."

Cable sighed, knowing there were going to be consequences, most of them falling on Kiziah—for traveling in two cars, for stopping in Waynesville and for separating—all when Fane wanted them to go directly to Ashburg.

He'd been with Fane longer. He understood the nature of vampires better than Kiziah did. He'd downplayed it when he and Kiziah talked as they drove, but he knew exactly how closely the three of them would be bonded once the third exchange of blood had taken place, just as he knew that with each exchange of blood, Fane's ability to command them would increase.

He also knew that Kiziah's freedom would soon be curtailed more than his own would ever be. Fane could turn off the dominant tendencies when it came to him, but with Kiziah, Fane was hard-wired not to relent. He was hard-wired to be possessive, protective. And the death of Fane's family, especially his mother, had only escalated the need in Fane.

Cable rubbed his cheek against Kiziah's hair. It was probably a mistake, but he wanted to give her a chance to go about life as though everything was normal—or as normal as it could be with the menacing presence of Fane hovering around them. "Meet you in the coffee shop or back here," he said, kissing her before traveling the half a block to a shop that reminded him of the one where he and Kiziah had met.

He placed his order and paid, then stepped aside, smiling as he thought about Madame Helki's reading and how it had led to Kiziah. How it had led to something he'd never even considered possible. Christ, he still couldn't believe she'd come into their lives, adapting and accepting not only Fane and him as lovers, but everything else as though she'd been born into it, created for it.

The coffee shop door opened and Cable looked up, fear rippling down his spine when he saw his two oldest brothers stepping inside. Fuck! He'd been sure they weren't being followed. He'd been thorough when he checked the cars.

"We can do this the easy way or the hard way," Levant said as he and Priest took up positions on either side of Cable. "We're going to make a quick trip to the bathroom together."

For a split second Cable considered throwing a punch and trying to escape, but worry for Kiziah kept him from doing it. His brothers had probably recognized her Suburban, but he didn't think they'd ever seen Fane's sports car. He couldn't be sure whether or not they knew Kiziah was here too, and down the street. If this was just about him, then he was safe. They wouldn't find additional bite marks on him. But one look at Kiziah's inner thigh…

"You're pushing the limits of brotherly love," Cable said, allowing himself to be guided into the bathroom, hoping that the sooner they saw he was "clean" the sooner they'd let him go.

"You know what we want," Levant said, following Cable into the small room and closing the door while Priest stood guard outside.

Cable stripped out of his shirt, turning without being told. "Why are you doing this?"

"To give Dad piece of mind."

"Wasn't the shotgun wedding enough for him?"

"Let's just get this over with. If your new wife is bite-free, the two of you can go about your business."

Cable's heart squeezed with panic. His stomach tightened. So they knew Kiziah was in town. "She's not stripping again in front of you."

"You're right. She's not. Deacon's collecting her. If you hurry then we'll take you to where she'll be so you can ease her through it while Deacon checks her."

Rage flashed through Cable and this time he did take a swing, his fist connecting solidly with Levant's stomach and making his brother grunt and curse before he returned the favor, his knuckles slamming into Cable's gut as he ducked a second punch.

The fight was over as soon as Priest waded in, making it two against one and forcing Cable to relent. His thoughts churning violently, swirling with the desire to get to Kiziah. He jerked his pants down, his breath heaving in and out of his chest as his body vibrated with tension. It took only a second for Levant to nod, acknowledging that they were done.

The three of them left the bathroom then, drawing a disgusted curse from a male customer and an embarrassed gasp from a woman. Another time, Cable might have found the reddening of Levant's face amusing, but not now, not when his thoughts centered on Kiziah.

Christ! He wanted to pound his brothers into the ground even though he knew they were just following his father's orders. "If Deacon scares her…" Cable said, a new fear forming when he realized how quickly the sky was darkening. How close they were to Fane being able to take his human shape.

"She's been through the routine before," Levant said and Cable's nostrils flared at the reminder of what had happened at the estate.

"Not too smart reminding him of that," Priest said, slowing to let Cable exit the coffee shop first, all three of them aware that Cable wouldn't try to escape if Deacon had Kiziah.

Kiziah knew she needed to make a run for it as soon as the bells over the entranceway of the shop signaled a new arrival and she looked up to see Cable's brother stepping inside. She didn't need the heavy pressure of Fane at her back to get her moving. Though she had the presence of mind to lean forward and whisper to the elderly woman on the other side of the counter, "Don't call the police. He's my brother-in-law," before bolting for the curtained doorway to the left of the counter and exiting through a back door she knew existed from her previous visits to the shop.

Footsteps sounded behind her. Cable's brother said, "Priest and Levant have Cable," but she didn't turn around.

Panic set in.

She was running as fast as she could but she knew that if she made it to the car she'd never get the door open and get in before he was on top of her. She couldn't afford to be caught and forced to strip. She didn't dare let them find Fane's bite.

Guilt filled Kiziah in a leap of intuition. They'd probably searched her car while it was parked in front of their family's estate. They would have found fliers about the psychic fair, fliers about the dreamcatchers she made. It wouldn't have taken a great leap to guess where she and Cable might go, or that they might stop in Waynesville to deliver the package that had been sitting in the passenger seat.

As she ran, her fear grew with the awareness of the rapidly approaching dusk. She could imagine what Fane's reaction would be when he took his human shape. His fury was already a tangible thing in the air around her, and despite everything, Kiziah knew that Cable loved his brothers.

She swerved into an alleyway, a tight narrow place not meant for anything other than trash cans and dumpsters. A cramp in her side made her gasp, and she knew she couldn't keep running.

Kiziah pulled her keys from her pocket, fisting her fingers around them before she stopped and doubled over, the hand containing the keys going to her knee while the other hand clutched her side. She didn't try to lessen the sound of her panting or keep the small whimpers of pain from escaping as Cable's brother rushed toward her.

At least there's only one of them. At least I have a chance.

One chance.

Within seconds he was next to her. His hand lightly grasping her shoulder as he moved around to stand in front of her, his legs slightly apart, his stance wide enough for her attack.

She struck without warning. The hand on her knee swinging upward, her fist striking his testicles with the precision of a boxer.

He dropped to his knees in an agonized moan and she fled, feeling guilty even as she rushed to the car and scrambled inside, shoving the keys into the ignition.

Shock jolted through Cable when he saw Kiziah run out of the alleyway and make it to the Suburban. A single thought formed and his body acted on it instantly. He ran, meeting Kiziah halfway down the street and sliding into the driver's seat while the car was still moving, the shift from her hands on the steering wheel to his, her foot on the pedal to his, smooth considering they weren't stunt doubles in an action movie.

"You okay?" he asked, feeling the tremor as her hand rested on his thigh.

"I am now."

Fane's energy hovered around them, a boiling mass of furious intent.

"Then let's get out of here," Cable said, covering her hand with his, squeezing it as they escaped the small town and raced for sanctuary in Ashburg.

* * * * *

Cable groaned when they got to the house and went inside, only to find Domino leaning against the wall in the hallway. Christ! Domino on a good day was enough to stir Fane's temper. And this day had gone rapidly downhill almost from the moment they'd left bed.

"This is Domino," Cable said and Kiziah shivered, looking at the man who'd been able to hypnotize her and compel her to leave the carnival, who'd made her bait for the Believer. She gasped when Fane shimmered into existence at her side. His body hard and firm. Naked. Aroused.

Domino straightened away from the wall, his gaze traveling over the three of them but coming to a rest on Fane, his eyebrows arching. "I see The Heat hasn't lessened its grip on you my friend, so I'll be quick—not that the sight of you fucking your kadine wouldn't be a tempting entertainment for me. She is beautiful." His teeth flashed. "And of course, Cable has his own charms, though they are outside my experience and inclinations."

"What do you want, Domino?" Fane asked.

"Only to tell you that the rest of us have managed to eliminate a large number of our enemy and will continue to hunt while you attend to other matters."

"And the one who calls himself The Apostle?"

The amusement left Domino's face. "Your revenge can wait until you've gained control of The Heat and The Hunger."

"You know where to find him?"

"Not yet."

"He's mine to destroy," Fane said.

"Understood. But you've only just gone through The Transformation. The temptation will be too great right now. You can no longer kill as a dhampir can." Domino's gaze shifted to encompass Cable and Kiziah. "The consequences of your actions don't fall solely to you any longer."

Fane hissed. A frustrated, angry sound. "You'll tell me when you find him?"

Domino took several long seconds before answering. "I'll tell you only after the third exchange has been made and the urges of our ancestors have been leashed by the taking of a kadine and a companion." Amusement once again flashed in obsidian eyes as Domino's gaze dropped to Fane's erection and his eyebrows went up. "As you're already primed for the task, I'll leave you to it."

"An excellent idea," Cable said, reaching around Kiziah and putting his hand on Fane's arm, his touch distracting Fane so that Domino was able to exit the house without incident.

Fane turned then and Kiziah took a step away from him when she saw the dark fury in his eyes. "You knew I wanted us to travel together," he said, crowding her until she was trapped between the wall and his hard body. "You knew I didn't want you to stop in Waynesville or to separate when you got there."

"I had a promise to keep," Kiziah said. "I have a life beyond you and Cable."

"Your life is mine," Fane said, flashing his fangs and sending a primitive fear along Kiziah's nerve endings.

He speared his fingers through her hair, holding her so that she couldn't look away from him, his expression so carnal, so possessive that she whimpered. His will already strong enough that she couldn't move or resist as he lowered his mouth to her neck, brushing his fangs against her skin, rubbing them against the wildly beating pulse of her jugular.

Fane struck without warning, the pain and shock of his fangs sliding through her skin rapidly transforming into ecstasy as he fed, his body aggressive, the hard line of his cock pressed against her belly. His thoughts pushing through her mental barriers, forging a pathway between them, insisting that she was his, that she would obey, that no one would take her from him or hurt her. His assault on her senses so intense that it became a struggle to think, to fight the waves of cloying darkness that began to press in on her.

With a hiss Fane lifted his mouth from her neck, his tongue swiping over her skin, and she became aware of the knife driven into the wall next to their faces, one of Cable's hands on its handle while the other pushed between them, circling Fane's cock as Cable's body pressed to Fane's back, his voice aroused and yet sounding a warning. "Stop, Fane. You've taken enough."

Fane turned his head slightly, his mouth only a breath away from Cable's. "I won't tolerate her disobedience. I *can't* tolerate it."

"And I won't let you make her a prisoner."

Fane's nostrils flared. His already dark eyes flashed with something primitive and alien. "You'll come to think as I do," he said, his voice a silky threat that made Kiziah shiver.

Cable took it in stride, his hand moving up and down on Fane's shaft, his head turning just enough to brush a kiss against Fane's shoulder. "Yeah, we'll see," he said, biting Fane lightly.

Fane shuddered. His body bucked against Kiziah's, heat moving through his eyes, a hunger that wouldn't be satisfied with blood alone.

"Yeah, we'll see," Fane said, echoing Cable's words but with deadly menace, his eyes boring into Kiziah's as he pulled Cable's hand from the knife's handle and pressed Cable's wrist to his mouth.

Cable grunted as Fane bit him, panted as Fane began sucking. And even without Fane's compulsion forcing her to watch as he fed from Cable, Kiziah couldn't have looked away.

Need filled her at the sight of it. Swelling her breasts and engorging her cunt lips. The desire intensifying at the look of pleasure on Cable's face. With the feel of his hand stroking Fane's cock, pumping up and down, brushing against her jeans, and making her desperate to open them and expose her erect clit. To press it against Fane's penis and feel Cable's knuckles against it as he touched Fane.

Their heightened arousal fed her own, and Kiziah went to her knees, her eyes not leaving Fane's until her mouth sought his cock. Cable's hand stilling as she took everything above it into her mouth, her tongue immediately swirling over the plump, sensitive head of Fane's penis.

Fane jerked, struggled, tried to fuck through Cable's hand in order to drive himself deeper into Kiziah's mouth.

"Not too much, Zia. He can't come until the exchanges are made and we're both inside you," Cable warned.

The Heat and Hunger twined together inside Fane, inseparable, demanding that he claim what belonged to him. With a mental command the knife pulled free of the wall, coming to Fane's hand like a bird of prey to its master, the sight of it stopping the torment of Kiziah's mouth as her eyes widened with surprise.

Fane sliced his inner thigh, issuing another silent command, this one to Kiziah, his will alone forcing her to leave his cock and press her lips to the wound, to drink. The sensation so heady that his body tightened, his back arched and his cock burned with the need to come, a hiss escaping when Cable used his hand to prevent it, to stave off orgasm while Kiziah whimpered and cried, making the second exchange.

It was ecstasy beyond imagine, unparalleled pleasure, the intensity of it consuming Fane, enthralling him until Cable sagged against him, muttering, "Christ," though he made no effort to pull his wrist from Fane's grasp. Fane stopped then, licking over the puncture marks even as he eased Kiziah away from his thigh so that his skin could knit back together.

Satisfaction filled him when he looked down at her, seeing her pleasure, her acceptance. "You will obey me," he said, caressing her cheek with his fingers before shifting, moving from between Kiziah and Cable, anticipation spiking through him when she immediately leaned forward, her hands going to Cable's jeans, her fingers deftly freeing Cable's cock, her mouth following, making Cable groan.

Fane closed the distance between them, one of his hands going to Kiziah's hair, the other going to the back of Cable's neck, pulling him forward so that their lips met and their tongues mated, rubbing and twining, neither of them relenting as they dueled in wet, dark heat — Kiziah held between them.

They were both breathing hard when the kiss ended, their cocks full and their balls heavy with the need to couple, to find release — with each other, with Kiziah. Fane summoned the knife from where he'd dropped it on the floor, this time using it to open a place on his neck, a symbolic gesture of trust. And as Cable willingly completed the second exchange, Fane couldn't resist repeating his earlier comment, this time in Cable's mind. *You will come to think as I do when it comes to Kiziah.*

Chapter Twelve

The night was a blur of sex. Of ravenous need. Of bonding. Of a burning hunger that went beyond the blood flowing through Kiziah's veins, a consuming need that claimed her soul and her heart.

The images of Cable and Fane together, the memory of them taking her, at the same time and individually, were seared into her mind for all time, the craving to repeat the night branded on every cell in her body.

Cable had told her that after the second exchange, after they'd come together—Fane's cock shoved into her channel while Cable's lodged in her ass—they would be sexually bonded. Tied together. But his words—and even her own imagination—hadn't prepared her for the reality.

Your life is mine, Fane said and long before sleep claimed her, he had demonstrated that truth with his body, his mind, his will— repeatedly proving how powerless she was against him.

Kiziah laughed softly. Or so Fane thought.

More than once during the night it had been two against one, the balance of power shifting as she and Cable commanded Fane's body, driving him to orgasm. Controlling his pleasure.

She stretched and turned, smiling when she saw how Fane was curled around Cable's back in the same way Cable had been curled around her, Fane's hand shoved between Cable's thighs as Cable's had been shoved between hers.

They were gorgeous. All it took was the sight of them—singly or together—but especially like this, intimately posed, to make her cunt and breasts flush with arousal. She didn't think she'd ever get enough of them—though she tried her best not to think about the centuries they would have ahead of them after the third exchange of blood had been made.

Such a lifespan seemed unnatural to her, a mixed blessing she hadn't looked for. She was sure that Cable had only scratched the surface of the padrall history, but even so, she could understand why the very first of them had elected to serve the vampires for material rewards instead of nonmaterial ones.

Cable shifted, his hand moving to cover Fane's where it rested on his cock, his eyelids fluttering open. His smile when his eyes met hers like a stroke of pure love.

She leaned in and kissed him. Her fingers playing over the bite Fane had given him. "One more to go."

"Second thoughts?"

"Just thoughts."

"Any that would interest me?"

Kiziah laughed. "It depends on how interested you are in sex."

Cable's hand left Fane's and went around Kiziah's waist, pulling her to him so that their lips were only inches apart. "With you and Fane, I'm always interested." His face grew serious. "It's going to be a harder adjustment for you, Zia. You're used to coming and going as you please. Last night wasn't as rough as I was afraid it would be. But that doesn't mean it'll always go like that." He pressed a kiss to her lips. "We can put it off if you need more time. We don't have to finish it in three consecutive nights."

Kiziah's hand went to Fane's upper arm, her fingers curling around it, feeling the smooth skin over firm muscles. "That wouldn't go over too well with him."

"Yeah. Waiting was against his nature even when he was a dhampir. But he'd do it, Zia."

"And if your family caught us again?"

Cable sighed, a small puff of air. "Then we'd be in trouble."

"I'm willing to finish what we started." She pressed her lips to his in reassurance. "I think us being together was in the cards."

He laughed, rubbing his mouth against hers. "Madame Helki's tarot cards?"

"Yeah." She shifted her hand from Fane's arm to Cable's chest. "Will your family forgive you?"

"My mother will accept it. I think my brothers will come around. We've talked about it before, how the padralls are trapped in a medieval world, how we need to gain some freedom for those of us born into it."

"And your father?"

Real sadness settled in Cable's eyes. "I don't know, Zia. I'll keep the door open and hope he comes around. But I won't count on it. I knew from the start what Fane was, what he would eventually become, the choice it might lead to."

Cable's mouth covered hers, his tongue gently parting her lips and sliding against hers, a slow, languid rub of heat and emotion, comfort and security, solidarity.

"Tonight's okay with me," Kiziah whispered when the kiss ended.

"I'm glad." He rubbed his nose against hers. "Want to get up? We've slept most of the day already. Fane will be up in a little while."

Kiziah snickered. "When is he not *up*?"

"Good question. Vampires are very sexual beings, especially when it comes to their kadines and companions."

Kiziah rolled over and slid from the bed while Cable disentangled himself from Fane, grinning when he finally got to his feet and reached for his jeans. "Since meeting you I always seem to be short of clothes."

"Not my fault if you had to abandon both of the sports cars." Her eyes trailed over his naked torso and then Fane's. "Not that I mind seeing you two flash a lot of skin."

Cable pulled her to him. "Careful, we might insist that you stay naked when we're alone." He gave her a quick kiss. "Unfortunately we're not alone now, and I don't think either one of us wants to deal with Fane's possessive streak if Domino sees you without anything on."

"Domino?" But as soon as Kiziah said it, she realized that her senses had heightened to the point where she could hear movement in the kitchen and smell a hint of coffee even though the bedroom door was closed. When she concentrated, the awareness of a supernatural presence that she'd always possessed hummed through her, yielding more information than it ever had. She could sense the alien influence in Domino, so strong that it nearly masked the human. She remembered Cable's answer when he'd first brought up the subject of vampires and she'd asked if Domino was one. *Almost.* "Is he close to turning?"

Cable zipped his jeans and took Kiziah's hand. "Maybe."

Domino was leaning against the counter when they entered the kitchen. Obsidian eyes flashed with humor and Cable suppressed a groan.

"So Fane lets you escape when The Sleep rules?" Domino said. "I'm surprised he doesn't keep you tethered to the bed."

"Why are you here?" Cable asked. "You're a little early if you've come just to jerk Fane's chain."

Domino laughed. "Believe it or not, I came to offer my assistance and protection."

"Somehow I can't see Fane inviting you into the bedroom."

Domino grinned. "True enough and I have no desire to find myself in a dogfight in which the winner gains a permanent mate."

Cable laughed. "I'm with Fane, it's going to be pure pleasure to see The Heat put a leash on you once you've gone through The Transformation."

"It'll never happen." Domino lifted his coffee cup. "The bitter taste of the herbs is nothing compared to the loss of freedom a mate imposes."

"Which brings us back to my original question. Why are you here?"

Domino's face grew serious. "You know what to expect after the third exchange has been made?"

Cable looked away. Oh yeah. He knew what to expect. Pain as his cells altered. Fiery heat coursing through his veins and arteries until balance was achieved between the human and the alien. None of it would be as bad as what a dhampir experienced during The Transformation, but it would be excruciating. And Kiziah would experience the same. Long moments of agony as opposed to the wild Heat and Hunger a kadine who'd been given her future mate's blood at birth and during the confirmation ceremony experienced. "Yeah, I know what to expect," he said, thinking of Domino's offer of assistance. "But I still can't see Fane inviting you into the bedroom."

"What are you two talking about?" Kiziah asked, trying to contain a growing uneasiness.

Cable pulled her into his arms, Kiziah's back to his front. "The last part is painful, Zia."

Her heart rate spiked. "How painful?"

His sigh did nothing to reassure her. "I've only read about it."

"But it's bad."

"Yeah." He tightened his arms around her. "It doesn't last for long. And you only have to go through it once."

"Sarael went through it?"

Cable swallowed the urge to admit that what Kiziah would go through was much harsher than what Sarael had experienced. "Yeah, she went through it."

"Okay, I can handle it," Kiziah said, forcing some of the anxiety out in a shaky exhale, the connection to Fane warning her that he was struggling to wake and join them in the kitchen, to take control of the situation. She looked at Domino, prepared to ask him to explain his offer, but Cable beat her to it, saying, "You'd better tell us what you have in mind before Fane comes storming in. He hasn't been a vampire long enough yet to issue a command in his sleep — but he's trying. And he's not going to be happy to wake and find you here."

Domino laughed. "True enough, and a test of strength is a show for another day. What I suggest is simple. One of you stays here. One of you leaves with me. A phone call when the first has gone through the changes and the three of you can be reunited."

Cable shook his head, but even as he did it, sensing Fane's absolute fury at the thought of one of them leaving, he remembered the vivid descriptions he'd read in the Santori histories. How Domino's ancestor had confided to the padrall serving as a scribe that it had been a mistake to make the third exchange and convert both his kadine and his male companion at the same time.

"I think it's a good idea," Kiziah said, pulling out of Cable's arms and turning to face him. Her heart thundering in her ears as she felt Fane's increased struggle to wake, his rage and possessiveness. Still she managed a small laugh as she took Cable's hands in hers. "And I think you should be first."

"You want to leave me to suffer his wrath and take the edge off him before he gets to you?"

"Self-preservation," Kiziah joked, leaning forward, her eyes going soft as she brushed her lips against Cable's. "I want you to be there when it's my turn. I'm willing to be there for you. But you and Fane have been a couple, and I'm okay with it just being the two of you first."

Cable hugged her to him. "Christ, Zia. We don't deserve you."

She returned the hug. "Well, you're stuck with me. But I'd better leave *now*, or I won't be able to."

Cable let her go, returning to the bedroom and stripping before flopping down next to Fane. The bond with Kiziah already strong enough that he could sense her moving further and further away from the house, just as he could sense Fane waking.

Cable braced himself. Prepared himself for Fane's anger and it came in a fury of movement, an attack that sent the blood pounding through Cable's body in a primal reaction even though his heart and mind knew that the deadly predator pinning him to the bed wasn't going to kill him.

"You let her leave," Fane said, his nostrils flaring, his face savage. His fangs fully extended, close enough to rip Cable's throat out if he desired.

"You know why," Cable said. "And you know she'll be back." He shifted, rubbing his cock against Fane's, watching as some of the rage fled in the presence of lust.

"I don't like it."

"She'll be safe with Domino."

Fane hissed, The Heat and Hunger twisting inside him like a wild thing despite the fact that he trusted Domino completely. Not just because of Domino's connection to his past, his family, but because Domino had seen him through The Transformation, had given him first blood, and both were tantamount to a sacrament between vampires. "I won't allow her this kind of freedom after the third exchange is made." Furious eyes met Cable's. "I *can't* allow her to defy me. I can't allow her to go unpunished."

"You'll have to," Cable said, moving again, the rub of his cock against Fane's flooding Fane's mind with more immediate desires, the deeply imprinted needs of his alien ancestors battling against his sexual cravings for Cable.

"I won't let you interfere with her punishment," Fane said.

Cable laughed. "Imagine you being possessive of a woman. Even the thought of it would have soured your mood not too long ago." His smile turned knowing. "If you need to get it out of your system before you can make the third exchange, then give me her punishment. I can take it."

Lust rushed through Fane, a wave of heat that consumed his anger. That made his cock pulse and leak, his body tighten to the point where it was him moving, him rubbing his cock against Cable's. "I was going to tie her to the bed. You've never allowed that. You've never wanted it."

"Do it. I'm not afraid."

Fane's lips curled, exposing deadly fangs. Frustration raged inside of him along with lust—at being outmaneuvered by Cable, at his inability to control Kiziah, at the loss of his own freedom to move around in a human form during the day.

With a hiss he levered himself up, calling a knife from the nightstand and using it to slash bindings from the sheet. But even as he secured Cable's wrists and ankles to the bed posts, Fane forced his own need to dominate into submission.

He would tie Cable because it would soothe the desire to strike out, and they would both gain pleasure from it. But Cable was mistaken if he thought the matter of Kiziah was settled. She *would* learn to obey, if not tonight, then in the future.

Fane settled again on Cable, pressing his mouth to Cable's, pressing his thoughts into Cable's mind. Unable to go forward until he had the final say with respect to the woman they now shared. *This isn't the end of it.*

But Cable only laughed, parting his lips and teasing Fane's tongue into a mating dance, into a carnal exchange that left them both panting, both breathless, both anxious to finish what they'd begun.

Fane closed his eyes, savoring the sensation, feeding on the wealth of emotion racing through Cable, their bond already deep enough—even without a single exchange of blood—for them to know what the other felt. Love poured into him and for a moment he was tempted to abandon his plan, to untie Cable so he could feel Cable's arms around him. But just as quickly as the impulse arose, another followed, the desire to have Cable writhing underneath him, to give him unparalleled ecstasy—an apology for the pain to come.

Fane moved lower, his mouth going to Cable's neck, his fangs grazing the skin, rubbing over a pulse that raced with lust, pausing there in mock threat, before he kissed his way to Cable's nipples, licking them, biting, toying with them as he compared them to Kiziah's in his mind, and remembered the pleasure he'd experienced at her breasts.

"Christ," Cable said, bucking, driving his cock against Fane's belly, then gasping when Fane's assault moved downward, Fane's mouth traveling over Cable's abdomen, pausing there as his hand circled Cable's penis, his touch so much different than Kiziah's and yet equally devastating.

"Christ," Cable repeated and Fane laughed, all traces of his earlier fury gone as his mouth went to Cable's cock, his lips and tongue driving Cable into a frenzy made more intense by the restraints. Reducing Cable to a primitive creature who sought only pleasure, whose body jerked and fought in a struggle for orgasm, his shout of release filling the room as well as Fane's heart. Echoing in a second coming when Fane turned his head and drove his fangs into Cable's inner thigh. Feeding there until Cable's heart stuttered in warning.

Fane swiped his tongue over the wound, then untied Cable before settling on top of him again, lowering his face and pressing his lips to Cable's. Their kiss gentle, not the usual struggle they enjoyed before coupling. But a soft communion, a sharing, a give-and-take.

"I love you," Fane said when he lifted his face, his voice gruff with the admission.

"Yeah, I know," Cable said, smiling, thinking it was the first time Fane had ever actually said it.

"It'll hurt. Even if it's only half of what I experienced during The Transformation, it'll hurt."

"Yeah. I know that too. The padralls who've witnessed and recorded it have made a point of writing about how agonizing the conversion process is. Just do it."

It humbled him that Cable was willing to sacrifice so much to be with him, made it easier for Fane to treat Cable as an equal, to resist the urges to completely dominate and control that he experienced with Kiziah. "Only after I do you."

Cable laughed, one of his hands tangling in Fane's hair, pulling him into a kiss that went from gentle to heated.

Fane shivered when Cable's hands trailed over his shoulders and back, bucked when one of them wedged between their bodies and took his cock.

Lust poured through Fane. The desire to fuck. And he pumped through Cable's closed fist, his breathing coming in pants, his cock burning, his balls full and heavy. "Your choice," he managed, willing to take Cable any way he could have him, his hips jerking when Cable's thumb brushed over the tip of his penis, sending arousal beading to the surface. His heart swelling, his soul acknowledging how deeply he cared for the human underneath him. For the man who balanced him, made him a better person. Offered him so much. Accepted so much.

Fane shifted position so that his hand could take Cable's cock, gliding over the smooth surface, the engorged head, making Cable pant and swear. "Christ, you always cheat!"

They knew each other's bodies so well that within minutes they were both close to orgasm, struggling to delay it, to savor the buildup even though they knew they had to finish what they'd started, not just for the sake of release but so they could summon Kiziah and claim their third.

"Your choice," Fane said, groaning when Cable released his cock and pushed against his chest, signaling that he should put some distance between them. But Fane yielded and the lust roared through him, doubling in intensity when Cable went to his hands and knees, allowing Fane to cover his body, to forge into his back entrance from behind. To fuck. Fane's vampire strength enabling him to open the vein on one wrist and press it to Cable's mouth even as he plunged in and out of Cable's anus while his other hand pumped Cable's shaft. Driving them both to an orgasm that left them shuddering, weak, sated — until the fiery effects of the third exchange arrived, burning through Cable's blood, a warning in the seconds before he writhed in pain.

Chapter Thirteen

"I'd like to go to the psychic fair," Kiziah said as soon as she and Domino put some distance between themselves and Fane.

His laugh was immediate. "So you enjoy living dangerously. I doubt even Cable would have let you leave if he knew where you'd want to be taken."

"Last night you said you'd eliminated a lot of the Believers."

"True. All but four, and only one of those is a danger to you."

"The Apostle?"

"Yes."

"Do you know where he is?"

"I will when the time comes to deliver him to Fane."

"Will you take me to the fair?"

"Yes. I'll take you." Domino glanced at her. Something in his eyes causing uneasiness to uncoil and spread through Kiziah. A sense of foreboding.

She turned and looked out the window, trying to gather her thoughts, her courage. Instead, her awareness of Domino increased—not as a gorgeous man but as a deadly predator.

In the close confines of the car, her sense of him was magnified far beyond what it had been in the house with Cable and Fane present. She'd asked if Domino was close to turning, and now the answer rubbed over every one of her nerve endings. *Oh yeah, Domino was very close to turning.* And underneath the human façade she could sense something as wild and driven by bloodlust as the alien cells which would turn him into a full-blooded vampire.

"Fear is an aphrodisiac to our kind. Doubly so for me," Domino said, the rough edge to his voice warning her that his body was reacting despite his intention to keep her safe.

"Because you're so close to changing?"

"That and because I already have a second form."

Kiziah turned away from the window. "You mean turning into mist?"

"That's a vampire's defense mechanism. A form I'll gain after The Transformation."

Her lips parted in surprise. "You're a shapeshifter? Like a werewolf?"

Some of the tension left his body. He laughed. "Not a werewolf, though I can take the form of a wolf."

Kiziah's thoughts whirled. Amusement and curiosity finding her when she remembered Domino's comment in the kitchen. *I have no desire to find myself in a dogfight in which the winner gains a permanent mate.* "Does Fane also change into a wolf?"

"No, he has only the vampire's second form. Have you seen his command of knives?"

"Yes."

"We're all born with at least one talent beyond those necessary for our survival. You've met Matteo?"

"Yes."

"Fire is his talent. Mine is the power to hypnotize and compel, more so than just a vampire or dhampir's ability to enthrall and confuse, to wipe out short-term memories and command during limited encounters."

Kiziah rubbed her palms over her jeans, vividly recalling her first encounter with Domino. The void that existed between leaving Madame Helki's tent and "waking" to find herself being stalked by the Believer. "I remembered your eyes."

"I wanted you to."

Her thoughts moved to the Believer who'd murdered Fane's family. "You said The Apostle is in the area. Has he been to the fair?"

"We're watching the entrances as well as the campgrounds and hotels. None of us have seen him, which is not surprising. Unlike many of the American recruits, he is not a hired thug or a social deviant. He's a true Believer. He wouldn't get too close to the psychics for the same reason we try to keep our distance." Domino shrugged. "The fair is very nearly over, it's possible that with so many of his brethren dead, he's decided to strike at another time."

Domino stopped the car near the front entrance, turning to look at Kiziah. "Be careful. You have enough of Fane's blood now to call humans to you, to mesmerize them. It can get out of hand if you don't control it."

"Control it how?" Kiziah asked, wanting to believe that he was just amusing himself at her expense but knowing that he wasn't.

"Our pheromones are triggered by strong emotion such as fear and lust, as well as by intent and hunger." He smiled, a flash of white teeth reflected in obsidian eyes. "You should be safe as long as you avoid imagining what Fane and Cable are doing."

No doubt just as Domino had intended, Kiziah immediately pictured Fane and Cable in bed, then became aware of changes within her own body, as if it was reaching out, calling, trying to draw others to it, even though she couldn't imagine intimacy with anyone other than Cable or Fane.

It was a confusing contradiction that Domino helped her to understand by saying, "For kadines the pheromones are intended as a defense mechanism. Once you've gone through the last of the changes, it will become second nature for you to control them, and you won't have to fear drawing humans to you accidentally." He glanced at the entrance to the psychic fair. "You should go now if you intend to visit your friends. I'll wait outside. But you don't have much time before Fane and Cable will arrive."

Kiziah's eyebrows drew together. "You're not taking me back to the house?"

Domino laughed. "Fane has always been short of patience. He'll come to collect you himself and probably rage all the way back to the bedroom."

Kiziah laughed, knowing he was right and she would no doubt end up with another demonstration of who was in control—which in turn caused the pheromones to flare and Domino's eyebrows to rise in amusement.

She slipped from the sports car and went inside, feeling a strange mix of homesickness and alienation at the familiar sights and sounds. In a heartbeat she knew this part of her life was over.

Even now she was drawing glances from many of the psychics, seeing puzzled frowns and curious expressions. Feeling the hum of their supernatural abilities against what she'd gained from Fane — recognizing traces of dark undercurrents, a willingness to take from her if a way could be found to do it. Her stomach tightened and she moved deeper into the building, consumed now with thoughts of finding Margo and Walt.

They'd gotten a good location for their booth and were doing a brisk business despite the fair being well into its final hour. "You're here!" Margo said, leaving her husband to handle their customers as she moved out of the booth and enfolded Kiziah in a fierce hug.

Kiziah returned the hug with equal fierceness. Had it only been three days since she'd played cards with them and come home to find Fane waiting for her in the Airstream? It seemed like a lifetime.

Margo put her hands on Kiziah's shoulders, keeping her less than an arm's length away as they drew apart. "You're much changed, just as your mother told me you'd be."

Pain and longing speared through Kiziah's heart. "You've seen her?"

A soft smile played over Margo's lips. "How your mother loved the tarot! She came to me in a dream. Standing in the center of the Wheel of Fortune. She told me you'd get here in time and I would see that you had found the path to your destiny. She left in an explosion of light that was bright enough to be The Sun."

Instead of being happy, fear coiled in Kiziah's stomach as she heard a different message in Margo's words. A warning about a bomb.

She told me you'd get here in time.

She left in an explosion.

Kiziah looked around, her mind jumping from thought to thought in a panic. The chaos ending when Margo asked, "Are you staying for the closing ceremony?"

Realization burst through Kiziah. Horror. "There's going to be one?"

"Yes."

And in that instant Kiziah guessed where the bomb would be. Somewhere outside. In a parked car maybe, or several of them. Close to where those attending the psychic fair would gather to chant and pray under the stars. The fairs didn't always end in a closing ceremony, it was a somewhat spontaneous event, a way of giving thanks and forming a connection with the townspeople.

She hugged Margo to her. Anguish making her chest so tight that she could hardly breathe. What if she was wrong? What if the bomb was inside? The Apostle could have had someone else bring it in. But would he have risked it if he was a true Believer? Would he have waited this long to detonate it?

"I've got to go. Please, please, try and get them to delay the ceremony. The dream was a warning. There may be a bomb outside."

Kiziah didn't wait until she got outside to tell Domino what she suspected, she called him, telling him about the ceremony. Grimacing when he began cursing violently. "Do you know what explosives smell like?" she asked, thinking about police and military dogs that were trained for the task though she guessed Domino wouldn't care to be equated to them.

"Yes." It was almost a growl.

"If you were to sniff around..."

"I'll give you the car. Get away from here. Call Fane or Cable, tell them you're going back to the house. They've already called me to say they were on their way." He paused. "Neither of them was pleased to learn that we were here."

Kiziah grimaced, emerging from the building and closing her cell phone as Domino got out of the car so that she could take the driver's seat. He tried to capture her gaze with his, but she avoided it by ducking her head and slipping into the car, closing the door so that only the window remained partly open. "There's not much time now."

He repeated his command, "Get away from here."

"I'm going," she said, feeling his will pressing against her but the lack of eye contact, the lack of a blood connection, as well as what she'd gained from Fane allowed her to resist without falling prey to his hypnosis, to drive away, not home but out of sight, so he would begin looking for any explosives while she began looking for The Apostle.

The thought of actually finding the Believer made her shiver with cold fear. But there was no way she could simply drive away and leave the people she'd grown up among to suffer or die at the hands of an enemy they didn't know existed. Not if she could do something to prevent it.

She told me you'd get here in time. Margo had said, and her words fed Kiziah's courage as she joined the crowd of protestors gathered outside the psychic fair and moved among them.

You have enough of Fane's blood now to call humans to you, to mesmerize them. Domino's warning provided her with a weapon she could use to delay The Apostle until Fane or Domino could deal with him.

She knew that Fane's blood had heightened all of her senses, but she had no reference point for what an explosive device would smell like. Fear and excitement were another matter though, the alien, predatory part of Fane that she carried inside her reacted to the fast beat of a pounding heart, the terror of prey, the smell of it.

Kiziah shivered again, her own heart jerking and racing, though she rushed to control her thoughts, her own fears, not wanting to release the pheromones as she searched among the protestors. She wished she knew what The Apostle looked like, wished now that she'd asked more questions, but the changes in her life had come so rapidly, and Cable's family had seemed a greater threat than the Believers.

She got to the last of the protestors and turned to look out at the parking lot. The Apostle would be there somewhere, to detonate the bomb, to see his handiwork firsthand. Didn't bombers feed on that?

The muscles in her stomach tightened when she saw the small restaurant across the street, the interior lit, indicating they were open. It would be the perfect place to watch, to wait.

No! Kiziah nearly stumbled as Fane and Cable's voices both ripped into her mind. The force of their combined will very nearly freezing her in place. They were very close now, and yet she couldn't afford to wait.

Even as she thought it, the protestors started chanting loudly as people began to emerge from the building housing the fair, their exit unhurried, an indication that Margo's warning about danger had gone unheeded.

I have to, Kiziah sent back, but the words felt as though they were trapped in wool, the connection that would allow her to speak mind-to-mind with Cable and Fane not yet fully in existence.

The possibility of it thrilled Kiziah, momentarily distracting her from her fear as she forced herself to hurry to the restaurant, telling herself as she opened the door and stepped inside that there was no reason for The Apostle to know who she was, to suspect that she knew what his intentions were.

"Seat yourself," a waitress called from behind the old-fashioned serving counter, her back turned to the entrance as she flirted with a muscled, apron-clad cook cubing chunks of beef with a heavy knife.

There were few customers but Kiziah knew immediately which one of them was The Apostle. He was seated at the window, looking out, his head turned so that she could see the red and black crucifix tattooed on his neck. Her gaze dropped to his hand, one bare, the smallest finger unnaturally short, one covered by a thin black glove, though the material didn't hide the fact that he was missing fingers, the trademark of a man who couldn't resist the lure of explosives.

Kiziah gathered her courage and moved toward him, the protective pheromones rising as a result of her own fear. "Okay if I join you?" she asked, sitting across from him, her presence drawing his attention away from the crowd gathered outside the psychic fair.

Their eyes met. Locked.

He blinked and tried to look away, as though some part of him knew what she was, what she intended to do, but his reaction only fed her fear, increasing the pheromones swirling around them.

Kiziah shivered as she saw his eyes glaze with lust. She nearly choked with nausea with the smell of it.

Sirens blared outside, distracting her. Causing her to glance out of the window, the release enough for his hand to go to his pocket. "No!" she said, reaching across the table, putting her hand on his arm, the touch filling her with revulsion, though it had the desired effect, stopping him, bringing his gaze to hers so that she could trap him again. The lust once again filling his eyes, the smell of it assaulting her, increasing her fear in a vicious cycle that had his tongue licking over his lips, his nostrils flaring.

Alarm moved through Kiziah as she sensed other customers moving toward the table. Drawn by the pheromones, their lust preceding them.

She jerked when the door to the restaurant opened in a rush of cold air and fury that confirmed what her awareness of the supernatural was already telling her. Fane and Cable had arrived.

"Get away from him," Fane said, the anger over her actions nothing compared to the hatred in his voice for The Apostle.

Kiziah hesitated, afraid to look away for fear that The Apostle would have time to reach into his pocket before Fane was close enough to stop him. She could hear Fane moving toward them, could sense another presence at her side. But before she could do anything, fingers closed around her arm, jerking her out of her chair, forcing her to turn and look into the face of a stranger unwittingly drawn to her, his eyes glazed, his skin flushed.

"I'll get her," Cable said as Fane's rage very nearly consumed him.

The Apostle's hand moved toward his pocket and Fane guessed his intent. There was no time to savor his revenge, no time to draw it out as he'd fantasized about.

With a mental command Fane wrenched the knife from the cook's fingers, hurling it at The Apostle, driving it through the bomber's throat with such force that his chair toppled, the blade's momentum carrying him backward and pinning his spasming, convulsing body to the floor as the detonation device tumbled from his pocket.

"A good use of your talent," Domino said, his appearance startling Kiziah. "Now I'll put mine to use and make a hero of the cook since you have arranged a perfect scenario and I have already located the devices and had an observant citizen report them to the police."

Kiziah's attention shifted to the cook and the waitress, to the other customers, all frozen in place, their eyes slightly glazed, probably a combination of shock and the heavy-duty pheromones in the air.

"Let's go," Cable said, taking Kiziah's arm as well as Fane's. "Domino can handle this."

The drive back to the house was made in silence — which surprised Kiziah given the intensity of emotion emanating from the two men in the car with her. Only when they'd gotten through the front door did Fane react in the manner she'd expected, crowding her, hissing and flashing his fangs as he stripped off her shirt and bra in a display that turned her on instead of terrorized her.

He pressed her backward against Cable, whose hands went immediately to the front of her jeans, unzipping them as his mouth found her neck, making her heart rush with excitement and her vulva swell when she felt the press of fangs against her skin.

She could tell that the two men were talking to each other, arguing mind-to-mind. She could guess the nature of what they were saying and decided to act before they reached a consensus.

Kiziah kicked off her shoes and wriggled out of her jeans, gasping when Cable's fingers slipped under the waistband of her panties and found her clit, circling, stroking, rubbing its head as though it was a tiny penis.

Fane cursed, he knew what Cable was doing, knew that Cable was using The Heat against him, and yet the sight of Cable's fingers toying with Kiziah's clit, the smell of her arousal, the feel of Cable's lust through the bond they now shared was overwhelming, compelling, a call to fuck that he couldn't resist.

You won't always win this way, Fane warned Cable, shedding his own clothing and kneeling in front of Kiziah, ripping her panties away so that he could see her pussy, could watch as Cable pleasured her. His own need to punish her fading as she grew slick with arousal, as her cunt lips parted, inviting his kiss, compelling him to lean forward and thrust his tongue into her, to gather her juices and eat at her feminine flesh.

Within seconds Kiziah was on the edge of orgasm, barely able to form a coherent thought. Her hands buried in Fane's hair, her body writhing, reacting to Cable's touch and the hungry stab of Fane's tongue. She arched and cried out in release, sagged against them, but it was only the beginning.

Fane rose to his feet. His eyes full of feral lust. His body vibrating with the need to dominate.

Without a word he claimed her mouth, fucked into it as aggressively as he'd fucked into her slit, forcing her to taste herself even as his hands moved around her body, wrenching the front of Cable's jeans open.

Cable groaned against Kiziah's neck, his cock a hard ridge against her buttocks. His breathing coming in pants next to her ear. He was close to coming just from the lust radiating off Fane, from the feel of Kiziah's slippery folds and erect clit as his fingers tunneled into the place Fane had abandoned.

Fane lifted his mouth from hers and stepped back, pulling Kiziah with him and sending an image to Cable. A picture that had Cable stripping out of his clothing and grasping his cock, holding it as he took a step backward so the wall braced him.

Cable's breath caught when Fane turned Kiziah to face him, commanded that she bend over and take Cable's penis into her mouth. But he didn't protest. Could only watch as she obeyed, her hands going to the wall on either side of his hips as her lips found him, as her tongue rubbed against the sensitive head of his penis in sweet torment.

"Christ!" It was a curse and a plea uttered as Cable's hand cupped her face, his fingers spearing through her hair, his body jerking, hunching over as he tried to forge deeper, to press more of his cock into the hot depths of her mouth. The dual sensation, the pleasure of taking her mouth as Fane's cock tunneled into her channel very nearly driving Cable to his knees.

It was too much. Too intense. Beyond anything he could have imagined. The bond formed with the third exchange of blood overwhelming, so close that his pleasure was Fane's just as Fane's with his. And when Fane leaned forward, pressing his mouth to Kiziah's shoulder, piercing her with his fangs, Cable cried out in ecstasy, his mouth seeking Fane's shoulder, his fangs driving into masculine flesh so that they all spun out of control.

Kiziah was boneless in Fane's arms as he carried her to the bedroom. She was completely sated until he placed her on the bed, lying down next to her and pulling her on top of him, positioning her so that his cock was buried in her channel.

"Ummm, nice," she whispered, pressing her lips to his, heat flaring to life in her cunt, in her breasts. The flames growing hotter when Cable's body joined theirs, his cock lodged at her back entrance, pushing in so that it lay against Fane's, separated by only a thin barrier and surrounded by her heat, both of them seemingly content to remain still, to savor an intimacy unlike any other, the three of them almost one.

"Ready for the third exchange?" Cable asked, brushing a kiss against Kiziah's shoulder.

She shivered, opened her mouth to ask how painful it was then thought better of it. Cable had made it through the final changes. "I'm ready."

He kissed her shoulder again, brushed his fangs against her skin as he began thrusting, his cock rubbing against Fane's, distracting Kiziah with pleasure even though she was aware of Fane summoning a knife, aware of him cutting his chest and guiding her mouth to the opening.

And then there was nothing but the dark ecstasy of feeding, of feeling Cable's fangs slide into her shoulder in the place Fane had bitten, of having two cocks pumping in and out of her, two men fucking her as they fucked each other, the three of them soon writhing, sweating, straining for a release like no other, a union unattainable by most.

A sweet release that plunged Kiziah into a hell of pain. A burning, searing place where cells attacked each other savagely and forced a change. Torturous moments that felt as though they lasted for hours, turning her into something neither wholly human nor completely alien, but the perfect balance of both.

"Almost there," Cable murmured against her ear as the agony subsided, only to be replaced by a consuming hunger, a savage need to draw blood. She fought then, a wild struggle to free herself from their grip, but Fane and Cable easily subdued her until the first rush of Heat and Hunger faded into a background hum, a need that only they could satisfy.

"I'm okay now," Kiziah whispered, dazed and yet strangely exhilarated, as though she stood on the threshold to a new world and only needed to take a single step to enter it.

Cable released her, but before she could move, Fane rolled her underneath him, filled her channel with his cock as he pinned her wrists to the bed. She whimpered in reaction, felt the heat coil in her belly as her canine teeth elongated. Cried out when he closed the distance between them, allowing her to drive her fangs into his neck, his pleasure blending with hers, merging with Cable's as he joined them, his penis sliding into Fane's back entrance.

Just as they'd done before the change, they stilled, savoring an intimacy unlike any other, three people very nearly one. *Feel it?* Cable asked.

Oh yeah, Kiziah said, retracting her fangs, the delight of being joined to Cable and Fane more heady even than the dark lure of vampire blood.

Cable's hand moved to tangle in Kiziah's hair. *It'll only get better.*

Especially when she learns to obey, Fane said, making both Cable and Kiziah smile as they began to move against him, to fuck, to demonstrate how capricious the Wheel of Fortune could be when linked to The Lovers, how easily the one with the most power could became the one with the least when pleasure was involved.

DAKOTAH'S READING

ဢ

Trademarks Acknowledgement

ഌ

The author acknowledges the trademarked status and trademark owners of the following wordmarks mentioned in this work of fiction:

Suburban: General Motors Corporation

Chapter One

It was time to leave. The tightness between Dakotah Flemming's shoulder blades, the sensation of being watched, the faint whiff of wolf she'd smelled on several occasions — all of it was confirmation of what her instincts had been urging for days.

She needed to get moving. Tomorrow. Sooner if she could find Roy and get her cut of the ride receipts. Tonight if she could still catch a bus out of the small town where the carnival had stopped, setting up in the hopes of drawing from the people coming for the psychic fair.

Fuck. If she'd known about the psychic fair, she would have bolted from the last town.

Her stomach twisted, exposing the lie for what it was. She'd caught faint traces of wolf in that town too, but she'd stuck around anyway, just in case Sarael called, needing help.

Dakotah shivered. Vague images of the man Sarael had been running from pressing in on her. Whatever he was, he wasn't human. He wasn't wolf. His scent was cold and alien even though she'd been aware of the blood rushing through his veins and heard his heart beating with lethal menace.

Her nose wrinkled in a silent snarl of denial as her womb fluttered and desire rippled across her abdomen before settling in her pussy. A lingering reaction to the potent pheromones the man had used to subdue and enthrall her.

She had a vague impression of talking to him, of being led to her trailer, of knowing she was in the presence of a predator more deadly than anything she'd encountered before. A man whose presence had stirred the wolf inside her. *It* wanted a mate like the male who'd claimed Sarael.

Dakotah's lips twisted. The wolf was mistaken in thinking that a mate would solve all their problems. The wolf hadn't seen men like those she'd been forced to service. The wolf hadn't been a part of her during those nightmare years. Hadn't watched through her eyes or experienced things through her body.

The wolf hadn't endured. Hadn't loathed and reviled the men she'd struck with whips and paddles while they pleaded with her in little-boy voices, begging for more punishment. Begging her to do degrading things to them.

Disgust curled in Dakotah's stomach. The wolf hadn't seen men like the ones who'd populated her world before she died—not literally—though maybe it had been like that. Maybe she had died in those dark woods and been reborn into something straight out of a horror film. She couldn't remember very much beyond escaping. Running. Bleeding. Hurting. The pain so intense that if she'd had the strength, she might have killed herself to end it.

Her hands balled into fists. Never. No matter how many men Victor Hale sent after her, she wouldn't die without a fight.

The wolf stirred and she forced herself to relax. If she couldn't get out of this town tonight, then she'd let it run. It might be a while before she could risk it again. She owed that part of herself a chance to escape from the deep cage it was forced to live in.

It had been a struggle at first—controlling the wolf, suppressing it, convincing it that only death would follow if its presence became known—especially to others who also had a second form. But a couple of chance encounters, fights that had left the wolf nearly savaged, lucky to escape, and it no longer believed that finding a pack was the answer.

Now the wolf moved deeper into the darkness of Dakotah's soul when it scented others like itself. Now it tried to contain any trace of itself for fear of triggering an attack. And in return, Dakotah ceded control when the wolf's form replaced her own, let it hunt deer and wallow in the kill, let it run free as long as it didn't threaten *innocent* human life.

Yeah. If she couldn't get out of this town tonight, she'd let the wolf run. It was cold enough outside that even horny teenage lovers would favor the backseat of a car over a blanket in the woods.

Dakotah looked around the small trailer that had been her home for the last year. A tin can on wheels. But a lump formed in her throat anyway, burning for a second until she swallowed it.

It'd been a good year. The safest she'd known in forever. Though the carnival still attracted its share of predators. Townies usually. Who thought the women would be easy.

But she'd managed to have some fun. To be around boys and men who were...decent. Around people who were decent.

She'd forgotten people could be like that. She'd forgotten that it didn't always come down to either using or being used. Maybe she'd never known it to begin with.

But it was still time to move on. At least she could leave knowing Sarael was okay.

Dakotah reached for the black leather jacket hanging on a hook next to the door and heard the slow, unmistakable gait of Helki, the carnival's ancient fortune-teller, drawing close to the trailer. She tensed. Bracing herself for the rattling of the door as the old woman stopped on the other side of it and knocked.

"You're leaving," Helki said when Dakotah opened the door and stepped back to allow the old woman to enter.

Dakotah shrugged, determined not to feed the fortune-teller any information. Even after a year of traveling with the carnival, of hearing Sarael's tales of Helki's tarot readings, of being around Sarael who actually believed in what the cards foretold — Dakotah remained skeptical. Not that truth couldn't be found in the cards — but that it couldn't be altered.

"You won't find Roy tonight," Helki said, her eyes dancing with mirth when Dakotah stiffened, giving away the fact that she'd been about to seek the carnival owner out.

"Where is he?"

Helki cackled, a sound she seemed to reserve for skeptics and fools. "He's got a couple of lady friends in this town. He'll be catting around all night and most of the morning."

"Thanks for coming by and saving me the trouble of looking for him." Dakotah shifted from one foot to the other before pressing forward, deciding it was better to get it over with than to play head games with the fortune-teller. "Is that all you wanted to tell me? Or did Sarael send a message?"

Helki's face softened at the mention of Sarael, the child she'd raised when Sarael's mother left her behind at the carnival. "No. Though you will see her sooner than you might think and be a part of her world for more years than you can imagine."

A burst of warmth filled Dakotah's heart, and for a moment she let herself believe, but then she ruthlessly pushed it aside. Sarael was already in Italy. And even if she did come back to the United States, there'd be no happy reunion. By tomorrow Dakotah would be gone. In another couple of days, she'd have a new name, a new identity, a new cell number. In a couple of days, Dakotah Flemming would no longer exist, though she had a feeling this name, this identity would be the hardest one she'd ever shed.

She'd adopted the name for the rugged wildness that could be found in the Dakotas. For the wolf. But over the last year, she felt as though she'd *become* Dakotah. It would bother her to... She shrugged the thought away. She couldn't afford to become sentimental over a name.

"So you swung by to save me the trouble of looking for Roy? Thanks," Dakotah said, her body tensing, her mind already guessing the reason behind Helki's visit.

It was a strange tradition at this carnival. A reading by Helki before you were allowed to stay. A reading by Helki before you left—if you intended to leave on good terms. She didn't plan on coming back. But the life she'd led had taught her it was smarter to leave doors open than to slam them shut. "You want to sit down?"

The skin around Helki's dark eyes crinkled with amusement. She answered by taking a seat and pulling a velvet-wrapped deck of tarot cards from the pocket of her coat.

Without being told, Dakotah took the chair opposite the fortune-teller and accepted the deck. Keeping her mind free of all thoughts as she shuffled then cut and restacked the deck, before handing it back to Helki.

For a long moment the old woman held the deck, her eyes closed as though she was listening to a story only she could hear. Dakotah grimaced and shifted in her chair, a tightness forming in her chest despite her desire to ignore what was going on in front of her, to reject the possibility that the reading was significant for *her*.

Helki's eyes snapped open and Dakotah's pulse jumped in response. The fortune-teller's knowing expression leaving Dakotah torn between amusement and irritation. But before she could think of anything to say, Helki placed three cards on the table between them. One after the other. The past. The present. The future.

Death.

Strength.

The Emperor.

Uneasiness moved through Dakotah, surprise. Wariness. But she forced herself to remain motionless, realizing in the instant she did so that it betrayed as much as movement would have.

Helki studied the cards, reaching out and laying her finger on the black-cloaked figure of Death, tracing over the scythe in his hands. "You have died and been reborn into a different person. It was a violent transition and death still stalks you in the form of a man who wants revenge." Her fingers moved to the lion depicted in Strength. "Where others have become monsters as a result of the things you have experienced, you have gained from them, the blending of your will and intellect with the beast within making you stronger." Helki's eyes sought Dakotah's and she gently tapped The Emperor. "The time will come when you will face the enemy who wants you dead, but you will not do so alone. Another change awaits you. This time at the hands of a man unlike any you have known before. A man who wants your life, not your death."

Without another word, Helki gathered the cards and stood, leaving Dakotah to stare at the place where they'd been—the tarot images forever burned into her memory. She shivered despite the warmth of the trailer, longing coiling around in her chest, weaving through her heart, momentarily wrapping her in hope until she tossed it off.

Helki had guessed correctly about the past. Had somehow glimpsed the wolf underneath Dakotah's skin and interpreted what it meant in the present. But the fortune-teller's vision didn't accurately reflect the future.

As much as the wolf might want a mate, Dakotah didn't have any illusion that such a thing was possible. Lovers, yes — though not often and never for longer than it took to gain release. It was foolish to wish for more, to hope for more, to allow herself to believe the future held anything but running and surviving.

* * * * *

Domino Santori watched as the fortune-teller left the trailer and made her way back to her own home on wheels, pausing for a moment to look in his direction, as though sensing him in the darkest shadows of the night.

He grimaced like a small boy caught at mischief and could easily imagine the flash of amusement in Helki's eyes, could very nearly hear her knowing cackle as she disappeared from view. No doubt she would share her thoughts tomorrow.

Within moments, the reason for his presence at the carnival emerged from the trailer Helki had just left. Dakotah.

Her scent reached him first, stirring his lust. Stirring the wolf's lust.

Domino smiled when Dakotah headed in the direction of the woods. He already knew them well. Not as a man. But as a wolf.

Anticipation roared through him. He had never run with a human who could shift into wolf form. Had never hunted with one. Never shared the night and the glory of chasing a deer or rabbit, killing it and feeding a hunger of the body and not The Hunger of his race.

He was dhampir. A soldier of the vampire race. A man born to protect his kind. He had the strengths of a vampire — the needs of one — and yet he could move about in the sun, feeding on the enemies he hunted, draining them of all life without sanction — at least until The Transformation, The Change occurred — turning him from dhampir to full vampire, a reproductively mature male who would have to deal with both The Hunger and The Heat.

He would lose his ability to move about in the sun in a human form, a price he was required to pay in order to secure the part of his alien heritage that would make him nearly impossible to kill, that extended his lifespan so it covered centuries instead of decades.

He would gain the ability to change into mist and dissipate into the air, the vampire's most effective self-defense mechanism, though unlike most vampires he would still have access to a physical shape—the wolf's—should he need to be out in the sunlight.

It was a shape he enjoyed. A wildness he embraced. One free of the rules that usually governed him—with the exception of one. Neither the dhampir nor the wolf were allowed to attack humans who didn't deserve to die.

He didn't expect to encounter such a human tonight, not when the woods were cold and unwelcoming. A perfect place to run in his other form.

Domino's cock pressed against his jeans, his balls grew heavy, aching to be free of the confining clothing. To hang between his legs in proud display in the presence of a female. *In the presence of a potential mate,* the wolf claimed, and the man laughed. He couldn't imagine craving only one particular cunt when there was such a variety of pleasure to be had among mortal women. He couldn't imagine finding a female whose mind interested him as much as her body, whose strength and courage he could admire, not for just a night but for the centuries that lay ahead for him.

Let others of his kind tie themselves to kadines—the human females created and raised for the purpose of being converted. Let others claim their brides and see them through the changes. Exchanging blood three times so the bodies of their mates were altered enough to enable them to bear a vampire's young, though they weren't fully vampire themselves.

It was a responsibility Domino didn't want. A cleverly disguised trap that led to loss of freedom.

To take a kadine was to be sexually bonded to her for centuries. The connection so deep that her happiness would become his, her sorrow his. Her life his, because without his blood, and his blood alone, she would die.

It was the ultimate insurance against betrayal. The ultimate insurance against one vampire coveting the mate of another. A complex design woven into their cells by ancient, alien ancestors. Ancestors who'd ruthlessly done what was necessary to survive, to adapt, to ensure that they wouldn't become extinct on the hostile, primitive world in which they found themselves.

Domino followed Dakotah as she moved deeper among the trees, each step a freeing of the wolf inside her. It amazed him how well she hid what she was. Fane had made no mention of it and he'd stationed himself at the carnival until Matteo Cabrelli had arrived from Italy in order to claim Sarael. Even Domino's own wolf hadn't been entirely certain until tonight. But as soon as she'd stepped from the trailer and bathed in the light of the moon, her focus on the woods — he'd known.

She stopped in a small clearing, a place that was little more than rocks and the half rotted trunk of a massive tree, lying on its side, a handful of its branches still reaching for the sky in silent supplication. Domino halted as well, making sure he was downwind of her, seeing a wariness in her body as she paused, searching the shadows as though she could feel him there, before relaxing and shedding her jacket, hanging it over a tree branch.

Her scent and clothed body alone had been enough to arouse him, but as the remainder of her clothing followed her jacket, his cock enlarged past the point he could continue to endure. With a silent groan he opened his jeans, taking himself in hand, unable to bear the thought of looking away from Dakotah even long enough to remove his own clothes.

She was magnificent. Stunning. Sleek lines and erotic curves. Dark nipples and dark hair between her thighs.

The wolf wanted to howl, to pounce. To feast on her scent and taste her. To mount her and thrust its penis into her hot, wet channel.

The man wanted the same.

When she moved out of sight again, slipping behind the fallen tree, Domino released his cock and quickly stripped. He crouched, tensing involuntarily, the remembered agony of his first change still present though the pain was no longer a part of each transformation.

When he stood again he was in wolf form, though no *canis lupus* would ever grow to be as massive as he was. Nor would their eyes be obsidian, as black as his coat.

She was wolf now too. The breeze informed him of that.

The majority of what human scent remained in the small clearing resided on the discarded clothing, with only a tiny hint lingering on fur — just enough so that one supernatural being would recognize another.

The wolf wanted to trot right over to her, to thrust its nose against her and wallow in the rich female smell. It wanted to explore her with its tongue. To chase and hunt with her before getting down to the business of covering her body and penetrating her, sending its cock into her wet heat in a frenzy of mating bliss.

But the man held back. Knowing it would be better to let Dakotah get deeper into the forest. To allow the wolf she kept suppressed to grow stronger before approaching her.

And so they ran together, separately at first, with the huge black wolf being careful to stay downwind of the smaller, lithe brown-gray female. But when a rabbit darted from a bush, its cotton tail a ball that instinct demanded be chased, Domino surged out of the shadows and into Dakotah's awareness.

The female wolf whirled, bracing for an attack, but when the larger male charged past her, intent on the rabbit, his scent carrying the unmistakable whiff of a being who was more than wolf, she raced after him. The wolf's will dominating despite the human soul struggling deep inside, trying to rise to the surface.

But the wolf would not yield. It recognized what the human did not. A mate.

There was no way the wolf was going to be denied. There was no way it was going to be pressed back into the cage it lived in — not until it had been mounted by the large male whose lush scent had sent it into heat, swelling its vulva and making its hormones rage.

She caught up to him easily, yipping in ecstasy, both of them plunging through thickets, immersed in the smell of dark woods and each other as they hunted together, the shared activity bonding them, their forms defining their behavior, so that when the hunt ended in a clearing without a kill, it was the female who approached the male, rubbing her body against his, offering him a chance to inhale her scent, to lick her — the escaped rabbit no longer of interest as they nuzzled and explored, growing more eager to mate with each passing moment.

It was a brief courtship, a hurried affair done before the humans could interfere. The female presenting herself to the male, bracing as he maneuvered into position, mounting her from the back and thrusting inside, his forelegs gripping her tightly as he rutted, the tip of his penis engorging until he could no longer slide in and out of her channel.

He dismounted then, his hind leg passing over her back as he turned to face the opposite direction, the wolf form allowing his penis to flex and twist as the swollen tip remained in her vagina. Ejaculating. The tie lasting until his testicles were empty of seed.

Chapter Two

The sun was attempting to burn through the heavy autumn fog when the large male wolf stirred, the human within waking also, both of them immediately aware of the smaller wolf curled at their back.

The wolf quivered with joy at having a mate, a companion. It whined with excitement, its body ready to nudge the female awake and cover her, tying again as it had done repeatedly throughout the night.

But the man's will prevailed, forcing the wolf to ease away from the female and escape. A denial of the wolf's claim of a mate echoing with each footstep as they returned to the spot where the human clothing lay in a damp pile on the ground. Where the wolf crouched, snarling, its instincts warring with those of the man, its protests absorbed and echoed in the alien cells even as the air shimmered and its form was lost.

Fuck!

Domino stood snarling and hissing. Naked in the cold, wet air, and yet he was unaware of anything beyond The Heat coursing through his body, the burning need to return to the spot he'd just escaped and take Dakotah in her human form, to rut on her as his fangs buried themselves in her flesh and he fed The Hunger.

For long moments he battled his primitive programming, taking his cock in hand and sliding up and down his shaft, the movement first heightening the need then easing it in a jet of steamy release. But the relief was short-lived, the urge to return to Dakotah a shout from every cell save what small part of him was still human.

The Heat and Hunger were a dual roar now, a demand and a seductive whisper that never relented. He was close to The Transformation. Closer than he'd let himself acknowledge.

With a curse Domino turned his back on the small clearing, on the half rotted tree trunk lying on its side, its branches reaching for the sky and draped with Dakotah's clothing. Despite the blueprint of creation and survival that his alien ancestors had designed for the vampire race, Domino didn't want a mate. And despite what the wolf might claim, he had done nothing more than fuck during the night. Done nothing more than enjoy a good run before finishing his business in Ashberg and leaving.

Frustration moved through him as he dressed. Irritation.

He'd hoped to hunt as a dhampir for a few more years. Hoped to retain the ability to move about during the day in a human shape for a little while longer. But his time of absolute freedom was nearly over.

Like all of his kind, he knew the symptoms well. He was close to changing. Too close to risk staying here much longer.

He needed to finish his business, to gain what remaining information he could and then destroy the last three Believers in the area. Enemies who belonged to a secret society committed to killing both his kind and anyone else not deemed human enough to suit them—though in truth, the men he'd hunted recently had been little more than twisted deviants. Afterward he would return to his parents' home where his father and brother could see him through the change and give him first blood.

Domino skirted the dirt and asphalt lot where the carnival had stopped and set up, preferring to avoid the sharp glance and biting comments of the fortune-teller, the knowing smiles and threats of a tarot reading. He would risk another encounter with her before he returned to his parents' home, but not now.

* * * * *

Dakotah woke alone. The wolf immediately lifting its muzzle to the sky, offering a long sad song of abandonment and pleading. Its howls adding to the eeriness of the fog-enshrouded day, the clearing with its shadow-trees and wet, heavy mist.

They rose as one being, the human and wolf very nearly equal in will, though their desires were divergent. Dakotah's thoughts centered on returning to the trailer, on leaving the carnival, her mind refusing to revisit the night or wonder about the male shapeshifter she'd spent it with. The wolf wanted to track its missing mate, to be by his side night and day. To forever abandon the lonely cage of its current life.

His trail led back to the clearing, his shape changing to that of a human, his scent one both Dakotah and the wolf would recognize again. The wolf yielded its form, accepting that it couldn't hunt for its mate on four legs, but the change of shape didn't reduce its determination to find the male who had claimed it.

Growling, the wolf slunk into the dark recesses where it was forced to hide, reduced to prey instead of living as it was meant to live, as a predator. But even in the darkness of its prison, the wolf's conviction was strong. It had found its mate and they would be together again.

Dakotah stopped at the trailer only long enough to shed her damp clothes and put on a drier version of the same outfit before leaving again. A smile formed on her lips when she spotted the carnival owner trying to slip away from his trailer, a man intent on not being noticed.

Too bad.

She resisted the urge to yell Roy's name, preferring instead to move to his side in the lifting fog. "Hot date?" she asked, catching him near the carousel.

Roy stopped, turning, enabling her to look down into his ancient, wrinkled face. She was curious despite herself as she remembered Helki's cackled, *He's got a couple of lady friends in this town. He'll be catting around all night and most of the morning.*

"Age is all in the mind," he said, his dark eyes gleaming with amusement, his laugh an echo of the fortune-teller's as he tapped his forehead with a gnarled finger. "You don't need pills and potions with the ladies if you know how to give them what they want."

"Then you know what I want?"

Roy's hand reached out and she stiffened automatically, bracing against the contact, willing to accept it even though she preferred not to be touched. Preferred to remain as separate as possible—except during those times when the need for sex became an itch that had to be scratched by someone other than herself.

Understanding flickered in Roy's eyes, along with a hint of something else—knowledge, the same glimmer Dakotah had seen in Helki's expression as she studied the tarot cards of Dakotah's reading. "Stay another day."

"I can't," Dakotah said. Knowing as soon as she said it that it was absolutely true. She could feel the change in the wolf. She was aware of its intention to find the large male and she couldn't allow that to happen.

It had taken her too long to master that part of herself. She couldn't risk losing control of it, though realization had slowly overtaken her as she'd returned to the carnival. The wolf in the woods was like none of the supernatural beings Victor Hale had sent after her. The wolf in the woods held traces of the same alien scent she'd encountered before. On Fane Mercier. And on the man who'd clamed Sarael.

The wolf stirred, savoring its future victory as Helki's words moved through Dakotah's mind. *You will see Sarael sooner than you might think and be a part of her world for more years than you can imagine.* But Dakotah pushed the prediction aside. She had no room for hope or sentiment. "I need to head out," she said, focusing on the carnival owner.

He nodded and pulled a wad of bills from his pocket as if expecting things to unfold just as they had.

* * * * *

Domino found the Believer named Byrd in a hotel room littered with liquor bottles and condoms. It had been a tedious task monitoring Byrd's activities, staying close enough to the Believer so that he could reinforce his commands periodically and gather information. But the sacrifice had been worth it. This trip alone—which had led to the deaths of several dozens of their enemy—had made the investment of Domino's time worthwhile. And yet he was more than happy to see it end.

Left to his own devices, Byrd was a rapist. A man who enjoyed breaking into houses and defiling the women within before stealing their money and jewelry. Domino's compulsions had kept the Believer from returning to his preferred forms of entertainment, but it required constant monitoring and Domino could no longer afford to do it or to take the risk that Byrd would slip his mental leash.

With a grimace, Domino kicked the sagging hotel bed. Repeating the action until Byrd opened bleary, reddened eyes, only to be immediately trapped in obsidian ones. "Where are the others?" Domino asked, an often repeated question when he dealt with the Believer.

Byrd's body twitched, as though he was trying to turn his head and look for his companions. "Must have gone after the girl."

Domino tensed, flashing back to the night Matteo had joined as he and Fane hunted. They'd first heard the Believers were after a female on that night. The confession coming from someone who claimed to have overheard it. But with each of their enemy questioned and then destroyed, no one else knew anything about her. And so Domino had come to believe there was no intended victim—though he had little doubt a woman would be taken and raped.

"What girl?" he asked, cursing himself for not hunting Byrd immediately after learning about the woman. But he'd been distracted by other matters—Sarael's escape from Matteo. Fane's conversion from dhampir to vampire. His own hunting, complicated by the closeness of the change and the distraction of Dakotah.

A growl escaped, a low rumble from the wolf at the reminder of the woman it considered its mate. Domino grimaced, suppressing that part of his nature. "What girl?" he asked again, his gaze boring into Byrd's. The Hunger waking, sliding irritably underneath his skin.

"A girl Chuck's been looking for. He said she was hotter than the whores we brought back last night. He got the go-ahead this morning to pick her up." Byrd licked his lips as his hand moved to his crotch, his smile widening. "We're going to have a good time tonight. As long as we deliver her alive, we can do anything we want with her."

The Hunger became a roar and Domino fought to keep his fangs from descending until after he'd gained all the useful information he could. It would be a pleasure to kill tonight, to sate The Hunger completely with not only blood but a life.

"Where are you taking the girl?"

Byrd's eyes went blank. "Chuck didn't say. Maybe back to Atlantic City."

"To those Chuck reports to?"

"I don't know for sure. Maybe not. I heard Chuck talking on his phone about money. Half for finding her. Half for delivering her."

"What's the woman's name?"

"Something weird. The name of a state."

Rage ripped through Domino. "Dakotah?"

Recognition turned Byrd's mouth upward in a smile that was his last. The word *yeah* forever trapped on his lips as Domino struck with savage fury, easily subduing the larger, heavier man as he drove his fangs into the Believer's neck.

It was over too quickly, too painlessly, as far as Domino was concerned. The meal too rushed and the hunt unsatisfying. But there was no time to waste or play. No time even to enjoy the blood which sated The Hunger even as The Heat grew more demanding.

* * * * *

Dakotah was aware of the two men almost as soon as she left the carnival. What few belongings she valued were packed in a knapsack that was slung casually over one shoulder so it wouldn't become a leash to hold her with. Her hands were buried in her jacket pockets, each caressing a knife hidden there — the handles black and the blades clean, though both had been covered in blood many times.

She cursed herself for not going the night before. For not blowing off her pay and leaving when her gut told her to.

Irritation moved along her spine. At herself. At the old fortune-teller. At the wolf — her own and the big male.

Even though *she* was in control, her body didn't feel as though it was completely hers. She felt edgy, restless beyond needing to run. She felt like she was in heat and it pissed her off.

Her lips pulled back in a baring of teeth. The men following her had picked the wrong day to take her on. They were human and she didn't feel remotely human at the moment.

She'd started walking in the direction of a nearby campground, one that had been popular among the psychics who'd come to Ashberg for the psychic fair. The fair was over but a large number of the rigs remained at the site and she felt sure she could hitch a ride, if not to the closest big city, at least to a different city, one where she could begin her disappearance, could begin the process of renaming and remaking herself.

If she ran she could probably get within sight of the campground without the men catching her—unless one of them was smart enough to go back for their car. Even without a breeze, she could smell the sweat and sex that clung to their skin, the stink of beer and cheap liquor. They were no match for her, especially if they could be separated, dealt with one at a time.

She needed to know if they were predators after any female or if they'd come for her in particular. It bothered her that she'd seen others with ornate crosses tattooed on their necks coming and going from the town and the carnival in the last couple of days. Men resembling these, conscienceless specimens of human garbage.

Their deaths would only be a crime if she got caught.

Dakotah veered into the woods when she heard one of the men say, "I'm going back for the car."

There was a curse behind her and she dropped the knapsack in a hidden pocket of shrubs and vine before she began jogging, luring them deeper into the forest of oak and pine, maple and cedar. Birch, the white of the trees like skeletal sentinels in a rapidly darkening land.

The wolf slid along Dakotah's nerve endings, willing her to stop and allow its form to rule. She would if she had to, if it came down to her life or death. But the wolf would end the chase in a flash of teeth, in screams as flesh and muscles parted from bones in a rush of hot blood. The wolf wouldn't stop to question, couldn't press the cold steel of a knife blade to throats and groins in order to demand answers.

Her pursuers had sense enough to be leery in a jungle of narrow trails and wet leaves instead of alleyways and garbage. They stayed together, cursing, their breath coming and going in short pants. When she'd drained them of their strength, Dakotah stopped and turned, facing her prey though they still maintained the illusion that she was theirs.

* * * * *

"Where is she?" Domino growled, whirling as the ancient fortune-teller entered the travel trailer.

"Gone."

"I can see that, old woman." He flashed his fangs. "The Believers are hunting her."

Helki laughed. "What kind of a mate would she be for you if she couldn't take care of herself, especially against mere humans?"

Obsidian eyes gleamed with menace. "I have no mate."

"The cards say otherwise." She nodded to the bed, to what remained of Dakotah's possessions, left there when the dresser and desk had been emptied. The tarot deck set apart from the rest. Three cards from it laid out on the dark blue comforter. The past, the present, the future.

Death. Strength. The Emperor.

A fourth and fifth, carelessly knocked to the floor when Domino handled her things. The Empress. The World.

"I don't have time for this foolishness."

The fortune-teller shrugged and stepped away from the door, her movement closing the distance between the two of them and leaving the exit clear. "Then go."

Domino snarled. Frustration and rage rippling through him along with unwilling respect. She knew how close he was to turning. He could read it in her eyes, and yet she tested him.

"I could force you to tell me what I want to know," he said, obsidian eyes meeting equally dark ones.

She reached up, smoothing calloused fingertips over his cheek. "So like your grandfather. Perhaps that's why I've always loved you best. Accept my words. Accept your destiny. Both lead to Dakotah." A small smile formed. "The wolves have already made their choice."

Domino scowled, knowing he'd been bested by his mother's mother. A woman who had managed to raise Sarael, a stolen kadine, without discovery. A woman who'd seen through the veil of his kind and peered into their world when her daughter, his mother, had been claimed and converted by his father.

"I want no mate."

Helki cackled. "Neither did your father that night he came to the carnival to hunt and discovered my Giselle." Her eyes danced with remembered amusement. "What a chase she gave him! What a chase she still gives him!"

Domino grimaced, preferring not to be reminded of The Heat that surrounded his parents. No doubt his mother would soon be pregnant, ready to bear and raise a second generation of sons, followed by more, two or three sons for each quarter of a century that she and his father were reproductively fertile.

"Have your say then," Domino grumbled.

The fortune-teller stroked her calloused fingertips over his cheek again. Her expression going from amused to serious. "I wouldn't have you spend the future alone, Domino, dependant on the herbs in order to control The Hunger." She grimaced with distaste. "Nor would I see you go to the padralls and have them create a kadine for you. A female raised with no freedom. No sense of who she really is other than one whose very existence is centered around becoming the perfect mate for a male she didn't choose. Accept what the cards say. What the wolf has already told you." She stepped away from him, leaning down to pick up the cards that had fallen to the floor.

Domino stiffened as she separated the third card from those already on the bed, joining it with the two he had brushed against earlier and knocked to the floor, positioning them in the shape of a V—the Emperor and the Empress connected to each other by The World.

"You see it?" Helki asked him, but Domino refused to be drawn into her game.

"I see nothing but the day fading and the night approaching."

Helki cackled, tapping The Emperor. "Oh, he is a stubborn one! Forceful and dominating. But what a protector he can be, a provider for those he cares about."

Her finger moved to the corner of The Empress. "An interesting card for your mate. She wouldn't see herself in it, but it contains her. Her life has been one of famine and drought instead of abundance. Of harsh choices and betrayal, and yet her soul has not been tarnished and her secret heart yearns for a man to prove that all men aren't like those who have come before him."

The fortune-teller's fingertips settled beneath The World, underscoring it. "The circle is complete. Two separate journeys now become one on a path that is lined with fulfillment, enjoyment, unity as it weaves its way into the future and takes form in the next generation of sons, soldiers to follow in their father's footsteps." She cackled. "And to give their father the same challenge that their father gave to his! You'll find your mate and those chasing her in the woods between here and the campground."

* * * * *

The men chasing Dakotah stopped in their tracks when they saw the knives in her hands. Wary, but not afraid. The one in the lead grinned, broken teeth in a filthy mouth. "This bitch is going to be better than the ones we had last night." He smacked his lips. "Oh yeah, unwilling women are always more fun."

"You think the guy who wants her will care if we knock her teeth out, Chuck? She's the kind that would bite a man's dick off just for spite."

"As long as she's alive, he don't care," Chuck said, retrieving a knife from his pocket before taking his jacket off and wrapping it around his arm. "Go around and get behind her on the trail. This place gives me the creeps. I want to be out of here before it gets much darker."

"What about fucking her?"

"You want to do it while I get the car and move it closer, fine, only she's got to be tied up. I've spent enough time in these shit-hole little towns. And I don't trust the guy not to figure out where we are and come get her himself — or send someone else — if we don't deliver soon."

"He wouldn't double-cross the order — "

"Bullshit. He's not a Believer."

Dakotah laughed, a sound without any true mirth. "Victor Hale isn't even human," she said, watching as Chuck's body jerked in reaction, verifying her suspicion about who had sent him, though the reference to the Believers puzzled her.

She smiled, a baring of teeth, relieved that they'd answered her questions without the necessity of her asking. They were after her and her enemy hadn't yet arrived. There was no reason to delay over their killing.

As the weaker of the two men slid into the woods, fighting vines and low branches in an attempt to get behind her, she lunged for the one named Chuck, growling in rage when his knife sliced along her shoulder and upper arm as one of her own drove into his stomach and ripped downward like a wolf's lethal disemboweling of its prey.

Chuck's scream was piercing, his movements violent as he tried to pry her off him. But the wolf was in a frenzy, driven by the hot, metallic smell of blood.

Dakotah barely felt his blows. She didn't hesitate to plunge the second knife into his back in the moment that the first blade ripped through his groin, internal organs emerging from torn clothing, trailing after her hand as she slashed at the inside of his thigh, deep enough to ensure that he would bleed out while she dealt with the other man.

She pulled away from him, turning, bracing for an attack that would never come. The second man lay in a crumpled heap at a dark stranger's feet. A man Dakotah had never seen before but whose scent she knew well.

Chapter Three

"Who are you?" Dakotah asked, knives held in front of her, refusing to give in to the wolf's joy at being reunited with the male from the previous night — even if he was in his human form.

"I am Domino Santori." An eyebrow lifted as his gaze dropped to the knives in her hands then upward, lingering on her breasts and making her nipples tighten and her cunt pulse. "Surely you don't need those. Not after we enjoyed each other's company last night."

Dakotah hesitated for a moment then closed the knives and returned them to her pockets before using her right hand to explore the extent of her injuries on the back of her left arm and shoulder, the touch sending pain rushing through her and making her gasp, her fingers coming away slick with blood.

Rage filled Domino at the sight of her bloody hand. A ferociousness that was beyond anything he'd ever experienced.

In the blink of an eye he was at her side, swamping her with the pheromones of his kind so that he could remove her jacket and shirt without the necessity of physically subduing her. She was mentally strong, but he was stronger, and he had an ally in her wolf.

Domino growled at the sight of her injury, snarled and cursed himself for not arriving soon enough to destroy both of the men who'd been pursuing her. *What had she been thinking to allow the Believers to catch her? Why hadn't she changed into her other form if she wanted them dead?*

He ran his tongue along the deep crevice of the knife wound, healing her even as her blood coated his tongue and fanned the flames of The Hunger. The Heat. And this time it was *his* wolf who worked against him, who joined forces with the alien inclinations of his ancestors so that Domino carried Dakotah deeper into the woods, away from the corpses of their enemy.

He'd had no intention of taking Dakotah again, either as wolf or man, but now Domino finished what he'd begun, stripped her of her remaining clothing before shedding his own, tossing it to the ground to form a rough shield against damp leaves and cold earth. The Heat was a fever in his blood. A pulsing, raging inferno in his cock. Her name the only one in his thoughts, her scent, the feel of her flesh against his the only things that mattered.

He allowed her to surface from the pheromones in the second before his body covered hers, his lips taking hers, his tongue thrusting against her, their skin so hot that steam rose around them.

Desire swamped Dakotah. Primitive. Familiar. Nature's celebration of life over death. Victory.

She'd experienced it each time she'd succeeding in killing one of the werewolves Victor Hale had sent after her — though until this instant she'd never given in to the heady need to mate, to rejoice in a wild thrashing of male joined to female. A tumultuous rutting that had nothing to do with love and everything to do with the continuation of the species, with survival.

Dakotah didn't hesitate, didn't question. She wrapped her legs around Domino's waist and welcomed him into her body. A deep moan vibrating in her throat when his thick cock stretched her, filled her, burned her from the inside out.

His hips pistoned hard, fast, pummeling in and out of her channel as though he wanted to hammer into her most private, untouched parts. His growls of pleasure and satisfaction feeding the frenzy inside her, driving her to take everything he had to offer.

He held her wrists to the ground and she allowed it, something she'd never done before. Where usually restraint triggered a savage need to escape, an almost mindless need to strike out and kill if necessary, it was different with Domino.

He had killed for her. His wolf had already coupled with hers.

Dakotah tightened her legs as orgasm neared, she bucked and writhed, fought for release, and he responded by giving her more of his weight, by thrusting harder, deeper than a human male was capable of doing, slamming against her cervix in a way that blurred the border between pain and pleasure, blended them so that there was no clear point where one ended and the other began.

A red haze filled Domino's mind, a hunger for more than sex, more than blood. But he fought off the programming of his alien cells, determined to fuck her throughout the night as he'd done in his wolf form and then walk away from her in the morning.

He wanted no mate. Needed no mate, despite the way his body craved her, despite the treacherous images going through his mind, the wish that she had fangs in her human form so she could sink them into him.

His gums ached as he kept his canines from descending, from plunging into Dakotah's soft neck in order to gorge on her as he fucked her. She was temptation beyond any he could have imagined. A wolf even in her human skin. A strong, wild creature that would never be completely tamed.

He growled as her legs tightened around his waist, responded by thrusting harder, deeper, her sheath a tight fist around his cock, resisting him even as it welcomed him. Causing the wolf he carried in his cells to rut furiously. To howl in frustration that its seed wasn't yet viable as orgasm roared through Domino's cock in a lava-hot rush to fill Dakotah.

Neither of them moved in the aftermath of release. Instead they remained coupled for long moments, panting, skin slick with sweat, hearts racing in chests pressed tightly together.

Dakotah was the first to stir, the instincts that had kept her alive for so long fighting to the surface, fighting to suppress the wolf, which had escaped its cage and was still shivering with joy at being reunited with the male it thought of as its mate.

Domino might have helped her this night, but she'd learned the hard way that the only person she could count on was herself. She needed to drag the bodies into the woods and be on her way. If she was lucky, she'd be long gone before the corpses were discovered.

She unhitched her legs from around Domino's waist, pulling her wrist from his grip and pressing her hand to his shoulder, urging him to roll off her. He complied with a grunt, disbelief filling him when she stood, pulling what clothing belonged to her out from under him as she did so.

He'd never had a woman rise from his bed with the intention of leaving unless he'd commanded her to do so. That this one thought she could escape him…

The same savage possessiveness he'd experienced before in her presence brought him to his feet, had him reaching for her, stalking her when she backed away from him. His cock hard and jutting out from his body in a bold display of intention.

A small thrill danced along Dakotah's spine at his show of dominance. At the desire she saw in his face and the way his penis was engorged and leaking, his balls heavy and full underneath it.

Wolf or man, he was a magnificent specimen of masculinity. An incredible example of a male in his prime.

He trigged memories from her past. Dreams and fantasies she'd once held as possibilities. Until she'd learned differently. Until those dreams and fantasies had become too painful a contrast to her reality. To what her life had become. A horror-show where only the strongest and the luckiest emerged alive. Where few emerged unbroken.

Only the flip of a coin had put her under dominatrix supervision and training. Had saved her from repeated rape, from becoming a cheap disposable commodity to the man her self-righteous grandmother and worthless father had turned her over to in order to wipe out her father's debt. If Victor Hale hadn't murdered them in retaliation for Dakotah killing his son, she might have returned one day to kill them herself.

A low growl sounded in her throat, threatening even to her own ears, and she forced her thoughts away from the past and back to the man who was stalking her, who'd tensed at the warning he heard, perhaps understanding there were places inside her so dark and full of fury that it would be a fight to the death if he stumbled into them.

"I want the night with you," Domino said, his voice stroking over her like a wolf's tongue. "Then I'll see to the bodies while you go on your way."

"Why?"

"A test of will." He smiled, a flash of white teeth, of mocking humor that intrigued her. "And because I don't believe in tarot readings given by meddling old fortune-tellers." He moved closer, the smile widening, his scent swirling around Dakotah along with his heat. "What about you? Do you believe?"

She thought about the reading Helki had forced on her. About The Emperor.

The time will come when you will face the enemy who wants you dead, but you will not do so alone. Another change awaits you. This time at the hands of a man unlike any you have known before. A man who wants your life, not your death.

And then her thoughts flashed to the day Helki had insisted on giving Sarael a reading. The day Matteo Cabrelli had come to claim her friend.

"I can feel the truth in them," Sarael had said, looking down at the three cards representing her past, her present and her future.

"You can change that truth," Dakotah had claimed, reaching over, flipping the cards so they lay facedown.

The lessons of Dakotah's past urged her to turn away from Domino and leave now. The wolf told her to stay.

She studied Domino for a long moment, wondering if it was only because their wolves had mated that she craved his touch, had allowed him to pin her down and take her roughly when she might have seriously injured or killed another man for trying it. Whatever the reason, it didn't matter.

In the end it was her secret heart, the place that still harbored forgotten dreams of happy-ever-after that held her in place. It was the knowledge that she couldn't run forever and that ultimately Victor Hale's wolves would find her and she would die in a savage fight, refusing to be hauled back to Atlantic City alive.

Why shouldn't she take what rare pleasure she could find that didn't involve her own hands and fingers or cheap toy substitutes? She couldn't afford to lose the entire night, but she would fuck him again and then walk away.

Dakotah shrugged. "I don't care what the tarot cards say. Once more and then I'm out of here. Take it or leave it."

Domino's nostrils flared as fire burned though his veins. The Heat responding to her challenge. Her taunt.

In his world, females were valued, treasured, cared for, loved, protected. But men ruled. Had always ruled. Would always rule, because only they were nearly indestructible.

The natural order of things was woven into the ancient fabric of vampire cells and Dakotah's words scraped over his nerve endings like sandpaper. Made him want to prove to her how wrong she was, how helpless she was.

It would take no effort at all to swamp her with the pheromones of his kind, to hypnotize her and command that she stay with him until *he* tired of her. Until *he* sent her on her way as he had so many other women. As he intended to do to so many more. She was a passing temptation, a fascination brought on by the nearness of The Transformation.

Domino moved into her, his cock straining to brush against her flat belly, to mark her with some of the seed coating its tip. His testicles were already heavy again, full, though until he became fully vampire there was no possibility of impregnating any female, and even afterward, only a kadine could carry his child, and he would not lose his freedom in such a manner.

Raw pleasure coursed through him at her boldness, the way she met his eyes, held her position, only stepping away from him as he crowded into her, physically forcing her to take one step and then another until her back was pressed against the smooth bark of a birch tree.

"I'll take it. I'll take you," he said, answering her challenge, his voice silky and dangerous, The Heat and The Hunger an incessant hum in his veins, feeding the desire to claim and dominate so that Domino knew a moment of real fear, worried that he was about to step into a carefully laid trap.

He shook it off. Told himself that if he intended to stay free of the responsibility of a mate, if he intended to avoid sexually bonding himself to one female, then he might as well strengthen his control and his will with this one, where the risk was reduced. He hadn't yet been through The Transformation, hadn't given her his blood. But even so, he wouldn't gamble by taking her blood, by leaving her unrestrained.

He took the clothing she'd collected but hadn't yet put on away from her, dropping everything but the bra to the ground before gathering her wrists. She immediately guessed what he was planning, and he read the intention to resist him in her eyes.

Domino had no choice but to swamp her with pheromones. He couldn't allow her to fight him. Couldn't allow her to become afraid.

Fear was a heady aphrodisiac to his kind. The lure of it, the ease with which it became an addiction in itself was part of the reason laws existed forbidding full vampires from killing their prey by draining them of life, from feeding on both their blood and their fear.

Only the dhampirs, the soldiers, were allowed to drain their enemies completely — a compensation woven into their design perhaps, for the years of service they gave before they became fully vampire. Or maybe it was because they retained their human shape, their ability to be out in the sun. Because The Hunger didn't whisper as loudly in them, wasn't yet as dangerous to them. Still, none of them could afford for their existence to become widely known, especially now, in a world with advanced technology.

If he weren't so close to The Transformation, so close to being ruled by The Heat and Hunger, then he wouldn't feel the need to partially restrain her. But her challenge, the wolf's claim that she was his mate, his own obsession with her — one that had started when he'd arrived in the previous town to hunt the Believers and assist in guarding Sarael — all converged in an emotional flashpoint that put both her life and his freedom at risk.

Domino ruthlessly captured her in obsidian eyes, pushed into her mind and spoke the thoughts he forced on her. "You will allow me to bind you."

The wolf rose within him and insisted that its mate not be treated as prey, insisted that she know the tethering was for her own protection, and Domino added, "You will not fight the restraints. They are for your own safety."

And unbidden, he said, "They are for your pleasure."

He used her bra to lash her unresisting wrists together before lifting her arms over her head and securing them to a limb. Desire rushed through him at the sight of her naked and tethered, a swirl of uneasiness following in its wake at how much it satisfied something inside of him to see her like that when he'd never done it to another female, never thought to do it.

A different hunger rose, the hunger to have her submit to it willingly, and Domino hissed. He stepped back from her, considered freeing Dakotah as the uneasiness gave way to unwelcome realization.

All those created and raised to be kadines were trained to accept being bound and restrained, to expect it, even to welcome it as proof that their mates knew how to keep them safe when The Hunger and Heat became dangerously intense. There were vampires who'd killed their kadines accidentally. Who'd forgotten in their pleasure what lurked in the most primitive parts of their being.

It was a dark ecstasy like no other, to take from a willing partner until their heart stuttered in warning, to know the pleasure they gained from the bite was so great that those they took from would trade their life for it.

It was an unparalleled high to take everything—as their ancestors had once done when they were trying to adapt to the hostile world they found themselves on—when they were experimenting, speeding the evolutionary process by taking the form of their prey, moving into its still warm body and possessing it thoroughly. A possessiveness that had evolved as his species had evolved, had been tweaked and modified until it became focused solely on their mates. And yet at the vampire's core, they retained parts of what they had originated from, ruthless, alien predators. Beings so feared and deadly that they weren't welcomed on any world.

Domino hissed again, taking his cock in hand and thinking he should free Dakotah. Send her on her way so he could deal with the bodies of the Believers and then return to his parents' home to await The Transformation.

Maybe he would have. Maybe he could have. But a breeze swirled into existence, assaulting him with their mingled scents, filling his nostrils with the smell of sex—and he was lost.

"You will not fight the restraints. They are for your safety, your pleasure," Domino repeated, stepping into her so their bodies touched, releasing her from his hypnotic gaze.

He slowly reduced the pheromones swamping her senses and leaving her dazed and malleable. Felt his own lust intensify when dark eyes met his, when the hunger he saw there was a reflection of the woman's desire and not enthrallment.

Domino captured her lips and thrust his tongue inside her mouth, taking control of the kiss just as he intended to take control of her body. She fought him, not as prey but as one who considered herself his equal, and he relished the challenge. Anticipated the moment when she would beg for her climax and scream his name when he gave it to her.

His hands slid from her wrists down her immobilized arms, the feel of her sleek muscles and smooth skin a sensory treat. She wasn't as well endowed as the women he usually took, but as his hands covered her breasts with their tight, dark nipples, he found them more desirable than any he had ever caressed.

The wolf approved of her sleek lines. The man echoed that approval, and Domino's lips left Dakotah's in order to trail kisses downward.

She groaned at the first brush of his tongue over her nipple. Jerked at the second. Struggled, arched into him with the third, her voice a husky command as she told him to suck her, to bite her.

He growled in response, wrapped his arms around her, yielded to her demands because it suited him, because suddenly her breasts had become his world and he wanted nothing more than to suckle, to mark her with rough pleasure.

Dakotah threw back her head as hot sensation coursed through her body. She strained against the tether, not remembering the moment when she'd allowed him to tie her but no longer caring. He made her feel alive in a way she'd never felt before.

She wanted him to bite her, to suck. To move lower and do the same to her cunt, her clit.

She wanted to feel his tongue fucking in and out of her body. Wanted to hear his hungry growls and watch his face grow flushed and tense with desire as he gripped his cock to keep from coming.

Dangerous fantasy filled Domino's mind. Images of allowing his fangs to descend so he could truly suckle at Dakotah's breast. He ached with the need for it. With the desire to do it. Until the temptation grew so great he had to force himself to release her nipple, to kiss downward, lingering over her smooth belly before rubbing his cheek against the dark brown pubic hair. He buried his nose in it, the wolf demanding that he inhale her scent, take it deep within his lungs, before the man was free to reach his destination. A clit engorged and erect, made for a man's mouth and tongue, for a woman's pleasure. Cunt lips flushed, opened, begging for him to kiss and suck them.

He was lost with the first taste. The Heat controlling so that for long moments he fed on her cries of pleasure, his cock pulsing and straining with each hoarse plea for him to fuck her, to let her come. The wolf wallowing in the scent of its mate, working itself into a frenzy that would only be satisfied with mounting her, tying with her, breeding her.

Domino tried to suppress the wolf's desires. But the more he ate Dakotah, the more she writhed against him, begging as he'd longed to hear her do, her voice low and husky, stroking over him like fur, the more insistent the wolf became. Its desires merged completely with The Heat so that fiery talons scraped at Domino's resolve to walk away from this female.

It had started out a challenge. A dare. But from the moment Domino's lips touched her skin, Dakotah was lost in pleasure. A pleasure so intense that all she could do was press against him, arch into him. Demand that he give her more of it.

His lips and tongue had become her world. His scent a heated fragrance that blended perfectly with the night and was more potent than any drug she'd ever been forced to take.

Desire roared through her veins. Not the victory of life over death. Not the wolf's craving for a mate. But the need of her human heart for contact and intimacy.

Each thrust of his tongue sent a jolt of searing heat to her nipples. Each suck on her clit had her pushing against firm masculine lips in a demand that he take more. That he take all.

A tiny part of her mind argued that she should be fighting the restraints. Fighting to keep herself separate. Fighting for release so she could make her escape. But those thoughts, those urges were lost under his sensual assault, under waves of incredible sensation.

She'd never known anything like it. And probably would never experience it again.

She still couldn't believe she'd allowed him to bind her wrists. Allowed him to strip away her freedom. But she was beyond caring.

"Now," she ordered, and without warning, The Hunger flamed to life in Domino and he fought to keep from turning his head and sinking his fangs into her inner thigh. The wild beat of her pulse blending with the sounds of her pleasure to become a chant in Domino's mind. *Mine! Mine! Mine!*

The sheer ferocity of it forced him away from the heaven of Dakotah's slick, wet folds and had him lunging to his feet before the last of his control slipped. He lifted her easily, pressed her back to the smooth bark of the tree and plunged his cock into her channel, rutting on her wildly as she wrapped her legs around him and clung, accepting the wild mating, both of them raising their faces to the moon and bathing in its light in the moment of climax.

It was a dangerous ecstasy. A challenge to fate. To the wolves. To themselves.

And they both retreated when the last tremor subsided. When skin cooled and night sounds closed in on them.

Without a word, Domino freed her and stepped back. Wild emotion and the wolf swirled and seethed inside him as he watched her dress. As he dressed in turn and followed her back to where the bodies of the Believers lay.

"You'll take care of them?" Dakotah asked, retrieving her shirt and jacket and putting them on, the words barely registering as Domino's nostrils flared, the scent of so much blood overwhelming him, making his body shudder as The Hunger snarled and raged like a caged beast.

He gasped and went to his knees as pain racked his body. Realized in that instant that The Transformation was on him, raking like talons through his internal organs and across his skin, the alien cells finally free to do what they'd been programmed to do, to destroy anything human within him. "Get out of here," he growled when Dakotah crouched at his side.

"What's wrong?"

Obsidian eyes trapped brown ones. The wolf demanding that its mate be sent to safety. "Leave!" Domino hissed before pain drove him the rest of the distance to the ground.

Chapter Four

Dakotah stumbled to a halt at the spot where she'd discarded her backpack when she made the decision to lure her pursuers into the woods. Confusion reigned, disorientation, but a glance down at her clothing, some of it blood-stained, brought memory rushing back, at least to the point where Domino had growled, "Get out of here."

Beyond that there was nothing, only the compulsion to leave. *Her own?* She rubbed her forehead. It's what she'd intended until Domino fell to the ground.

She fought against the nothingness. Remembered staring into obsidian eyes just before everything was lost.

Fear ripped through her. Anger. Disbelief. Rage when she realized that whatever he'd done to send her away, he'd also done when she would have fought him over being tied. And yet…

She snarled, hating the fact that what he'd done to her had led to pleasure beyond anything she'd ever experienced, beyond anything she'd thought she was capable of feeling after what she'd seen and done in order to survive. It would serve him right if she left him writhing in pain.

She knew she wouldn't. She couldn't. Even though it was a weakness. To care. To feel. To not be able to walk away.

Dakotah retrieved her backpack and returned to Domino who'd managed to get to his feet and drag the bodies into the woods, who'd even managed to make it a little way down the trail before going to his hands and knees.

He was sweating, panting, shaking.

And not happy to see her.

"Leave," he growled, lifting his head, but she wasn't about to let him capture her mind again.

"Where's your house? Or your car?" One of them had to be nearby since he'd appeared wearing clothes and not naked from shifting to human form.

Domino forced himself to get to his feet, the wolf urging him to trap her again and give her a more explicit command—knowing that the bloodlust following The Transformation might lead to her death if she was anywhere near the full vampire Domino would soon become. But the man, the dhampir, resisted this time as the pain subsided enough to allow him to think rather than just react.

It was too late now to get to his parents' home. But if he could get to the house he was renting, there was a chance he could survive The Transformation without becoming rogue. Without succumbing to the full force of The Hunger and leaving a trail of bodies behind as he killed the innocent along with the guilty as he fed.

If he could get to a place of safety, then he could contact Fane and Fane would come, if not in time to see him through the change, then in time to offer first blood.

Domino grimaced at the thought of Fane's presence. Of the jokes and taunts he'd no doubt have to endure in the centuries ahead—payback for those he'd often delivered to Fane. But he trusted Fane with his life. He'd stood with Fane and seen him though The Transformation, given him first blood, and he knew Fane wouldn't hesitate to do the same for him.

If there was time.

Domino could feel the pain building again. Stretching inside him, the alien cells ready for a fresh assault on anything human. He managed to tell Dakotah where he'd parked and gave her directions to the house, allowed her to drape his arm over her shoulder and help him leave the woods, but he was hardly aware of either time or distance as he used what control and will remained in order to keep upright and moving.

He was shifting back and forth between man and wolf, his clothing shredded and hanging off his body by the time Dakotah managed to get Domino into the house and into the bedroom. And as bizarre as the sight was, it was easier for her to deal with than his pain alone.

At first she'd been terrified that he had rabies. But other than panting heavily, the wolf gave no signs of being in distress.

Dakotah shivered as Domino's human form took shape and began writhing on the bed, gasping. His words incoherent. Her stomach tightened, not only at the sight of his suffering but with the worry that what he was experiencing was something she'd have to endure in the future.

He stilled, seemed to be fighting the pain. "Cuffs. In the dresser," he gasped, rolling to his side and spearing her with eyes holding something so alien that only instinct kept her from bolting. "Cuffs. Put them on me." This time it was a hiss.

A chill swept up Dakotah's spine at the sight of his fangs. She braced herself, expecting hair to begin sprouting on his face and hands, a nightmare image of a werewolf caught in the middle of two forms. Instead his eyes filled with flames, as though his very soul was being burned away. And for an instant there was nothing of either the man or the wolf, nothing except a dangerous, inhuman predator whose intent to kill her was a scream in every cell of Dakotah's body.

She remained still, focused, knowing that to turn her back was to accept death. And as she watched, the flames receded, the man gritting his teeth as a wave of agony ripped through his body.

Escape was a fleeting thought, turned aside. Dakotah rushed to the dresser, rapidly tossing the contents of its drawers onto the floor as she looked for the cuffs he'd fought so hard to tell her about.

She found them, but the sight of the cuffs had her trembling, reluctant to touch them. They were silver, studded with some type of gem, bloodstone maybe. But the silver alone was enough to make her break out in a sweat. To make her hands clench and unclench as she steeled herself to touch them.

She shuddered, remembering the red cast of Domino's eyes, then forced herself to take the cuffs from their velvet-lined case, to endure when a burning numbness spread through her as she returned to the bed.

He snarled and hissed as she fumbled to get the first band around his wrist. Tried to escape when she went to do the second, so that she moved to his ankles and secured them, then waited until he was bucking in pain, barely aware of her presence as she secured the last band.

Horror raged through Dakotah with sharp talons, tearing her up on the inside as she watched his suffering, watched as his back arched and spasmed so violently that she thought it would break, his arms and legs paralyzed by the silver and bloodstone.

In the nightmare that was her life before she killed Victor Hale's son and escaped, she'd been paid to inflict pain, had mastered the art of wielding a whip or a paddle, of taking those she was forced to serve to the destination they desired. She'd learned to close her mind to their screams, their suffering, to watch it mechanically and alter her techniques as necessary, to take some of them to the edge of death itself—and feel nothing during the process.

But Domino's suffering tore through her. Frightened her. Made the wolf pace and whine while the woman found tears she wouldn't have believed she still possessed running down her cheeks.

With the bands on he remained in human form, alternating between periods of pain and brief moments when he lay panting, his body coated in sweat, seemingly focused inward, unaware of her presence.

She didn't know whether he'd appreciate her touch or not, but she couldn't remain in the room with him and do nothing. When he stilled again, she moved to the bathroom and wet a hand towel, then returned, wiping the sweat from his chest first though he hissed and jerked, nearly catching her in gleaming obsidian eyes when she looked at his face.

Dakotah managed to break away, her heart thundering in her chest at the reminder of his ability to hypnotize. He'd been unaware of her before, but now she could feel the intensity of his gaze as she retreated to the bathroom. It burned into her, causing primal instinct to roar to the surface and urge her to run. Even the wolf danced nervously inside her, though it insisted she stay.

Just as her own conscience did.

Dakotah closed her eyes for a moment, willing that conscience away. She didn't need this. She didn't owe him anything. And if she did, she'd paid him back by not walking away and leaving him in the woods.

She had her own set of problems. If the men Victor Hale sent after her managed to take her alive... Fuck.

Dakotah rinsed the cloth and turned, stepping back into the bedroom, her heart thundering as adrenaline surged through her at the sight of the silver bands lying on an empty bed.

She dropped the moistened cloth and took a step toward the bedroom door as the air around her seemed to thicken with deadly menace. The threat so real that even the wolf wanted to flee.

But there was no time to escape.

No time even to react as Domino shimmered into existence and attacked.

There was only The Hunger.

The wild rush as blood poured into starving cells.

There was no man. No wolf.

Only a host form feeding.

A drive to survive, because survival was the only thing that mattered.

The Hunger ruled unchecked, unchallenged, until The Heat rose, reshaping the savagery, allowing the man and the wolf to emerge and take possession of the shell, though both man and wolf burned with the twin flames of Heat and Hunger.

The wolf was the first to react. To recognize that its mate was dying and protest with its entire being and will.

The man acted, using his fangs to rip into his wrist before pressing it against silken lips, his voice a command that had to be obeyed. "Drink." And with each swallow the flames receded, surrendering, leaving the wolf yipping with pleasure and Domino staring down at Dakotah, denying the truth to himself even as she opened her eyes and his cock surged to life so that he could fuck his bride.

"Leave," he growled, ignoring what both the wolf and his body told him. Determined not to fall into the neatly laid out trap beneath him. One fuck was all it would take to bind himself to her sexually.

Too late, the wolf claimed but Domino refused to believe it. He rolled off Dakotah, eyes narrowing and nostrils flaring when he saw the mark on her neck where he'd bitten her.

A howl of denial formed in his mind, blending with the wolf's howl of joy, the chorus bringing The Heat to life so only sheer force of will kept him from pouncing on Dakotah, from pulling her down and underneath his body when she scrambled to her feet and backed away from him, intent on doing as he'd commanded and leaving.

Dakotah was beyond fear. Beyond even shock.

Vampire.

The single word ricocheted around and around in her thoughts. Even his scent had changed, reminding her of the man who'd claimed Sarael, though the wolf's familiar presence was blended with the cold, alien taint that now identified Domino.

Fire burned through Dakotah's veins. Need, despite the fact he'd very nearly killed her.

But she had no intention of giving in to the wolf's yearning or her own body's demands. She had no intention of taking a chance and becoming vampire. The wolf she could accept, had learned to accept, but she wouldn't lose the rest of her humanity. She wouldn't lose what little control she had over her life. His command echoed through her, this time done without hypnotism, and yet she *had* to obey, knew instinctively that if they shared more blood, his will would rule. He would become The Emperor of the cards.

Bile rose in Dakotah's throat as the fortune-teller's words rang with finality. *Another change awaits you. This time at the hands of a man unlike any you have known before. A man who wants your life, not your death.* But just as she'd counseled Sarael, Dakotah refused to believe the reading held the *only* truth. She grabbed her knapsack from where she'd dropped it just inside the front door and rushed into the night, determined to put as much distance between herself and Domino as she could.

She headed in the direction of the campground, memories pressing in on her as she loped along the edge of the woods.

Memories of another night, another man who'd attacked her—changed her—dying in the process.

A growl escaped. Her lips pulling back in a snarl as feral hatred filled her.

Not for Domino.

The wolf wouldn't allow that, and Dakotah wouldn't lie to herself.

Domino had commanded her to leave when they were in the woods but she'd gone back. She'd chosen to involve herself—forgotten a lifetime of painful lessons—and paid a price for it. Though she couldn't guess what the true cost was yet.

Her blood burned. Her body burned.

Each step away from Domino was an act of will. A test of resolve. Making her push herself until finally she halted, lungs burning and sides aching from running.

Fuck! What was she going to do now?

The wolf was rioting inside her. Fighting her as it hadn't fought since those early days. The days after she'd been taken from her prison in Atlantic City and delivered to Anthony Hale's estate at the edge of the Pine Barrens.

Despite her value, the money she brought in for services rendered, men didn't say no to the Hale family. Men didn't ask questions about the women taken to Anthony's estate and never seen again.

The feral hatred for Anthony Hale—and his father—was a wildness inside Dakotah. A living thing, fed by something alien…something she'd gained from Domino's blood.

Not a thirst for revenge. Anthony Hale was dead. But a primordial *need* to hunt her enemy, to invade his home and destroy him. To kill Victor Hale.

Dakotah forced the thoughts away. Attacking Victor Hale would be suicide. She'd been running since she was taken to his son's home.

She'd thought Anthony was just another sick pervert when he'd shown her into the den, his smile vicious as he'd said, "I've got a little entertainment planned. You can take off your clothing or leave it on. Either way, you're going to get fucked in a way you've never been fucked before."

When he left her alone, she'd found the hidden cameras and more—a weapon for herself in the pokers next to the fireplace.

She'd braced herself for anything. Except for the sight of the door being opened and a wolf entering the room, its penis extending beyond its foreskin.

It attacked without hesitation, ripping at her clothing and leaving her bleeding, fighting to keep from becoming someone else's sick entertainment. The drive to not only save herself but to escape had been the sole focus, the years of "disciplining" clients giving her the strength and knowledge—the rage—to wield the fireplace poker with deadly efficiency and aim.

The wolf collapsed, blood and bone and brain oozing onto the carpet as its form altered and Anthony Hale lay at her feet.

She'd escaped. Or thought she had.

You have died and been reborn into a different person.

A grim smile settled on Dakotah's face. Death, the card of her past. The fortune-teller got that one right.

She forced herself to straighten and keep walking. Forward. Toward the campground, though it was a struggle to keep from turning around, from going back, from giving in to the voice that said there was no changing the truth of what had happened between Domino and her. What had happened between their wolves.

Dakotah hoped Domino was suffering as much as she was.

* * * * *

The wine glass shattered as Domino slammed it against the kitchen counter in frustration. The herbs weren't helping to still the clamoring. To silence the insidious whisper of The Hunger urging him to leave the house and hunt as it tried to regain what it had lost when The Heat rose in Domino.

But Domino wasn't so arrogant in his confidence that he would risk becoming rogue. If he hunted this night, it would end in death. A human's first, but perhaps his own in the end.

He knew the sweet ecstasy of killing as he fed, he knew how hard it was to resist the temptation to take everything. How the beat of any human heart would beckon and tempt. Tonight, it would be nearly impossible to resist The Hunger.

The Transformation had left him vulnerable. Dakotah's absence made it worse. If he left the house, the herbs he'd ingested wouldn't hold against the bloodlust.

Wild emotion raged through Domino, stripping him of his ability to deny the truth. Whether it was the mating of their wolves or the fact that he'd taken her in the woods immediately before The Transformation and the sharing of blood—it didn't matter. What shouldn't be—was. The very trap he'd planned to avoid had caught him unprepared.

He'd bound himself to her sexually.

A hiss escaped as he thought about her out in the night— drawing men to her with the pheromone lure she would gain from his blood. Free to fuck them if she wanted to while his cock would now fill only for her.

He hadn't wanted the responsibility of a kadine, had thought he'd rather enjoy the pleasures to be found in a thousand different pussies, but now… The Heat made him crave and ache for only one. It promised fulfillment beyond anything he could imagine as the blueprint designed by his alien ancestors unfolded and Dakotah was at its center.

Fuck!

A snarl escaped as his cock responded to the word. As his mind flooded with images of what they'd already done, what he still wanted to do.

Domino pushed away from the counter and reached for his cell phone. Irritation scraping along every nerve ending at the necessity of asking for help.

* * * * *

Dakotah probably shouldn't have been surprised to see Fane's sleek black sports car at the campground. He and Cable had been a fixture around the carnival in the days before Sarael left. She'd even teased Sarael about them, though she knew Sarael wouldn't pursue either man and she wasn't entirely certain that the men were interested in women. They always smelled of wild sex and darkness. Of each other.

She paused in the shadows, wary as she remembered what else they smelled like. Or at least what Fane's scent reminded her of. Domino's. As well as the man who'd hunted for and claimed Sarael.

Dakotah didn't trust many people, but she trusted Cable. She wasn't drawn to the pain of others and yet Fane's was a darkness that filled his soul, reminding her of her own. There'd been times when she'd wondered if Fane's scent meant he could shift forms, the contrast between the hot beat of a human's heart and the coldly alien aura making her speculate that if he had another shape, it was something reptile.

She didn't know the details of either of their lives. She hadn't asked. The carnival was a refuge, a place to hide, the men and women there all running from something, hiding from something, even if it was just themselves.

As she watched, Fane and Cable emerged from a travel trailer. Laughing, the sight of Fane's animated face a shock. But not nearly as much of one as seeing the blonde woman between them, her hands held in theirs.

Longing filled Dakotah and she tried to squelch it. Automatically. Ruthlessly. As she'd done for most of her life.

But the longing wouldn't yield. The fortune-teller's prophecy and the wolf's claim pressed in on her with the image of Domino, filled her mind and heart with thoughts and dreams she'd put away long ago. Even before she'd gone to live with her father and his mother. Even before the first of her mother's never ending string of "boyfriends" tried to molest her.

The door to the travel trailer closed, leaving the others in the yellow glow of a porch light. And as if sensing her presence, Fane's face turned in Dakotah's direction. He said something then nuzzled against the woman's neck before letting her hand go. Rather than climb into the sports car, she slid into the passenger seat of a Suburban while Fane and Cable moved toward Dakotah.

Dakotah's hands went instinctively to her jacket pockets, curling around the handles of the knives there. The move making Fane's lips pull back in a flash of teeth that reminded her of Domino.

Surprise rippled through her when the very knives she held concealed in her jacket became an invisible leash, pulling her toward Fane. She knew he was skilled with knives, they'd thrown them at targets, challenging each other in fun as the carnies had gathered to unwind when their booths were closed and their rides shut down for the night.

"We're all born with talents beyond what's necessary to survive," Fane said when she was standing in front of him, reeling with the knowledge that like Domino, Fane's scent had changed since the last time she saw him, making her guess that he was now a vampire.

"Let me guess, yours is knives."

"Yes."

She took her hands out of her pockets and included Cable in her glance. "What are you two doing here?"

Fane's eyes danced with amusement. "Our bride wished to visit with her friends and the timing was right. Domino called. Apparently he allowed his own bride to escape then thought better of it."

Dakotah took a step backward but was halted by Cable's hand on her arm and his sympathetic, caring expression. "You can't run from this," he said and she heard the absolute certainty and truth in his voice.

"I can try."

He shrugged. Smiled slightly, deflating her resolve before it had formed, piercing it with words. "He needs you. Right now he can't even leave the house for fear of what he might do before he finds you."

Fane grinned. "A sight I can hardly wait to see for myself."

"Come back with us, Dakotah," Cable said. "It's not safe for you to be away from him."

"It hasn't been safe for me for a long time, Cable."

"It'll be worse now. His blood has changed you." Cable grimaced. "Men won't see the No Trespassing signs you've got posted. You'll be fighting them off wherever you go."

She frowned in disbelief. "Like I'm doing now?"

"I'm already bound to Fane. Come back to the house with us. There are things you need to know." Cable squeezed her arm. "Don't turn this into a fight. You won't win. You can't. Not against what Fane and Domino are."

Fuck. She could hear Cable's sincerity.

"Just roll over?" she asked, but there was no heat in her words. One of the lessons she'd learned early on was the importance of adapting, compartmentalizing. You didn't survive otherwise. And sometimes you didn't survive anyway.

She knew Cable was telling the truth. Her blood burned and with each step she'd taken away from Domino, a knot had formed in her chest, tightening to the point of pain and panic. But what really scared her was that part of her wanted to go back—and not just the part that was wolf.

She'd made it this far by sheer force of will. She believed she could make it even further. She could make it alone. And that was a salve to her pride, along with the knowledge that whatever she and Domino had done to themselves and each other—or more accurately, whatever their wolves had set into motion—he hadn't asked for it any more than she had.

"I'll go back with you, but Fane is wrong. I'm not Domino's bride."

Chapter Five

Joy rushed through Domino when Dakotah walked into the house of her own free will. The sight of her loosened the tight knot of rage and frustration that had been a leaden weight in his chest. The sight of her sent his cock jerking to attention in a rush of blood that left him dizzy—until he saw Fane's mocking smile. "If you're smart, you won't say anything," Domino said.

Fane's smile widened. "What's to be said? Other than, *He who laughs last, laughs best*."

Domino hissed, flashing his fangs though he knew it would have no effect on Fane. He shifted his attention to Dakotah and his nostrils flared when he became aware of Cable's scent on her arm. He wanted to rip her jacket off her, to get rid of the smell of another man, but her wary expression warned him against giving in to the primitive impulse.

Dakotah took the last step and closed the distance between them. Their bodies touched. Relief soaked in even without the feel of skin against skin. And still it wasn't enough for Domino. He pulled her into his arms, covered her lips with his and thrust his tongue against hers.

She tasted of woman and darkness.

Of blood.

And courage.

And him.

He plundered her mouth and she responded by softening, her body molding itself to his as her tongue tangled and battled, rubbed and enticed in a greeting that made his heart race and his cock throb.

Anticipation rose. The Heat burning more intensely than The Hunger and Domino embraced its fiery flame. Envisioned taking her into the bedroom and fucking her as he should have done earlier instead of sending her away. Envisioned taking her as his bride and seeing the truth of it in her eyes.

But as quickly as he thought it, she stiffened and tried to pull away, and in the process stirred the need to dominate, to claim. To be what he was designed to be.

His fangs elongated and he forced himself to end the kiss. The Heat ruled for the moment, but The Hunger was a deadly presence just underneath the surface of his skin. One taste of her blood… He lifted his mouth from hers and stepped away, his eyes traveling over her, his gaze possessive and hot as realization dawned.

He still saw sleek lines and a body that made him want to cover it with his own. To rut like a wolf and make love like a man. But now he also saw her strength of will and found a courage he could admire. There was no fear in her despite the fact he'd very nearly killed her.

She was a woman he could easily imagine at his side, at his back in the centuries that lay ahead. She was what he'd never imagined he might have. Even if the wariness in her eyes warned him she didn't truly understand or accept what they already were to each other, what they would soon be to one another.

"You need to feed," Fane said, drawing Domino's attention away from Dakotah, his words striking against The Hunger like a match and causing it to roar through Domino's veins.

Domino couldn't resist shooting a glance in Cable's direction and then Kiziah's, his eyes lingering over her blonde beauty in a way guaranteed to scrape over Fane's nerve endings. "You're offering your kadine? Your companion?"

This time it was Fane who hissed, flashing his fangs. "You know better."

Dakotah caught the look of amusement Cable and Kiziah shared before Cable said, "Zia and I are going to go camp out in front of the fireplace."

The rest of them followed, going deeper into the house. Dakotah acutely aware of the man walking behind her.

Without even touching, the lust was there. The need. Not just the wolf's, but Dakotah's own desire. Without a word the anticipation was building. As though the night could be spent in only one way. Sating a hunger that transcended the body. A hunger of the soul. The heart.

Cable and Kiziah settled on the thick carpeting in front of the fireplace, their attention fixed on one another. Dakotah took a seat at the end of the couch and Domino sat next to her, crowding against her so that they were once again touching.

Fane surprised her, sitting on Domino's other side and unbuttoning the sleeve of his shirt then pulling it back. "You need blood, Domino, to fully sate The Hunger." His eyes met Dakotah's, dark and serious. "If you weren't important to him, he would have killed you to sate the bloodlust that rides us with The Transformation. It's almost impossible to stop. It's a miracle that he did."

"It was a close thing," she said, remembering how she hadn't even put up a fight, how good it had felt, even when she knew he was killing her.

There were men she'd been forced to service who required erotic asphyxiation — men willing to skate the edge of death for their sexual pleasure. She'd hated them, hated what they forced her to do to them. It revolted her. They revolted her.

She got to her feet and moved to stand behind the chair. Torn. Confused by her own reaction to Domino. The fact that she didn't hate him, wasn't even sickened by what had happened between them after his Transformation. He watched her through hooded eyes as he lifted Fane's wrist to his mouth and fed.

Dakotah responded to the sight of it, her labia swelling, her breasts growing full and heavy. It was an act of communion, primitive and sacred at the same time. Sexual and yet not sexual.

Her womb fluttered and her nipples hardened. Desire moved through her. To be what Domino needed. To have him take *her* blood instead of Fane's.

Domino released Fane's wrist and stood, his focus on Dakotah. His eyes reflecting the heat that was burning through her.

Fane rose from the sofa and joined Cable and Kiziah on the rug in front of the fireplace, Kiziah's soft, embarrassed laughter causing Dakotah to look away from Domino, to watch as Cable and Fane positioned Kiziah between them, their hands and mouths roaming over her body, turning her laughter into weak protests, and then into sighs and whimpers and muted pleas.

"Does it turn you on to watch them?" Domino asked, trapping Dakotah between his body and the back of the chair. His hands sliding around, cupping her breasts, tweaking her nipples through clothing that was suddenly too restrictive. Making her folds grow slippery with the feel of his erection pressed against her ass.

"I've seen shows like this before," she said. *I've been in them.* And yet even as she said the words, thought them, she knew they weren't completely true. If it was only sex, she would have turned away by now. But it was more than sex, more than pleasure. The love she saw on their faces was a seduction of her senses, a torment to her heart.

"Have you really?" he whispered against her neck. "Have you really seen *this* show before? Once we've formed a bond, it's impossible for us to have sex outside of it. But among close friends and family, we sometimes share the pleasure that we take in those who have become our world. The kadines — or male companions — whose blood sates us, whose bodies succor us, whose existence gives deeper meaning to our own. It's not a trap I thought to find myself in, but here I am." His fingers tightened on her nipples, becoming almost painful as he warned, "Don't fight me, Dakotah. You can't win and neither of us can change what's happened between us."

Dakotah shivered as his words slid through her. In that moment she believed. In that moment she allowed herself to be caught up in the dream.

She didn't protest when his fingers replicated Fane's and Cable's movements, stripping her of her jacket and shirt and bra as they were doing to Kiziah. She whimpered as Kiziah whimpered, longed to feel Domino's mouth suckling at her breasts, hungrily eating her as Fane and Cable were doing to Kiziah.

"You're aroused," Domino said, smoothing over the tight crowns of her breasts, tugging at her nipples before moving lower, his hands hot against her belly, their nearness to her cunt making her suck in her breath, making her want to open her jeans so that he could cup her mound. "Admit it. Admit that you're aroused."

"You know I am. You can smell it."

His hand stroked over her stomach. Teased along the waistband of her pants. And she pushed against his erection, ground against it, needing more as Cable stripped Kiziah of her skirt and panties and pressed his face to her cunt. Kiziah's cry of pleasure scraping over Dakotah with razor-sharp talons of need.

"You liked the feel of my mouth on you in the woods," Domino said, tormenting Dakotah by unzipping her jeans, his fingertips sliding inside her panties, tracing the line of her pubic hair.

She tried to turn in his arms, to turn the tables on him, but he held her in place with his superior strength. Buried his face in her neck, seducing her with the feel of lips and fangs, so that she very nearly begged him to bite her.

Lust burned through Domino. Sparked by the sight of Fane with Kiziah and Cable, fed by Dakotah's willing participation.

The scent of her arousal inflamed him, tested his control. Both The Heat and the wolf urged him to take her, to bury his cock in her, to spend the rest of the night fucking her. But the man wanted to savor these moments. To use them to ease Dakotah into his world. To get better acquainted with his bride.

The word no longer felt awkward on his lips or unexpected in his thoughts. Domino grimaced — no doubt his grandmother would chortle with pleasure that her predictions had come true.

But there was nothing to be done about it and he wouldn't change it if he could. Dakotah was his bride, she would be his kadine. Already he craved it as much as he'd once craved his freedom. The desire for it was hardwired into him, but her earlier actions had made it more than what he'd always imagined it would be. He's seen it as a trap. Now he saw it as a doorway. And the need to go through it was overwhelming. She was already everything to him.

He kissed along her spine. Inhaled her scent as he smoothed his hands over her hips and down her legs, pushing her clothing in front of them. Following with his mouth, licking the base of her spine, gently biting a sleek buttock before moving lower, to torment the back of her knees with his tongue as he removed her shoes so that her jeans and panties could fall to the floor.

She was muscle and tawny skin, lean and feminine. Her lines like the wolf's, beautiful to him. Arousing.

Domino stood, shimmering into mist in order to shed his clothing, returning to human form in the blink of an eye so he could press against Dakotah. So he could drink her in through his skin.

In front of them Cable was scrambling out of his jeans, the firelight dancing off his flesh. Stark need written on his face as he took his cock in hand, its tip glistening with arousal.

With a groan Domino rubbed his cock against Dakotah, covered her mound with his fingers and rejoiced in her wetness, in the stab of her clit against his palm. She pushed back against him, spreading her legs and leaning forward, trying to draw him into her depths.

He resisted. Pressed her more firmly against the back of the chair so he could withstand the temptation she presented for a few moments longer. "Have you really seen this show before?" he asked, returning to their earlier conversation, his lips pulling back in a silent snarl. "Have you experienced it?"

Dakotah's cunt clinched as Cable pulled Kiziah on top of him. She whimpered when Cable thrust upward, his face a mask of pleasure as his cock slid home. And then Fane joined them, forging into Kiziah's back entrance, the three of them going still, as though they were savoring the instant when they first joined, as though they were so closely bound together that they were one person.

"No," Dakotah said, answering Domino's question. Longing filling her as she looked at the three people making love in front of the fireplace. "No, I've never seen this show before."

Domino brushed his fangs against her neck, the need to dominate pressing in on him along with the wolf's urge to cover its mate. The desire to erase any memory she had of other men, other lovers, was a burning ache in his gut. "I will kill any man who tries to take you from me."

"You already have," Dakotah said, thinking about the two men who'd followed her into the woods. Shuddering as she thought about Victor Hale—a man she'd never met but who was determined to see her dead. "There will be more of them."

"And they will die too," Domino said, his voice without inflection. His absolute confidence filling her with a security she'd never known before. A shimmering vision of safety that she was hesitant to believe in.

Already Domino could sense something of her emotions, and already it wasn't enough. He found himself longing for the second blood exchange and then the third—so he could touch her thoughts at will, so he could know who she was.

He kissed her shoulder, cupped her breast while the fingers of his other hand pushed into her sheath. He gloried in how wet and slick she was, how the muscles of her channel clamped down on him, tried to hold him inside of her. "Do you want me to take you now?" he asked, his cock full, pulsing, leaking as both Fane and Cable began moving in and out of their bride's body.

Dakotah had never wanted anything so badly. Never thought that anything sexual could touch the deepest parts of her—that she'd allow it to reach her. But seeing Fane and Cable and Kiziah, being with Domino…

She hungered like a beggar at the edge of a feast. Felt starved as though she'd lived through a lifetime of famine. The pain of her need was soul-deep, wrenching, squeezing her chest so the only thing she could say was yes. Her voice whisper-soft, her answer triggering a fierce possessiveness in Domino, a driving desire to see to her safety and happiness.

He positioned her so her hands were braced on the back of the chair, teased her by sliding his cock back and forth along her cunt lips, stroking over her clit as he coated himself with her arousal.

When she would have impaled herself on him, he resisted, tormenting them both by delaying. Pushing the need higher until her skin was coated with a fine sheen of sweat, until his testicles ached for release and his cock screamed for the feel of her wet channel and feminine heat.

Only then did he give in to what nature demanded, thrusting all the way into her in a forceful stroke meant to claim, to dominate, to reach her heart and take her soul. She moaned, a husky sound that had his nostrils flaring, his muscles tensing, fighting against the urge to piston in and out and spew his seed within seconds of mounting her.

"Watch them," he growled, subduing the fierce urge to rut by focusing on the rhythm in front of him, by matching what Cable and Fane were doing with their bride.

And Dakotah watched, soaking in the raw emotion and passion as she breathed the heavy musk of arousal, became consumed by it. Wanted it for herself. And Domino.

She looked away, tilted her head so that dark eyes met obsidian ones, in challenge, in demand, and he answered her call, snarling with need as his thrusts became more aggressive, as their awareness of what the others were doing faded until the only thing that mattered was finding release and pleasure in each other.

Domino took her to the ground with his penis still embedded in her, the wolf demanding a closer contact, a true covering of its mate. Dakotah's wolf wanting the same, so that she readily went to her hands and knees, readily lowered her upper body, enabling Domino's cock to thrust deeper.

He wanted to sink his fangs into her as they fucked, but settled for gripping her shoulder with his teeth, pressing his chest against her back and pinning her with his weight, taking her as a man though the movements and instincts were those of the wolf. He wanted to consume her, to be so closely melded that they were one body, one mind, one being, the ancient stamp of his ancestors so strong that there was no thought to resist. No point in denying it.

Domino settled more heavily on her, a show of strength and dominance, and she responded by yielding more of herself. Accepting all that he had to give, letting him take her as no man ever had, letting him touch her heart and soul where the others had gotten a body devoid of feeling, a hollow vessel to sate their needs with.

He didn't allow either of them a release until they were both panting, writhing, burning, the sweat pouring off them, their bodies closely attuned, his thoughts pressing into hers. Pounding into her with each thrust. *Mine! Mine! Mine!* The presence and fierceness of his words as overwhelming as the rush of orgasm that took her, leaving her dizzy, shaken, trying to pull back, to retreat to safer ground.

Domino wouldn't allow it.

He scooped her up and carried her from the room, though not before Dakotah saw Fane and Cable and Kiziah wrapped in a cocoon of love, holding one another tightly as they basked in the afterglow of their own pleasure. The flames in the fireplace not nearly as bright or as hot as what they found in each other.

She expected Domino to toss her onto the bed, but instead he moved through the bedroom and into the bathroom, depositing her in the shower stall and joining her there, making her scream then laugh when a blast of cold water hit them both before steamy hot water followed in a soothing caress. He pressed her against the wall, eyes dancing, lips trailing wet, sucking kisses along her neck and shoulders, her breasts, playful now where only moments before he'd been intense.

It was a welcome relief to Dakotah. A different type of seduction. And she responded to it, petting him in return, nipping and kissing as she slid down his body. His mock growls making her smile against his slick skin, filling her heart with a lightness she'd never associated with sex.

She stopped to torture tight male nipples, reveled in his honest moans of pleasure, in the way his body shuddered, pressing and rubbing against hers, enticing her to lick and suck, his cock already hard again, thick and full and waiting for her attention.

But she refused to be hurried despite its pulsing insistence. She grasped his nipple between her teeth, tugging as he'd done to her earlier, teasing it with her tongue as his fingers clenched and unclenched in her hair.

Only when his head was thrown back, his body arched, tense, did she slip lower, cupping his testicles in her hand, measuring their fullness and weight as she nuzzled his cock, inhaled his scent, the wolf inside shivering with joy, urging her to taste him, to know him through all her senses.

Domino's growls turned into moans, and then became her name. Repeated over and over again as she let him press through her lips. Her hands and mouth controlling the depth of his pleasure, the length of it, driving him higher and higher, until there was no hint of their earlier playfulness. Until there was only fevered need and the satisfaction of giving and receiving beyond anything ever experienced with another partner.

She was a heady addiction for Domino. The end result hardwired into him. Each taking fed The Heat and erased the memory of those who had come before her. Bound him more tightly to Dakotah until his reality centered on her. On what she would become for him. His kadine. His mate. The mother of his children. And he rejoiced in her presence in his life.

He took her to the floor of the shower stall, pinned her there, testing his control by burying his face between her thighs, the hot rush of her arousal warring for his attention with the wild thundering of her blood. He wanted to sink his fangs into her inner thigh but thrust his tongue into her cunt instead, fucking in and out, consuming her, lifting his head only to suck her clit, to attack it with his tongue as she writhed and strained against him, her voice husky then hoarse as she begged him for more, and he savored the sound, enjoyed the erotic retribution for what she'd done to him. Ignored her pleas as she'd ignored his until his own needs matched hers. Only then did he swallow her release—jerking away when the temptation to take her blood became too great—and with a growl he levered himself over her, his eyes capturing and holding hers as he pierced her with his cock, fucked her as the hot water rained down on them.

Chapter Six

Dakotah woke up with Domino pressed tightly against her back, his arm draped over her side, insurance that she'd stay put.

Or maybe she woke up pressed tightly against his chest, snuggled close as though needing Domino's warmth and intimacy.

Either way, it was a first. To wake up in someone's arms.

She lay still for long moments, savoring it, thinking about it, wondering if it was an illusion. Wondering if the night before had really been about more than sex.

It was daytime now. She could feel it even though heavy drapes covered the windows.

Dakotah turned in Domino's arms, surprise filling her when she realized that she could see him as clearly as if the room had been flooded with sunlight. The knowledge that she'd gained another edge, one she might need to survive, pleased her, but it also made her wonder what other changes had occurred from taking his blood.

Uneasiness skittered along her spine when she thought about how difficult it had been for her to leave him and go to the campground. How she'd almost felt relieved when it became obvious that Fane and Cable intended to take her back to Domino, whether she was willing or not.

And yet despite her misgivings, her doubts, Dakotah's womb fluttered as she looked at Domino's ultramasculine features. Her body grew heavy as need and lust gathered, pulsing through her veins in thick, slow waves, like blood-red water pulled from a deep internal well.

She had so many questions. Questions she needed answers to.

Dakotah shivered, remembering the nightmare days after surviving Anthony Hale's attack. The lost memories. The lost periods of time. Waking up naked and covered in blood. The terror she'd experienced, wondering if she'd learn that the wolf had killed a child or an innocent. The relief each time there'd been no whisper of lives lost.

There was so much blood on her hands. But none of it coated her conscience.

There were so many things she'd had to do in order to survive. Choices forced on her and she could live with them, burying them in the darkness of the past as she kept moving into the future.

She'd made the decision to return to the clearing, to help Domino back to the house. And yet she still had no idea what that decision had cost her.

She needed to know. Needed to deal with it.

The smell of bacon and coffee drifted in, diverting her thoughts, drawing her attention away from the man next her. Her sense of smell and her hearing expanded so that she knew there was only one person in the kitchen. Kiziah. The footsteps were light, and there was a faint, feminine smell underneath that of the bacon and coffee.

Dakotah slipped from the bed and dressed, taking her backpack with her as she left the bedroom. Kiziah looked up from the stove when she walked in, her face turning pink with embarrassment before she ducked her head and mumbled, "There's enough for two if you want something to eat."

It took Dakotah a second to realize what was causing the other woman's face to flame with color. She almost laughed. Though the sound of it would have held more pain than amusement.

Fuck. There'd been no room in her life for shyness or sensibilities when it came to sex. No room for shame unless she wanted it to destroy her.

Dakotah moved to the counter and retrieved a coffee mug from the cabinet, feeling suddenly awkward, her mind scrambling for something to say to put Kiziah at ease. Finally deciding to part with a measure of truth, even if the words tasted bitter on her tongue. "There's nothing to be embarrassed about. At least what you've got with them is real. Most of what I've seen and done isn't."

Kiziah's head jerked up, her face flushing again, though her eyes widened with surprise and a measure of confusion. "You're

Jory Strong

Domino's…you're going to be his kadine. I think it doesn't get any more real than that."

Dakotah's heart raced at the words but she shrugged. "I don't know what I am to him yet. I helped him out when he was in a jam and he almost killed me in return."

"You're not terrified of him, or of Fane," Kiziah said and there was a wealth of curiosity in her voice.

"I've seen a lot scarier things."

Kiziah's mouth gaped slightly. She reached for a couple of plates, filling them both with bacon, eggs and toast before handing one of them to Dakotah. "I know it's closer to dinnertime. I'm still adjusting to being up during the night and sleeping during the day."

They moved to the kitchen table. Dakotah said, "So they sleep during the day?"

"If they stay in their human form." Kiziah buttered her toast, hesitating. "They…evaporate…for lack of a better word in sunlight, though I guess Domino has a choice between changing into a wolf or turning into tiny particles."

Dakotah stilled, surprised Kiziah knew Domino could shift his form, though she probably shouldn't have been. "What about Fane?"

Kiziah shook her head. "Fane's just Fane. Cable told me there are certain lines of vampires and dhampirs who have other shapes. You're either born with the ability or you're not."

Dakotah remembered Fane's words. She remembered the pull he had on her knives. She'd already guessed what Domino's special ability was, but she wanted to hear it confirmed. "Fane's talent is knives. Domino's is hypnotism, isn't it?"

Kiziah shuddered. "Oh yeah."

"He's done it to you?"

"The first time I encountered him. Then a second time, the night I met Fane."

Dakotah picked up a piece of bacon. After she'd finally gained control of the wolf, she'd haunted libraries and bookstores, reading everything she could about the supernatural, though not believing most of it. "I thought dhampirs were supposed to be vampire hunters."

"They can be. But mainly they're soldiers for the vampire race until they go through The Transformation and become vampires themselves. Fane and Domino were both dhampir. Cable was—is— well, I'm not sure what his status is now. Before Fane made him a companion, Cable was a padrall, a member of an order that has served vampires since the very beginning. He was born into it." Kiziah took a sip of coffee. "I guess it's no surprise that if vampires and dhampirs and padralls exist then there are also secret societies like the Believers that try and kill them—or anyone associated with them." She shuddered. "But you already know that. While I was visiting some of my friends at the campground, Cable and Fane were getting rid of the bodies of the two men who attacked you in the woods."

Dakotah frowned as worry filled her. Even though she'd heard them use the word *Believers*, she'd thought they were ordinary scum trying to earn fast money by turning her over to Victor Hale. But if there were more of them… She clamped down on her fear before it could grow and paralyze her. "You're sure they were members of some secret society?"

"Did they have elaborate crosses tattooed on their necks?"

Dakota nodded and remembered the other men she'd seen hanging around the carnival, not just in Ashberg but in the town before, Kenton, men who'd had the same tattoo.

"Fane says that the Believers in the United States favor the cross tattoos." Kiziah smiled tentatively. "You don't have to worry about them, at least for a while. Supposedly those are the last of them in the area."

Dakotah shrugged. The last of the Believers maybe. But she had a feeling the place would soon be overrun with werewolves.

Her nostrils flared slightly, taking in Kiziah's scent. Human and something else. Just as Cable's was now. She had no way of knowing whether they were strong enough to survive a werewolf attack, and yet if her trail led to them, Victor Hale or his men wouldn't think twice about killing them or trying to use them to find her.

"You should leave Ashberg and stay away from the carnival," Dakotah said. "I've got enemies hunting me."

Kiziah's coffee cup wobbled slightly. "What kind of enemies?"

Dakotah hesitated, not used to sharing information about herself. But she didn't know yet what she was going to do. Whether she was going to stay or go. If she left, she wanted a clear conscience, or as much of one as she could manage. "Werewolves."

"They exist too?" Kiziah put the coffee cup down quickly, as though she was worried about dropping it, then laughed softly. "I shouldn't be surprised. I guess I've still got a lot to get used to." Heat rushed to her face. "Fane and Cable have been a big adjustment."

Curiosity got the better of Dakotah. The need to understand her own situation along with the sense that Kiziah was willing to talk opened a door Dakotah rarely allowed herself to acknowledge, much less touch. Even before she'd killed Anthony Hale and started running, she'd learned the hard way not to ask others about their lives or to share the details of her own.

"Fane and Cable hung out at the carnival for a while," Dakotah said. "I was surprised to see them with a woman."

Kiziah's color heightened. "*I* was a surprise to them too. Especially to Fane." She met Dakotah's eyes. "Has Madame Helki ever given you a reading?"

Dakotah grimaced and Kiziah laughed. "Did she predict Domino? I think she saw Cable and Fane in my cards. And the reading she did for Cable led him to me."

"She's a meddlesome old woman," Dakotah said without heat, uncomfortable at how accurate the fortune-teller's predictions had become.

Kiziah cocked her head and grinned. "So she gave you a reading?"

"Yes."

"And you don't want to talk about it."

Dakotah couldn't help but laugh. Kiziah reminded her of Sarael. Both of them openhearted, willing to talk or listen but also willing to back off.

She relented, touching the bite mark on her neck. "Yeah, I think it's safe to say that Helki predicted Domino."

"Well, good luck with him. I'm just glad I have Cable to help me with Fane. If you haven't already guessed, vampires are hard-wired to…control their women. And it doesn't help that they can read your thoughts, shuffle through your memories and freeze you in place with a command." Kiziah laughed, flushing with color, before adding, "But there are compensations."

Dakotah reached for her coffee cup as she tried to still the riot of emotion and thought swirling inside her. Her gut churned at the idea of Domino—or anyone—seeing her memories, seeing the things she'd had to do to survive. "Can you read Fane's thoughts?"

"Yes. And Cable's. We're all connected now." She hesitated then added, "It happens after the third exchange."

Dakotah frowned, myth and reality at odds in her mind. Her senses told her Kiziah and Cable were still partially human while Fane and Domino weren't human at all. "You're not a vampire."

"No. I'm different than I was. Fane's blood changed me. But I'll never be vampire. Neither will Cable. They can't fully convert humans, though they can adapt us." Kiziah grimaced. "And they can give us a major headache. At least that's what a certain vampire who claims it's Domino's responsibility to tell you what you need to know is doing right now."

"Fane's wrong. I'm not Domino's responsibility. He helped me out, I helped him out. We're even and free to go our separate ways."

Kiziah's eyebrows drew together. "It's not safe to do that. He's sexually bonded to you. And you'll attract a lot of unwanted attention until you've made the second exchange and can control the pheromones. Even then they can get out of hand. At least with the third it becomes more natural, so you don't have to think about it." Kiziah sighed. "Not that I ever go anywhere alone anymore." She stood and gathered her dishes, carrying them to the sink.

Dakotah did the same, thinking about what she'd learned, mad at herself for feeling…hollow inside at the prospect of Domino wanting her only because he'd sexually bonded himself to her. He hadn't meant to—she wasn't going to lie to herself about it. He didn't know her. Though he would—all too well if he could see her memories. And then what? She guessed there was no such thing as an amicable divorce from a vampire. "I'm going to head out for a while," she said, and felt both the wolf's and Domino's protest.

The silverware Kiziah was washing clattered to the bottom of the sink. "Don't. I mean, if you need to get out of the house for awhile, at least let Cable and I go with you."

Dakotah pushed away from the counter. "Thanks for the offer, but I need some space." She could feel Domino struggling, concentrating, and she guessed he was trying to take his wolf form. If he succeeded, he'd have her pinned before she could get out of the front door. If she left on foot, he'd just track her down.

She grabbed her backpack and delayed long enough to take his car keys. The wolf howling in protest as she drove away, the first hints of Domino's will pressing in on her, demanding that she return.

She fought the wolf. She fought him. She fought herself and kept going, driving to the beach. Glad for the cold and the fog that was already starting to form as it got closer to sunset. It was weather guaranteed to keep people inside.

She hadn't been lying. She needed space, time.

For a long while she just sat in Domino's car, surrounded by his scent. Taking comfort in it though she saw it as a weakness in herself — a weakness she didn't have the energy to fight.

In her mind's eye she replayed events and conversations, analyzed them. Once again saw the spread of tarot cards. Death. Strength. The Emperor. Heard her challenge to Domino in the woods. *I don't care what the tarot cards say.* And she hadn't.

They only give one possibility, she'd once told Sarael. *You can change that truth.* And she'd believed her own words. Ignored both the promise and the warning that The Emperor card presented.

And in the end she had not only walked right into the future Helki predicted but escaped it and then willingly returned — twice.

Dakotah rubbed her heart. The tight knot returning when she thought about Kiziah's revelations. About Domino having access to her memories. Memories she never visited.

A cold shiver slid up her spine at the idea of his gaining control to the point he could freeze her in place with a thought. That was more threatening than his ability to hypnotize — something she'd avoided thinking about.

Dakotah forced herself from the car. Forced herself to leave the warmth and security, the comfort. To step out into the cold. The act a physical reminder of her reality.

She walked. Not far. Just far enough to come to a decision.

Both Cable and Kiziah had told her she'd be fighting men off wherever she went. She had no reason to doubt them and every reason to believe them. Her blood burned, her body felt different, was different. And yet there had to be a way to turn it to her advantage — just as she'd done with the wolf. To use what she'd gained from Domino to help her survive. To help her do more than just survive.

For the first time since she'd learned that Victor Hale was determined to make her pay for killing his son, Dakotah let herself believe she could do more than just run and hide, do more than fight to the death when cornered. If she could gain control of the pheromones, use the vampire lure to get through the men Victor had guarding him, then she could end it once and for all.

One more death, just a little more blood on her hands and it'd be settled.

Or maybe she'd be dead.

Either way, she could stop running — at least from Victor Hale.

Domino was a different story. He may have ordered her to leave once and allowed her to leave a second time, inadvertently let her escape this time, but she doubted he would let her get away from him again.

Their wolves might claim to be mated. Domino himself may have come to accept it — but right now he was operating on the physical level, doing what nature had programmed him to do. She wished it was more than that. And for an instant, longing coiled around in her chest, wrapping her in hope — just as it had when Helki read the cards. But just like then, she tossed it off.

She wasn't ready to trust in the cards. She wasn't going to roll over and expose her belly and neck. To risk her heart.

Dakotah got in the car, grimacing at the thought of encountering Helki. But the carnival was the safest place to go, at least for what she had in mind. She couldn't gain control over the pheromones by walking into a bar. The situation would be too unpredictable, too dangerous. Not that it would be fun fighting off carnies she'd come to think of as friends. But she thought she could subdue them without killing them. And though the prospect of asking Helki for help made Dakotah grind her teeth, she would ask for it if she had to.

If she could find the old fortune-teller and the carnival.

Dakotah got out of the car and looked around at the empty, moonlit field where only a day before the carnival had been set up.

The scent of it remained. Hot dogs and cotton candy. Metal and fuel. The unique smells of hundreds of strangers mixed with those of the carnies Dakotah had traveled with for the last year.

It got to her. Made her feel raw. The unexpectedness of seeing emptiness where her world had been solid and real was like a chilling glimpse into the future. And she turned away from it, had only a fleeting second to become aware of sound and movement before the sharp sting of a dart slammed into her chest, the tranquilizer taking effect, pulling her into darkness even as she ripped it from her body.

* * * * *

Domino came out of the bedroom growling, bristling, ready to bite when Fane shimmered into place in front of Kiziah, his eyes alight with amusement.

Cable walked in a second later. "We'll help you find her," he said, skirting Domino and Fane in order to kiss Kiziah.

Fane grinned. "We'll help you *after* you drink your herbs. And while you do it, I'll regale you with advice on the claiming and taming of a kadine so that you'll be more successful the next time we return her to you."

Kiziah reached over and pinched Fane's naked ass cheek. "Or better yet, you'll go get dressed before you make Domino mad enough to castrate you while I cheer him on. *The claiming and taming of a kadine.* That's *not* a story *you're* going to be telling anytime soon."

Cable laughed, hugging Kiziah's back to his chest as he curled his hand around Fane's forearm, pulling him into the embrace, teasing Fane by saying, "We're still on our honeymoon. It's not a good thing to upset your wife when you're on your honeymoon." He glanced down at Fane's erection. "Unless you plan on going back to same-sex-only encounters."

Fane growled, kissing both Cable and Kiziah, then shimmered out of sight.

Kiziah sighed. "I'm sorry, Domino. I…"

Domino shook his head. "You didn't do anything wrong. You didn't say anything wrong. I'm grateful to you for telling her what you did. And for learning something about her enemies."

Cable rubbed his cheek against Kiziah's hair. "I can make enquiries. She's got your mark on her neck. The Weres don't want a war with the vampires. I can get the word out that she belongs to you."

Domino grimaced. "No doubt the story of my failure to hold on to my bride will grow with each telling."

Fane strolled in, zipping his jeans. "Or you could simply let her go and endure the herbs. You have long claimed you don't want a kadine. Her lifespan is short against our own. With her death you'd be a free man again."

Domino's eyes flashed to red. His lips pulled back to reveal deadly fangs. "She is mine and she won't escape that fate."

Fane grinned, stopping next to Domino and offering his wrist in a gesture of trust. "Then perhaps you'd better feed so we won't need a leash when we go out in public with you."

Chapter Seven

Domino followed the scent to the edge of the woods, rage burning through him with each step. He stopped just inside the tree line, crouched, inhaled deeply. The Were who'd waited here was a dead man.

Behind him Cable stopped talking into his cell phone, the tiny click signaling that he'd closed it. "Fane says there was a man asking about Dakotah at the campground. His scent is Were. So far no one noticed what he was driving, but Kiziah's still talking to the people she knows there."

Domino nodded and stood. Turning so the field where the carnival had been was spread out in front of him, empty except for Fane's sports car and his own. It surprised him that Dakotah had come back here. It gave him reason to hope that maybe she hadn't decided to run. A grim smile settled on his face. Maybe she'd even decided to consult with the fortune-teller. That would have made his grandmother's day.

"Just one of them?" Cable asked. "Male?"

"Yeah. Here for several hours. Long enough to piss on a lot of trees."

"I'm surprised he didn't take your car."

Domino shrugged. "For all he knew, it was stolen."

Cable nodded and they left the woods, heading to the cars. Domino tight with anger and worry. The scent was fresh. The picture it presented a movie he could easily view.

A lone hunter had waited in the woods. Fired when Dakotah arrived.

The dart had struck her but she'd had the strength and intelligence to remove it quickly. But then she'd fallen next to the car, the dart rolling underneath. The ground absorbing her scent, her heat. Telling him she'd lain there for awhile.

The hunter had made a phone call probably. To the man at the campground maybe. Or perhaps to another. That man had come, had stood next to Dakotah.

Domino knelt beside the tire again, hissing, reacting to the scent of fear lingering near where Dakotah had lain. They'd seen his mark on her. They'd known what it meant. And yet they'd taken her all the same.

They'd invited their own deaths.

* * * * *

Dakotah fought through the drug-induced darkness. Its cloying presence sickening her, reminding her of things she'd long ago forced herself to forget.

Nausea rolled over her and she closed her eyes. Held her breath. Willed herself not to heave. Not to let on that she was waking up.

The first wave passed, followed by long moments of choppiness, clarity and confusion, dizziness, of pulsing gray and black bursts of color at the edge of her consciousness, by heat, as though her blood was burning away the foreign substance in her body. When it was done she was panting silently, coated in a light sheen of sweat. But she was alert. Strong. Though not strong enough to escape the duct tape that bound her wrists behind her, then bound them again to ankles that had been similarly taped, her knees bent so that her ankles and wrists met in the center of her back.

Dakotah clenched her teeth to keep from growling and snarling in rage. From opening her mouth and howling with frustration. The wolf inside echoing her own horror and anger at being caught and rendered helpless by Victor Hale's men.

Werewolves. The car reeked of human perspiration and flesh overlaid on the wolf's scent. It smelled of steak and beer, cheap cologne and fear.

"I don't like this," the driver whined and Dakotah zeroed in on him, tasted his nervousness, knew he was afraid.

"You're not paid to like it. You're paid to forget about it."

"The vampires—"

"Are Victor's problem. We told him she was marked and he said bring her anyway. For all we know, he's going to tell her that he forgives her for killing his son."

"You don't believe that."

"That's my story. And by the time Victor is done with her, there won't be enough of her left to identify." The man laughed. "Even if someone decided they wanted to analyze a lot of wolf shit. Nothing like a group hunt followed by a group fuck and a nice group feast to keep things in the pack so to speak."

"Count me out."

"You get invited. You participate. Or else you join her. There are guys who are horny enough to fuck a log when they change. You'll do if they can't get a turn at her. I'm hoping Victor invites me. She's going to be a fighter. Has to have been to take out Anthony. He spent most of his time thinking with his dick, but he wasn't a lightweight when it came to breaking bones and ripping fur."

The two men lapsed into silence, their scents deepening in opposite directions, becoming more pronounced. One with greater fear. One growing heavy with lust.

Dakotah's lips pulled back in a snarl. A silent, fleeting rebellion. But she was a fighter. And she knew better than most how sex could equal survival.

Kiziah and Cable had both said that men would be drawn to her. They'd made it sound as though it would happen whether she invited the attention or not. But she wasn't going to waste time waiting for the pheromones to build.

She closed her eyes and thought of Domino. Pictured the scene in the woods, her hands bound as he knelt before her, worshipping her with his mouth. His tongue wicked as he slid it in and out of her channel, then up and over her clit. His lips and teeth tormenting the swollen knob until she was trying to fuck him with it, to shove herself down his throat as arousal seeped from her slit and coated her inner thighs.

Now that she knew what he was, she wanted him to bite her there. To take her to heights of ecstasy she would never experience elsewhere. She wanted—

The car screeched to a halt, jarring Dakotah from her fantasy and into a sauna of pheromones and lust. Car doors opened then rough hands were jerking her from the back seat, pawing at her clothing.

Fear came with the cold air. Not her own, but the weaker man's. And yet there was arousal where there hadn't been before. "We can't do her by the side of the road."

His companion grunted. "Take her legs then."

She let them take her to the woods. Let them think she wasn't fully aware of what they were doing. But with each step, she could feel some of the mad haze of lust leaving under the burden of carrying her and the fresh air.

She thought about Domino again, imagined his cock sliding back and forth across her cunt lips as they'd watched Cable and Fane make love to Kiziah. As Domino's words had seduced her.

The fantasy played out in one part of her mind, compartmentalized this time, so she would be ready when opportunity presented itself.

The two men stopped just inside the woods, in a small patch of wet pine needles and trampled grass. A place that smelled of deer and rabbits.

Pain seared through Dakotah's shoulders and thighs when they dropped her on her back, her arms and legs trapped and bound underneath her. The more aggressive of the two leaned over her, his breath hot and rank, his hands and fingers rough as he tore at her clothing.

She opened her eyes and trapped him with her gaze. Watched as his eyes grew more glazed, as mindless lust consumed him.

The wolf rose inside her, pressing against her skin. Urging her to free it, to let it rip their enemy's throat out.

She'd thought to wait, suspected they'd free her ankles before they tried to rape her. She'd wondered if she could enthrall the men and then command them with her voice, guessed it was part of a vampire's arsenal. But the wolf's solution was simple. Efficient. Brutal.

Adrenaline surged through her. The same wild rush that preceded the change and yet the energy raced to her face, tingling, burning, the wolf prepared to claim only a part of her.

She'd never changed partially, never believed she could or been tempted to try it. But she felt the wolf's determination. Its resolve. None but its mate would claim the body it lived in.

Dakotah licked her lips, watched as the man's face went slack. As his tongue duplicated her movement, wetting his own. The stench of his arousal burning her nose. Adding to the pressure, the sense of impending change, the elongation into a snout, a muzzle full of deadly teeth.

The wolf drew itself into a crouch. Its focus entirely on their enemy as his face lowered. As his throat got close enough for an attack. When it sprang, Dakotah ceded control, her face burning first with the fury of the change and then from the hot rush of blood that poured over her.

It was over within seconds. Leaving her ribs and chest and abdomen sore from where his fists and knees had landed. Leaving her coated with blood and covered by death. The body heavy where it lay on top of her.

Leaving her alone. Still bound. But alone. The sight of the attack and the blood ridding the fearful man of his lust and sending him running.

Dakotah wriggled out from underneath the dead man and turned on her side to relieve the pressure on her shoulders. For a brief instant she contemplated changing. But the wolf's body wasn't flexible enough to endure the position she was bound in, and the pain would be excruciating unless the duct tape gave with the wolf's struggles. Instead she wriggled and squirmed, moved along the body next to her and smiled with feral pleasure when she explored his jacket, using her nose and cheek and finding the outline of a knife. Using her teeth to work it upward until it dropped to the blood-soaked ground.

Savage victory filled her at the sight of the black-handled knife. At the sight of one of *her* knives.

She rolled over, working herself into position. The movements slow and painful, awkward. The effort to grasp the knife, to open it, to cut the tape, excruciating.

But she succeeded.

Dakotah stood and lifted her face to the sky. To the moon. The wolf inside howling. The woman reveling in the moment, in the fierce satisfaction of surviving.

When the wild emotion settled, she turned her attention to the corpse at her feet and went through the dead man's pockets. Finding her second knife along with her cell phone. The sight of it bringing the question, *What now?*

The wolf's answer was simple. Return to their mate.

Dakotah hesitated for only a second before agreeing. Before calling Cable, knowing as she did that it would be Domino who came.

* * * * *

It humbled Domino that she'd called. Sent an uncomfortable, unstable mix of emotions cascading through him. Instinct and alien heritage demanded that he assert his dominance and punish her for leaving the safety of the house when she knew he didn't want her to go. And yet his heart demanded that he hold back. That he recognize the progress he'd made with her. She didn't yet *need* him, not as he needed her, but she'd called Cable anyway, knowing that Cable would turn the information over to him.

He didn't know what her life had been like before arriving at the carnival, but his grandmother's words offered a clue. They rang through his mind and made his heart ache.

Her life has been one of famine and drought instead of abundance. Of harsh choices and betrayal.

That Dakotah had sought refuge in the carnival told him much. That she'd survived the last attack as well as this one, by her own courage and intelligence, told him more.

Resolve stiffened his spine. Anticipation stiffened his cock. She would no longer fight her battles alone. She was his. And he would let nothing threaten or harm her.

* * * * *

Dakotah stepped out of the trees when Domino entered the clearing. The wolf whined and quivered inside her, wanting to race to him. To rub against him. To lick at his lips in greeting. The woman stood her ground despite the tightening of her body, the slick swell of her vulva.

Domino's nostrils flared. His fangs elongated.

She was covered in blood. The clearing reeked of it. And yet it wasn't The Hunger that compelled him to close the distance between them, it was The Heat.

A hundred hearts could have thundered around them, but it was only hers that could hold his interest. He wanted to drive his fangs into her. To feed, not to sate a hunger of the body, but to sate one of the soul. He wanted to take her to the edge of human death and then fill her with his own blood, his own existence.

He'd never imagined how desperately he could want it, crave it, need it. "Never again, Dakotah," he growled. "Never again will you be unguarded, unprotected."

She licked her lips and he leaned in, duplicating her action, tracing the path her tongue had taken. Taking her scent and taste and leaving his own.

Dakotah shivered. The men she'd been forced to service, the ones she'd known even before then, the life she'd led—none of them had prepared her for Domino.

There were parts of her that argued against trusting him, against believing what he offered was real and not an illusion. But the wolf was stronger and the hum of the blood they shared too loud to ignore.

She licked her lips again, tasting him as she'd done on other occasions. Her heart expanding in her chest, the secret places inside spilling out, flooding her with a happiness she couldn't deal with.

She stepped back, put some distance between them. Buried her hands in her pockets and took comfort in the cool feel of the knives.

His nostrils flared slightly, as though he could smell the steel, as if her retreat bothered him.

She tensed and met his eyes, knowing what she was risking and yet offering a challenge all the same. He surprised her by smiling. A flash of lethal fangs. "Do you think I want a mate with no mind of her own? No courage of her own?"

Dakotah rubbed her thumb over the handle of one blade, remembering how she'd woken up in the clearing alone after they'd run together as wolves. "Did you want a mate at all?"

"No. But now that I have one, I find that I want to keep her." He took a step forward, his eyes daring her to retreat as he once again closed the distance between the two of them. "Now that I have one, I find I'm consumed with thoughts of her, with the need to know she's safe." His voice was low and husky, seductive. "I crave her in ways I never imagined possible." His eyes flashed with amusement. "She's The Empress to my Emperor. My World if the tarot cards are to be believed."

Dakotah laughed. She couldn't help herself. "You really did let Helki read for you."

"I came back when I learned you were being hunted by the Believers and found you'd left the carnival. She's a stubborn old woman. She wouldn't tell me where you'd gone until I submitted to a reading."

"You could have hypnotized her."

"I could have. But to do so in that circumstance would have been a breach of trust and a great show of disrespect." He leaned down, brushed a feather-soft kiss across Dakotah's lips. "Another time, in a different situation, I wouldn't have hesitated despite my ties to her. My…nature demands certain things of me."

"So there are no promises?"

"What promises would you have?"

Dakotah turned away from him. Feeling lost. Confused.

Her thoughts went to those moments when she'd been braced against the chair. When she'd watched Fane and Cable with Kiziah, when she'd seen pleasure that was an expression of love, passion that sprung from the heart. When she'd hungered like a beggar at the edge of a feast. Felt starved as though she'd lived through a lifetime of famine.

What promises did she want? What promises would she believe?

Her life was full of lies and deceit. Betrayal and loneliness.

Only in the last year had she found it possible to trust even a little bit—though she'd held her secrets close.

"Who is behind these attacks on you?" Domino asked, surprised at how the play of her emotions stirred his own, caused his heart to ache and tempered his behavior. From the moment he'd learned that she'd been taken, he'd resolved to find her, to reclaim her. To not allow her out of his sight until the second and third exchanges had been made. And yet now… His grandmother's words rang in his mind and echoed through every cell.

Her secret heart yearns for a man to prove that all men aren't like those who have come before him.

It shocked him how desperately he wanted to be the man who proved himself to be different from the rest. How much he wanted her to come to him willingly. Not because of the wolf. Not because of the blood-tie. But because he was her choice.

"Tell me who's behind the attacks," he repeated, "and I will see that they end."

"In exchange for what?"

He grimaced, realizing he should have seen the question coming. But he didn't want to bargain with her. He couldn't. It would be a lie if he told her she could leave him now.

"I will do it because I can and I must, Dakotah."

He moved into her personal space and curled his hands around her forearms. Relief surging through him when she didn't stiffen or pull away.

She licked her lips and he wanted to lean in and cover them. To savor her taste and explore her mouth with his tongue.

The night was melting away and despite the tension between them, he was hard, hungry. Aching.

Dakotah closed her eyes. Hearing Helki's words.

The time will come when you will face the enemy who wants you dead, but you will not do so alone. Another change awaits you. This time at the hands of a man unlike any you have known before. A man who wants your life, not your death.

And like Sarael before her, she could feel the truth in them. A truth she couldn't run from. A truth she wasn't sure she wanted to run from.

"Victor Hale. His pack is in Atlantic City." She opened her eyes and met Domino's. "I killed his son and ended up a werewolf in the process."

Domino shrugged. "What matters is whether or not he wants to join his son in death. The choice will be his."

"And us?"

This time Domino did lean in and cover her mouth, his lips gently sucking at hers until she willingly opened them and invited his tongue into her mouth. "You have seen the effects of what you gained from ingesting my blood?" he asked when the kiss ended.

"Yes."

"It will get worse until the second exchange is made. I will leave the choice of when the exchange is done up to you despite the fact that every instinct I possess demands we do it tonight." He lifted his hand and stroked her cheek. "I can allow you that choice, but not the choice of whether or not you will remain with me."

Dakotah nodded, admitting to herself that she wanted to be with him. She was tired of running. Tired of fighting. At least for tonight. "We can't leave the body here," she said just as Fane appeared.

He flashed a smile as his gaze swept over the dead man, then Dakotah's blood-soaked clothing, before landing on Domino. "The trail of your courtship seems to be littered with corpses. How many more nights will I have to spend disposing of them rather than attending to the needs of my own kadine?"

"Don't bother with this one at all," Domino said. "Send for the padralls and have them deliver it to the wolves in Atlantic City, along with a message. Dakotah is mine. Regardless of whose blood changed her into a Were, it is only mine that matters now. Victor Hale's hunt stops now with a blood pledge or a challenge."

Chapter Eight

Fane's eyes widened slightly. "And if he is foolish enough to choose a challenge? Or those around him make the choice for him?"

"I'm taking Dakotah to the house Matteo rented for his claiming of Sarael."

Fane nodded. "Cable, Kiziah and I will return to Kenton as well. There are more than enough dhampirs and vampires still in the area should their presence become necessary."

"What does it mean, a blood pledge or a challenge?" Dakotah asked.

Fane's gaze shifted to her. "A challenge is a fight to the death. Domino in your place against your enemy. Wolf against wolf. Or man against man."

"And the other?"

"A blood pledge in this case means the wolves guarantee that Victor Hale will no longer hunt or have you hunted. It is a promise made with the lives of every member of his pack—along with any related to them who are in the generation before or after—put up as collateral. If the pledge is broken, then we will call their debt and exact retribution."

Horror washed through Dakotah. "So the innocent die with the guilty?"

Fane shrugged. "For the most part we leave each other alone, but when their business interferes with ours, we are the masters. We're alive long after they become dust and ash underneath our feet. Over the centuries they have learned to police their own or we will do it for them."

Dakotah shivered, unable to pull her eyes away from Fane as she remembered the times they'd joked when he and Cable hung around the carnival. It had been an easy camaraderie, though she'd sensed he wasn't an enemy she'd want. But now, looking at him, hearing his words, she realized just how ruthless, how alien he was.

Her gaze moved to Domino, who was watching her intently, whose expression gave away nothing, who had the power to take her mind if he desired. She should be terrified of him, but instead her secret heart, the place that still harbored forgotten dreams of happy-ever-after, of a prince charming who would rescue her and take her to safety, kept her fear at bay, just as it had the last time they were in the woods with the body of her enemy nearby.

He was a dark, alien prince. And she was capable of rescuing herself.

Their lives could just as easily be a nightmare as a fairytale.

But she trusted him. With her life.

And that realization *did* scare her.

"Let's get out of here," she said, afraid that if too much more time passed, doubts and panic would rush in and push her into running.

Domino took her arm as though sensing how close she was to bolting. "We will stop by the house here in Ashberg so Dakotah can get cleaned up. Cable and Kiziah are there?"

Fane grinned. "I will call ahead and send them back to Kenton, in case you and Dakotah want to linger long enough to enjoy the fireplace as we did last night."

* * * * *

And after she'd taken a shower and gotten dressed, that's where Dakotah found Domino, standing next to the fireplace, its heat filling the room, its flames reflecting off him. He took a swallow from a wine glass and set it on the mantel. She wrinkled her nose at the smell of the pungent herbs mixed with wine. Even from across the room, the odor offended her, burning her nostrils as she moved to stand opposite him. "What's that?" she asked, tilting her head toward the glass.

"Something to keep The Hunger at bay." His eyes darkened and his face tightened as his gaze slid over her, the scent of arousal joining the mix of wine and herbs. "Though it does nothing for The Heat."

Dakotah reached for the glass, grimacing as she brought it closer to her mouth. He smiled slightly but didn't stop her from taking a sip, though in truth, she barely wet her lips before putting the glass back down on the mantel. "What happens if you don't drink it?"

"Eventually the whisper of The Hunger becomes a temptation and a command that can't be ignored. Then we kill. And are declared rogue and hunted depending on the circumstances and whether or not rehabilitation is possible." He reached over and cupped her face, stroked her mouth with his thumb. "Only the taking of a mate frees us from the necessity of using the herbs. The sharing and mixing of blood changes us so The Hunger is completely sated when we feed from our chosen one."

Dakotah turned her face so that her lips rubbed against his palm. Her tongue darted out, tasting him. "Kiziah said you're sexually bonded to me."

His nostrils flared slightly and something primitive moved through his eyes. "I am."

Dakotah had no desire to have sex with anyone else. The wolf bristled at the thought of it, and yet she *could* if she wanted to. "I'm not sexually bonded to you."

"Yet." His hand moved to her hair, his fingers grasped the dark strands, trapping her as he leaned in, stopping when his lips hovered over hers. "There is no escape, Dakotah, only the choice as to when the second and third exchanges are made."

He closed the distance, covered her mouth with his. The strength of his hands, the hardness of his body, the fierceness of the need pouring off him all contrasting sharply with the gentleness of his kiss, the slow, seductive dance of his tongue against hers.

Her heart jerked and raced when his fangs extended, tempting her curiosity just as the smell of the herbs and wine had. He groaned when she traced the deadly canines with her tongue, pressed his lower body more tightly to hers so that she could feel the rigid length of his erection.

Of their own accord her hands went to the front of his shirt, trailed down the center of it, releasing the buttons one at a time, not stopping until she'd undone the sole button at the waistband of his jeans. "Dakotah," he warned and she laughed softly.

It was exhilarating playing with him, dangerous. Like teasing a wolf.

But then she wasn't afraid of wolves.

She unzipped him, catching his gasp in her mouth and his cock in her hand as she became the aggressor, as she rubbed her tongue against his and explored his straining shaft and heavy balls with her fingers.

He let her, though she knew he could easily take control. And she marveled at how much pleasure it gave her to command his body.

She'd dominated hundreds of men because it meant her continued survival. She'd controlled them. Reduced them to pleading and begging. Been the embodiment of their sexual fantasies. And it had left her cold. Compartmentalized. Wishing only to escape from the hell she found herself in.

But now she found herself in a sensual heaven. Where her blood burned and her body ached.

She knelt, pulling his jeans down with her, pausing to take off his shoes and socks before removing his pants and looking up his body. Marveling at his masculine beauty. He was firm muscle and hard male. Enthralling even without the pheromones of his kind.

The wolf quivered with joy and anticipation, the woman mimicked the movement, shivering, suddenly sorry she'd bothered dressing. The feel of her clothing was an irritation against her skin, a confining presence that needed to be shed.

She stood and stripped. Boldly meeting Domino's gaze. Her breasts swelling and her nipples tightening as his eyes traveled over her body. His nostrils flaring and his lips parting.

She spread her legs when he got to the dark pubic hair, let him see her flushed, swollen cunt lips and the moisture that was gathered there. A wet, silent summons.

When he dropped to his knees, she buried her fingers in his hair and draped one thigh over his shoulder. Nearly howled with pleasure when his tongue went to her slit, his hungry bites and licks and sucks making her grind herself against his face.

The Heat roared through Domino. The taste of her arousal was almost as addicting as that of her blood.

He wanted to drive his fangs into her thigh, to mix pleasure with pain and find ecstasy. He wanted to consume her. To feast. To fuck. To claim.

But he forced himself to please her instead. To thrust his tongue deep into her channel then retreat to swirl it over her erect clit. To press his lips to her lower ones in an erotic kiss meant to capture then leave that nectar-covered flesh in order to suck on her engorged knob.

She fought the pleasure even as she writhed against him in order to gain more of it. The sound of his name in between her whimpers and deep-throated moans rewarding him and holding him in check.

She would beg for his bite. Beg for the second exchange of blood.

He wanted it to be her choice. He needed it to be her choice. The words he'd said in the woods had come from his heart. He wanted a mate with a mind of her own. With courage of her own.

Domino ate at her until her back bowed and she convulsed with orgasm, flooding his senses with her release. His cock bobbed in warning and only the tight fist of his hand around his penis kept him from spewing his seed across his own stomach. He groaned and looked up, his mouth still buried between her thighs, his lips and tongue pressed to her wet flesh.

The wildness he saw in her eyes rushed through him like a lightning bolt, stripping away the man and the wolf, so that only the vampire remained, a creature of Heat and Hunger.

"Bite me," she said.

Domino turned his face into her thigh, knowing he was damning himself. But there was no way to ignore her command. No way to ignore the temptation she presented.

His fangs slid through her skin, hitting the artery there with easy accuracy. The hot rush of her blood intoxicating, an addiction he had no hope of curing. It fed The Hunger while The Heat drove him to slide his hand up and down his cock, to palm the head as his tongue lapped at her silky flesh, to resume pumping in time to the movement of his throat as he swallowed. Until Heat and Hunger once again merged, blending together into a single flame that burned with Dakotah's name, danced in time to her heartbeat. Thundering, racing, spiking with orgasm as jets of semen rushed through his cock. Slowing, stuttering, nearly extinguishing as he sealed the bite and pulled his mouth away, catching her easily as she collapsed.

Every instinct demanded he open a vein and force her to drink, that he make the second exchange when she was too weak and dazed to fight the choice. Domino stood instead, pausing to ensure she wasn't in danger of dying before retrieving a hand-stitched quilt from the sofa.

He wrapped her in it and settled her on the couch, then dressed himself and doused the fire in the fireplace. It took only a moment to gather her clothes and pick her up. To take her to the car.

He trapped her in obsidian when she stirred and opened her eyes, commanded her to sleep. They were hours away from Matteo's house. And she was too great a distraction. Too great a temptation.

He wasn't sure he could fight the demands of his nature if they stayed here. And if she gave in, accepted his blood, asked for it, then they would fuck the rest of the night. His cock would fill time and time again in order to sate the need a second exchange would generate, in order to cement the bond that tied them together sexually until one of them died.

"Sleep," he whispered, brushing his fingers over her cheek, her lips, kissing her softly before bringing the engine of the powerful sports car to life and leaving Ashberg, his thoughts going to the edict he'd issued. He would know by sunrise whether there was to be a challenge or a pledge.

* * * * *

Dakotah woke to a fantasyscape. Flickering candles and scented air. The crackle of logs burning in the fireplace. A dark prince offering her a goblet of wine.

"Drink," Domino said, pressing the ornate cup to her hand, its warmth seeping into her palm as the smell of heated wine mixed with some type of herb wafted upward.

She drank. Not even stopping to question.

When she was done she handed the heavy cup back to him, noticing for the first time that she was naked underneath the sheets and propped up against a mound of pillows in a bed made for carnal pleasure.

She shivered when she saw the cuffs dangling from the post at the foot of the bed. Domino laughed, setting the cup on the nightstand before rolling to his side, his cock a hard, heated presence against her thigh and hip. "For kadines who need to be disciplined," he said, splaying his fingers over her belly and making her cunt clench and flare in reaction.

Dakotah remembered the conversation he'd had with Fane. "We're back in Kenton? This is where Sarael was taken?"

"Yes."

It felt strange to end up here. A circle closing.

By the time she stumbled into the carnival, she had almost become a feral animal. Intent only on running, on surviving. On staying one step ahead of Victor Hale.

But as she'd traveled with the carnival, shared a home on wheels with Sarael, she'd slowly become human again. Found that it didn't have to hurt to care about someone. And she'd cared about Sarael. She'd worried for her.

Dakotah's gaze went to the cuffs dangling from the post and she frowned. Domino laughed again, leaned in so that his face blocked her view. "She was created for Matteo. From the moment of her birth, Sarael belonged to him. You will see her again and you can judge her happiness for yourself."

His hand moved from Dakotah's abdomen to her breast, his fingers tracing over a hardened, puckered nipple, his expression serious. "There is little separation between a kadine and the one who claims her. Her misery becomes his. Her joy is his as well."

"Along with her thoughts and memories," Dakotah said, the wine which had soothed only seconds before now churning in her stomach.

Domino stilled, her emotions battering him, warning him they were moving into dangerous, treacherous territory. It would be so easy to calm her, to remove her worries. To smooth them over so nothing stood in the way of his claiming her completely.

"It works both ways," he said, closing the distance between their faces, his tongue lightly tracing her lips before his mouth sucked at hers in a gentle kiss. "There are no secrets between a male and his kadine."

When she would have turned her head, his hand left her breast and cupped her cheek. Holding her in position, deepening the kiss, though it remained soft, persuasive. A heated rub of slick heat and wet desire. "There is nothing you can't know about me," he whispered, his gaze meeting hers. "The good and the bad."

Dakotah closed her eyes, tried to close her mind and her heart, but it was useless. She'd come this far. She'd pushed the boundaries of her trust further than she would have thought possible.

"I've been with a lot of men," she said, hating the starkness of her voice. "Not by choice, but it doesn't matter. You'll see everything I've done."

His nostrils flared. Rage roared through him. Flashing red in his eyes and causing her to flinch and try to pull away.

Domino was on her in an instant. His weight holding her to the mattress and pillows as his eyes bored into hers. "If it wasn't your choice, Dakotah, then I will kill any man who has touched you." He leaned in, his mouth hovering over hers once again. "And I will enjoy every kill."

Shock rippled through her, holding her as motionless as his eyes and will. She knew he spoke the truth. She felt it in every cell of her body. And for a second she filled with hate and the savage need for revenge. Allowed old, violent fantasies to resurface. "How?" she asked and this time her voice sounded hard, brittle, even to her own ears.

Domino smiled, a flash of fangs and ruthlessness. Alien despite the human flesh, despite the candles with their dancing flames, the trappings of romance he'd provided before waking her and offering her herbs and wine.

"Easily, Dakotah. I could have them hunt and kill each other if it would please you. I could command them to kill themselves."

She shivered at just how powerful he was. "You wouldn't end up being hunted by vampires and dhampirs for doing that?"

"Only if I risked exposing us by killing while feeding." He pressed his mouth to hers briefly. "Shall I pledge to kill all those who have hurt or used you? Make it my gift to you for becoming my kadine?"

She licked her lips and his eyes darkened, desire moving through them. She knew he was serious. His offer genuine. His intent to free her from the demons of her past, not to enslave her.

He could make her his kadine without her consent. He could make her want to belong to him. But instead he was trying to give her a choice even though there really was no choice. Their wolves had decided that first night in the forest. Their blood had already mixed and mingled.

He was her future. She was his.

The Emperor to her Empress.

Dakotah wriggled her hand and he freed her wrist. She smoothed her knuckles over his cheek. When his sensual lips tilted upward in response to her touch, she smiled and allowed a lightness to fill her heart and chase away the old hatred and pain. "No," she said. "Let the past stay in the past. I don't want to spend my future revisiting it. Reliving it. Killing because of it." She tangled her fingers in his hair, rubbed her mouth against his. "The night will be over soon, isn't there something we have to do before that happens?"

Joy filled Domino. Intense and overwhelming. He rolled, startling her and making her laugh as he shifted her to the dominant position, forcing her to straddle him.

Her eyes widened when he reached over and lifted a small dagger from the nightstand, handing it to her with a teasing smile.

"You have already demonstrated how handy you are with a blade. Choose a spot and take what I have to offer."

Dakotah took the knife and leaned down, bracing herself on one elbow, her wet slit rubbing and sliding against his cock, her nipple aligned to his, two hard tight points pressed to one another. "Aren't you worried what I might decide to cut?" she teased.

He laughed, looking fully human. A confident male sure of his woman. "And cheat yourself of the pleasure you'll soon get only from me?"

She put the tip of the blade against his throat, lightly traced the pulse beating there in a steady, unhurried rhythm, then moved downward, following the trail of his blood until the blade was poised above his nipple. Only his cock reacted, jerking, striking her clit, the head leaking against her belly, causing more of her arousal to escape, to coat his shaft and roll down to his testicles.

His eyes were molten stone, dark temptation in a face she could spend a lifetime looking at. He hissed when she cut him. Then threw back his head with a groan when her mouth covered both the wound and the nipple.

Ecstasy tore through Domino as she fed. A wild rush that had him writhing underneath her, his hands spearing through her hair, holding her to his chest.

He nearly came when her fingers reached for his cock, when they guided him to her entrance and she impaled herself on him.

It took all of his control not to roll her to her back, to become the aggressor as his ancestors had programmed him to be. But the gift she was giving him was one he would treasure always. And so he let her feed. Let *her* take him. Control him. Ride him to a dizzying, all-encompassing climax, her mouth finally leaving his chest as her own pleasure crested.

Only then did he give in to ancient instincts. Become what the blueprint of his cells demanded. What The Heat coursing through them both demanded, his body taking hers time and time again, leading hers in a dance of pleasure, need and release, until they were both weak, sated, ready to welcome The Sleep as the first rays of the sun breached the darkness.

It was a peace beyond anything Domino had ever known. A happiness he could find no words for. Broken only by the sound of his cell phone ringing, its demand muted by the jeans encasing it. The sound of it jarring him from the warmth of Dakotah's arms and body.

With a groan he rolled to the edge of the bed and fished through the clothing on the floor until he retrieved the phone. Fane. Which meant the wolves in Atlantic City had reached a decision on whether there was to be a challenge or a blood pledge.

Chapter Nine

"Even Victor Hale's allies don't trust him with their lives," Fane said as soon as Domino answered the phone. "They didn't allow him a choice. They elected to throw him into the ring with you. The padralls accepted on your behalf and agreed to a challenge after sunset—tonight. I could have changed it but then thought better of it." There was a hint of amusement in Fane's voice that immediately grated on Domino's nerves. "It gives you the choice as to whether or not you want to make the third exchange with Dakotah before fighting her enemy. After all, her life would be forfeit as well should you bind her to you and then lose."

Domino's nostril flared. "Perhaps I will rip out two throats tonight."

Fane laughed. "I see you still harbor delusions that you could best me."

"It's no delusion," Domino growled.

"Dementia then. But on a serious note, I have asked Cable to assist with the arrangements and ensure there is no opportunity for mischief or deceit—though the presence of so many dhampirs and vampires will drive the point home to the wolves that we are prepared to slaughter them all."

"It's no less than the truth."

"And it's good they're reminded of it. For the sake of my bride, who claims we are on our honeymoon and begs for my attention, I hope we're not delayed here any longer. I'll see you tonight."

Domino closed the phone and dropped it onto the pile of clothing next to the bed before repositioning himself beside Dakotah and pulling her into his arms. She was tense and he could feel the wild mix of her emotions. "Don't think to leave me," he said. "Don't think to take Victor Hale on by yourself."

"It's not your fight."

He laughed. Warmed despite the way her heart raced against his chest and her body vibrated with concern. He didn't need the third exchange to know what she was thinking. What she was contemplating.

"It will hardly be a fight at all. Do you have so little faith in my abilities?" He rolled, trapping her underneath him. Her gaze caught in his. "From the time we are children we are trained in the use of restraints. Will you force me to bind you in order to keep you from doing something foolish? Or would you rather I simply command you not to leave the bed during the day?"

Dakotah opened her mouth to challenge him, to dare him, to insist he let her fight her own battles, but the words didn't come. The wolf held them back until they dissolved on her tongue, replaced by a different demand. "I want to be there when you fight."

He snarled in response. A gut reaction. A need to know she was safe. That her enemy couldn't reach her.

Her face tightened. The eyes that moments before had been soft and yielding became polished stones, reflections of the wall she was prepared to build between them.

"Only if you stand with Fane," Domino said, forcing the words out, hating that his heart thrilled at the sight of her satisfaction, at the way her body relaxed underneath his. He tightened his grip on her, wanting to meld them into one being. "Do I tether you to the bed or command you? Or will you give me your promise to stay by my side while The Sleep holds me? To be next to me when I wake?"

Her eyebrow lifted in amused challenge and happiness uncurled in his chest and belly. "I assume any promise will exclude bathroom breaks and trips to the kitchen?"

He growled softly. "Say the words, Dakotah."

"I'll stay."

He resettled them, spooning her back to his chest and curling his arm around her, holding her tightly to him in a gesture that made her feel cherished rather than imprisoned.

Outside, beyond the heavy drapes, the sun rose higher. She was aware of it though she couldn't see it. Just as she was acutely aware of Domino's skin pressed to hers, his heart beating, slowing as a heavy lethargy descended, pulling her under, The Sleep taking her as it took him.

* * * * *

Domino knew the moment she left the bed. It was nearing sunset. The lethargy clung to him, but because of the wolf, The Sleep didn't hold him as mercilessly as it did other vampires. He followed her movements by sound, smiled when she went into the bathroom and filled the old-fashioned tub Matteo had insisted be installed.

When she slid into the water, Domino forced himself to stand, the wolf aiding him against The Sleep. The Heat and Hunger also rising, allies instead of adversaries. Wanting him to be close to Dakotah in order to make the third exchange.

He halted in the bathroom doorway, his cock going to rigid attention at the sight of her in the tub, her head thrown back, her eyes closed as her hands smoothed soap over slick female curves.

The scent of her filled his nostrils. The desire for her filled his soul.

She tilted her head and opened eyes dark with need and lust. "Join me?"

His cock led the way, jutting out in front of him as he moved to the tub.

She laughed, a husky sound that added to his torment. He groaned when she took his shaft in her hand and brushed her thumb over the engorged head, stroking until the tip was wet. Then she used his cock to guide him into the tub and position him where she wanted him, at the other end, so that she could rise onto her knees and straddle him.

The blood burned through Dakotah's veins. Whispered and hinted of an ecstasy yet to be experienced, an ecstasy beyond what she'd already had with Domino.

There was no fighting the call of blood to blood. Of body to body. The yearning of the soul and heart.

There was no denying the truth of what they were to each other. The wolf's truth. The truth revealed in the tarot cards. The truth she and Domino had both come to accept.

They belonged together.

Her fingers speared through his hair, holding him still for her kiss, an exploration of lips and tongue, a savoring, a taste of desire found in wet heated darkness and the smooth glide of female against male. He let her control the kiss though his hands moved to her back, his fingers traced her spine and sent shivers of delight along her nerve endings, then moved to her sides, her hips as his cock stroked her folds, her clit. Sending heat spiraling through her.

She groaned and rose higher in the tub, rubbed her nipple back and forth across his lips. Taunting him by not allowing him to latch on and feast despite his growls of frustration.

He retaliated by filling her channel with his cock, by securing her so she couldn't fuck herself on him as his fingers went to her clit, stroking, teasing, making her sheath fist and unfist around a thick, pulsing shaft that remained stationary.

Dakotah relented, stilled, brought him to her breast and held him there as he suckled, the pull of his mouth sending ice-hot shards of need straight to her engorged knob so that it strained against his fingers, jerked under his caress. So that she whispered, "Please."

He took control then. Shifting, plundering her body with his cock as his fangs sank into her breast. Dark urges filling him, whispering for him to take her to the edge of human death, to the point where her heart stuttered in warning. But he resisted, wanting more than a single fuck in the tub before finishing what they had started.

And so he fed, holding her tightly to him, their thrashing sending water cascading over the edge of the tub. Her scream of release echoing off the walls of the bathroom. His own muffled against her flesh.

Domino rose from the tub, his mouth still pressed to her breast, his cock still embedded in her cunt. The strength he'd gained from his alien ancestors allowed him to take her to the bedroom, to settle them both on the thick pile of rugs in front of the fireplace.

Only then did he lift his head, sealing the puncture marks above her nipple with his tongue before kissing up her body, stopping when his mouth was above hers, his eyes locked with hers. There wasn't much time left before they'd have to leave. Fane or Cable or both of them would arrive shortly to escort them to the place where the challenge would be met and answered in death.

Victor Hale's death.

Domino didn't doubt for an instant that Dakotah's enemy would die tonight.

He understood her need to be present. And was reconciled to it.

It was his own reluctance to make the third exchange without ensuring himself that she understood what it meant that surprised him.

The Heat and Hunger, the alien stamp of his ancestors, had no conscience when it came to the taking of a kadine. Even the wolf felt nothing beyond the rightness of its claim to Dakotah's wolf as its mate.

But the man needed more.

Domino brushed his lips against Dakotah's, groaning when the movement slid his cock deeper into her body and her slick muscles clamped down on him, tightened as though afraid he would try to leave.

Dakotah could feel his hesitation, his uncertainty and if she'd been in doubt as to where her future lay, then his delay, his desire that she accept him without the thrall of pheromones or the instinct of the wolf, would have allayed her fears. His concern was a wedge driven into a heart that had been locked shut, forcing it open, so the love held there for the future could finally be freed.

"We'll have to leave soon," he said, but made no attempt to escape from her body or her arms.

"Then we'll have to hurry and finish what we started."

He settled more heavily on her. "There'll be pain."

"I assumed there would be."

"My death would trigger your own."

She laughed. "What happened to your assertion that taking on Victor Hale would hardly be a fight at all?"

Domino growled, a playful sound echoing the joy cascading through him, flooding him with happiness before The Heat and The Hunger moved in, asserting its claim.

With a groan he pulled from her body and flipped her to her stomach. His hands and mouth, the sharp nip of his teeth driving her to her elbows and knees, positioning her so that her nipples pressed against the heavy fiber of the carpet. Her thighs spread, exposing wet pubic hair and folds pulled back to reveal a rosy cleft, flushed and parted, seeping with desire. He traced the glistening skin with his tongue, rubbed over her erect clit, tortured them both with the brush of fangs against the flesh of her inner thigh.

She whimpered, a nearly wolf-like sound that made his cock jerk and leak. That made him taste her arousal again, growl with frustration. The urge to lick and suck, to bathe his face in her need warring with the necessity of finishing what they'd started.

He lingered between her thighs as long as he could. Until his cock was flexing, bobbing, smearing liquid heat on his abdomen. Until his balls burned and ached. Then he mounted her in a smooth motion, shoved all the way into her in one thrust, stopping only when his testicles were pressed tightly to her body, trapped between her hot mound and his muscled thighs.

There was no thought beyond that point. There was only The Hunger and The Heat. Driving him to slash his wrist and press it to her mouth. To pierce her shoulder with his fangs and feed. To fuck. Endless moments of dark ecstasy. Of sharing so profound that life and death blended into exquisite release.

Followed by pain so searing that it seemed to last an eternity. A physical pain for Dakotah. An agony of the heart and soul, the mind for Domino, who could only hold her, his strength keeping her from hurting herself as her cells attacked one another, savagely and forever altering what she was, turning her into something not human or wolf, or completely alien, but the perfect blending of the three.

She was panting, exhausted, shaking by the time it was over. But it was the sight of her tears that very nearly undid Domino. "It's over now," he whispered, kissing her, nuzzling her as a wolf comforts its mate. Absorbing her tears, sharing them. Baring his throat and pressing it to her mouth. A promise. A show of trust.

Take my blood, Dakotah, he said, the command so clear that for a moment she thought he'd spoken it out loud. But when he repeated the words in her mind, she knew she hadn't imagined them. And then he shifted, spearing his fingers through her hair, controlling the range of her movement as he rubbed his neck against her mouth.

In an instant the pain and trauma of the transformation was forgotten. Her sole reality became the beat of his pulse against her lips. She cried out, arched as her canine teeth elongated into fangs.

She burned.

With Heat. With Hunger.

A scorching wave that made her struggle wildly in his arms until it passed. Then he once again offered his throat. This time as his penis slid into her channel in a gentle homecoming.

Now, Dakotah.

And she bit. Fed as they made love. Both of them gaining strength from the intimacy of their joining. The sacredness of the mixing and sharing of blood.

When it was done they lay together, limbs entangled. Two still joined into one. Content. Until the first tendril of doubt, the first tug of a heartstring, the first brush of mind against mind. A tentative exploration. Domino wanting to know what she felt for him, why she'd made the second and third exchanges — even though he knew he should accept her gift without question. Domino seeing glimpses of her past. Of the men. Of the things she'd been forced to do and endure.

She jerked as though he'd slapped her and tried to close her mind. He tightened his grip on her, rolled so she was trapped underneath him, captured by his body and his eyes. "I will kill all of them," he said, letting her feel the extent of his rage at what had been done to her, his desire for revenge and retribution. Letting her feel too his awe at her courage, her endurance, her intelligence. His amazement that she'd survived where few would have, grown stronger where others would have been broken and crushed.

That she'd been willing to trust and give herself to him nearly reduced him to tears, and he allowed her to feel that as well, though he repeated his comment, not holding back his lethal nature, what he was capable of. "I will kill all of them."

Dakotah's heart stuttered in her chest, not from a brush with death this time but from the immensity of the life now shimmering in front of her. *There is little separation between a kadine and the one who claims her. There are no secrets between a male and his kadine.*

Domino had told her as much and she'd believed him, and yet the reality was so much more. It was very nearly overwhelming.

With a thought she could know anything about him. See anything of his past. Read his intentions for the future.

But it was his emotions that held her enthralled. The intensity of what he felt for her. Admiration and respect where a part of her had feared there would be disgust, contempt. A turning away. The banquet replaced by famine.

"Forget about them," Dakotah said as she tugged, freeing her wrists from where he held them pinned to the thick rugs, tangling her fingers in his hair, and guiding his mouth to hers, pressing her lips to him, kissing him. Letting her actions speak for her, letting the carefully guarded secret place in her heart open, letting him see how he'd become the dream she'd locked away and not dared to look at again until he'd come into her life.

The kiss was like the sharing of their blood. A primitive and sacred communion. A starting point.

Soon tenderness gave way to desire. The past to the present. And Domino rose above her, but not before he'd stumbled upon a cold shiver of fear over his gaining control to the point where he could freeze her in place with a thought.

He sent a warning in the instant before he commanded her body, pinning her wrists to her sides and her ankles to the carpet, her legs spread so that he could kneel between them.

Her heart raced in reaction, her pulse jumped and made him fight to keep his fangs from descending. And even though she fought the restraint, she didn't demand that he let her go as he lowered his mouth and captured a dark nipple. Pulling and sucking on it until the thundering in her veins was a molten fire fueled by The Heat.

He took her to the edge with his lips at her breast, his fingers on her clit, tugging and stroking, gripping and releasing. Brought her close to climax repeatedly but didn't allow her a release.

Dakotah thrashed and arched, held in place by his thoughts alone. She felt the full measure of his power over her but also his desire to do what was right, to never abuse her. She felt his need to dominate, to protect, to possess. To be everything to her. And she accepted it. Even reveled in it. Though it didn't make her submissive.

"Now," she demanded, meeting his gaze in challenge, watching as his face tightened and his nostrils flared. As something alien moved through his eyes.

He hissed, letting her see his fangs, but she saw it as a victory, an acknowledgement of her own power, an indication of how aroused he was that some of his control had slipped.

The wild urges of his ancestors screamed in Domino's cock. Demanding that he subdue her, answer her challenge in a way that would prove his mastery. That would make her as submissive as the kadines created and raised for his race.

But as quickly as the thought came, the wolf bristled and the man laughed silently — all in the second before The Heat made it impossible to delay, to play, even to tease.

With a thought he freed one of her hands, erotic images pressing in on him as he said, "Pleasure yourself. Let me see you come from the touch of your own hand."

And satisfaction rushed through him when her fingers went to her slit, her clit — not because he'd commanded it of her, but because he'd asked it, because she could read his fantasies and was willing to make them his reality.

He had to take his cock in hand in order to stave off orgasm as she manipulated her engorged knob and drove her fingers into her channel, sliding in and out as the smell of her arousal invaded his senses, enflamed him. Made him want to cover her and thrust into her. To surround himself with her wet heat and slick feminine flesh.

He resisted the temptation. Hissed when he saw her knowing smile. Waited until she jerked under her own hand, her cunt burning against her fingers, clenching and unclenching. And then he fell on her. Freed her so that she could wrap her arms and legs around him and hold him tight as he fucked her, loved her, became one with her.

They were still naked in front of the fire when Fane arrived. His amusement as he plopped down in a chair as though he intended to watch them grated over Domino's nerves and made Dakotah smile.

Domino rose to his feet, flashing his fangs when Fane's gaze traveled over Dakotah's body as she stood.

She slipped her arm through Domino's, laughing, her heart light, the bond with Domino allowing her to see that beneath their outward sparring, the two men had a history, a deep loyalty to one another. "Don't waste yourself on him," she joked, leading Domino back to the bedroom. "You can't afford to let him weaken you before the challenge."

Her comment earned her a flash of fangs and a growl while Fane laughed in the other room. But all too soon the humor was gone, replaced by somber watchfulness as they left the house and arrived at the site of the challenge. The lightheartedness replaced by the unmistakable smell of nervousness as a handful of wolves gathered at the edge of a small moonlit patch of bare earth surrounded by a dense forest of trees.

Even without the deepening of her senses that Dakotah had gained with Domino's blood, she was aware of vampires and dhampirs in the woods around them. The cold, alien presence they projected made chill bumps rise along her arms. And though she couldn't see them or count them, she knew they greatly outnumbered the wolves.

The wolves knew it too. They huddled together in a defensive pack. Separating themselves from the naked man who waited at the center of the clearing. Their positioning a silent statement that Victor Hale stood on his own. That his fate was his own.

Dakotah squeezed Domino's hand. A thousand thoughts tumbling through her mind. Including the belief that it should be her going into the clearing.

Don't even consider it, Dakotah, he said. Obsidian eyes meeting hers, warning her with a look that he would take complete control if she pushed him.

Hurry up and get it over with then, she said. Confident he would win, though her heart raced with the fear that something would go wrong and he would die because of her.

Domino pulled her to him, poured love and the promise of a future together into her with a kiss, then set her aside. His gaze meeting Fane's in a silent communication that had Fane moving closer, his shoulder against Dakotah's, as Domino stripped and entered the clearing.

The wolves moved forward in a tight knot and Dakotah tensed. Fane took her arm and said, "Don't worry. The pack elders are only going to state the terms agreed on by the padralls and hear Domino's formal acceptance of them before the challenge begins."

It was done in a second and the wolves retreated. Then Victor Hale shifted into a grey wolf. Attacked. No doubt hoping to catch Domino as he changed form.

But where Domino had been, the black wolf shimmered into existence. Its bulk larger than the grey wolf's. Its speed and savagery stunning. The product of an evolution far more intricate and ruthless than the one that had created Victor Hale.

It was over in a fury of movement, of breaking bones and torn flesh, of blood loss and spilled internal organs. The grey wolf's life pouring into the dirt, its body changing for a final time, becoming a human corpse to be disposed of.

Domino trotted over to where Dakotah stood. The wolf not wanting to relinquish its form when the moon was out and the forest called. *Run with me.* And Dakotah's wolf shivered with joy, pressed against her skin in remembered pleasure.

She laughed, thinking about what had happened the last time they ran. *You mean mate with you.*

He play-bowed, obsidian eyes dancing with joy. *That too.*

Next to her Fane laughed and said, "Oh how the mighty have fallen." But Dakotah couldn't resist Domino's call. She stripped and handed her clothes to Fane, then changed and darted for the trees, the black wolf bounding after her.

Epilogue

Palazzo dei Venti Oscuri. Palace of Dark Winds.

One look at it and Dakotah could see how Matteo Cabrelli's home got its name. It loomed high above the ocean as though daring the sea and air and earth to challenge it. To try and topple it from its perch along the cliffs.

Dakotah's stomach tightened, though her heart raced with anticipation. She even managed a smile when she remembered Helki's assertion that she would see Sarael again sooner than she might think and be a part of Sarael's world for more years than she could imagine.

Next to her, Domino laughed softly, pulling Dakotah more tightly against him in the backseat of the limousine that was now making the slow climb upward. *It's a good thing my mother's mother is so sure of her readings and her visions that she never needs to say "I told you so."*

He picked Dakotah's left hand up and brought it to his mouth, kissing the jeweled and scripted band he'd given her. *The Empress to my Emperor, with The World before us.*

She pressed her forehead to his, bathing in the wash of his emotions. The love she felt there. The respect. The acceptance.

It still felt like a fairytale. A dream. An impossible reality.

Where she'd once been alone, now her life was full. Not just with him, but with his family. With Cable and Fane and Kiziah, who were waiting above, in Matteo's home, along with Sarael and the man Dakotah could only vaguely remember.

"I was there that night," Domino said and she instantly saw his memory of it. Felt the relief he'd experienced knowing Matteo was already sexually bonded to Sarael.

She laughed when she saw Domino's resolve to both feed from and fuck her before leaving the area, and she couldn't resist lowering her hand and tracing over the erection pressed against the fabric of his jeans. Couldn't stop herself from nuzzling his neck, from letting her fangs descend so she could torment him by brushing them over a pulse that was suddenly dancing.

Dakotah smiled against his skin, feminine satisfaction roaring through her at the way he was tense, his breath coming faster, his desire merging with her own, The Heat flaring hot and bright, a single flame contained in separate bodies. *You got more than you bargained for when you fucked and fed from me,* she teased.

His hand moved to her breast, his fingers going to her nipple with deadly precision, making her gasp as her cunt clenched. *Do you hear me complaining?*

She laughed and closed her eyes, savoring the scent and feel of him, wondering if there was time to make love before they got to Matteo's estate.

Only if you intend to greet our host and hostess with the sight of your naked ass, Domino teased, flashing her an image that had her pulling away from him. Brown eyes meeting amused obsidian ones.

"I love you," she said, the words coming easier now. Though there were still days when she caught herself probing his thoughts, ensuring herself that he loved her in return. That it was more than a sexual bonding, more than a mating of their wolves.

Domino pulled her into his lap as the heavy gates of Matteo's estate swung open, his heart aching for all the pain she'd endured during her life.

Once he couldn't have imagined finding a female whose mind interested him as much as her body, whose strength and courage he could admire, not for just a night but for the centuries that lay ahead for him. But now he couldn't imagine life without her. "You're my world, Dakotah. Everything I could want not only in a kadine but in a companion."

The limousine stopped and the door swung open, making Dakotah blink in momentary confusion at the man standing there. A man who looked like Cable and yet wasn't. Domino shifted, his movement propelling her out of the limo but not before she felt his curiosity.

"What are you doing here, Levant?" Domino asked as he exited the car, his thoughts informing Dakotah that the man in front of them was Cable's brother.

Levant's face tightened. "We've come to work among the *espandral.*"

He refers to the padrall order responsible for creating the kadines and molding them into what their mates desire, Domino sent to Dakotah, though to Levant he said, "Is that the royal *we*, or did your brothers come with you?"

"Priest and Deacon are also here." Levant tilted his head. "If you'll follow me, I'll take you to where Matteo and the others are waiting."

"You've been reduced to servant?" Domino asked and Dakotah frowned at his needling of Cable's brother.

But Levant took it in stride. "Hardly. Though being Matteo's servant would be preferable to what awaits."

The wealth displayed in Matteo's home was breathtaking and more than once Domino caught Dakotah when she stumbled, distracted by the view and the art, the sheer beauty and glitter of the scene around her as they climbed elegant staircases and walked down hallways that seemed as though they belonged in another era.

They do, Domino said. *As Matteo does. He is not like Fane or me. He was never dhampir. He marked his life in centuries from the moment of his birth.* Domino laughed. *So you don't need to worry about watching as he pleasures his kadine or having Sarael see you in the same situation. He's much too old-fashioned for that.* Domino nuzzled the side of Dakotah's face. *But later, after they've retired...no doubt Fane and Cable would enjoy a night in front of the fireplace with their woman.*

And Dakotah laughed in spite of herself. Shivered at the images his words brought to mind. The play of them in her thoughts holding her attention until they entered the room where the others were waiting.

She took in Fane and Kiziah, standing with Cable and two men who could only be Deacon and Priest. But then she found Sarael. Smiling. Hurrying toward her. Matteo following in her wake.

There was a hesitation on Sarael's part when she reached Dakotah, a small barrier that belonged in the past, and Dakotah disposed of it by pulling Sarael into a hug. The need to keep others separate no longer necessary for her survival.

When they moved apart, Matteo positioned Sarael so her back was to his front, his arms around her waist in a possessive display that had her blushing and laughing, exchanging a glance with Dakotah. The happiness there easy for Dakotah to see. To recognize. Because it was a happiness echoed in her own heart.

Enjoy An Excerpt From:
SKYE'S TRAIL

Detective Rico Santana knew there was going to be hell to pay. One way or the other, there always was when *she* was involved. If not from Rivera, his captain, then from the unrelenting lust and the lack of sleep that always followed any encounter with Skye Delano.

¡Carajo! He lusted after her. Maybe if he fucked her, it would get her out of his system.

Rico gritted his teeth against the need he could already feel building, the anticipation. Now he was sorry he'd brought along backup. If he just had some time alone with her he'd...

Shit. He needed saving...from himself. Fucking Skye would be professional suicide—maybe even personal suicide. Rico had a feeling that once would never be enough with her.

He hit the turn signal and eased the unmarked police car toward an empty parking space. Out of the corner of his eye he saw Cia Caldwell's tight disapproving frown. She was the newest member of the department, and as far as he knew, she'd never had any personal contact with Skye. She'd heard the stories though, and read the captain's file.

His mistake was calling Skye from the bullpen. When he'd looked up, Detective Caldwell was standing next to his cubicle. "Rivera is going to ream you," she'd said before the phone had even hit its cradle.

"It'll be dark soon. They're not going to find those kids without Skye's help."

Cia squared her shoulders. "I'm going with you."

A ripple of anger shot through Rico. He didn't need a babysitter.

A flash of sanity followed. Yeah, maybe it'd be better.

The captain was going to be pissed enough. At least this way Rivera would see it was all about finding the kids—not about finding an excuse to see Skye again.

¡Carajo! How could he be so hard when right now the only thing he should be thinking about was two missing kids?

Rico parked the sedan in front of Skye's apartment complex. Caldwell had her door open before he could even turn off the engine. He grimaced and looked down at the bulge in the front of his pants. "Wait here," he said.

Caldwell's mutinous expression let him know what she thought of his order. But he was the senior detective and she was new.

Heart racing, he got out of the car. Every time he saw Skye the lust that rolled through his system made him think of standing in front of a wave of molten lava.

Rico braced himself as he took the stairs up to her apartment and rang the bell. It was going to be worse this time. He knew that. Always before he'd seen her at a crime scene or the station. He'd never been alone with her in a place that might lead to something physical.

The cop in him said he was crazy to go into this situation without backup. The man said he was a fool not to try and fuck her.

When the door swung open, Rico knew he couldn't keep denying what his body was telling him. Shit. Everything about Skye whispered of sex and dark mystery, danger. She was beautiful temptation, silver-blonde hair and jet-black lashes framing hypnotic pale blue eyes.

In that second he didn't care whether the rumors about her were true or not. She was a fantasy. His fantasy.

Rivera had warned him off her after the last search, when the perps responsible for kidnapping a couple of kids had turned up dead. The captain had told him more as a friend than as a commanding officer that a personal relationship with Skye could be the end of his career.

Rico was a cop first. Came from a family of cops. Above everything else, that's what he was, what he'd always wanted to be. A cop.

So he'd kept his distance. Avoided her. Until now.

Now the only thing he could think about was pressing her back into the apartment and taking her against the wall. On the floor. Eventually in the bed.

¡Carajo! The things he wanted to do to her, the things he wanted to let her do to him, actually shocked him.

"You came quick," she said and his heart jumped at her choice of words. He wondered if she'd guessed how badly he wanted her. Fuck, he'd be lucky if he lasted one stroke before shooting his load into her.

For a minute all he could do was stare into her eyes. He thought he saw desire in them but he wasn't sure if it was real or imagined. All his cop instincts failed him when he was around her.

He tried to focus on the reason he was here. The kids.

It helped—some. "Are you ready?" he asked.

Skye studied the raven-haired cop standing in front of her. She could feel the lust pouring off of him, could read the fantasies even without delving into his mind.

Her body craved his, had from the first moment they'd met.

It'd be so easy to get involved with him.

So easy but so dangerous.

So very, very dangerous.

She stepped out of the apartment and locked the door behind her. "Ready."

Now Available!

Ellora's Cavemen:
Dreams of the Oasis I

Featuring:

Myla Jackson, Liddy Midnight, Nicole Austin, Allyson James, Paige Cuccaro, Jory Strong

A special edition anthology of six sizzling stories from Ellora's Cave's Mistresses of Romantica.
Edited by Raelene Gorlinsky

Call Me Barbarian by Liddy Midnight

Princess Cedilla enjoys unprecedented privilege in a society where women are neither seen nor heard. Her life changes when twin barbarian gladiators enter the arena. One glance and Cedilla is irrevocably bound to these Southern warriors—and revealed as half-barbarian herself. Whether in the arena or the bedchamber, Asterix and Apostroph live for the moment—until they find their destined mate. When Cedilla is banished by the Emperor, they devote themselves to satisfying her wildest desires. But the Empire needs Cedilla, and the Empire is intolerant of barbarians...

Dragonmagic by Allyson James

It's hell to be a dragon enslaved. Arys, a powerful silver dragon in human form, is bound to a witch who uses his magic and his body to pleasure her in every way imaginable. When Arys spies Naida, a young woman just coming into her powers, watching Arys performing erotic acts with the witch, he knows that Naida is the key to his freedom. First he must convince Naida she's his true mate and that the power of their sexual play, and her love, will release him.

Fallen For You by Paige Cuccaro

For ten thousand years, Zade's warrior mentality kept him focused on the Watcher's mission—rid the world of the Oscurità fallen angels. And then the witch Isabel came under his care. The Oscurità will be coming to posses her or kill her, drawn by her burgeoning powers. Isabel is a temptation they can't ignore, but neither can Zade. If he succumbs to his feelings, Zade's frozen soul could destroy Isabel. If he resists, his unsatisfied need may cost him everything. To save all he holds dear, Zade must trust that Isabel was born for him, and he has fallen for her.

Spontaneous Combustion by Nicole Austin

Dr. Madailein Flannagan's carnal desires are blazing deep inside, and her best friend Jake Cruise is just the man to fan the flames. But the sexy, bad boy firefighter goes for equally bad girls, and Maddy's afraid she's just not his type. Although lately she has been fantasizing about Jake and a few of his friends… Jake thinks that Maddy is way out of his league, but he knows that she can't refuse a challenge. And he's come up with an irresistible dare guaranteed to send her body up in flames, gain her submission, and maybe even win her heart.

The Ambassador's Widow by Myla Jackson

Chameleon Agent Andre Batello is sent on assignment to "fill in" for an ambassador who died the night before a long-negotiated peace treaty is due to be signed. As part of a special team of individuals with the ability to assume another's identity based on a single strand of DNA, Andre's mission is to infiltrate the ambassador's life and sign that treaty. The one major glitch in his mission: he didn't plan on falling in love with the ambassador's widow.

The Joining by Jory Strong

On the water world of Qumaar, Siria Chaton is a prisoner of her talent. With her credits dwindling, she has few options and little hope for a future. Until Jett and Mozaiic du'Zehren enter her life.

After five years of being a couple, Jett and Mozaiic have gained permission to add a third, a woman, to their joining. They can't believe their good fortune when the woman assigned to them is a water diviner. Now if only she'll accept them as lovers and come home with them to the forbidden desert planet of Adjara.

Now Available
from
Cerridwen Press

Hocus Pocus

By Teresa Roblin

Shy and quiet Amanda Santorelli is unhappy watching the world go by around her. When her well-meaning but wacky aunt casts an assertiveness spell on her, Amanda's orderly world is turned upside down. Unable to control herself, Amanda blurts out whatever is on her mind every time someone asks her a question. Trying to outwit the spell only makes matters worse. With no control over her own mouth, it's only a matter of time before someone discovers the object of her secret obsession.

Mark Abbott is happy with the way his unassuming assistant runs his office. But all of a sudden she's become a new person—both in attitude and appearance—and he's not sure he likes the effect on his orderly work routine. With each passing day, he finds himself waiting to see what will come out of her mouth next. Before long, he can no longer deny the truth—the new Amanda is seriously making him reconsider his vow never to mix business with pleasure.

Mark doesn't know if it's love—or if he's just a victim of Hocus Pocus.

erridwen, the Celtic Goddess of wisdom, was the muse who brought inspiration to storytellers and those in the creative arts. Cerridwen Press encompasses the best and most innovative stories in all genres of today's fiction. Visit our site and discover the newest titles by talented authors who still get inspired - much like the ancient storytellers did, once upon a time.

Cerridwen Press

www.cerridwenpress.com

Why an electronic book?

We live in the Information Age—an exciting time in the history of human civilization, in which technology rules supreme and continues to progress in leaps and bounds every minute of every day. For a multitude of reasons, more and more avid literary fans are opting to purchase e-books instead of paper books. The question from those not yet initiated into the world of electronic reading is simply: *Why?*

1. *Price.* An electronic title at Ellora's Cave Publishing and Cerridwen Press runs anywhere from 40% to 75% less than the cover price of the exact same title in paperback format. Why? Basic mathematics and cost. It is less expensive to publish an e-book (no paper and printing, no warehousing and shipping) than it is to publish a paperback, so the savings are passed along to the consumer.

2. *Space.* Running out of room in your house for your books? That is one worry you will never have with electronic books. For a low one-time cost, you can purchase a handheld device specifically designed for e-reading. Many e-readers have large, convenient screens for viewing. Better yet, hundreds of titles can be stored within your new library—on a single microchip. There are a variety of e-readers from different manufacturers. You can also read e-books on your PC or laptop computer. (Please note that Ellora's Cave does not endorse any specific brands. You can check our websites at www.ellorascave.com or

www.cerridwenpress.com for information we make available to new consumers.)

3. *Mobility*. Because your new e-library consists of only a microchip within a small, easily transportable e-reader, your entire cache of books can be taken with you wherever you go.

4. *Personal Viewing Preferences.* Are the words you are currently reading too small? Too large? Too… ANNOYING? Paperback books cannot be modified according to personal preferences, but e-books can.

5. *Instant Gratification.* Is it the middle of the night and all the bookstores near you are closed? Are you tired of waiting days, sometimes weeks, for bookstores to ship the novels you bought? Ellora's Cave Publishing sells instantaneous downloads twenty-four hours a day, seven days a week, every day of the year. Our webstore is never closed. Our e-book delivery system is 100% automated, meaning your order is filled as soon as you pay for it.

Those are a few of the top reasons why electronic books are replacing paperbacks for many avid readers.

As always, Ellora's Cave and Cerridwen Press welcome your questions and comments. We invite you to email us at Comments@ellorascave.com or write to us directly at Ellora's Cave Publishing Inc., 1056 Home Avenue, Akron, OH 44310-3502.

THE
☥ ELLORA'S CAVE ☥
LIBRARY

Stay up to date with Ellora's Cave Titles in
Print with our Quarterly Catalog.

TO RECIEVE A CATALOG,
SEND AN EMAIL WITH YOUR NAME
AND MAILING ADDRESS TO:

CATALOG@ELLORASCAVE.COM

OR SEND A LETTER OR POSTCARD
WITH YOUR MAILING ADDRESS TO:

CATALOG REQUEST
c/o ELLORA'S CAVE PUBLISHING, INC.
1056 HOME AVENUE
AKRON, OHIO 44310-3502